A Maryland Witch in Arthur King's Court

Catherine Mesick

Copyright © 2020 by Catherine Mesick.
Cover Design by Melody Simmons.

All rights reserved. Published by Scofflaw Publishing.

ISBN: 978-0-9986631-6-6

Witches of Crabtree Bay: Book 2

A Maryland Witch in Arthur King's Court

Catherine Mesick

Chapter One

"Is that Chloe? I want to talk to Chloe Bartlett."

The voice on the phone was high and querulous.

I recognized it only too well.

"Yes, Mr. Clementine. It's me."

"Don't you take that tone of voice with me, my girl," he replied. "I've donated a lot of money to that library of yours. If not for me, you wouldn't even have the lights on in that place."

That wasn't quite true, but he had been a generous patron. I took a deep breath and willed myself to be patient.

"What can I do for you, Mr. Clementine?"

I asked the question to be polite, but I already knew what he wanted—it was the third Tuesday of the month.

"Now I want you to take this down," Mr. Clementine said. "Do you hear me? Do you have pen and paper?"

"Yes, Mr. Clementine. I'm ready to write it down."

"I want *Robertson's History of Rome, Volume One.* That's Ro-bert-son with an apostrophe 's' at the end. Make sure it's a history of *Rome.* Not anywhere else. And I want *Volume One,* not *Volume Two.* Do you understand that?"

"Yes, Mr. Clementine." I glanced at the little clock on the phone. I'd only been talking to him for about sixty seconds, but it felt like ten minutes. "You want *Robertson's History of Rome, Volume One*—not *Volume Two*."

"I want *Volume One*," Mr. Clementine said peevishly, as if that wasn't what I had just said.

"I understand," I said. "You want *Volume One*."

"It's important."

"I understand," I said again.

"Did you write it down?"

"Yes—I wrote it down."

"Good. Because you brought the wrong book last time, and that was a complete waste of a day for me. I can't afford to lose time because of your mistakes."

I felt myself bristling—I had *not* brought the wrong book.

But I knew there would be no point in trying to explain that to Mr. Clementine.

He continued. "I want that book. Do you hear me? Bring it by my house today at eleven thirty. Don't be late."

Without waiting for a response, he hung up.

"The library doesn't deliver, Mr. Clementine," I muttered to myself angrily. "It's not like ordering a pizza."

But I realized there was no point in grumbling. I had gotten myself into this situation, and I wasn't ready to get out of it.

At least not yet.

I was just sighing to myself and checking to make sure that we actually had the book he wanted in the system when I caught sight of a swift movement out of the corner of my eye.

I paused with my fingers over the keyboard.

I turned quickly.

I was just in time to see a tall form disappearing behind the stacks in the graphic novel section.

As I watched, a dark-haired, dark-eyed man peered around the corner of a bookcase.

He saw me looking at him and quickly darted back out of sight.

"Mike?" I said.

I wasn't supposed to speak out loud in the library unless I was on the phone, but I was so startled that the word slipped out.

The man reappeared and smiled sheepishly.

It was indeed Professor Mike Fellowes.

He was the very definition of tall, dark, and handsome, and my heart gave a little flutter when I saw him.

It had been a little while since we'd seen each other.

He stepped out from behind the bookcase and moved toward me.

"Chloe—" he said.

Even in a whisper, his voice sent a tingle through me when he said my name.

"Chloe, I—"

But Mike got no further.

Another man was also hiding in the graphic novel section, and he stepped out also.

This man was tall, but not as tall as Mike, and he had longish blond hair with streaks of gold running through it. He was tan and athletic, and he wore a tight T-shirt that showed off his muscular torso.

His name was Joe Osgood, and he was often to be found perusing the comic books section and sneaking peeks over at me.

Mike, however, was a surprise.

Joe elbowed his way in front of Mike and walked over to the circulation desk where I stood.

"Hi, Chloe," he said. "How's it going?"

I glanced over at Mrs. Ludlow, who was eyeing me severely over the top of her silver-framed glasses. She hadn't liked my conversation with Mr. Clementine on the phone, and she looked like she wasn't going to like what was about to happen, either.

For that matter, I wasn't sure I was going to like what was about to happen.

Joe leaned on the desk, and Mike quickly started toward us.

I wasn't entirely certain, but I thought I saw Mike's nostrils flare—something I'd never seen him do before.

A storm was definitely brewing.

Joe was staring at me, and his normally guileless blue eyes held a hint of challenge in them.

But that challenge wasn't directed at me.

It was directed at the man behind him.

Mike came to stand just behind Joe, and he folded his arms across his chest.

"So how's it going?" Joe said again.

I drew in breath to say something I hoped would be pacific when Mike interrupted.

"What do you think you're doing?" he demanded.

There was a clear challenge in his tone, and once again, that challenge wasn't directed at me.

It was directed at Joe.

Joe slanted a glance back at Mike.

"I'm talking to my girl—my friend. I'm talking to Chloe, who's my friend."

"Is that so?" Somehow Mike's arms seemed to fold even harder.

Joe pushed himself off the desk and turned to face Mike.

I felt an urge to reach out and grab Joe's arm, but I restrained myself.

"Yeah, that's so," Joe said. "Do you have something you want to say about it?"

The atmosphere suddenly grew very tense, and I was aware of the fact that all eyes in the library were turned toward the confrontation at the circulation desk.

"Yes," Mike grated out. "I do have something I want to say about it."

"Oh yeah?" Joe said. "Well, I have something I want to say, too."

Mike arched a mocking eyebrow. He could be very superior and condescending when he wanted to be, and apparently this was one of those times.

"This ought to be good. Go ahead."

A sneer twisted Joe's good-natured face.

"July the Fourth."

He only spoke three words, but the effect on Mike was electric. He turned pale and his mouth dropped open. His arms dropped to his sides, and his hands clenched into fists.

Then he turned without a word and stormed out of the library.

Joe stared after his vanquished foe, and a smirk lit up his face.

"Guess I showed him."

"Oh, Joe," I said softly.

I wanted to run after Mike.

But I knew that now was not the time—not yet.

"Well, I suppose I should be going, too," Joe said. "I've got to get some work in today."

I held out a hand. "Joe, wait. Don't—"

He paused and looked back at me.

"Don't go after him," I finished. "Let Mike leave before you go out there."

"Don't worry." Joe looked very pleased with himself. "I'm sure he got in his car quickly—I doubt he's even out there anymore. Besides, I won't rub it in."

I frowned. "Rub what in?"

But Joe simply smiled and left the library.

If he'd been insinuating what I thought he'd been insinuating, that was probably wise.

I wasn't some kind of prize to be won.

"Everything okay?" said a new voice.

I turned to see Rita Cavanaugh, the head librarian, walking up to the circulation desk.

Her black hair was pulled back into a chic chignon, and she was wearing a beautifully cut gray dress that was ideal for the hot summer weather and showed off her coffee-colored skin to perfection.

Somehow, even working in a dusty library, Rita always managed to look as if she'd just stepped off the cover of a magazine.

I, on the other hand, had a feeling that I was looking more than a little frazzled.

I could actually feel my curly brown hair frizzing even harder and working its way free of the careless ponytail I'd wrapped it in.

Dealing with three unreasonable men all at once could do that to you.

I blew a column of air up into my hair.

Rita gave me an understanding smile. "Looks like I arrived just in time."

"Yes, you did," I said. I glanced at the clock on my computer. "Mr. Clementine just called, and I've got to take his book over to him. And then I was just looking the book up when Mike and Joe started to have their thing."

Rita continued to look calm and unperturbed. "Don't worry. I've got you covered."

I happened to glance down then and noticed for the first time that she was carrying a book in her hands.

"The Robertson book!" I exclaimed.

I glanced around.

"Sorry," I whispered.

"I happened to overhear you while you were talking to Mr. Clementine," Rita said. "So I took the liberty of pulling it from the shelves. It's *Volume One*. Just like he wanted."

She paused significantly. "We have *Volume Two* also."

"Thanks," I said. "I'd better take that one, too."

Rita gave me a conspirator's smile and then turned to get the second book.

I began to gather up my stuff and glanced at the clock on the phone.

I'd need to hurry if I wanted to get there by eleven thirty.

Rita soon returned with *Volume Two*, but she hesitated before she gave it to me.

"You don't have to this," she said. "We don't make house calls."

"I know," I said.

"Then why do you do it? Why take a book over to that cantankerous, rude old man?"

"I feel sorry for him," I said.

Rita gave me a sympathetic look, and I accepted the book from her.

Then I left the library.

As I walked out the doors, I was immediately hit by a blast of the July heat.

The humidity was no joke, either, and beads of sweat began to form quickly as I settled into my very hot car and hoped that the air-conditioning would kick in soon.

Then I drove over to Camelot.

Camelot was the housing development, country club, and golf course that Mr. Otis Clementine had built, though it wasn't really the main source of his wealth.

Mr. Clementine was, as he had said, a generous donor to the library—and to many other institutions and charities besides—and over the course of his life he had amassed a vast fortune.

Most of his money came from the Brian's Baskets discount stores that he owned all over the country. The stores sold food and clothing, electronics and housewares, cleaners, toiletries, and all manner of products made out of plastic.

He was by all accounts a business genius, and he only dabbled a little in real estate.

So naturally, his dabbling was highly successful.

Mr. Clementine had actually been born and raised right here in Crabtree Bay, and though he certainly could have lived anywhere, he'd always promised himself that he'd build a castle and a kingdom here.

And he'd done just that with Camelot.

As I turned into the exclusive housing development, I could see Mr. Clementine's house on a hill, dominating the landscape and looking down on all the other houses.

His house was immense, it was made of gray stone, and it even had a tall tower with a pointed roof.

It was, indeed, a castle.

I drove along, wincing just a little as I always did, as I glanced at the street names in the housing development.

Excalibur Avenue.

Round Table Terrace.

Lancelot's Love Lane.

There was even the inexplicably named Guinevere's Gauntlet.

And then there was the largest street in the development—the one that led up to the towering stone house on the horizon and had no outlet.

Arthur King's Court.

I could never figure out why he had chosen to transpose the name that way.

I supposed it was Mr. Clementine's idea of a joke.

But after having been acquainted with Mr. Clementine for a few months, I had a feeling that the joke wasn't something others were supposed to laugh at.

Instead, it was likely to be his way of laughing at us.

There was a glint from the tower up above, and I had a feeling that Mr. Clementine was sitting up there, watching me.

I continued on up the hill to the house, and I was surprised as I always was that there was no gate.

On the contrary, the house had a long, wide path up to it with no obstructions, and a circular drive curled around the front providing ample parking and access.

It was almost as if he were inviting people in—although I knew that likely wasn't the case.

According to his housekeeper, Mr. Clementine very seldom entertained.

I parked the car and went up to the door, and that same housekeeper answered when I rang the doorbell.

Daphne Minton was a plump, middle-aged woman with brown hair cut into the same kind of sleek, shiny bob that I'd always wanted to try, but I knew my curly hair wouldn't allow.

Daphne also had a good-natured face and a friendly manner that was somehow off-putting at the same time.

She was both welcoming and forbidding—a quality which I imagined served her well when dealing with tradesmen, contractors, or visitors. She always gave me a strange feeling of ambiguity—I never knew where I stood with her.

"Welcome back, Chloe," she said.

She ushered me into the house and closed the door behind me.

The interior was all wood and stone and sparsely furnished—I supposed to make it look more like an ancient castle. The only real decoration in the vast front room was an enormous painting of the owner of the house that hung on the wall near the door.

It showed Otis Clementine as a much younger man. He'd had sallow cheeks and a deep, defiant cleft in his chin. His rich, dark auburn hair was swept back from his high forehead, and his piercing blue eyes stared out at the world like he meant to rule it all.

I paused to stare at the painting—somehow it made me shiver this morning.

Daphne cleared her throat and then twitched her finger at me impatiently.

"Mr. Clementine is waiting."

Then she nodded significantly toward the stone staircase on my right.

I sighed. I had a sneaking suspicion that there was actually an elevator somewhere, but I trudged toward the stairs like I always did.

I got the distinct impression that somewhere up above, Mr. Clementine was laughing at me.

Climbing up the first flight was never that bad, and the next floor up actually changed from heavy stone to light, airy, very modern living quarters.

I climbed up to the next floor, and then I had to pause just a moment to catch my breath. The truth was Mr. Clementine's tower wasn't really that high up—the slenderness of the tower and the fact that the house itself sat on a hill gave the illusion of greater height.

From the current floor, I opened a wooden door and entered the tower.

Then I climbed up two more flights, pausing once on the landing between them to catch my breath and look out the window at Mr. Clementine's expansive back lawn.

Then I reached the top and found myself facing a closed wooden door.

I knocked.

Mr. Clementine's voice floated out, just as high and querulous as it had been on the phone.

"Come in."

Otis Clementine was in his late seventies, and his once-thick auburn hair—so vibrant in his portrait—had faded to white and thinned considerably. But his piercing blue eyes were just as sharp as ever, and he regarded me with a malevolent twinkle as I entered the room.

"Chloe, my girl! So you've finally arrived. Enjoy your walk?"

Mr. Clementine's witty quip was followed by raucous laughter, and I was more sure than ever that there was an elevator concealed nearby.

Mr. Clementine wiped at his eyes with a slightly shaky hand. Then he fixed me with his sharp blue eyes again.

"Still, you're young—you shouldn't mind a few stairs! How old are you?"

The question was impertinent—and delivered that way—but I decided to answer it. The sooner our meeting was over, the better. And arguing with him would just prolong it—I knew that from experience.

"I'm twenty-three."

"So I was right. Thirty-three! Just like my son Christopher."

I sighed. Mr. Clementine's habit of being contradictory was so ingrained that I didn't even think he realized he did it anymore.

He continued. "He's the older of the two, too. But insists on being called 'Christopher.' Won't take a nickname and be called Chris like a sensible boy would do. Then there's his younger brother. *His* name is Robert, but he goes by 'Bobby.' *He's* not too good for a nickname."

Mr. Clementine shot a glance over at me.

"Don't just stand there hovering in the doorway, girl. Come in and have a seat. I want to have a look at my book—make sure you've brought the right one."

I was reluctant to enter the room, but I stepped forward.

As I'd counseled myself before, the sooner I got this over with, the sooner I could leave.

"So you brought the book, did you?"

"Yes, I did," I said as I sat down.

Mr. Clementine held out a slightly trembling hand.

"Give it to me."

I passed over the book.

Mr. Clementine's eyes were a bit weak, and I waited while he looked it over. I happened to notice a magnifying glass resting on a beautiful, ornate box decorated with sunflowers. I thought of offering the glass to him, but I figured he knew it was there and would use it if he wanted it.

As he continued to look the book over, a spiteful gleam came into his eyes.

But this time—thanks to Rita—I was ready for him.

"Nope," Mr. Clementine declared emphatically. "This isn't the book. This is *Robertson's History of Rome, Volume One.*"

"Yes," I said. "That's the book you asked for."

"No, it isn't. Not a bit of it. I distinctly asked for *Volume Two. Volume One* is no good to me."

His eyes glittered in triumph.

I felt a twinge of irritation, even though I was expecting that answer. Mr. Clementine always did this. No matter what book I brought over, he always said that I had to return tomorrow with a different one.

But this time, I simply reached into my bag and pulled out the other book.

"As it so happens," I said sweetly. "I also have *Volume Two* right here."

Mr. Clementine's triumph turned to astonishment as I handed the book over.

As he examined the book, his astonishment turned to anger as he realized that I had indeed brought him *Volume Two* also.

"Confound you, girl!"

Realizing he'd admitted to his little scheme, he quickly covered his ire.

"Thank you for the book. Yes—this is the one I wanted."

He cast another one of his piercing looks my way.

"You're a clever one, aren't you? You remind me of my wife, Clytie. Not in looks or coloring, but in cleverness. Clytie always was a sharp one. She knew how to think circles around me."

Mr. Clementine paused and his expression grew dreamy.

He ran his gnarled hands over the box with the sunflowers, and it seemed for a moment that he forgot I was there.

Then a malicious twinkle lit up his eye.

"So tell me, clever girl, do you know what the name 'Clytie' means?"

"Yes," I said.

Mr. Clementine looked startled. "Yes?"

"Yes—it's a Greek name. It means 'lovely one.' The Clytie of Greek myth fell in love with Apollo, but he didn't love her back. So she turned into a—"

"Sunflower," Mr. Clementine said.

"In the later versions, yes. But in the earliest stories, she turned into a heliotrope."

"Nonsense. It was a sunflower. The sunflower turns to follow the sun—just as Clytie turned to follow Apollo wherever he went in the sky. My Clytie went to follow the sun, too."

"Sunflowers don't actually do that," I said. "That's just an old wives' tale."

Anger flashed in Mr. Clementine's eyes. "Chloe's a Greek name, too. Did you know that?"

"Yes. And so's Daphne for that matter."

"Daphne? Who's Daphne?"

"Daphne—your housekeeper."

Mr. Clementine gave a bark of laughter. "Old Minton? Now there's an old wives' tale. She couldn't be less like Clytie if she tried. My Clytie was a blonde—a beautiful blonde. I never did care for brunettes."

He shot me another look, and I could tell he was baiting me.

He reached for a magazine that was lying near the sunflower box and pushed it over to me.

"That's my kind of girl. In fact, that *is* my girl—Heather."

On the cover of *Eastern Shore Today*, a beautiful girl with close-cropped blond hair and a dazzling smile cavorted on a beach in a white sundress.

"She's lovely," I said. "Is she your daughter?"

Mr. Clementine sputtered. "My daughter? She's my girlfriend. I've got all boys—four of them. She just had my latest one a year ago—Jaden."

"Oh," I said, startled. "She'll make a beautiful bride."

"Bride?" Mr. Clementine sputtered even louder. "Clytie was my only wife. I'd never marry that girl. She can't hold a candle to my Clytie."

I felt vaguely embarrassed. I wasn't really interested in Mr. Clementine's personal life. The white dress must have suggested the idea of a wedding to me.

That, and Mr. Clementine's constant use of the word "wife."

He continued. "No—Clytie was my only wife. But I lost her."

I felt a rush of sympathy for the combative man in front of me. "She died?"

"She did eventually—at least according to the media. But I lost her when she left me. She was only twenty-two. She took off to follow the sun—just like her namesake did with Apollo."

Mr. Clementine ran his hands over the box again.

"She ran off to Italy. Became a successful actress. She took my son with her. She'd be about fifty-seven now if she'd lived."

"Your son?" I said.

Mr. Clementine had so many sons that it was getting hard for me to keep track of them all.

"Brian," he replied curtly.

"Brian?" I said. "As in—"

"Brian's Baskets. Exactly. I built that business up for him. And someday I'm going to give it to him. I've just got to find him first. He'd be about thirty-six now."

Mr. Clementine looked up at me. "I only saw him once, you know, when he was a baby. But he was just like me. Just like me! He had my ambition, my drive—my everything! And someday I will find him. He left a trail of breadcrumbs—"

His voice trailed off.

"Do you know the tale of Hansel and Gretel, my girl?" Mr. Clementine asked abruptly.

"Yes, of course."

"They left a trail of breadcrumbs, too, and I mean to follow them all the way to my son."

"But—" I began.

"Yes? Out with it!"

"The trail of breadcrumbs didn't work for Hansel and Gretel," I said. "The birds ate the breadcrumbs up, and they couldn't find their way back home again."

Mr. Clementine stared at me for a long moment.

Then he gave a short bark of laughter.

"You have an answer for everything, don't you, girl? Like I said, you're a smart one. Just like my Clytie. Someday you'll find out that I've—"

He stopped. "But that won't be for years now. I'm hale and hearty. Strong as a bull. That day's not coming for a long time."

Before I could ask what he meant, Mr. Clementine thumped one of his hands on the book in front of him.

"Thank you for the book. You may go now."

I stood up, ruffled by the abrupt dismissal, and headed for the door.

"And, Chloe—"

Mr. Clementine's words drew me back, and I turned.

"Don't think I've forgotten," he said.

"Forgotten what?"

"The others are starting to forget. But I haven't."

Mr. Clementine leaned forward and spoke the words distinctly.

"I know you're a witch."

I turned on my heel and left the room.

Mr. Clementine's laughter followed me down the stairs.

Chapter Two

Witch.

I sighed to myself.

There was that word again.

And it was true—but he was supposed to forget.

They were all supposed to forget.

And most people had.

Most people in our little town of Crabtree Bay didn't remember that I and my two sisters had been outed as witches in a newspaper article just last month.

The article had caused quite a stir at the time, but our protective symbol had done its work.

I was sitting now in my car in front of Mr. Clementine's house where I had paused to catch my breath.

I was feeling just a little shaky, and I hadn't felt like I could drive away just yet—even though I really wanted to.

I took off the gold ring I always wore and looked at the tiny symbol engraved inside the band:

It was the symbol that had originally been developed by my ancestor, Mary Bartlett, and it had kept my family's abilities secret for three hundred years.

And then a stranger had made our symbol public and told everyone all about us—our history—everything.

I shivered just a little—the memory of the day I had first seen our symbol being waved around in public still made my breath catch and my heart race—for more than one reason.

The symbol was our secret and it protected us—and until that day I had never seen it in public before.

I had feared for the safety of my family.

And then there was the person who had been waving it around—the handsome *and* infuriating Professor Mike Fellowes from Henrietta College.

He was the same one who had splashed my family's history all over the local paper, *The Morning Cider*, and the one who had just been peering around a bookcase at me over at the Crabtree Bay Public Library.

I slipped my gold ring back on my finger and rested my head on the steering wheel for just a moment.

I closed my eyes.

Every time I saw Mike, I felt a little tingle run through me, and this time had been no exception.

Mike was good-looking and funny and smart—if occasionally irritating, something I couldn't seem to stop reminding myself of—and I still remembered the times we had kissed.

The two of us had been getting along really well, and then things had suddenly gone horribly wrong.

As Joe had said, there had been the Fourth of July.

I straightened up and drove back to the library.

The rest of the day passed in a bit of a blur, and before I knew it, Stu, our other librarian, and Emily, our page, were coming in to take over the night shift. Many of our library patrons believed that I was also a librarian, but in reality, I actually lacked the necessary degree—I was formally known as a library assistant. My professional career had actually begun in the publishing industry in New York, but had quickly fizzled out. And then I had found myself back in Crabtree Bay and staying with my sister Alberta—and happily so.

But some days, life in a small town felt oppressively close, and today I longed for the anonymity of the big city.

Mr. Clementine had said that he knew I was a witch, and while I doubted he would go to the press about it, he would likely make caustic comments about it from now on. And the incident this morning with Joe and Mike would likely set tongues wagging—after a very bizarre incident last month involving some figures from my past, I was already getting a reputation as a shameless flirt who destroyed men's lives.

Now that Joe and Mike had been arguing over me publicly, that would only add to the gossip mill for those who were so inclined.

I sighed to myself and drove to my sister Alberta's house.

I was only staying with my sister until I found a place of my own— I hadn't yet found an apartment for myself since moving back to Maryland four months ago.

Of course, I hadn't really been looking that hard—and Alberta seemed like she liked having me around.

She certainly hadn't done any grumbling about it, and Alberta wasn't the type to remain silent when she was displeased.

As I arrived at the house, I noticed that my sister Rafaela's car was there also.

I was momentarily puzzled—I hadn't known that she was coming over.

I went inside.

As I stepped into the blissfully cool, air-conditioned house, my sister Alberta came flying into the living room, her eyes wide with alarm.

Alberta Bogdana Bartlett Delaney, or Alberta Bartlett as she was more commonly known, was twenty-eight years old and a tax attorney. However, she didn't look like most people's conception of a member of that profession. She had flame-red hair, bright green eyes, and I had heard her described as gorgeous on more than one occasion.

She was also a witch like me, and she derived her powers from the element of fire. The element suited her, too—Alberta was bold and fiery—definitely the fighter in the family.

And at the moment, she seemed to be engaged in a battle of some kind.

"Stop her!" she cried.

I looked around, puzzled, for a moment, and then I saw a streak of black and red surging toward me.

It was Alberta's cat, Sibyl.

And she appeared to have something crimson all over her face.

"Stop her!" Alberta cried. "Don't let her get to the furniture!"

Alberta's living room was done up in neutral shades—mostly white and cream—and I could understand how she might be concerned about red stains getting on the sofa.

I moved to intercept Sibyl, but she quickly dodged around me.

Alberta had better luck, however, and she soon scooped up her errant pet into her arms.

Sibyl turned her red-smeared face toward me and let out a tiny meow.

I wrinkled my nose at a familiar scent. "Is that tomato sauce?"

"Yes—I was going to make pizza tonight. I made my own sauce last night in preparation. And then I got out the container just now and took off the lid, and Sibyl jumped right up on the counter and stuck her face in it."

Alberta sighed and looked down at her cat. "Now I don't think I can use it."

I leaned closer and wrinkled my nose again. "It smells a little sour."

"That's just Sibyl's tuna breath you're smelling," Alberta said frostily. "There's *nothing* wrong with my sauce."

"No—no, of course not," I said hastily. "So since the sauce is ruined, do you think we should just order a pizza or two?"

Alberta sighed again. "I guess we'll have to."

"Armando's?"

"Naturally."

I felt a rush of relief. Armando's pizza was terrific, and Alberta's cooking was uncertain at best. She was a marvelous baker, but anything she did using the stovetop rather than the oven tended to have mixed results.

Alberta turned toward the stairs. "I'm going to go rinse this stuff off Sibyl's face before she gets it all over everything. Can you do the ordering?"

"I'd love to," I said.

Alberta cast me a suspicious glance, but she kept going.

As she ascended the stairs, Sibyl looked down at me, her orange eyes blending in with her bright red face.

"Thank you," I mouthed to her.

Alberta glanced back at me again, and I quickly turned to find my phone.

I ordered one large pizza with extra cheese and one large pizza with half pepperoni and half olives.

I loved cheese, and I knew both Alberta and Rafaela would eat it, too. The pepperoni was for Alberta, and the olives were for Rafaela—whom I was assuming was here, though I hadn't seen her yet.

As I set down my phone, I found Rafaela standing right beside me.

She seemed to have materialized out of nowhere, and I jumped just a little.

"So are you saving us from her pizza?" she asked in a low voice.

Rafaela Serena Bartlett Delaney, or Rafaela Bartlett, was twenty-five, and she worked as a physician's assistant. She had big blue-green eyes, and her hair was an unusual shade of brown mixed with gold. She was a witch—just like Alberta and me—and she derived her powers from the element of water. Water governed both emotion and health, and Rafaela was a sensitive, gifted healer, which made her extraordinarily adept at her chosen profession.

My powers, on the other hand, derived from all four elements—earth, air, fire, and water—which Alberta said made me vague and unreliable when working magic. My powers were as different from my sisters' as my coloring was. My eyes were brown, where their eyes were light, my hair was dark and curly, where theirs was straight and lighter in color, and with my powers I could make things grow—not just plants—but other things, too—like ideas.

Despite our differences, everyone knew we were sisters right away when they met us—there was a strong family resemblance.

And no one in town knew we were witches—at least not until last month when Mike had published his newspaper article revealing our family's history and symbol. Revealing the symbol enabled people to remember the unusual things we could do when ordinarily they would forget. But the sensation that had been caused by Mike's article had already died down, eclipsed by more exciting news.

So people were starting to forget the symbol again and to forget about us.

Except Mike, of course—he still seemed to remember—though I knew he didn't actually believe in any of it.

And then there was Mr. Clementine.

He clearly still remembered, too.

Although his remembering probably wouldn't amount to much more than taunts on my monthly visits to him, something about it gave me pause.

I didn't know what about it disturbed me, though.

"Chloe?" Rafaela said softly. "Is everything okay?"

She was staring at me with her big, soulful eyes, as sensitive as ever.

I could tell she sensed I was worried about something.

"It's nothing," I said. "And I did just order pizza—but I'm not the one who saved us. That was Sibyl."

"Sibyl?"

"Yes. She apparently stuck her face in the sauce—ruined the whole batch."

"That's odd," Rafaela said. "Cats don't usually like things that are acidic."

"Well, she is a smart cat," I said. "Maybe she really was trying to save us." I glanced at her. "So where did you come from? I didn't see you when I came in."

Rafaela held up a brown paper bag. "I was out back gathering some of your herbs. You really do a marvelous job with the dandelion root—not to mention the tansy."

Rafaela's tone was overbright and just a touch too complimentary. She wasn't openly disparaging of my abilities like Alberta was, but she was often so encouraging that I knew she thought I needed the praise. She, like Alberta, didn't necessarily have a lot of confidence in my powers.

"So do you think Alberta's going to be occupied for a few minutes?" Rafaela asked, her tone still low.

There was a crash from overhead, and Alberta's muffled swearing drifted down to us.

"I think right now she's struggling to get a cat into the bathtub," I said. "What's up?"

"It's just that Alberta doesn't seem quite like herself lately."

We both glanced up as a fresh stream of swearing started above us.

"I don't know," I said. "She certainly sounds like her usual self to me."

"I think," Rafaela said slowly, "that Alberta is keeping a secret from us. I think she's up to something."

"Like what?"

"I don't know. Have you noticed anything different about her lately?"

I frowned a little. "Now that you mention it, I *had* been wondering."

"Yes?" Rafaela said.

"She's usually such a workaholic," I said. "She typically leaves for work before dawn and sometimes doesn't get back till after midnight. Certainly many nights she doesn't get in until after I've gone to sleep. But lately, she's been getting home on time like a normal person, and sometimes I even see her in the morning before I leave. She hasn't been home this much since last month when we had all the trouble."

Rafaela nodded, her eyes full of concern. "That's it exactly. She's not working like she used to."

"Well, surely that's a good thing?"

Rafaela sighed. "I don't know. If that's all it was, I wouldn't be so concerned. But Peter stopped by the clinic the other day. He said Alberta's been brushing him off lately—avoiding him. He's worried that she's not interested in him anymore."

Peter Gambelli was a local restauranteur, and Alberta had begun seeing him about a month ago. I'd thought they were getting along well, but now it seemed as if there might be trouble.

"Is that why you're here tonight?" I asked. "Not that I'm not glad to see you. But you work nearly as much as Alberta does, and I haven't seen you much since last month's incident."

Rafaela blushed a little. "Yes—and I'm sorry. I didn't mean to ignore you guys—but I've been so wrapped up in my patients that I haven't been around much. In fact, when Peter asked me about Alberta, I didn't know what to tell him. I haven't seen her lately, so I thought I would come by tonight, maybe read her emotions—see if I can figure out what's going on."

She glanced at me. "You haven't noticed anything else strange about Alberta lately, have you? Apart from her work hours?"

There was a fresh burst of swearing from overhead, and Sibyl ran downstairs, soaking wet, but with her face clean.

"No stranger than usual," I said.

Rafaela directed another glance at me, this one much sharper.

"What's wrong?" she said.

"Nothing really," I replied. "Just work. It's no big deal."

The pizza arrived at that moment, and I was grateful for the interruption—Rafaela's big, soulful eyes could be really disturbing when she was reading my feelings.

Alberta soon reappeared, too, and before long we were all ensconced in her dining room, enjoying Armando's delicious pizza.

As I bit into my first slice, I pulled away a long string of melted cheese—the sure sign of a good piece of pizza.

While I was focused on eating, Rafaela made several attempts to draw Alberta out about what she was feeling and doing lately, but Alberta rebuffed her firmly.

And then, somehow, the two of them became focused on me.

"All right, out with it," Alberta said.

"Out with what?" I replied.

"You're clearly stressed out about something," Rafaela said. "You should tell us what it is."

We went through all of my usual troubles at work—strange patrons, Joe, people who were eating in the library, and I negatived them all.

"I've got it!" Alberta exclaimed. "It's the third Tuesday of the month, isn't it? It's Otis Clementine that's bothering you."

Rafaela frowned a little. "He's the one who always wants you to bring him two books, right? One on Tuesday, and then another one on Wednesday after he claims you've brought the wrong book?"

"Yes," I said. "But this time I think I outsmarted him—or really Rita did. I brought two books this time."

"So then what's the problem?" Alberta asked.

I told them briefly about how he remembered I was a witch—and I told them my concerns about our symbol.

Alberta waved a dismissive hand. "Oh, the symbol. Who cares if a few people still remember? It's only been about a month. Soon the rest of them will forget, too."

Rafaela gave me a long look. "What is it that concerns you exactly? Do you think he'll make it public again?"

"No—I don't," I said. "It's just that I have a vague feeling that something is wrong."

I realized that that was it. An idea was tugging on my mind.

Alberta snorted. "What's wrong is that you keep going over there. Just tell the bony old coot you won't stand for it—you don't make house calls."

"You can do that, you know," Rafaela said quietly. "You don't have to take things to him personally."

"I know," I said. "It's just that—"

"What?" Rafaela's eyes were mild and curious.

I thought back to the way Mr. Clementine had looked when he was talking about his eldest son, Brian.

"I feel sorry for him," I said.

Alberta snorted again, but I knew it was true. I'd felt sorry for him ever since the first time I'd heard his voice on the phone—high, tremulous, and demanding.

"So—what then?" Alberta was staring at me. "What do you think you can do?"

"I think I can help him," I said slowly.

"With what? He's one of the richest men in the country."

"I think he's lonely," I said—though that wasn't really it. Desolate and desperate were two other words that occurred to me.

"Ridiculous," Alberta replied. "The man's surrounded by people constantly, and I hear he's got a girlfriend a quarter of his age. Not to mention a new baby."

"I know," I said. "But—"

"But nothing." Alberta was adamant.

My phone buzzed then, and I jumped up, glad for the interruption. I hurried to pick it up, and I hoped it was Mike.

Maybe he'd finally decided to talk to me again.

But the text was actually from my mother.

Give me a call tonight. And don't tell your sisters.

Chapter Three

That night, after Rafaela had left and Alberta had gotten busy in the kitchen baking something, I went up to my room to call my mother.

She answered on the first ring.

"Hi, honey."

Her voice was warm and calm, and she sounded untroubled.

I thought I'd sensed some urgency in her text, but perhaps I'd been wrong.

"Hey, Mom. What's up?"

There was a pause, and I could picture her frowning.

Maura Everly Bartlett Delaney had once been known as Maura Marian Bartlett Everly, but after her marriage to my dad, she had dropped her middle name, "Marian," and had kept her father's last name, "Everly." She had also kept the name "Bartlett," as had everyone in our family line, in honor of Mary Bartlett, our ancestor who had first come to these shores. In fact, it was common for the women in my family to drop their other names and just use "Bartlett" as a surname. So my full name was actually Chloe Anastasia Bartlett Delaney, but I went by Chloe Bartlett in my everyday interactions, and I always gave Bartlett as my surname—just as my sisters did.

It was a way for the women in my family to honor our heritage and our illustrious ancestor.

The silence on my mom's end continued, and I pictured her frown deepening and her blond brows drawing together over her blue eyes.

My mom was a witch who drew her powers from the element of water, like Rafaela did, and usually she was very in tune with her daughters' emotional states.

But tonight I felt like I was the one reading her emotions—though maybe that wasn't such a great feat.

When talking to someone on the phone, a long pause usually meant that something was wrong.

"Mom?" I prompted.

"I don't want you to tell your sisters," Maura said in a rush. "At least not yet."

"Okay—I won't. But I still don't know what this is about."

Maura sighed softly.

"Is Dad there?" I asked, hoping to jog the conversation.

Whenever I called, I was typically put on speaker phone so I could talk to both of them. I pictured Richard Delaney with his glasses on his nose, his hair still dark but sprinkled with silver, sitting in his easy chair in their rental home in Florida.

Both Mom and Dad had taken early retirement after his illness earlier in the year, and they were currently spending an extended vacation in the sunny climes of the South, trying to decide if they wanted to spend retirement down there or remain in their house in Maryland.

"Your father's here," Maura replied. "But he's fallen asleep in his chair. He looked so comfortable that I didn't want to wake him."

"Okay—so please just tell me," I said.

"It's about the runes, dear, and the wards. I don't think they're working."

I was startled. "What?"

My mother maintained rune stones around the town of Crabtree Bay that did two things—they let us know if any magic was performed within the city limits that wasn't performed by us—and they worked to discourage other magic workers from entering the town. The warding off aspect of the protective runes was more of a suggestion than an absolute barrier. Other magic workers would feel an aversion to entering the town—but the wards wouldn't actually physically stop them from coming in.

When my mother didn't continue, I peppered her with questions.

"What's wrong with the runes? Why aren't the wards working? And how long have you known?"

"I've known since last month," Maura replied, answering my last question. "Ever since all the trouble you had."

I remembered that Alberta had found our rune stones last month, defaced and covered up, and competing rune stones had been placed beside them.

"But I thought you had gotten everything working again," I said. "With your connective magic and your charts and that app you found."

The weirdest part had been the app—I hadn't known there was one for witchcraft.

"Well, I had—sort of. But there's only so much I can do remotely. And the rune stones weren't really working that well, even after my fix. I could tell from here that magic was being worked at the time, but if you recall you didn't feel the finger-tingling like you were supposed to, did you?"

"No, I didn't."

"Neither did I."

Finger-tingling was a sign that all of us—Mom included—were supposed to feel whenever someone who wasn't us performed magic in the town—no matter the distance. The rune stones were connected to all of us through a spell of Mom's, and I remembered that last month I had noticed that that telltale sign wasn't working.

"So what are you saying?" I asked. "Do you think someone's performing magic right now that we don't know about?"

There was a long pause, and I felt myself growing worried.

"Mom?"

"Oh, honey." She sighed. "I'm just not sure. My connective magic and my charts and *my app*—" Here I could sense a smile in her voice, and it made me relax a little. "All these things are telling me that there's low-level magic that's not ours in Crabtree Bay all the time now."

"So then, is there any danger?"

"I can't really pinpoint any specific spells," Maura said. "It's just sort of all around—ambient. I don't *think* there's any danger. And it's also possible my methods are malfunctioning. What I'd really like is for you to look into it. And that's why I didn't want you to tell your sisters."

"I don't quite follow," I said.

"Maybe I'm wrong," Maura replied, and I could picture her frowning again. "But I don't think your sisters are quite up to this. Alberta would go charging out, making lots of waves, and putting our magic workers—if they do indeed exist—on alert. And Rafaela might get worried—maybe freeze up like she does sometimes."

"Alberta does have some subtlety," I said. "And Rafaela doesn't so much freeze up as start dreaming—she does that to find answers. Besides, I'm not sure they'd agree with you about my abilities."

"Chloe," Maura said firmly, "you shouldn't let your sisters' talk put you off things. I know they disapprove sometimes of the fact that you draw on so many elements, but I still think that gives you some special abilities—ones you haven't even tapped yet. I think you're the one best equipped to deal with this."

"Okay," I said. "So what am I doing exactly?"

"Just look into things, like I said. I'm not getting any spikes like I did last month with all the spellcasting. This time there's just constant, low-level activity—sort of a background hum. I'd like to know where it's coming from. And I'm also curious about why our fingers don't tingle anymore—see if you can find out if anything is working to cloud or sever the connective magic."

"So check on the runes stones, too?" I said.

"Yes."

"Last time you sent Alberta to do that."

"I know, dear." Maura paused again. "This time I really think it's a job for you."

I paused myself then. "Do you think the Crabtree Coven is involved?"

Maura sighed. "I really don't know. Somehow I doubt it, though. And if it is them, they don't appear to be very active. And I don't think there's any danger—otherwise, I'd come up and do it myself."

We turned to other topics then—Dad's health and what I and my sisters had been up to—what Mom had been up to.

Eventually, Maura got ready to sign off.

"Well, have a good night, honey. And I don't want to alarm you or anyone else. Just have a look around and see what you find. It could just be that my runes aren't working properly."

"I'll check into things," I said.

"Thanks, honey."

"Good night, Mom."

"Good night."

With that, she was gone.

I sat for a moment, just thinking about what Mom had said. I was a little disturbed to hear that there was low-level magic around us all the time, but maybe Mom was right—maybe the rune stones were just malfunctioning.

I glanced over at my little family of flowerpots. They, like the rune stones, employed connective magic to stay attuned to us—and this particular bit of magic stemmed from a spell I had created myself. There were four flowers in four pots—one for each member of my family. There was a yellow daffodil for my mom, a dark-purple iris for my dad, a red rose for Alberta, and a blue hydrangea for Rafaela. The flowers were tied their biorhythms, and as long as the flowers were healthy and thriving, I knew that my family members were, too—no matter how far away they were.

By the same token, any sign of poor health or damage to any of the flowers was a sign that a member of my family was ill or in trouble—or worse.

Out of curiosity, I got up and walked over to the windowsill to examine my plants.

All four of the flowers were thriving, but a vague sense of restlessness and unease remained with me, and I realized what was causing it.

It was the mention of the Crabtree Coven.

Of course, Mom hadn't mentioned them—I had. And she didn't seem to think they were behind the current rune trouble—if it was, in fact, trouble and not just a malfunction.

I moved uneasily as I thought of them, however. The Crabtree Coven could sort of be called our rivals—for lack of a better term—though they were supposed to be long gone now. They'd been banished from the town two hundred years ago, and my family had worked since then to make sure they stayed out.

Recently, however, we'd found evidence that suggested they'd returned to town. But after a big flurry of activity last month, including spells, power outages, and bizarre weather, everything had calmed down again.

It was entirely possible this rune thing would turn out to be no big deal.

But as I got ready for bed and turned out the lights, I couldn't help but feel a little twinge of doubt.

In the morning, Alberta was long gone by the time I made it down to the kitchen for breakfast. She typically left before dawn—though she'd been doing that less often lately—and I didn't usually need to get to work until nine.

Even though Alberta was gone, I could tell she'd been busy, as the kitchen was full of the delicious scent of baking. I investigated and found a coffee cake reposing in a plastic container on the counter. It was still a little bit warm, and it was delightfully sticky, and I cut myself a piece and savored it as I waited for my coffee to percolate.

Once my coffee was ready, and I had drunk enough of it to feel recognizably human again, I cut myself another piece.

Since no one else was around, I couldn't resist licking my fingers, too.

Then I gathered up my stuff and went outside.

It was already warm and humid, and I knew we had another scorching day ahead of us.

I paused to pick up the local paper, *The Morning Cider*, which was lying on the step. Aside from last month's flurry of sensational headlines that had referenced me and my family, there was seldom anything of interest for me in its pages.

This morning its headlines were properly sedate and community-centered, and I dropped the paper in the house before closing the door and locking it.

Then I drove to work.

The Crabtree Bay Public Library was a pretty brick building in a quiet, leafy neighborhood. Only a month ago, this same building had been defaced by graffiti—the word "WITCH" had been scrawled across it in black spray paint. But the library had been covered in graffiti before—usually with much more colorful language—and this latest incident seemed to have been forgotten already.

Nobody—except for two notable exceptions—seemed to remember that I'd been called that any longer, and neither of those two people—Mike and Mr. Clementine—were likely to contact me today. I'd outmaneuvered Mr. Clementine, and Mike had left in a huff and still seemed to be angry with me.

One of those things I was happy about.

And the other I wasn't.

I found a good parking space near the library, and I sighed as I got out of the car.

I was already perspiring, since my car's air-conditioning hadn't had a chance to kick in yet, and I paused to pull my crisply curling hair into a ponytail.

Then I unlocked the book drop and went into the library.

The morning started with our usual stampede of patrons, and then things settled down into a quiet rhythm after the initial rush was over.

Around ten thirty, I noticed that a familiar pair of clear blue eyes was peering around a corner at me, and I realized that Joe Osgood was back at his post. Ever since I had arrived in town four months ago, Joe had been coming to the library to pretend to read comic books and peer around the corner of a bookshelf at me. Most days it was just a minor irritation—and Joe was a really nice guy. I did like talking to him on the occasions when he actually came over to speak to me.

But today his presence just reminded me that Joe was here alone, and Mike wasn't with him, trying to peer at me also.

It was really out of character for Mike to do something like that, and the two of them clearly didn't get along, so it was probably for the best that he wasn't here.

But all the same, I felt a little pang at his absence.

There was a scuffling sound then, and I quickly looked back over at the graphic novel section.

Joe's blue eyes had disappeared, and for just a moment, I saw a flash of dark hair.

Then the scuffling sound returned.

I continued to stare at the graphic novel section, and the scuffling increased. It was punctuated by one short, sharp word.

"Dude!"

I got up then and went to investigate.

As I rounded the corner of the comic book section, I could see Joe grappling with a tall, dark-haired man whose back was to me.

Joe had his hands bunched in the front of the man's shirt, and the man also had his hands wrapped up in the front collar of Joe's polo shirt.

The two were wrenching each other back and forth, and they were also both gripping flowers as they did so.

Joe had a pink one, and the man had a red one.

The whole thing was very bizarre.

They continued their flower-adorned wrestling for several more moments, and then Joe managed to turn the other man so that I could see his profile.

"Mike?" I said.

Both Joe and Mike froze.

"Mike?" I said again. "What are you doing?"

The two men let go of each other and quickly stepped apart.

Mike looked at me sheepishly. "Oh, hello, Chloe. I didn't realize you were there. This isn't—uh—what it looks like."

Joe's face was truculent. "He started it."

I looked from the tall blond-haired man to the even taller dark-haired man.

Then I looked at both the flowers.

"So what is going on here?" I said. "Because it's really not obvious to me."

Mike stepped forward and held out a slightly crumpled rose.

"I—uh—came here to give this to you."

Joe elbowed his way in front of him.

"He was just copying me. I came here to give you this."

Joe held out a pink tiger lily that also looked a little worse for wear.

"Oh, wow," I said. "I honestly don't know what to say."

"I do," Joe replied. He smirked at Mike. "*Anybody* could give Chloe a rose—but I happen to know that Chloe loves tiger lilies. So my flower is better."

Mike looked aghast, and Joe turned to me for confirmation.

"I do love tiger lilies," I said. "But—"

At that moment, the phone at the circulation desk rang, and I turned toward it.

"I'd better get that," I said. "You two stay right here, and try not to get involved in any more flower-based fights while I'm gone. I'll be right back."

I held out a hand as if willing the two of them to stay put, and then I hurried toward the shrill ring of the phone.

A few of our patrons frowned at me as I rushed past.

They didn't like it when I let the library phone ring too long.

I lifted the handset from its cradle, and a voice—high, demanding—and familiar—filled my ear.

"Is that Chloe? I want to talk to Chloe."

I was stunned. "Mr. Clementine?"

"You brought me the wrong book. Do you hear me? It's the wrong one!"

"But—I brought *Volume One* and *Volume Two*," I protested. "How can they both be the wrong book?"

"Because there's a *Volume Three*, smart girl—that's how. *Volume Three* is the one I need. I want you to bring it over right away."

"What's wrong?" said a quiet voice. "I heard a ruckus."

I looked around.

Rita had materialized by my side.

I put a hand over the receiver. I didn't have time to explain about Mike and Joe, so I just focused on my most immediate problem.

"It's Mr. Clementine."

He continued to squawk over the phone, and Rita's warm brown eyes filled with sympathy.

"I thought you took care of that," she whispered.

"So did I," I said. "But now he says *Robertson's History of Rome* has a *Volume Three*, and he needs it immediately."

"What do you want to do?"

"I'll take it to him," I replied. "But this is absolutely the last time. I'm finally fed up."

Rita gave my arm a squeeze. "I'll go find it."

I managed to calm Mr. Clementine down long enough to get him off the phone.

And then I turned around eagerly, looking for Mike.

But Mike had disappeared.

Chapter Four

"Stupid, stupid, stupid," I muttered to myself. Eleven fifteen on the third Wednesday of the month would once again find me driving over to Mr. Clementine's house with a special-delivery book.

I thought I'd outsmarted him, but apparently he was ornery enough to request yet another book in order to win his little game.

And the worst part about it was that he'd interrupted me right when I'd had a chance to talk to Mike.

Mike—who had shown up with a flower to give to me.

I felt a pang as I thought of him.

He had shown up two days in a row at the library now—and surely bringing a rose meant that he finally wanted to talk to me.

And then I had to go running to answer that cantankerous man's phone call.

I would have dropped my head on the steering wheel if I hadn't been driving.

I wondered how I was going to fix this.

I could just spy Mr. Clementine's tall castle-house off in the distance when something suddenly flew straight at my windshield.

I swerved quickly and then slammed on the brakes. Nothing hit the car, but I put it in park and got out anyway.

I was just in time to see a blush-colored bird flapping busily away to the trees of a nearby wood—almost as if it were escaping from something. It looked to be a dove, and I was really glad I hadn't struck it.

I wondered what had made the little creature so frantic to get away, and I looked around.

The road was quiet, and the day was hot, and there was nothing in the sky except for one pink cloud that was shaped just a little like a question mark.

It seemed to me that the cloud was parked directly over Mr. Clementine's house.

I knew that was just an optical illusion, however, and after watching the dove disappear into the woods, I got back in the car and continued on my way.

I soon reached Mr. Clementine's house and parked in the circular drive for the second time in as many days. I got out of the car with my bag weighed down by the heavy book, and I went up to the door to knock.

Daphne Minton answered in her usual friendly but off-putting fashion, and if she was surprised to see me, her calm blue eyes didn't betray it.

I sighed to myself—I supposed I was foolish to believe I'd outmaneuvered Otis Clementine.

Daphne had just closed the door behind me when a sturdy knock sounded and reverberated through the stone room.

She blinked and stared at the door as if she couldn't quite believe what she was hearing, and then the knock sounded again.

She turned to me in mute appeal.

"Not expecting anyone?" I said.

Daphne huffed. "This is *most* irregular. Mr. Clementine keeps a very strict, well-organized schedule, and I am always informed when he has a visitor. I am positive that you are the only one scheduled for eleven thirty today."

"I was scheduled for today?" I said.

"Of course. And you're fifteen minutes late."

"So then Mr. Clementine didn't just call me on the spur of the moment? He had planned all along to—"

Daphne was staring at me as if I'd just grown two heads, and I stopped.

"You were definitely on the schedule," she said firmly.

The knock sounded yet again, and this time it was starting to sound impatient.

"Maybe you should see who that is," I suggested gently.

Daphne hesitated for just a moment and then reached out and opened the door.

A man with dark hair and a thick, dark beard rushed into the room. His eyes were wide and urgent, and he quickly pulled what looked like a gold badge out of his jacket pocket.

As he held it up, I noticed that there was dirt under his fingernails.

"I'm Detective Dave Ortiz," the man said in an angry, accusing voice. "I have reason to believe that a homicide is in progress on these premises."

Daphne was livid. "How dare you—"

"No, ma'am, how dare you? You're standing in my way."

Daphne had indeed moved to stand in front of the man and was impeding his forward progress.

She sputtered. "In your way? This is a private house. You have no right—*no right*—to come in here!"

Dave's eyes were blazing. "This is the home of Otis Clementine, isn't it?"

"Yes, of course."

"Then, ma'am, I am here to tell you that he's in danger this very minute."

Daphne began to sputter once more. "Nonsense! Absolute nonsense!"

Dave reached into his jacket pocket once again and pulled out a phone. His fingers played over the surface quickly, and then he held it up.

The phone's speaker squawked to life.

"Help me ... help me—" A crackle of static. "—pushed me. Down the stairs. Help ..."

The voice, hoarse and tremulous, clearly belonged to Mr. Clementine.

There was a beep and a time stamp then.

Eleven thirty-five.

"That was just ten minutes ago, ma'am," Dave said to Daphne. "Do you recognize that voice?"

Daphne stuttered, looking perplexed. "Why, yes. I—I—"

"It's Mr. Clementine, isn't it?"

"Yes—"

"Then get out of my way!"

Dave rushed past her and headed for the stone stairs.

"But—you don't know where he is!" Daphne cried. "You don't know this house!"

Dave kept running, taking the stairs two at a time.

"Then you'd better come and show me!" he shouted over his shoulder.

Daphne and I glanced at each other.

Then we both ran for the stairs.

Dave pounded up the stairs ahead of us, and we lost sight of him pretty quickly.

Eventually, we reached the tower, and we saw him up above us on the landing.

"Stop!"

His voice, stern and commanding, echoed in the stone cylinder of the tower.

Daphne and I both paused on the stairs.

"Don't be ridiculous!" Daphne huffed. "I live here, you know. I will not be forbidden to—"

"Stop!" Dave commanded again. "Don't take another step!"

Daphne let out another irritated puff of air, but she remained where she was.

Dave crouched down, and I could see that there was a dark mass on the floor that he was examining.

I felt a chill run through me.

At that same moment, I caught a little flutter of motion out of the corner of my eye.

There was a series of thin, staggered windows set into the stone wall, and I thought I could see the figure of a tall person running across the back lawn.

I peered closer.

The figure was wearing a baseball cap and appeared to have short blond hair.

The figure was also clearing fleeing.

"Daphne? Detective Ortiz?" I said. "I think you need to see this."

But Daphne wasn't listening.

"What—*what* is so important that you won't let us go up the stairs?"

I stared at her.

She clearly hadn't noticed the dark, unmoving mass on the landing.

Dave flew down the stairs and pushed his face close to Daphne's.

"You'd better hope we can revive him," he snarled.

I tugged on his sleeve and pointed out the window.

He turned swiftly, but the figure had gone.

"What?" he snapped, turning back to me.

"There was someone running away—" I began.

"What do you mean 'revive him'?" Daphne said sharply.

She was pale and trembling.

Dave got out his cell phone. I could see he was dialing 9-1-1.

He spoke curtly to the operator, requesting emergency medical assistance.

Then he turned back to us.

He pointed a finger first at Daphne, then at me.

"You and you—out!"

"But I saw someone—" I began.

"I don't understand." Daphne's voice rose shrilly. "What's going on?"

She was trembling violently.

She had finally figured out what was wrong—despite her words to the contrary.

I put an arm around her.

"Come on, Daphne," I said gently. "Let's go downstairs."

I figured I could tell Dave about what I'd seen later.

For his part, he hurried up the stairs and began to perform CPR on the prone form on the landing.

But I had a terrible feeling it would all be too late.

Daphne continued to tremble as I led her down the many stairs, and I realized I didn't quite know where I was taking her—I was really only familiar with the stone foyer and Mr. Clementine's tower-top aerie.

I figured the foyer was the best place to take her—I'd spied some benches there before, and we could wait for the paramedics.

The ambulance soon arrived, and a group of EMTs rushed in with a stretcher.

Daphne roused herself enough to show them that there was indeed an elevator, and they were whisked upstairs.

After a few minutes, Dave came back down using the stairs.

He was staring daggers at me.

He came to stand in front of me where I sat next to Daphne on a stone bench.

"I want to talk to you," he said.

Daphne looked up at him sharply.

"What? Why?"

Dave turned a stern face on her.

"Because a man is dead, ma'am. That's why. And I need to get some answers."

I felt another chill run through me.

It wasn't as though I hadn't known after seeing that far-too-still form. But I had hoped—

Daphne's voice cut into my thoughts.

"You're sure? But maybe the paramedics—"

Dave shook his head.

"He was dead before they arrived. They'll be bringing him down soon."

A little gasp escaped Daphne's lips.

Dave turned back to me.

"So who are you anyway?"

"I'm Chloe Bartlett," I replied.

"And what are you doing here, Ms. Bartlett?"

"I work at the library, and Mr. Clementine needed a book. So I brought it to him."

I had a vague feeling that I should ask for a lawyer, but at the same time, I felt deeply numb.

I couldn't believe Mr. Clementine was gone.

Dave was staring at me with a blazing intensity.

"Since when do libraries deliver books?" he said. He leaned closer. "What were you really doing here?"

I stared back at him. "Just what are you implying?"

Dave shrugged and an unpleasant grin spread across his face.

"Oh—I don't know. A pretty girl like you … coming here with a flimsy excuse … I have a feeling you were—how shall I put this? Mr. Clementine's special friend."

"What?" I said.

"Ridiculous!" Daphne said. "Just ridiculous!"

"Is it?" Dave's malicious grin deepened. "I'm going to suggest that you've been Mr. Clementine's friend for quite some time, and you came here today to get some extra money out of him. When he wouldn't cooperate, you pushed him down the stairs to his death."

Daphne jumped to her feet.

"Stop this! Stop this at once!"

Dave turned his unpleasant grin on her. "Don't worry, ma'am. I'll get to you soon enough."

"This is absolutely outrageous!" Daphne sputtered. "Mr. Clementine has never had an inappropriate relationship with this young lady. In fact, he barely knew her."

Dave smirked. "Is that so?"

"Yes, that's so. And I don't believe for a moment that Mr. Clementine was purposefully pushed down the stairs. I'm sure it was just a terrible, unfortunate accident."

"Oh? Then how do you explain my phone message?"

Daphne wavered for just a moment.

Then she became stiff and formal.

"I don't know a thing about that. Besides, that phone message had a time stamp on it."

"So?"

Daphne gave Dave a tiny, unpleasant smile of her own.

"So, Chloe didn't arrive here at the house until well after the time indicated on that message. And we have a camera outside that will prove it."

Dave went very red in the face, and Daphne stared at him in triumph.

I thought for just a moment that Dave was going to explode, but instead, he seemed to regroup, and he became calm.

"There's no need to get upset, ma'am. I'm just gathering pertinent information."

"If it's information you're after," I interjected, "I saw something you should know about."

Daphne and Dave turned as one to look at me.

"I saw someone running across the lawn," I said. "When we were all standing on the stairs. I think whoever it was had climbed down from the wall of the house—right under Mr. Clementine's office."

Daphne stared at me, startled.

Dave appeared disbelieving.

"How convenient," he said.

"It's not convenient at all," I said shortly. "In fact, this whole thing is horrible."

"I quite agree," Daphne said. "This *has* been horrible. You should be offering us sympathy—not grilling us."

At that moment, there was a quiet hiss from somewhere close by, and then there were various clinks and creaks as three paramedics wheeled a gurney out into the foyer.

I stood up, and Daphne quickly moved to my side.

"Look away, dear," she said. "I don't think you should see this."

Her voice was the kindest I'd ever heard it, and she took me by the shoulders firmly and turned me so that I didn't see the body being wheeled out.

"What is this stuff?" said a male voice.

"I don't know," replied another. "But it was all over the floor back there—blue and gray grit."

"Hold that steady!" cried a third voice. "Careful now. We're almost at the door."

I could hear the paramedics calling out further directions to each other, and it sounded as if they were still trying to revive Mr. Clementine.

I supposed they didn't want to give up hope.

After they left, Dave turned toward me and drew in breath to speak, but Daphne interrupted him.

"Detective, this badgering has gone on long enough. I insist that you leave Chloe alone."

Dave swung toward her. "Oh, you do, do you? Who are you anyway?"

"That," Daphne said with a great deal of asperity, "is the question you should have asked *first*. I am Daphne Minton. I am Mr. Clementine's housekeeper."

Dave smirked. "Not anymore."

Daphne's eyes widened to an alarming degree, and I thought for just a moment that she was going to rush toward him.

But to my relief, she remained where she was, and her manner became severe.

"Detective Ortiz," she said. "Will you join me in the kitchen?"

He smirked again. "I don't see that that's—"

"Detective Ortiz!" Daphne's voice rang out sternly and echoed in the stone foyer.

The detective appeared taken aback, but he quickly recovered himself.

"Of course, Ms. Minton," he said, his voice tinged with sarcasm. "Lead the way."

Daphne turned and marched away stiffly.

The detective moved to follow her, and then he turned back to me and held out a warning finger.

"*Don't* leave. I'm not done with you yet."

He turned on his heel, and he and Daphne disappeared from the room, their footsteps echoing down the hall.

I went to sit down on the stone bench again.

As I waited, I found my attention drawn to the large portrait of Mr. Clementine that hung near the door. He really had been handsome when he was younger with his thick auburn hair and his strong cleft chin.

I stood up and walked over to the painting.

As I stared at it, it seemed to me that there was something sad about the eyes, and in the next moment, I thought I heard a gentle sigh.

I turned quickly, but I was alone in the foyer.

At the same time, I felt a chill run through me, and I had the strangest feeling that there was a presence in the room.

I could feel the hair on my arms and the back of my neck standing up.

And then in the next moment, there was the quietest whisper—it was so quiet that I might have imagined it.

Help me.

Chapter Five

That afternoon when I got home, both my sisters met me at the door.

As soon as I stepped into the house, they enveloped me in a hug.

"Oh, sweetie, I'm so sorry," Rafaela said.

"You poor thing!" Alberta cried. "What an awful time you must have had!"

I stepped back from their embrace, and I could see them staring at me.

Rafaela's blue-green eyes were full of worry and sympathy.

Alberta had gone a little red in the face, and she looked as if she wanted to go out and slay some dragons for me.

And there was something else—a delicious scent in the air.

I inhaled deeply. "Are those brownies?"

"Not just brownies," Alberta said, taking me by the shoulders and steering me toward the dining room. "Cream cheese brownies."

"I love cream cheese brownies," I said as I was deposited in a chair.

"I know you do," Alberta replied. She patted me on the hand and then hurried into the kitchen.

In a moment, she returned with a plate of brownies and a glass of milk, which she set down in front of me.

She sat down next to me, and Rafaela sat down on my other side.

"And I'll make whatever you want for dinner," Rafaela said.

She was a marvelous cook, and all manner of cheesy delights began to dance in my head.

Whenever I needed comfort food, I always reached for the cheese.

I bit into the first brownie. It was warm—fresh from the oven—and the cream cheese added just a little bit of tang to it.

It was absolutely perfect.

I closed my eyes. "Thank you, Alberta. This is just what I needed."

She patted my hand again. "I know, darling. You've been through a lot. Take another one."

She pushed the plate toward me.

I smiled at her. Alberta was definitely a "feeder"—whenever someone was worried or in trouble, she started baking.

I continued eating, and my sisters continued to stare at me with worry in their eyes.

And then a thought struck me.

"I'm happy to see you," I said. "But what are you guys doing home?"

"What are we doing home?" Alberta said, incredulous. "We *had* to come home. We couldn't let you go through this alone."

"Of course, dear," Rafaela said, reaching over to pat my back. "After you called us, we had to come to you. We couldn't let you come home to an empty house."

I had called both of them while I waited for Detective Ortiz to return, and then after I called them, I had called Rita. Rita had insisted that I not return to work, and I was greatly relieved. And of course I had known that she and my sisters would be supportive, but I had been unprepared for their great outpouring of sympathy and affection.

Now that I was in trouble, they were here for me, and I felt myself relaxing just a little bit as I started on my second brownie.

"Tell us all about it," Rafaela said. "Every single detail."

So I told them about how I thought I'd outmaneuvered Mr. Clementine—but he'd called anyway. I told them about Mike and Joe's scuffling at the library. And I told them all about the sad discovery of

Mr. Clementine's body and the fact that Detective Ortiz believed he'd been purposefully pushed down the stairs.

I also told them about the detective's apparent belief that I'd had something to do with it—and about the vague presence I'd felt at the end.

"Nonsense," Alberta said when I'd finished. Her eyes were blazing.

"Which part?" I said.

"All of it," she replied promptly. "But particularly the part with Detective Ortiz blaming you for that man's death. Like the housekeeper said, they have cameras and they'll clearly show what time you arrived at the house."

Rafaela's blue-green eyes were thoughtful. "What about the other stuff? Do you think the detective was right that Mr. Clementine was pushed? And what about the presence Chloe felt?"

Alberta snorted a little and then reined herself in.

"You know, I don't know. I'm pretty skeptical about the fall—I really think it could just have been an accident—"

Rafaela interrupted. "But the phone call—"

"Yes, I know. I'm still wondering if Mr. Clementine didn't just trip and then call the police in a panic."

She frowned. "And I'm a little surprised that they took Mr. Clementine to the hospital. If he was already dead, and they believed it was a crime, then they should have left him in place. The fact that they took him to the hospital makes it sound more like they thought it was an accident."

"Maybe they thought they could still revive him," Rafaela said. "You never want to give up on a patient."

"I don't know," Alberta replied. "He sounded pretty much gone to me."

"But what about Chloe's feeling?"

Alberta glanced at me, and I could see the skepticism in her eyes.

"I'm sure you're sincere," she said. "But none of us has the ability to communicate with spirits. And it's also not a talent that runs in our family. Are you sure you didn't just imagine it?"

"No," I said firmly. "The feeling was real. So was the whispering."

"It *was* a stressful situation," Alberta said. "And you were waiting for that cop to come back—"

"It happened."

"Your mind could have been playing tricks on you."

"I'm not crazy."

"I didn't say you were crazy."

"It happened and that's final."

I took a swig of my milk and set it down with purpose.

"Fine. Whatever," Alberta replied.

She mumbled something else under her breath, but I was in no mood to make an issue of it.

Rafaela just looked distressed.

"We're fine, Raf," I said. "*I'm* fine. And tomorrow's my day off. Things will be back to normal soon."

Rafaela took my hand, and I could see that her eyes were a little misty.

"I know," she said. "It's just that this is a lot for you to go through."

Both of my sisters got up then and wrapped me in a hug.

And suddenly I felt safe and home and welcome.

That night, after Rafaela had made us a marvelous macaroni-and-cheese dinner with extra sharp white cheddar, and then departed with one last hug, I sat up in my room thinking over what had happened at Mr. Clementine's house.

The feeling that had come to me while I gazed at his portrait was still with me, and I was more sure than ever that what I had experienced was real and *not* my imagination.

I had felt sadness—and fear.

There had definitely been fear.

And I had a strong feeling that I needed to go back and have another look.

Then I felt something—the germ of an idea growing in my mind.

I had a feeling that Mr. Clementine had been reaching out to me—that he needed my help with something.

Despite the fact that Alberta didn't believe in my feelings, I knew that Mr. Clementine had a message for me.

And I was going to find out what it was.

I turned out my light and went to bed.

In the morning, I awoke to find that I had a series of voicemail messages from my mom and a series of texts from Mike.

I called my mother first, and she answered on the first ring.

"Oh, honey," she said. "Are you all right?"

Our talk was quick. Mom was taking Dad to a doctor's appointment this morning, but she did want to know how I was doing.

And she was wondering why I hadn't called her and she'd had to find out about my ill-fated visit to Mr. Clementine's house from my sisters.

Truthfully, I hadn't even thought of it.

Everything seemed to happen so quickly, and the need to tell Rita and my sisters was more immediate.

Mom fussed over me a little, and then she told me not to worry about the other matter—the rune stones and whether or not they were working properly.

As she mentioned the rune stones, I frowned a little. I'd forgotten about them in all the commotion, but now I wondered about them—and about the low-level magic that she'd said was present in Crabtree Bay all the time now.

There was a little tug at the back of my mind, and the germ of an idea that had appeared last night seemed to sprout just a little.

I was puzzled, but Mom went on with her torrent of words—things she'd apparently been waiting to say all night—and I didn't have time to think about it.

"So take care of yourself, honey," she concluded. "And please don't worry about anything else. I'll call you again soon. And lean on your sisters. They'll be there for you. Gotta run. Love you."

She hung up, and I quickly texted Mike.

Moments after I hit send, my phone rang.

It was Mike.

"Chloe?" he said. "Are you okay?"

I was surprised to hear the concern in his voice. I could picture his handsome face, his dark brows creased with worry.

"Yes, I'm all right," I said. "How did you—"

"Why didn't you call me?" he demanded. "Chloe, you promised me once that you would always call me if you were in trouble."

I felt a flutter of happiness run through me.

I remembered that he had said that.

But I hadn't realized that he remembered it, too.

I felt a spark of hope ignite within me.

"I—I'm sorry," I said. "I guess I just didn't think of it." I paused. "You are talking about Mr. Clementine, right?"

Mike sighed in exasperation.

"Of course I'm talking about Mr. Clementine."

"How did you find out?"

"How did I find out? Chloe, you're present on the scene when a man is found murdered, and you think no one's going to be talking about it?"

"Murdered?" I said sharply. "Is that what everyone's saying?"

"Yes." Mike sounded confused. "Isn't that the impression you got from being there? It's even in the little local paper this morning."

"That *is* what the police seemed to think," I replied. "But others seemed to doubt it."

Mostly my sister, I thought to myself.

But I remembered then that Daphne, the housekeeper, had thought it was an accident, too.

"Well, in any event," Mike said, clearing his throat, "I was wondering if you might come by to see me. I need—I mean—I would like to talk to you—to tell you something. I imagine you'll have to leave for work soon. But maybe you could come over at lunch?"

I felt another little flutter of happiness.

"You want to see me?"

"I—er—yes. And the library isn't really conducive to conversation."

"That's true enough," I replied. "And today's actually my day off, so I can definitely come to see you."

"You can? That's wonderful!" Mike quickly cleared his throat again. "I mean, that's good news—I'm glad you can make it. I'm here at the school right now—what time would you like to come by?"

I almost said "now," but I was afraid that would sound too eager.

At the same time, an idea began to tug at the back of my mind—there was something I needed to do first.

I glanced at the clock by my bed.

"How about eleven o'clock?" I said.

"Perfect," Mike replied. "I'll be here. I can't wait to—"

He paused. "It'll be good to see you again. And Chloe—"

"Yes?"

"Sorry about the flower thing yesterday."

"That's okay," I said. "These things happen."

"They do?" Mike sounded startled.

"Well, maybe not that particular thing," I admitted. "People don't fight with flowers in the library too often—but we do get our fair share of strange occurrences."

"Ah, I see."

Mike sounded uncomfortable, and I winced a little.

I'd been trying to sound reassuring and somehow it hadn't worked out that way at all.

"Okay—so I'll see you later?" Mike said.

"See you later," I replied.

We both hung up, and I sat for a moment staring down at my phone.

The conversation hadn't gone quite the way I'd hoped, but at least Mike wanted to see me.

I pushed myself to get up and get ready for the day—I would need to get moving if I wanted to run my errand before I saw Mike.

I was soon downstairs brewing myself a cup of coffee.

Alberta had left for the day, but the kitchen was still warm, and I could smell the scent of something delicious lingering in the air. I investigated and found two loaves of banana bread nestled in a plastic container.

I cut myself two slices and then sat down with my coffee.

Once I had finished every delectable crumb and imbibed every last drop of energizing coffee, I gathered up my things and headed outside.

I was going to do some investigating.

Mom had told me not to worry about the rune stones, but somehow I had a feeling that that was exactly what I should be doing.

So I stepped out into the hot, muggy morning, and I paused to pick up the local paper, which was lying on the step.

As Mike had said, *The Morning Cider* was mostly concerned this morning with Mr. Clementine's demise, and the headline on the front page trumpeted, "Local Businessman Murdered!"

I read through the lead article quickly.

The paper did seem to believe that Mr. Clementine had been the victim of a homicide, and it declared a push down the stairs of his tower as the likeliest cause of death. It also said that the police were soliciting information and gave a phone number for reporting tips.

I noticed with relief that I wasn't mentioned anywhere—Mike must have heard about my involvement somewhere else.

I scanned through the rest of the paper quickly.

There were other articles—brief sketches, really—about Mr. Clementine—his life, his work, his family—and there were also other articles about the crime and speculation about who could be responsible.

There was no information I didn't know already, however, so I folded up the paper and put it in the house.

Then I got in my car and drove to the outskirts of the city.

There were four rune stones in total, set up by one of our ancestors long ago, and each one sat at the far boundaries of Crabtree Bay. They formed a protective barrier around the town, working to ward off any unauthorized magic workers, and they also alerted us whenever any magic was performed in the city limits that wasn't performed by a member of our family. Whenever that second thing happened—outsider magic being worked—the rune stones were supposed to cause our fingertips to tingle. But as Mom had pointed out, outsider magic had been performed as recently as last month, and no finger-tingling or other indicators had occurred.

I reached the location of the first rune stone and got out of my car.

I was parked on the gravel shoulder of a lonely country road, and I walked down into the grass toward a little copse of trees.

The rune stone was nestled at the base of a towering oak.

The sun was fierce as I made my way over to the mighty tree through the dry grass, and I was relieved when I reached its shade.

I kneeled down to find the stone.

It was partially hidden by the grass, but it was just as I remembered it—it was a speckled white-and-black piece of granite, shaped like an egg, with runes carved into it.

I didn't know what most of the runes did, but I did know that they did their job—or at least they had until recently. I looked the stone over, and as far as I could see, it showed no sign of damage or defacement—the blue paint that an unknown vandal had coated the stone with last month had been completely washed away.

As far as I could tell, the rune stone was in good condition.

I sat back on my heels just staring down at it for a little while.

Then I got back in my car and drove to the next one.

The second rune stone was placed just outside a long-abandoned cemetery. The cemetery itself was really quite pretty—the headstones were a light dove gray, and they were largely overgrown with scraggy weeds and blue wildflowers. All writings and carvings on the gravestones had been worn down by wind and rain, giving them a muted, gentle look. The entire place had an atmosphere of profound calm and peace.

The rune stone I was looking for sat outside what had once been the front gate, and it, like the headstones, was surrounded by scrubby weeds and flowers.

This stone was a brick of layered gray slate, its runes carved clearly and deep, and it was unaffected by the ravages of weather that had worn down the words on the stone memorials. Like the first one, it also appeared to be fine, and I was puzzled as I looked it over. No matter how I examined it, it seemed to be in good working order, and I set it down.

I began to wonder if there really was nothing wrong with them.

The third rune stone—a porous, chunky piece of yellow limestone—was hidden beside the bank of a tiny, trickling brook, and that one looked okay, too.

The fourth one was hidden in the shadow of an old stone building that had probably once been a house. Part of a crumbling chimney still rose several feet high, and portions of three outside walls and one interior room still stood. There was also a stone wall like a fence, largely intact, that ran around the house and a large bare patch that likely been a garden long ago.

The rune stone sat twenty paces from the stone wall, and I found it lying in a patch of scraggly grass.

I picked it up and looked it over—it was a pale, triangular hunk of sandstone with faint striations running through it. This one looked fine, too.

I suddenly remembered that there was an incantation I could use to check the functioning of the rune stones, and I mentally kicked myself for not thinking of it before.

The incantation actually worked to ascertain the health of a person—Rafaela had taught it to me. And since the rune stones were tied to us through connective magic, the spell, oddly enough, could also be used on the stones—even though they weren't alive.

The stone would glow a faint green if all was well. And it would glow red it if wasn't.

I whispered the words to the stone and imbued each one with my own power and magic—it was the intent more so than the words themselves that made the incantation work.

After I said the words, I waited—I knew it would take a few moments for the magic to take effect.

And the incantation would work on all the stones—what was true for one would be true for them all.

After a few moments, the stone began to grow warm, and I knew that the magic was working.

As I watched, the rune stone began to glow with the slightest tinge of green.

I frowned—apparently the stones were working after all.

There was a soft flutter then, and I looked around quickly. Perched on the stone wall twenty paces away, settling its wings, was a pale pink dove like the one I had seen on my way to Mr. Clementine's house. Its dark, beady eyes were trained on me, and as the green glow faded from the stone, the dove unfurled its wings again. Then it settled down and continued to stare in my direction.

I stared back, and the dove didn't look away.

As I set the stone down and walked away, the dove launched itself from the wall and flew overhead, somehow keeping pace with me.

I had the funniest feeling that it was watching me.

Chapter Six

It was getting late, and soon it would be time for me to meet up with Mike.

I hurried away from the creepy bird back to my car, and I was relieved to see that it turned away from me and veered off.

Actually, "creepy" was really the wrong word—the dove was really quite lovely.

But it was also watchful in a way that left me feeling profoundly unsettled.

I was glad I would be seeing Mike soon—I knew the sight of him would dispel the shadows that the bird seemed to have brought with it.

I sighed and settled into my car—that was really the thing about it. I would be glad to see Mike, even if he wasn't glad to see me.

But then again, he had called me.

Would he be happy to see me?

Was he still angry with me?

I couldn't answer any of those questions at the moment, so I started the car and began to drive.

Another thirty minutes' worth of travel brought me back within the environs of the school where Mike taught.

Henrietta College was home to about fifteen hundred students, both grad and undergrad, and it sat on a small, pretty campus that was still leafy and green despite the scorching heat of the summer. A reduced number of classes were in session for the summer semester, and Mike, I knew, was teaching one undergraduate course and one graduate at the moment. He was Professor of English and Folklore Studies, with a heavy emphasis on the folklore.

Mike was very interested in folktales, in superstitions, in tales of magic and the supernatural, and he had a compelling reason for his interest—he didn't believe in any of it. He was, in fact, determined to debunk all stories of the supernatural and prove that they actually had a factual basis that would explain them away.

And though he remembered that I was a witch, he didn't believe in such things himself. He believed *I* believed it, and while he respected my belief, he couldn't actually credit it.

Mike, in fact, respected all the belief systems he studied—even if he thought they were erroneous.

I sighed softly to myself as I parked in one of the college's largely empty parking lots, and then I got out of my car and began my walk to Mike's building.

When I'd first come to Henrietta College to visit Mike—to yell at him, really—I'd wondered if the buildings had controlled access, and I'd ended up sneaking into his building along with a group of students.

As it turned out, the school's buildings *did* have controlled access, but the card reader on Mike's building was currently broken and anyone could walk in.

Of course, Mike had actually invited me this time, so he surely would have let me in even if the card reader had been working.

As it was, I walked right up to the charming brick building and went inside.

Mike's office was on the second floor. I climbed up the wide steps with the ornate wooden banister painted in white and walked down the hall to his door.

It was standing slightly ajar, and I peered inside.

Mike looked up and saw me, and his whole face lit up.

I pulled back quickly, though I didn't know why.

I supposed I was afraid that that happy look on his face wouldn't last.

I heard quick footsteps then, and the door was suddenly pulled open.

Mike was standing in front of me, his dark eyes full of concern.

I drew in my breath sharply.

Sometimes I was startled by just how handsome he was.

"Chloe," Mike said, and he made a slight move toward me.

For just a second, I thought he was going to pull me into his arms, and I found myself leaning toward him.

But he pulled back at the last moment and stood stiffly by the door.

"Chloe," he said again, and this time his tone was more formal.

"It's good to see you," he concluded. "Won't you come in?"

He moved to his desk and then waved me to a chair.

I perched uncertainly on the edge of it.

"You wanted to see me?" I said.

"I—yes." Mike seated himself and then leaned forward on his desk.

His dark eyes were full of concern once again, and I found myself wishing for the closeness we'd started to share before it was all shattered.

"Are you okay?" he said softly.

I thought over the events of the last twenty-four hours, and I could honestly say that I was still feeling very shaken and rattled.

But I hesitated to admit that to Mike. He'd seemed concerned about the Mr. Clementine situation yesterday on the phone, but I wondered if this could be about something else.

Maybe this was actually about the Fourth of July and he finally wanted to have it out.

"What do you mean?" I said cautiously.

Mike was incredulous. "What do I mean? You were present at the house where a man was found murdered, and you have to ask me what I mean?"

So Mike really did care.

I felt a rush of warmth run through me.

"I—I'm okay, I guess," I said. "Considering everything."

Mike was staring at me steadily. "Considering everything? Chloe, I was so worried about you."

He leaned forward again. "Are you really okay?"

"Yes, I'm—" I was going to say I was fine, but that wasn't exactly true. But I knew I would be fine eventually.

"Chloe, I know I asked you this before, but why didn't you call me?" A look flitted across Mike's face that I couldn't quite place. "You said you didn't think of it. Why was that? Why wouldn't you think of me?"

"I—" I said.

"What?"

"It's just that I didn't know if you still meant that after— everything."

"After what?" Mike said.

I looked up at him. "After July the Fourth."

I took a deep breath.

One of us had finally said it.

The events of the day came flooding back to me.

Mike and I had planned to go on a romantic little picnic and then watch the fireworks in the evening.

I had prepared a simple lunch with cheese and grapes and a delicious crusty bread that Alberta had baked. I'd also made cucumber and cream cheese sandwiches, and I'd included cold slices of chicken and turkey ham. To drink, there was a peach iced tea I'd brewed that was pretty good, even if I did say so myself, and Alberta had also donated two slices of a truly divine blueberry cheesecake.

So all in all, the meal wasn't actually that simple, but somehow it felt simple and easy and *right*—because I was preparing it all for Mike.

I'd wrapped up the lunch in a checkered cloth and placed it all in a pretty wicker basket.

Then I'd driven out to the town green where the fireworks were to be held and set out my picnic on a blanket.

And *then* I'd waited patiently for Mike.

He never showed up.

Time passed and more and more people appeared and sat around me.

And I was sitting alone with my picnic.

Eventually, enough time—two hours—went by that I knew it was no accident—Mike wasn't simply late, he wasn't coming at all.

I had been stood up.

I felt tears pricking my eyes.

And then Joe Osgood had shown up at just that moment.

He was happy to see me, as he always was, and he sat down on the blanket to say hello.

He noticed I was unhappy, and eventually the whole story came out.

Along with the story came a few tears.

He was soon consoling me, and before long, we started eating the lunch I had packed.

There was no reason to let it go to waste.

By the time Joe and I had started on the cheesecake, I had forgotten about Mike, and I was starting to have a good time.

And then I heard a gasp.

I looked up to see Mike, silhouetted against the late afternoon sky, staring at us with his mouth open.

The day was very hot, and his dark hair was curling just a little in the humidity.

He was also drenched in sweat.

I jumped up and began to pepper him with questions.

But Mike simply turned on his heel and strode away.

I considered running after him, but *he* was the one who was hours late without any explanation.

I knew Mike wasn't happy to see Joe, but I was sure he could see that it was all perfectly innocent—it wasn't like I had purposefully invited Joe.

So I sat back down and stayed with Joe until the sun went down and the sky deepened to night. Then we watched the fireworks together.

After that Mike and I didn't really speak to each other.

We did run into each other in town a couple of times, but we didn't call or text, and the times when we did see one another were awkward.

It wasn't that I didn't want to talk to Mike—I did—but I just didn't know how.

And I wasn't sure why he appeared to be angry—after all, he was the one who had left me all alone and hadn't even bothered to call.

I thought Mike owed it to me to contact me with some sort of apology, but so far, he'd said nothing.

And I was beginning to think it was all over before it had ever really started.

But then he'd shown up at the library, and now we were here.

And I'd finally said the words.

Mike's face went pale, and then it turned red.

"July the Fourth," he muttered.

"Mike," I said, "what's going on here? One minute you won't talk to me, and the next minute you're telling me you're worried about me."

His face went even redder. "I *am* worried about you."

"Then talk to me. I think you owe me an explanation."

Mike sat up stiffly in his chair. "I owe you an explanation?"

"Yes."

Mike scoffed. "If anything, I think I should be the one asking questions here."

I looked into his face, and I saw a glimpse of the sneering, arrogant person he had been on the day when I'd first met him.

I felt my anger flare.

"And what questions did you want to ask exactly?"

Mike sat forward in his chair. "So what about you and Joe Osgood?"

"What about him?"

Mike stared at me, and I could see anger flicker in his eyes.

"Are you seeing him?"

"What?" I said. "No. Don't be crazy."

"Oh, really? Because the two of you looked awfully cozy that day."

"And what about you?" I said hotly. "Where were you?"

Mike grew stiff and formal. "You might have waited for me."

"I *did* wait for you. I waited for *hours*."

"You're exaggerating."

"No, I'm not," I said. "I waited and waited. And I texted and called. You never answered me."

"So you found yourself a new boy toy?"

"Don't call Joe that. And he found me. He happened to walk by, and he saw me. He could tell that I was upset."

"And you didn't mind that a bit, did you?" Mike sneered.

"I admit that I didn't mind the company," I said, "because you stood me up."

"I didn't," Mike said.

"You did."

"You couldn't wait an hour for me?"

"It was a lot more like three."

Mike jumped to his feet. "You threw me over for another guy."

I jumped to my feet, too. "You abandoned me without a word of explanation."

The two of us stood for a moment, staring at each other and breathing hard.

As I stared into his eyes, I thought I saw a flicker of regret—and fear.

"Oh, Mike," I said. "What really happened that day?"

I sat down, and after a moment, Mike did, too.

He sighed heavily and looked away.

"Mike?" I prompted.

"You'll think I'm—" he muttered, and the rest of the sentence was lost.

"What was that?" I said.

He finally looked at me. "You'll think I'm a fool."

"No, I won't. Please just tell me what happened."

Mike heaved another sigh and placed both of his elbows on the desk in front of him.

"I had car trouble."

"That's not so—"

"I had car trouble and my cell phone was dead. I hadn't charged it properly, and I was stuck out on a small country road with no way to call for help and no way to call you to let you know what happened."

"Oh," I said.

"And I was out on that road in the first place because I was looking for some wildflowers for you—I know you like unusual flowers like that tiger lily Joe brought you."

Tiger lilies weren't all that unusual, and Mike wasn't likely to find anything genuinely exotic growing along the side of the road, but I decided not to tell him that.

"Oh, Mike," was all I said.

He fell silent again.

"Mike," I began after a few moments. "This doesn't sound so terrible—"

"You don't know what was wrong with the car," he said irritably.

"What *was* wrong with the car?"

Mike glanced at me and then looked away again.

"I had a flat tire, and I didn't know how to fix it."

I stared at him, stunned.

"You don't—"

"No."

He darted another glance at me and then smiled a little sheepishly.

"I imagine you need tools of some kind. Possibly a wrench? You certainly can't get those bolts off with your hands."

I tried not to smile.

"Yes, you do need a few tools. And a jack wouldn't hurt, either."

Mike put his head in his hands. "A jack. Of course. That's why people cart those things around."

"So how *did* you get rescued?" I said. "I presume you were rescued?"

"A man in a pickup truck came by," Mike said from behind his hands. "He took pity on me and changed the tire for me."

"So you did have a spare?" I said.

Mike dropped his hands and sat back in his chair. "Yes—I did at least have that. Of course this was after several hours had passed."

"Hence your late arrival."

Mike nodded.

"To sum up," I said. "You had car trouble. And your phone had died. Why didn't you just tell me all this?"

Mike's face went red again.

"I didn't want you to know that I didn't know how to change a tire. A man should know how to change a tire."

Once again, I tried not to smile.

Mike's face went redder still.

"And then there was *him*."

I sighed. "I'm really sorry about Joe. It wasn't intentional—I promise. And I'm not in love with him, and nothing happened on that night or any other. I don't prefer him—it's just that I was afraid you had decided you didn't like me and you weren't coming. And he was so happy to see me—it just made me feel better. But I really wish it had been you I'd spent the day with."

Mike was staring at me with a stunned expression on his face.

"You mean that?"

"Yes."

"And you really don't prefer him?"

"No." I allowed myself a small smile. "And I'll even show you how to change a tire if you would like."

Mike's sheepish smile returned. "That would be nice. And I'm—sorry—I didn't tell you this before. I'm also sorry we haven't spent time together lately. I've really missed you."

I felt another rush of warmth run through me, and I wanted to jump up and run around the desk to hug Mike.

But I stayed where I was.

After a moment, Mike shot a furtive glance at me.

"Chloe, do you mind if—that is, do you think we could start over again?"

This time, I had an impulse to reach my hand out to him across the desk, and I went with it.

Mike leaned forward to take my hand in his, and I felt a little tingle run through me.

"I would like that," I said.

Our contact was broken far too soon, but Mike gave me an earnest look that was nearly as good.

"You really are all right?" he asked. "You weren't traumatized by being present at a murder? Now that we know what we know?"

"What do we know?" I asked sharply. "Has it been confirmed as a murder? I seemed to recall that there was some question about that— it might have been an accident."

Mike waved a hand. "It's all over the place. Someone got a hold of the coroner's report. It was definitely murder. That's what I wanted to talk to you about. I wanted to know if you'd heard—and I wanted to make sure that you were all right, considering—everything."

"Oh," I said. "Was it in *The Morning Cider*? The coroner's report, I mean. I don't think I saw anything about that."

Mike smirked a little. "I don't know if our esteemed local paper covered it or not. But it *is* all over the place online."

"Online?"

"Yes. Otis Clementine was a very wealthy man. He may not have been a household name exactly, but when a man with that kind of money dies, media outlets take notice. There are camera crews all over town."

"So it was murder," I said softly. "And he was deliberately pushed. I wonder how they can tell. I suppose it's the angle of the body?"

"Pushed?" Mike said. "No—he wasn't pushed. Or at least if he was, that wasn't what killed him."

"Then what was it?"

"He was strangled."

Chapter Seven

I went home to think things over—and I had a lot to think about.

Mike and I appeared to be back on, and my heart fluttered a little as I remembered our tête-à-tête.

But as wonderful as that was, thoughts of Mr. Clementine crowded into my mind and pushed everything else out.

He had been strangled.

So his death was murder after all—just as I'd thought from the beginning.

I remembered, too, the strange feeling that I'd had at his house— that he was asking me for help.

I had a duty—an obligation—to find out who the murderer was and help that troubled spirit.

And I had a funny feeling that I was the only person who could.

As I walked into the house, I was hit by the marvelous smell of baked goods, and I thought I could hear someone rattling around in the kitchen.

"Alberta?" I said, puzzled.

It wasn't like her to be home in the middle of the afternoon on a weekday.

She poked her head out of the kitchen and looked out into the living room where I stood, setting down my things.

"Oh, good—you're home," she said, and her eyes were bright with excitement. "Come in here and taste this."

She didn't have to tell me twice.

I hurried into the kitchen, and I could see a baking sheet with two neat rows of golden-brown croissants.

"I just took these out," Alberta said. "You can be the first to try one."

"I don't think I've ever had a croissant straight from the oven before," I murmured.

Alberta turned to the refrigerator to get something, and I selected a croissant and picked it up.

It was hot, and it burned my fingers, but I pulled off one of the pointed ends anyway, and popped it in my mouth.

The croissant was warm and buttery, and it melted in my mouth in the best possible way.

Alberta was turning back toward me with a dish of the Irish butter she always had in the house.

"Oh," she said, "I was going to offer you—"

"That's okay," I said, popping another bit of the croissant in my mouth. "Don't need it. These are buttery enough, believe me."

Alberta eyed me a little uncertainly, which was rare for her. "So they're okay?"

"They're marvelous," I said. "So is that why you're home now—in the middle of the day? You ditched work so you could come home and bake?"

"I—uh—yes," Alberta said, suddenly evasive. Her eyes actually shifted from side to side, and I could tell there was something she didn't want to tell me. Alberta was naturally straightforward, and dissembling didn't sit well on her.

"Have another croissant," she said.

Once again, she didn't have to tell me twice. I accepted a second one gladly and savored the warm buttery taste of it.

"So I'm worried about Rafaela," she said abruptly.

Whether this was a ploy to distract me, or a genuine concern for her, I didn't know.

Whatever it was, it worked.

"Why are you worried?"

Alberta began to fiddle with one of her emerald earrings—a habit she had when she was unusually concerned about something.

"I think she's up to something—I think she's hiding something."

"Like what?"

"I don't know. I even looked on her Facebook page, but I didn't find anything."

"Wait, what?" I said, startled. "Since when do you have a Facebook page?"

Alberta looked away, evasive once again.

"I didn't say I had a Facebook page—I just looked on Rafaela's. You don't necessarily need a page yourself to look at someone else's."

"That's true, I suppose," I said. "But since when do you go on Facebook at all—even to look? I thought you couldn't stand social media."

"I don't like it, but sometimes a person needs to use it—like now."

I sighed. "But you didn't see anything unusual?"

"No."

I gave Alberta an impish grin. "Then you didn't really need to use it."

Alberta scowled. "I'm serious, Chloe. Something's going on with her."

"Speaking of things you really need to use," I said, "I think you're going to need to do some scrying."

Alberta was startled. "What? Why?"

I told her briefly about my meeting with Mike—and about the revelation that Mr. Clementine had been strangled.

"Okay," Alberta said when I had finished my tale. "There's a lot to unpack in there. You and Mike are back on?"

"Yes," I said. "I think so. And to be fair, we were never really 'on' in the first place. We were just getting to know each other when the whole thing blew up. But that's not what I need your help with—what I really need is your scrying ability."

"Oh, Chloe, I don't know," Alberta replied.

"Otis Clementine was strangled. There's no way that was an accident."

Alberta sighed. "Maybe later. Right now I'm tired."

"Tired from what?" I said. "Playing hooky?"

Alberta opened her mouth to retort, and then decided not to say anything.

"That's what I thought," I said.

Alberta sighed again wearily. "You say it was in the coroner's report?"

"Yes—Mike saw it online. I'm sure it's easy enough to look up. Besides, like I told you before, I saw someone leaving the house right after we found Mr. Clementine. Someone was running away across the back lawn."

Alberta shot me a sharp glance then. "Chloe—you're not getting too involved in this, are you? I mean, after all, this is a matter for the police, and you're not a cop."

I bristled. "So only you get to help the police?"

Alberta shook her head. "That was different. I only did that twice, and in both cases, I had a very strong feeling about it."

"Well, I have a strong feeling about this."

"Ah, yes—your ghostly visitation. I keep telling you none of us can see spirits."

"Okay," I said. "Maybe I'm not 'seeing spirits.' Maybe I'm just receiving a message from a spirit this one time. It's not out of the realm of possibility for me to have a one-time contact, is it? Especially since I was present when something really terrible happened?"

Alberta grumbled a little under her breath, but I could tell my point had gone home.

"Maybe I'll do some scrying," she said at last. "But later. I'm not really up to it at the moment—I need to be in the right frame of mind."

"Thank you, Alberta," I said.

71

"I said 'maybe,' " she cautioned. "There's a possibility that I may not do it after all."

I smiled at this little speech—I was pretty sure that that was actually a yes.

"Little sisters," Alberta muttered to herself.

My phone rang then, and I hurried over to my purse to see who it was.

I frowned at the caller ID as I picked it up.

It was a new acquaintance of mine—Detective Mia Coleman.

After a moment's pause, I decided to answer.

"Hello?"

"Is that Chloe Bartlett?" Mia's voice was warm and friendly over the phone.

"Yes, this is Chloe."

"How have you been?"

I frowned a little more—her tone was inviting and sociable, and Mia and I weren't exactly friends. We'd met when I was accused of trying to kill a local woman and her cleaning lady, and I had been one of Detective Mia's main suspects.

Though I'd been cleared eventually, we weren't exactly in the habit of calling each other up to chat.

"I'm doing well," I said in response to Mia's question. "How can I help you?"

"It's been a little while since we've chatted. I was wondering if you wouldn't mind coming down to the station—I've got a few questions to ask you."

"What?" I said, startled.

"I already went to your place of employment," Mia said smoothly. "They said you had the day off, so I was hoping you would have some time to come down and visit."

"What?" I said again. "Is this about Mr. Clementine? I've already spoken to Detective Ortiz. He knows I'm not responsible—no matter what he might say."

"This is just a little talk." Mia's tone was soothing. "Gal to gal. We know you were present at the scene, and we'd like you to help us out—maybe fill in a few details. It would mean a lot."

I sighed to myself—Mia's voice was friendly, but I could hear the determination in it. She was going to get me down to the station—one way or another.

"I'll come down," I said heavily. "What time do you want to see me?"

"Do you have any time now?"

I glanced around at Alberta, who was watching me anxiously.

"I can do it now," I said.

"Wonderful," Mia said. "I'll see you soon."

I set down my phone.

Alberta hurried over to me. "Who was that?"

"Detective Mia," I replied.

"Detective Mia?" Alberta said in surprise—she was acquainted with the detective, too. "What does she want?"

"She wants me to come down to the station to talk about what happened at Mr. Clementine's house."

Alberta frowned. "But you already gave a statement to Detective What's-his-name."

"Ortiz," I said. "And, yes, that's true. I don't know why they need to see me again."

"Are you going to go?"

I thought for a moment.

"Yes. I think I should—I think it's important."

Alberta's expression grew stormy. "You call me if you need anything—anything at all. I may not be a defense attorney, but I'll stop them if they get too troublesome. No one's railroading my sister."

"Thanks, Alberta," I said.

I picked up my purse and headed to the door.

I appreciated Alberta's concern, but I was anxious to get this meeting with the police over and done with.

I drove to the station.

Once inside, I stopped at the little window with bulletproof glass in the lobby.

The young man behind the glass made a phone call, and Detective Mia came out to greet me.

Mia Coleman had black hair and rich brown skin, and she was dressed in a well-tailored, plum-colored suit.

She broke into a wide smile that I remembered well when she saw me, and she extended a hand in greeting.

"Chloe Bartlett—how good to see you."

Her hand was warm and firm when I clasped it, and she placed her other hand over mine and gave me a friendly pat.

I could see I was in for the charm treatment.

But I wasn't quite sure why.

"Thank you so much for coming in today. Would you please follow me?"

She led me to the big metal door she had just come through, and as we passed inside, two young officers in uniform brushed past us.

"—and there's been another break-in," the first officer was saying.

"But I was still finishing my lunch," the second one protested.

As if to prove his point, he popped the last bit of what looked like a sandwich into his mouth.

"Besides," the second one continued, "don't those things always happen at night? What's the rush to get over there? It's been hours already."

"Come *on*," the first one responded.

The two of them disappeared from view, and the heavy, metal door slammed closed after them.

"Chloe?" Mia prompted. "My desk is this way."

I turned to see Mia waiting for me, and I hurried to follow her.

I hadn't realized I had stopped to watch the other two cops.

Mia ushered me to her desk, and I sat down on a metal chair that had been placed next to it. Mia's desk had several neat piles of folders stacked on it, and I noticed that another desk was set right next to it, just beyond a low-walled cubicle. This desk, however, was anything but neat, and piles of paper, knickknacks, and a handful of assorted picture frames all fought for space.

Whoever usually occupied the desk wasn't present.

Mia smiled at me.

"So, Chloe—"

"Why aren't we in one of the rooms?" I blurted out.

Mia blinked, startled. "I'm sorry—what was that?"

"Last time I was here, you took me into a room in the back to ask me questions—it was just the two of us. Why are we staying out here this time?"

Mia smiled. "Like I said, this is just a friendly chat—"

"So the rooms in the back are just for suspects?"

Mia's smile grew a little strained. "Not necessarily. It's up to the individual officer where he or she conducts business."

She waited for a moment to see if I would respond to that, and when I didn't say anything, she continued.

"So, Chloe, if you don't mind, I'd like to go over a few of the things you said on Wednesday. I understand, for example, that you saw someone leaving the scene?"

"Yes," I said.

"Perhaps if you could tell me what happened again? Starting from the time you arrived at Mr. Clementine's house."

I started to tell my story again, and Mia opened a folder and stared down at a set of handwritten notes. From time to time, she jotted down another note in the margins, but for the most part, she just listened.

When I was finished, she consulted the notes again.

"Tell me one more time about the person you saw running across the lawn."

"It was someone tall," I said. "Or at least I think it was someone tall—it's hard to tell when you're looking down from above. The person had a baseball cap on, and I thought I could see some short blond hair sticking out at the base of it."

Mia glanced down at her notes. "I noticed that when you described the person, you avoided saying anything about gender. Could you tell if it was a man or a woman?"

"No—I couldn't say for sure. I only saw the person from the back. And he or she was wearing baggy sweats."

I glanced at the notes in front of Detective Mia curiously. "Are those Detective Ortiz's notes?"

"No. They're mine."

"Why isn't he talking to me? Not that I'm complaining—it's just that I thought he was running this case."

And I genuinely wasn't complaining—I had no real desire to see Detective Ortiz ever again.

Mia glanced over at the desk next to her.

"Yes—he was running the case. But he's come down with the flu."

"The flu?" I said, surprised. "He looked perfectly healthy to me."

"That's the thing with the flu." Detective Mia was rueful. "Sudden onset is one of the symptoms—it'll hit you out of nowhere. So I'm working the case while he's indisposed."

"May I ask you a question?" I said.

Mia glanced at me sharply. "Of course."

"Detective Ortiz," I said slowly. "He's a little intense, isn't he?"

Mia relaxed a little—as if she'd expected me to ask something else. "Yes—yes, he is."

She said the words with a certain fondness.

"Don't you think he's maybe a little too intense?" I said. "Maybe a little overzealous?"

I was still smarting from some of the things he'd said.

Mia smiled a little. "I suppose he can seem that way. But he's really a good guy—and he comes from a long line of cops. His dad was one, and so was his grandfather—and I believe his father was one, too. We've even got a picture of Dave in the case out front as a teenager in the Police Athletic League. He wanted to be a cop his entire life, and he believes very strongly in protecting people. If he seems a little overzealous, it's just because he's serious about his job—and about bringing the bad guys to justice."

Mia paused. "Is there anything else you'd like to tell me? Anything at all?"

"No," I said.

I'd told her everything—except for the part about the feeling of sadness and fear in the house—and the feeling that Mr. Clementine needed my help.

But I could hardly tell her any of that—she wouldn't believe me, and if even she did, she couldn't help me anyway.

Mia continued to stare at me expectantly.

I stared back at her.

"Did you notice anything that interested you in your professional capacity?" she asked.

"In my professional capacity?" I said, puzzled.

"Yes."

"As a library assistant?"

"No—as a practitioner of magic."

She said the words lightly, but she was watching me carefully.

"What do you mean?" I said, instantly on alert.

Mia smiled. "I seem to recall a newspaper article about a month back that claimed you and your sisters believe you're witches."

I stared at her. "You remember that?"

"Yes."

You're not supposed to, I thought to myself.

Here was yet another person who wasn't forgetting. I wondered how many others remembered—and I began to wonder if our symbol had been irreparably damaged.

But I didn't have time to worry about that.

Mia looked down at her notes again.

"Are there magical ways to do away with someone?" she said suddenly.

I stared at her in shock—I assumed that was the reaction she'd been going for.

"What?"

"Are there magical means to end a human life?"

"I thought Mr. Clementine was strangled," I said.

Mia eyed me suspiciously.

"It was in the coroner's report," I said quickly. "It's all over the news."

"Yes, it is—that's true." Mia seemed to relax a little, but she continued. "And it's the autopsy actually—that's a public record. The coroner's report won't be available for a little while yet—and that'll be more in depth."

"So if you know that he was strangled, why are you asking me about magical means?"

Mia gave me a broad smile.

"What do you know about the witch in the woods?"

"The what?" I said.

"The children around here say there's a witch who lives in the woods and tries to lure the little ones out there—she even lives in a gingerbread house."

I stared at Detective Mia. "Are you joking right now?"

"No, I assure you I am not. They say you can only find her by following a trail of breadcrumbs, and they also say that in addition to luring children, she also sells spells—dangerous ones. Ones you can use to get rid of people."

"Breadcrumbs," I murmured softly.

"What's that?" Mia said.

"Nothing."

"So how about it? Is she one of yours?"

"One of ours?" I said.

"Is she part of your coven?"

"We do not have a coven," I said with dignity.

Mia smiled again. "So you're just sister witches?"

I caught the note of sarcasm, but I couldn't quite tell what she was getting at. "Something like that."

"Then—"

"I don't know who she is," I said.

"You don't?"

"No."

"They also say she keeps a dove that spies for her."

"A dove?" I said, sitting forward. "What color?"

"What color?" Mia said. "Are you saying you've seen it?"

"I—don't know," I said somewhat lamely.

"Have you seen it?" Mia's voice rose.

"I mean, I have seen a dove—twice in fact. But it could have just been an ordinary bird."

The detective suddenly seemed deflated. "Yes, that's true, isn't it? A dove isn't really much to go on."

She seemed to be talking more to herself than to me.

Mia continued trying to pump me for information, and I tried to find out more about this mysterious woman with a house in the woods. But I didn't know anything else, and all Mia had was rumors.

In the end, we were both disappointed.

I left the police station and walked out to my car.

As I drove home, all I could think about was a blush-colored dove sitting on a crumbling stone wall, watching me.

Chapter Eight

That night I sat up in my room, staring at my plants.

They were perfectly healthy—all of their colors were bright and none of them had dropped any petals or leaves—and that meant that my family was perfectly healthy, too.

But I wasn't really concerned about their health at the moment. I could feel an idea growing at the back of my mind once again, and I wanted to look at something else that was growing, thriving.

Maybe that would help the idea along.

When I'd arrived home, Alberta was still baking croissants, which was a little odd, since I didn't know how many croissants we could really use—Alberta had already baked several dozen. And then Rafaela, who had planned to have dinner with us, had called to say she couldn't make it.

Alberta thought this was odd, but I didn't—Rafaela frequently worked odd hours at the clinic and could always be counted on to come in and work extra hours if they found themselves short-staffed.

On the other hand, Alberta did *not* think Detective Mia's tale of a witch in the woods was odd. She didn't believe a word of it, and said it was just a story children told to scare each other—and besides, *she'd* never heard of it.

She also didn't believe there was anything in my sightings of a dove.

But I wasn't so sure that the stories could be dismissed so easily. I resolved to look into them as soon as possible.

But first, I had to look into what had happened to Mr. Clementine.

Now that I knew he'd been strangled—and that there was a possibility that there was a magic element to the crime—I knew there was no one else who could solve this.

It was even clearer to me now that I had a duty to find the killer.

Alberta had been in a particularly truculent mood—possibly due to my lack of concern over Rafaela's doings—and I hadn't asked her about scrying again.

I would do so—but just a little later. And I wanted to think a little more about what I would ask her to find.

First, I had to get back into Mr. Clementine's house.

I had to see if I could find the presence I had sensed before.

In the morning, I was up before my alarm, and I hurried downstairs.

Alberta was already gone, which was a little more like her normal routine, but when I looked for a croissant to have for breakfast, I found that they were all gone.

That was definitely not normal.

I looked around a little more, but the croissants were nowhere to be found.

I figured Alberta must have taken them into her office, but her office wasn't really that large—I wasn't sure what they would do with several dozen croissants.

But that was a mystery for another time, and I got myself a cup of coffee, an apple, and an energy bar for breakfast.

Then I hurried out the door.

The Morning Cider was sitting on the doorstep, and its headline caught my attention:

"Bold Burglar Strikes Again!"

I skimmed over the article quickly.

Apparently, two jewelry stores had been burglarized in the last two months—one was part of a large chain and the other was a small mom-

and-pop store. But in both cases, the security system and the cameras had been disabled first, and then a back door had been broken open with very little force.

And then both stores had been completely been cleaned out.

The paper was speculating that both burglaries had been committed by the same person—and that a crime spree was beginning.

That was probably an exaggeration, but all the same I felt a little unsettled.

Then I shrugged the story off—it was probably just the paper trying to be sensational.

I got in my car and drove to work.

The day started off with the usual morning rush, and once it died down a bit, I stood with my hand hovering over my cell phone. I was considering taking it outside and using it.

I wanted to call Daphne Minton and ask her if I could come to the house, but I was having trouble coming up with a pretext for the visit—other than the obvious one.

As I stood in an agony of indecision, the library phone rang, startling me.

The caller ID said "Watley and Hurtzel," and below that was a number with a local area code.

I frowned a little as I answered it—I wondered if it could be a telemarketer.

We'd been getting quite a few calls that were spoofed to look like local calls lately.

"Thank you for calling the Crabtree Bay Public Library," I said. "This is Chloe. How may I help you?"

The man on the other end cleared his throat.

"This is—uh—Lee Hurtzel. Am I speaking with Chloe Bartlett?"

"Yes," I said cautiously.

The man sounded as if he wasn't used to talking on the phone—so he clearly wasn't a telemarketer. But all the same, there was something in his tone of voice that gave me pause.

He sounded like someone who'd been caught doing something he shouldn't do.

"I'm sorry—what was that?" the man said. "You'll have to forgive me—I'm a little hard of hearing."

"Yes, this is Chloe Bartlett," I said more clearly. "How can I help you, Mr. Hurtzel?"

The man chuckled, sounding natural for the first time. "Please call me Lee. Mr. Hurtzel is my father."

I had to smile at that—Lee Hurtzel sounded as if he could be a grandfather himself.

"How can I help you, Lee?"

"Well, now, Chloe, I'll tell you—it's a most peculiar thing."

He hesitated, and I waited patiently. It sounded as if Lee was just getting warmed up.

After a moment, he continued.

"I take my duties and the trust my clients place in me seriously—very seriously."

He paused.

"Chloe—I was fortunate to be the attorney for the late Mr. Otis Clementine, and he placed an enormous amount of faith and trust in me. And before he passed, he enjoined me to fulfill a task for him in the event of his demise, and now that he has shuffled off this mortal coil, I find myself in the position of needing to discharge that task."

Lee paused again.

"Chloe, I would esteem it a great kindness if you would stop by my office sometime today—entirely at your convenience, of course."

I was startled. "I'm sorry, Lee. I don't quite understand."

"Without getting into particulars," he replied, "I can tell you that the task I need to fulfill has to do with you."

"With me?"

"Yes, ma'am."

"I don't see how that's possible," I said. "What kind of task is it?"

Even though I couldn't see him, I could tell that Lee stirred uneasily.

"If you don't mind," he said, "I'd rather not divulge that over the phone. I'd feel—safer—if you could come to my office so I could tell you about it in person."

I glanced up at the people who were seated at the tables near the circulation desk.

A few of my regular patrons were staring at me—they typically disapproved when I had conversations on the library phone—and conversations on cell phones were strictly forbidden.

Mrs. Ludlow—one of my regulars who'd already been angered earlier in the week by my phone calls—was giving me a particularly baleful glance over the top of her silver-rimmed glasses.

And then there were the patrons who weren't paying any attention to me at all. One of them was Tom Patterson, a recent college graduate who was absorbed in a car magazine. Tom had asked me if I could help him with some job applications online, and I'd agreed to do it during my lunch hour—that was really the only time I could give him my undivided attention.

The trouble was that that was the only time I could offer Lee Hurtzel, too.

And I couldn't disappoint Tom.

"Does it have to be today?" I said into the phone.

I could hear Lee shifting a little. "Today would be best—if you can manage it. It's a matter of some urgency."

"I'm afraid I won't be able to leave the library until about five thirty," I replied. "How late does your office stay open?"

Lee chuckled a little. "I have spent many nights burning the midnight oil here. Any time after five thirty is fine. My secretary will have gone for the day, but the front door will be open. Just come on in. My office isn't hard to find."

"Okay," I said, still feeling a little uncertain.

"You'll come, then?"

"Yes, I will."

"Thank you, Chloe. I'll see you this evening."

Lee Hurtzel gave me his address and then hung up, and I replaced the receiver in its cradle.

I was feeling more than a little disturbed by the call—and the appointment—but a patron came up to the desk to check out a book and several movies, and I was quickly occupied again.

I couldn't imagine what business Mr. Clementine's attorney could have with me, and it seemed to me that he had been feeling ill at ease during the phone call.

I wondered why he had called if he really didn't want to.

But I knew I would have to wait several more hours before I could find out.

The day did indeed get busy again, and at lunchtime I was able to help Tom submit his resume to no less than three places.

After that, I got back to work again.

I wondered a few times if I should try calling Daphne Minton to set up an appointment with her, too, but I was feeling too unsettled about my meeting with Lee to attempt to talk to her.

I would have to get that over with first.

The end of the day did roll around eventually, and Stu and Emily came in to relieve Rita and me.

Then I got in my car and drove to the address that Lee had given me.

The office of Watley and Hurtzel, Attorneys at Law, was located in our historic downtown area, where the houses and buildings were made of brick, and the streets were paved with cobblestones.

The neighborhood was fashionable, and the rents were high—it was the perfect location for an old and venerable law firm.

Lee's office was red brick with white shutters like all of the other buildings on the street, and parking appeared to be nonexistent.

I did eventually find a spot in the tiny parking lot of the nearby post office, and as I slotted into the space, I prayed I wouldn't be towed.

Then I hurried to Lee's office.

The front door was indeed open—as he'd said—and I stepped into a tastefully furnished waiting room full of dark wood. The receptionist's desk was also empty—as Lee had indicated it might be—and there was an open doorway standing just beyond it.

I stepped through it and found myself standing in a short hallway.

There was an open door on my left, and I walked over to it.

Before I reached it, however, I could see the sign on the door: "Lee J. Hurtzel, Jr., Esq."

I tapped on the door and a slightly husky voice rasped, "Come in."

I stepped inside.

The room was bigger than it appeared to be from the outside, and Lee Hurtzel's desk was set near a window off to the side—which was why I hadn't been able to see him from the doorway.

The man himself rose as I entered.

He cleared his throat. "Chloe Bartlett?"

"Yes," I said.

The man smiled and stepped forward. "I'm Lee Hurtzel. Thank you for coming."

Lee was a tall, distinguished-looking man of about sixty with a full head of gray hair and an equally full gray mustache. I felt very much like I should call him "Mr. Hurtzel," but he'd already said how he felt about that.

He held out his hand, and I shook it, and then he extended that same hand toward a nearby chair.

"Would you care to take a seat?"

I settled myself and my purse in the chair, and Lee sat down behind the desk across from me.

He paused for a moment in thought, and my eyes roamed over the shelves of leather-bound books that rose up toward the ceiling behind him—lawbooks, I presumed.

Eventually, Lee cleared his throat once again. "I apologize for all the sounds I'm making. I hear there's a flu going around. I hope that's not what this is."

He paused again, and after a moment, he seemed to come to a decision.

"Chloe, there's no easy way to say this, so I'll just come out and tell it to you straight. A lawyer's job is to uphold the law—maybe not in the same way that a police officer does—but it's still our job to make sure that the laws of this land are followed. And it's also our job to carry out the wishes of our clients—they place a lot of trust in us, and we have to act in a way that makes us worthy of that trust."

Lee paused yet again. "And sometimes those two things conflict with one another."

I was puzzled. "What do you mean?"

Lee leaned forward and rested his hands on the desk in front of him.

"Otis Clementine was a client of mine, as I have said. But he was also a very dear friend."

He hesitated.

Coming from another man, the words might have seemed insincere—I got the impression that Mr. Clementine hadn't had many friends—not real ones, at least.

But when Lee Hurtzel said he'd been Mr. Clementine's friend, I believed him.

Lee continued. "So when Otis asked me to do something for him in the event of his demise, I agreed—despite the somewhat questionable legality of situation."

I looked up sharply at that.

"You see, Chloe, when a person dies—particularly a very wealthy individual like Mr. Clementine—the estate goes into probate. All the heirs are notified of what they've inherited, all dispositions of property and money are looked into very carefully, and there is also a period of time during which people may contest the will if they so choose. The entire process can take up to a year, and again, in the case of someone as wealthy as Mr. Clementine, the process can take even longer."

Lee took a deep breath. "What this typically means is that the heirs don't receive their inheritance until after the probate process is finished. But in this particular case, Mr. Clementine wanted me to give you something immediately, should he pass away. The item in question is something quite valuable—something that should definitely be included in an inventory of the estate. Mr. Clementine has instructed me to say that the item has been lost."

Lee cleared his throat, clearly uncomfortable.

Then he stood and walked to a picture on the wall.

He pulled the picture to the side to reveal a wall safe, and then he punched a combination of numbers into the keypad.

The door opened after that, and Lee extracted an object, which he gave to me.

I looked it over—it was the box with the sunflowers that I had seen in Mr. Clementine's office.

And I could hear something rattling around inside it.

I looked up at Lee, puzzled.

"Go ahead and open it," he said as he seated himself once again.

I stared at the pretty, gold-colored box with the sunflower pattern for just a moment, and then I pried the lid off carefully.

Inside was a black-velvet ring box and a white glove trimmed with brightly colored jewels.

I picked up the glove first, and a heavy key dropped out of it, landing in the box with a clatter. The key was old-fashioned looking with an ornate handle and a long stem, and I looked it over for a moment before turning back to the glove. The glove was small with slender fingers, and it looked like it would only fit a lady's hand. Jewels in red, blue, and green adorned the cuff, and right above them sat two initials, "GG."

"I don't believe those are real jewels," Lee said. "They're only glass. But the ring is real enough."

I set the glove down again and picked up the ring box. Inside was a huge, dazzling diamond flanked on either side by stones the color of sunshine.

"Wow," I said.

"The ring was recently appraised at a little over half a million dollars," Lee said. "And it's possible that it could go for even more at auction."

"Wow," I said again.

"There's an inscription on the inside of the band, if you'd care to read it."

I took the ring out of the box carefully and examined the band. It was made of a silvery metal that I assumed was platinum, and I could just make out a few words etched on the inside:

"For one who truly loves."

Then two letters:

"CC."

I looked up at Lee.

"I don't quite understand."

Lee reached into a drawer and pulled out an envelope.

"Mr. Clementine also wrote you a letter. He asked me to read it to you after you'd opened the box."

He cleared his throat and began to read.

"Dear Chloe. I have been wrong about a lot of people in my life— but I don't think I'm wrong about you.

"I have entrusted one of my most prized possessions to you. It's the ring I gave my wife—and unfortunately, it's also the ring she gave back to me when she left me. It was also my mother's ring, and she and my father had a long and happy life together. The ring is now yours, and you may keep it if you wish. But what I would really like for you to do is give it to someone who deserves it.

"I have a feeling you aren't motivated by money, and I think that you will genuinely do your best to find someone who is worthy of this ring. Though I never said it, I appreciated the assistance you gave me, and I have a lot of faith in you. Thank you for putting up with the temper and vagaries of an old man.

"And for what it's worth, I think she really did love me.

"I know I loved her.

"Yours in all sincerity, Otis Clementine."

Lee finished the letter and folded it up again.

I looked at him and then looked at the ring in my hand.

"He wants *me* to give this ring to someone?"

Lee shifted a little. "Does that mean you don't intend to keep it?"

"Of course I don't intend to keep it," I replied. "I've only known Mr. Clementine for a few months, and this ring clearly meant a lot to him. It should go to someone in his family."

I paused. "He does want it to go to someone in his family, doesn't he?"

Lee smiled. "You're a very unusual person, you know that? I do believe you mean what you say. As far as whether the ring needs to go to a family member, I don't believe that is specified. Would you like to read it over yourself?"

He held the letter out.

I took it and read it over again.

Then I looked up at Lee. "How did this box come into your possession anyway? I saw it on Mr. Clementine's desk just a few days ago."

Lee reddened. "As soon as I heard news of Mr. Clementine's demise, I went over to his house to get it. It was his most particular wish that I do so."

Then he nodded his head in the direction of the letter I was still holding.

"He also gave me instructions to burn his letter."

I committed the contents to memory and then handed it back to Lee.

"So this is all highly illegal," I said.

Lee reddened again. "It's certainly not typical practice for me to remove a valuable piece of property from a client's estate and dispose of it myself. But Mr. Clementine made me promise to do it—and I never break a promise."

Lee drew himself up with dignity and then continued. "And as far as the estate is concerned, it doesn't exist. Mr. Clementine never included it in any of the official inventories of his assets. And when he had it appraised, he actually took it out of the country and did it under an assumed name. He didn't want the world to know that his wife sent it back to him—as far as everyone knows, she died with it in her possession, and she died overseas. What became of it was a mystery. And I don't believe that that ring is famous—at least not anymore.

"That being said, there is some risk in this. And if you choose not to accept, I understand completely."

I looked at Lee for a long time, and then I looked down at the ring.

Mr. Clementine had said he had faith in me.

"I'll do it," I said. "I'll give the ring to someone who deserves it."

Lee stared at me, and I could see a number of emotions at war in his face—guilt, pride, and something that looked like compassion.

"On behalf of my old friend," he said, "I thank you."

He pulled another envelope out of a drawer and handed it over to me.

"I want you to take this with you."

I looked the envelope over.

It was sealed.

"What is it?" I said.

Lee's lips twitched. "It's a confession. I've detailed my entire role in this little affair and declared you completely innocent—and entirely ignorant—of what was going on here. That way, if there's ever any fuss over the ring and what you do with it—any legal trouble for instance—you'll be entirely absolved of wrongdoing. I believe you should be safe, but as you've said, this enterprise is highly illegal. And I don't want you getting into trouble because of me."

"Oh, no," I said. "I can't—"

Lee held up a hand. "Please. You must take it. It's the only way I'll sleep tonight. Or indeed on any other night."

"Okay," I said. I could tell Lee wasn't going to take no for an answer. "Thank you."

He relaxed visibly. Then took a sheet of paper out of a folder on his desk.

"There's one last piece of business to attend to. There will be a reading of Mr. Clementine's will on Monday. He was most particular that a reading should take place—though such things aren't really done anymore—and he asked me to invite you in the event that such a thing did occur. I've taken the liberty of printing out the details."

I accepted the sheet of paper from Lee and read it over.

"Thank you," I said. "I'll be there."

"Oh, and one last thing, Miss Bartlett. I'm not going to forbid you to mention the ring to anyone—in fact, it may be better if a few close associates such as a family member or a financial advisor know of its existence. But I would counsel you to exercise extreme caution in choosing whom to tell about it. Please promise me that you'll reveal your possession of the ring only to those whom you trust and only when it's necessary. Please don't give out the information casually."

"I promise," I said.

"Then on behalf of my dear friend Otis Clementine, once again, I thank you for taking this on."

I nodded, a little embarrassed.

We exchanged a few pleasantries, and then Lee walked me to the door.

As I stepped out into the hot, muggy summer evening, I had the strangest feeling that I'd just agreed to more than one thing.

Chapter Nine

"Crazy," Alberta said. "Completely crazy."

We were sitting in the kitchen eating dinner, and I had just finished telling her about my meeting with Lee. As if in response to her words, Alberta's cat, Sibyl, came into the room with a heavy coating of dust bunnies on her chin, side whiskers, and the little whiskers that grew over her eyes. The wispy clumps of dust created the illusion of a snowy beard and eyebrows, and Sibyl now looked like a tiny Santa Claus.

Alberta stood up.

"Sibyl, not again."

She moved toward the cat, who fled from the room, leaving tiny wisps of dust floating behind her in the air.

We could hear her galloping up the stairs.

"That cat," Alberta said, sitting down again. "She did the same think this morning before I left for work—she waltzed in here covered in dust. I have no idea where she got it from. This house is spotless."

Alberta's house was indeed spotless—so much so that I often wondered if she used magic to do it. There was nothing wrong with using magic to assist with housekeeping, of course, but for some reason our mother had frowned on it.

Perhaps she thought it was too obvious and could draw undue attention to our abilities.

Alberta shot me a peevish look.

"Maybe she got it from your room."

I shifted a little guiltily—that was entirely possible.

Alberta never went into my room, and I had been a bit remiss about cleaning.

There certainly could be a few dust bunnies under my bed.

"Just finish eating," I said soothingly. "You've barely touched your food."

Alberta grumbled a little, but she picked up her fork again.

I had made chicken parmesan, and I thought it was quite good—even if I did say so myself.

The chicken was juicy and tender, the breadcrumbs were golden brown and had just the right level of crispiness, and the tomato sauce was both tangy and hearty. And then of course, there was the parmesan and provolone cheeses melted together, and just a little brown on top.

And Alberta had whipped up an angel food cake—apparently in the middle of all her croissant-baking—and it sat next to the stove looking light and fluffy as a cloud.

I was really looking forward to dessert.

Alberta ate a few more mouthfuls of the chicken and then really began to dig in.

"This is pretty good," she said grudgingly.

I wanted to ask Alberta what had happened to the croissants this morning, but I decided now wouldn't be an ideal time—I still wanted to ask her about scrying, and my telling her about my meeting with Lee Hurtzel had put her in a bad mood.

"Crazy," she said again, as if she could read my thoughts.

"Should I not have told you?" I asked.

Alberta sighed. "No—I'm glad you told me. But I will have to deny any knowledge of the existence of the ring if it ever comes up. I'll have to do that to protect you."

"So you think I shouldn't have agreed to it? You think I shouldn't have accepted the ring?"

"No," Alberta said slowly. "That's a decision you have to make yourself—and you did make it. Though I agree with Lee Hurtzel that

that's a piece of property the court should know about and have a say in as far as its disposition. If anything, Lee shouldn't have put you in this position."

She paused. "Did Mr. Clementine's 'ghost' have anything to do with your decision?"

"It might have," I said.

Alberta sighed again—this time in a loud and unnecessarily theatrical manner. "I knew it."

It seemed to me that my chances of getting her to do any scrying for me tonight were growing ever more remote. I cast about for something that would cheer her up.

"How's Peter?" I said.

I wasn't entirely sure what type of reaction I had expected, but the one that I got really surprised me.

Alberta's face went very pale. Then it went equally red.

She'd apparently been about to finish a bite of chicken parmesan, and she paused and appeared to swallow it with difficulty.

Then she took a very long drink of water, staring at me the whole time.

Then she set the glass down.

"Peter," she said, "is fine."

"Are you sure? Because you seem a little—"

"He's fine," she said with emphasis.

As Rafaela had pointed out to me, Peter had gone from being a regular—if recent—fixture in our daily lives to missing in action.

I'd hoped that Rafaela was misinterpreting things, but clearly something was up that Alberta didn't want to tell me about.

Before I could comment on that, Alberta went on—almost as if she could read my thoughts.

"And Rafaela's acting crazy, too. Just like you."

"Oh," I said. "How's that?"

"I asked her over to dinner again tonight," Alberta said darkly. "And she begged off once again. Something's wrong—I just know it."

I suppressed a giggle.

95

Given the uncertain nature of Alberta's cooking, I could entirely understand why Rafaela might turn her down two times in a row.

I decided that this wasn't necessarily the best time to bring that up, either, and then I made the decision not to broach the topic of scrying at all. Alberta was obviously not in a good mood, and scrying required clarity and calmness.

It would have to wait for another time.

Besides, I realized I was still working out the details of what I needed her to look for.

Alberta continued. "I wonder if she's dating someone?"

"Rafaela?" I said. "She would have told us."

Alberta shook her head. "Not if something's wrong."

"What could be wrong? Have you heard something?"

"No."

"Alberta, you're not making sense."

Alberta suddenly stood up in an almost distracted manner and went to the refrigerator.

"What are you doing?" I said.

"I need to get the raspberry sauce for the angel food cake. It should sit out and warm up a little before we pour it on the cake."

"But you haven't finished your dinner yet," I protested.

"I know. It'll take a little while for it to get to room temperature, and I don't want to nuke it—it destroys the flavor."

Sibyl wandered back into the kitchen then, still wearing her white beard and eyebrows.

"It's a conspiracy," Alberta muttered.

That night I sat up in my room looking over at my family of flowers once again.

All of them, including Rafaela's, looked perfectly healthy—despite Alberta's misgivings.

And yet, Alberta was genuinely worried about her—that much I could tell.

I squinted my eyes at Rafaela's flower, trying to see if there was something I had missed—but it still looked fine.

I sighed.

I thought of Mike then, and I stood up and wandered over to the flowers.

As I looked them over, I wondered vaguely if I should add one for Mike.

I felt myself blushing, despite the fact that no one else was in the room, and I told myself not to be silly.

It was far too soon—I barely knew Mike—and besides, there was no guarantee that our relationship would ever progress to a point at which it was serious.

But it was a nice idea all the same, and I felt a little glow inside.

I decided I would call Mike.

I walked over to my purse and dug out my phone.

I wanted to hear the sound of his voice, and it suddenly occurred to me that he might be able to help me.

Mike, as usual, answered the phone very quickly.

"Hey, Chloe."

He sounded so happy that I couldn't help but smile.

"Hey, Mike. Do you have a second?"

"Sure. What's up?"

I took a deep breath. I wasn't quite sure how to bring up the subject I wanted to discuss.

So I just plunged right into it.

"Mike, what do you know about local witches?"

He laughed—a full-voiced, hearty sound.

I listened for just a moment, realizing that I liked the sound of it.

"You're kidding, right?" Mike said when he could catch his breath.

"No—I'm not kidding at all."

Mike quickly sobered.

"Well, I—um—I didn't mean to ... I mean, after all, I *do* know you—"

He sounded uncertain, and I rushed to reassure him.

"It's okay," I said. "I'm not offended. It's just that—in addition to being an expert on world folklore, you're also an expert on local folklore, right?"

"I certainly am." I could picture Mike puffing himself up with pride as he said the words. "I dare say I am the world's foremost authority on this region."

"Then, what do you know about a witch in the woods?"

Mike paused for a long time. "Chloe, what's this about?"

"I need to do some—investigating."

Mike sighed heavily. "I have a terrible feeling that you're about to get involved in something dangerous. What is it this time?"

"It's about Mr. Clementine—"

Mike drew in his breath sharply. "I knew it! This is all my fault."

I could picture Mike going pale as he went on in a rush.

"I should never have told you what that coroner's report said."

This time I was offended. "I would have found out on my own. As you said, the news was all over the internet. And besides, it's the autopsy report, not the coroner's report."

Mike sighed again. "What's going on here, Chloe? Do you think you're going to figure out who killed him?"

"Yes," I said.

I could picture Mike's look of disapproval.

"You're not a cop."

"I know. Alberta said the same thing. But I was present when he was found, and—"

"Yes?" Mike prompted.

"I had the strangest feeling that he wanted me to help him."

"And just who is 'he'?"

" 'He' is Mr. Clementine."

There was a long pause, and I could sense Mike's incredulity.

He was a professor of folklore who didn't believe in the supernatural—perhaps that was why he was good at studying it.

He could be dispassionate about it.

"Chloe—"

I could hear a world of frustration in the way he said my name. Mike continued.

"So now you're talking to ghosts? That is what you meant, isn't it?"

"No—I wasn't talking to anyone. It was just a feeling. But it was a very powerful feeling. And there might have been a whisper—"

"This is a job for the police, Chloe. They don't want you poking around in their business."

I felt my anger flare. "I've done it before."

"You got lucky."

"I didn't get lucky," I said. "I figured things out. Besides, you said you would always help me. You said that if I was going to do anything crazy that you wanted to be in on it."

Mike surprised me by chuckling.

"So you admit that this is crazy?"

I felt another spark of anger. "Crazy?"

"Oh, Chloe," Mike said. "I don't want to start arguing again. Especially not when I just got you—"

"Got me what?"

"Got you back."

I had a moment for that to sink in before Mike went on.

"I don't want to stop you from doing anything. It's just that I don't want you to get hurt. Otis Clementine was *murdered*. Somebody strangled him. And that person is still out there. Who knows what will happen if you get involved?"

I felt a chill run through me as Mike said the words.

"And then there's the police," Mike said. "I have to imagine that interfering with a police investigation is some kind of crime. I don't want you to get arrested. Or do you think your friend Detective Mia is going to save you?"

I had to chuckle at that.

Mia and I weren't exactly friends.

"Chloe, I'm serious," Mike said.

"I know," I replied. "It's just—"

Mike waited.

"It's just that you sound like my dad."

"I am twenty-seven to your twenty-three," Mike said with dignity.

I laughed—at that moment, he actually sounded his age.

"Chloe, this is no laughing matter."

"All right, Professor," I said.

"So I take it you're *determined*—"

"I'm not determined," I said quietly. "Someone asked me for help. And he can no longer help himself."

Mike sighed again. "You're going to be the death of me."

"Does that mean you'll help me?"

"Apparently you can't ignore a plea for help and neither can I. What do you need me to do?"

"Oh, Mike," I breathed. "That's wonderful. You're wonderful. Thank you."

"Never mind that the plea you're listening to is imaginary—"

"What was that?"

"Nothing," Mike said. "Just tell me what kind of trouble I'm going to get into this time."

"Don't worry," I said. "I just need a little of your expertise. I do all the dangerous stuff."

"Oh, you do, do you?"

I could picture Mike's raised eyebrow.

"We'll see about that," he said.

"I'm going to start by interviewing Mr. Clementine's friends and family," I said breezily, as if I had had that plan in mind all along when in reality it had only just popped into my head. "And I'll also talk to his business associates—though it's been my experience that murders are most often committed by the people closest to the victim."

"Your experience?" Mike sounded amused. "Don't you work in a library?"

"My experience from reading books," I clarified. "I read a lot of true crime."

"Ah, I see. And where do I come in? You still haven't told me."

"With a witch in the woods."

"You mentioned that before," Mike said. "What exactly do you mean?"

"It was something Detective Mia said when she interviewed me. She hinted—though she didn't say it outright—that there might be a supernatural element to this crime. She then asked me if I knew about a witch who lived in the woods around here. She was wondering if the witch might be associated with my family."

"So Detective Mia really is on this case?"

"There was another detective on the scene," I said. "But apparently he's come down with the flu. Mia's taken over—at least for now."

"Well, I'm a little surprised to hear about the angle the good detective is taking on this. When I met her, I thought she seemed much more sensible than that."

Mike was trying to needle me, and it worked.

"So do you know anything or not?" I said, irritated.

"I'm surprised you don't know," he replied. "I thought you said folklore was your favorite section of the library."

I was startled to hear him say that—and pleased that he'd remembered.

"Yes," I said. "That's true."

"Well?"

"Well what?"

"Don't you know already?" Mike said.

"I think I've made it clear that I don't," I replied.

"I know," Mike said. "I just wanted to hear you say that. As it so happens, Henrietta College has an excellent collection of—"

He stopped suddenly.

"You know—I wonder if the detective could be referring to the Hansel and Gretel house?"

"The—"

"Hansel and Gretel house," Mike repeated. "The rumors are pretty vague—really just stories kids tell each other around campfires. But I bet I could find out something about it."

"A Hansel and Gretel house?" I said doubtfully. "That doesn't sound very serious."

"There's supposed to be a witch there," Mike said. "I'll get to work on it and give you a call in the morning."

"Are you sure, Mike?" I said, feeling the stirrings of misgivings. "I don't like the idea of your sitting up all night working on this."

"Don't worry," Mike said, and I could picture him smirking. "Henrietta College's archives are largely digitized, and I have access from my home computer. It's not like I'll be poring over ancient tomes in a dusty library. Besides, you've got me intrigued, and you know I work fast."

"You do indeed," I replied.

"What's wrong?" Mike said. "Why are you pulling back all of a sudden? Didn't you just ask me to look into this?"

"I did. It's just—"

"What?"

"I don't know," I said. Suddenly, my head felt hazy and my chest felt tight.

"Well, like I said, don't worry. I'll look this stuff up, and then I'll call you in the morning. Good night, Chloe."

Mike hung up, and I sat for several moments holding my phone.

Then I got up to look at my plants once again.

As I lingered by them, I glanced out the nearby window, and I thought I saw a swift movement somewhere out in the night—something light colored. I pulled back the curtains quickly to get a better view, but whatever it was, it fluttered away before I could get a good look at it.

I stared out into the night for a long time, but there was no further movement.

Eventually, I left the window and got ready for bed.

As I drifted off to sleep that night, I had the strangest feeling that I was being watched by a blush-colored dove.

Chapter Ten

On Saturday morning, I woke up before dawn, and the whole house was silent—even Alberta wasn't up yet.

I looked around in the kitchen and was delighted to find a pan of strudel in the refrigerator—Alberta must have made it after I'd gone up to my room. As I made myself a cup of coffee and warmed up some strudel in the microwave, it occurred to me that Alberta had been baking a lot lately—even by her standards.

She often baked just for the joy of it—but I also knew that she sometimes baked when she was upset.

I thought again of Peter Gambelli, and I wondered why he hadn't been around lately.

The icing on the strudel melted beautifully in the microwave, and I had a very enjoyable breakfast.

While I ate, I got out my phone and did a little searching online. I tried to find a mention of a witch in the woods of Crabtree Bay, or anything about a "Hansel and Gretel" house, but any searches about witches in our area just brought up the article from a month ago about me and my sisters.

I had to smile ruefully at that.

Then I searched on Mr. Clementine to see if there were any new developments that were available to the public—anything else the police might have released.

But most of the news stories were about the search for Mr. Clementine's missing son Brian. Apparently—as Mr. Clementine himself had told me—he'd had no contact with his son for most of his life and had been searching for him for years. The media outlets speculated that Brian could be worth hundreds of millions of dollars after his father's estate was settled.

However, there was no word on his whereabouts.

I sighed and put away my phone. Research was hard to do on such a small device. I'd have to make use of the library computers later.

I finished up the last of my strudel quickly, and then I was out the door.

I wanted to see if I could find the dove that seemed to keep popping up. There was no reason for me to believe that I could find one bird in all of the great outdoors.

But I had to try.

I drove out to the ruined stone house where I had seen a dove sitting the wall, seemingly watching me, but this time, as I approached, I could see that the wall was empty.

I checked on the rune stone, too, just to be sure—but it looked much the same as it had last time.

As far as I could tell, it was fine.

I drove out to the other three rune stones, also, to check them, but they all appeared to be in good working order.

All the while, I kept an eye out for the dove.

But this time it didn't put in an appearance.

I began to wonder if I was making too big a deal out of the little bird's appearances.

Maybe it was all just a coincidence.

I got in the car and decided to turn toward home—but then I suddenly thought of Mr. Clementine's house.

It was early in the morning on a Saturday.

Maybe I could find a way to slip into the house before everyone was awake, and have a look around.

I wanted to see if I could find that feeling that had come to me before.

So with dawn just beginning to light up the sky, I began to drive over to Mr. Clementine's palatial home.

As I saw the house's tower looming on the horizon, I noticed a curiously shaped pink cloud floating near the tower—it appeared to be shaped a bit like a question mark.

I frowned as I ducked my head to peer out the windshield at it.

It seemed to me that that cloud had been hanging over the house the last time I'd been here.

I told myself not to be ridiculous.

This, too, was probably a coincidence.

I drove into the community of Camelot, and I wound past Round Table Terrace, Lancelot's Love Lane, and Guinevere's Gauntlet on my way up the hill to Arthur King's Court.

From a distance, the house looked peaceful, and I couldn't see any activity outside or any cars parked in the circular front drive.

I continued on up the hill, and I parked at a little distance from the house.

Then I got out of the car and walked up to the front door.

As I paused at the broad double doors, I glanced up at the camera that was pointed rather obviously in my direction. I knew, of course, that my visit here was being recorded and that I wouldn't be able to deny it if the police asked about it.

But there was nothing wrong with my visiting Mr. Clementine's house, and anybody who was here could simply deny me entry if they chose.

I raised my hand to knock, and then I hesitated.

Some instinct told me to try the handle first.

My hand dropped to the knob, and I tried it.

It turned easily.

Then I pushed on the door, and it swung open.

I glanced into the front hall—everything was quiet, and the household didn't appear to be stirring yet.

I stepped inside and closed the door behind me, lest some noise from outside draw attention to the fact that the door was open.

The entrance hall was dimly lit—the light from the sunrise had yet to filter in through the windows—and the stone room was cold and somehow oppressive.

I stood for a moment, listening, but I couldn't discern any signs of movement in the house.

I stepped further in.

Soon I found myself standing in front of the portrait of Mr. Clementine that dominated the hall.

This more youthful incarnation of Mr. Clementine still had the rich dark auburn hair, the defiant cleft chin, and the arrogant, challenging tilt of the head it had had before. But the eyes—the eyes that were full of determination—and still more arrogance—had somehow changed.

The painting was the same—it had to be.

But somehow the eyes were sad—sad and knowing in a way that they hadn't been before.

Something had changed.

"You see it, too, don't you?" said a voice.

I turned, startled, to see a girl about my age standing behind me.

"Oh," I said, trying to think of a good reason for my being there. "I—um. That is, I—"

"You're Chloe, aren't you?" the young woman said.

"Yes," I said, hoping her recognition of me would buy me some time.

The girl had red hair and a smattering of freckles across her nose, and wide, guileless eyes. The jeans and T-shirt she wore were crisp and clean and yet somehow plain and unfashionable. All the same, they couldn't disguise that she had a lithe, healthy body, probably due to a lot of outdoor work.

When I'd been in school, there had been town girls and country girls.

This was clearly a country girl.

I cast about, still trying to think of an excuse, but as the girl continued to look at me calmly, I realized I didn't have to have one just yet.

The girl clearly wasn't going to raise the alarm.

I decided just to be straightforward.

"Yes, I'm Chloe—Chloe Bartlett. I've been here a few times before. I probably should have knocked, but the door was open."

The girl nodded. "I seen you before. I seen you the day they found him."

She glanced at the portrait meaningfully.

"Yes," I said simply.

"I seen you before that, too. You used to bring lie-barry books."

I winced at the pronunciation of "library," but I ordered myself not to say anything.

Bringing it up would be impolite, and besides, the girl hadn't thrown me out yet.

I owed her some courtesy for that at least.

"So why was the door unlocked?" I asked.

The girl shrugged. "I don't know. A lot of strange things have happened lately."

She eyed me furtively, as if she wanted to say more.

"What's your name?" I asked.

"Marianne. I'm Marianne Mozer. I used to work for Mr. Clementine. I do yard work and sometimes I clean inside the house. I guess I work for Daphne Minton now."

"Does Daphne live in this house?" I asked.

"Yes."

"Did she always?"

"Yes—she's lived here for years," Marianne said. "I don't know how long that will last now that he's gone. I guess that will depend on who gets the house next."

She paused, and a note of pride crept into her voice. "I been invited to the reading of the will."

"Me, too," I said.

Any remaining reticence on Marianne's part seemed to be swept away by my admission, and she relaxed visibly.

"Is that why you're here now? Something to do with the will?"

"No," I said. Marianne was staring at me with a trusting look in her eyes, and I decided to continue being straightforward. "When I was here before, I had a strange feeling—"

Marianne nodded vigorously. "Like he ain't gone." She glanced at the picture again.

I stared at her. "Yes."

"You psychic?"

"No," I said. "At least I don't think so. Are you?"

"No," Marianne replied. "But me and him had a special bond."

She glanced up at the portrait and then smiled as if at a private joke.

"He always said I wasn't his type. But he said it friendly-like. He used to talk to me sometimes—said he couldn't talk to her."

"Her?" I said.

"Old Minton. That's what me and him used to call her. He never called her Daphne."

"So does anyone else live here?" I asked.

"No. It was just him and Daphne. The girlfriend and the baby used to visit sometimes, but they don't live here. Mostly he would go over to visit her—I heard he got her a condo. And sometimes there are business guests, and me and some of the other workers stay overnight sometimes when there's a lot to do—parties and such. But none of us live here."

"It's a big house for two people," I said.

Marianne shrugged. "I think he meant it to be for a family once. But that never really worked out."

"How do you know that?"

"He told me."

"Did he tell you anything else?" I asked.

"Like what?"

"Like—did anything special or unusual happen before he died? Did he argue with anyone, for instance? Did anyone he didn't expect show up at the house?"

Marianne shook her head. "No—nothing like that happened—at least not that I know about. But I do know that he was looking for his son."

"His son?"

"Yes. His first one. The one he had with her—the one who ran off."

I sighed to myself—Marianne's tendency to just use pronouns and not use names made having a conversation a little difficult—especially since there were so many "hers" in Mr. Clementine's life.

"By 'her,' you mean his first wife, Clytie?"

Marianne nodded. "Yes. His first and only wife. He said there'd never be another one after her."

I recalled that Mr. Clementine had said something similar to me.

"So he was looking for his son Brian?" I asked.

"Yes—the one he named them Brian's Baskets after."

"Did he find him?" I asked.

Marianne shrugged again. "I don't know. But I do know he looked real hard—he told me he tried everything."

"So what can you tell me about the day Mr. Clementine was found? You said you were here that day and you saw me, right?"

"Yes, I seen you. You were here twice, and the policeman was here twice. And Old Minton—Daphne—was beside herself when she seen him. Didn't want him here at all, no ma'am."

She glanced at me. "I heard what you said, though, about there being someone outside—someone running away."

I seized on her words.

"Did you see anyone?" I said quickly.

"No." Marianne looked embarrassed. "But I wish I had. I was cleaning in the kitchen, and I heard all the commotion. So I came out and followed you all. I crept up the stairs after you quiet-like, so you all wouldn't know I was there, and I heard everything you said. I ran downstairs after you said that to see if I could see the person. But I didn't see nobody."

She glanced at me sharply. "Did you say the person was tall and blond—with short hair?"

"Yes," I said. "Or at least that's what I think I saw. It's hard to tell height from a distance."

Marianne nodded. "I bet it was her."

"Her?"

"She's got short hair like a boy, too. Always keeps it that way."

Marianne ran her fingers through her own long hair as if in silent rebuke.

I remembered, then, a magazine cover with a short-haired blonde that Mr. Clementine had showed me once.

"Do you mean Heather, his girlfriend?"

Marianne sniffed. "Yes—that's her. She's the one who done it. She knew Mr. Clementine was looking for his first son. She was afraid she and her son would be cut right out of the will."

"How do you know?"

"Because it's true. But she was too late. Mr. Clementine had already made his new will."

"He had?"

"Yes—he made two of them. The first one was witnessed by Old Minton and one of the gardeners a few years back. Then two months ago, he made a new one. It was witnessed by me and Ralph, the handy man."

Marianne smiled. "I think Ralph likes me."

"Wait—a new will?" I said. "Why did Mr. Clementine make a new will? And why so recently?"

"I don't know."

"Well, did something happen?" I said.

Marianne tossed her head. "I don't know. But Mr. Clementine said Old Minton would be mad. And he said he left me something in his new will, too. He said they would all be surprised."

"But why make a new will?" I persisted. "Something must have changed. Was he ill? Did he think he'd need one soon?"

"No," Marianne said. "Mr. Clementine was perfectly healthy—even if he was kind of old. I think—"

She paused, and her brow creased with effort.

"I think he thought someone might be after him. And it looks like he was right."

Marianne looked up at the portrait. After a moment she went on.

"She was here, you know."

"Who?" I said.

"The girlfriend."

"When?"

"Right after the news came out that he had died. But she was too late. That lawyer guy got here before her, and he left with something."

"He did?" I said, but I already knew what she was going to say.

Marianne nodded. "He left with a box—all covered with sunflowers. I reckon that's what *she* was looking for, too, because she went upstairs to his office and bedroom and searched through them. She came away, screaming, saying she couldn't find it."

Marianne paused and drew herself up with dignity. "She even accused me of taking it, but I didn't take nothing. Mr. Clementine said he remembered me in his will, and that's enough for me."

"Do you know why Heather wanted the box?" I asked—although if she knew what was in it, I could well imagine why.

"No," Marianne replied shortly.

"So this will—" I said. "Do you know—"

Marianne tossed her head again, suddenly sanctimonious. "I don't know nothing about what's in it, except he said people would be surprised, and there's something for me in it. You'll find out same as me what's in it when you go to the reading on Monday."

Marianne began to walk away as if the subject was closed.

"Wait," I said, and she turned back reluctantly.

"Do you mind if I have a look around?"

Marianne shrugged. "It's not my house. You can do as you like."

She walked away, her footsteps dying off down a long hall, and I was left standing in front of the portrait of Mr. Clementine.

He stared down at me with his sad, determined eyes.

Suddenly the feeling I had felt before—one of sadness and fear—rose up around me and nearly overwhelmed me. And in the middle of the feeling there was the barest whisper—or maybe it was only in my mind—two words, just like before:

Help me.

Chapter Eleven

I followed the feeling.

The feeling of sadness and fear was strong, and it swirled around me. But there was definitely a spot where the feeling was strongest, and I moved toward it.

It led me up the stairs.

I left the cold stone of the ground floor behind and continued up to the next level where everything was light and airy and much more modern.

I continued on up the stairs, still following the feeling, and I paused on the landing where Mr. Clementine's body had been found.

The feeling of sadness was even stronger here, and I thought I detected something new—a note of bewilderment.

Whatever had happened here had been a surprise to Mr. Clementine.

I stopped to look out the window, hoping to refresh my memory of the fleeing figure I'd seen, but my mind offered no new details, and the green, well-manicured lawn outside offered up no new clues.

If there had been any footprints or other telltale signs, they were surely gone by now—covered over by Mr. Clementine's excellent lawn care service. As I turned to move on, my feet scraped on something on the floor—and I bent down to see tiny bits of grit, colored both blue and gray. I remembered that one of the paramedics had mentioned something like that, and I reached out a finger to touch it.

Then I thought better of it and drew my hand back.

I continued on, spurred on by the feeling that tugged at me.

I made my way up to the top of Mr. Clementine's tower, and I found the door of his office standing open.

I walked in.

I'd been to Mr. Clementine's office a few times, of course, but I'd never been inside it without its owner being present, and now that he was gone, it felt strangely peaceful.

But despite the sense of peace, there was sadness there, too—not stronger in this spot, but somehow deeper—as if the sadness had come to rest here.

I took a look around.

The police had surely been here already, and I imagined any clues of vital importance had already been removed. But despite the fact that the office had probably been searched, it looked much the same as it had when I'd been here a few days ago.

The police had been very careful. The only real difference was that there was more blue-and-gray grit here.

In fact, there was quite a bit more—I stepped around it, careful not to disturb it.

Mr. Clementine's office was a strange mixture of disorder and neatness, and piles of clutter sat next to items that had clearly been carefully and meticulously arranged.

The desk in particular was like that—receipts and papers spilled out of folders and various heaps of clutter on one side, and the other side had folders that were neatly filed and labeled in wire racks.

I searched through everything quickly and found Detective Ortiz's cell phone number written down on multiple scraps of paper—it had a local exchange and the rest of the number was all zeros and eights, so it seemed like it wouldn't have been that hard to remember—but perhaps Mr. Clementine had wanted to be sure. Other than that, my examination of the desk didn't turn up anything that appeared to have any bearing on the current situation, so I drifted over to the bookshelves.

Here there was a smattering of books on business and the latest management fads—*Secrets of the Fortune 500*, *Whip Time Management Now!*—but they were vastly outnumbered by books on one particular topic—King Arthur.

Mr. Clementine's personal bookshelves were laden with books on magic, romance, knights, and chivalry, and all of them centered on King Arthur and his court. Most of the volumes were leather-bound in rich shades of red, blue, green, and brown, and many of them featured gilt trim.

I selected one book and leafed through it. The pages had gold edging, and each chapter began with a lavishly decorated first letter and a richly decorated border—like an illuminated manuscript. There were also highly detailed illustrations of knights, ladies, and fabulous monsters, as well as one illustration of the great king himself in the center of the book.

Clearly, Mr. Clementine was a fan.

Despite the intriguingly romantic nature of Mr. Clementine's personal library, it yielded no clues, and I paused to look out the window.

There were windows all around the room, both front and back, but this particular window looked out on a broad green swath of back lawn, and it seemed to be that this was the same view that could be seen from the landing below where Mr. Clementine had been found—we were just up a little higher.

So if this was the same view, had the blond intruder come into Mr. Clementine's office? Or had the person come in on the landing below?

And which way had that same intruder escaped?

I examined the window—it opened outward, swinging on a hinge, and the glass was heavy and framed in iron—no doubt it was supposed to look old-fashioned and medieval in style. There was a latch to close the window, but no real lock, and it would be easy enough to open from the outside—that is presuming that someone could get up that high to begin with.

I leaned out and glanced down, and it was certainly a long way down to the ground. But the stone of the outside wall provided plenty of handholds and footholds—that is, if someone were very good at climbing.

I realized then that the intruder had to have come in this way—the windows on the landing below were far too small.

This was the only window that was large enough to admit a full-grown human being.

I wondered if the police had noticed that, and I figured that it was very probable that they had.

And right by the window, within easy reach of the desk, was a telescope on a stand.

I wondered for a moment if Mr. Clementine had been interested in stargazing, but then I turned the telescope toward the window and looked into it.

Looking through a telescope during the day wasn't ideal, but I could still make out a row of stately homes that came into blurry view. As I panned over them, I suddenly came across a gap, and I angled the telescope down.

This time I could see the blurred outline of a little cottage, and as I moved the telescope to see what was next to it, another large, stately home popped into view.

I moved the telescope back to its original position and wondered once again.

I heard faint stirrings in the house below me, and I looked around the room—I realized that I didn't have much time left if I wanted to get out of the house without being seen by someone who might be less forgiving than Marianne.

I decided to have one last look through the desk and then leave.

I wasn't entirely sure what I was looking for, but I wanted to make sure that I looked through everything.

After all, the feeling had led me here.

I'd searched the top of the desk, but I hadn't looked through the drawers.

The top left one had a stack of magazines, including the one Mr. Clementine had shown me with his girlfriend on the cover.

Sure enough, as Marianne had said, her hair was short.

The drawers below it had neatly labeled files that I didn't have time to look through, so I started on the drawers on the right.

And there in the top drawer, I found something that gave me pause.

Lying there all alone was a framed photograph.

I drew it out.

The photograph was a little yellow and somewhat grainy—it had probably been taken with an actual camera. In the photo, a beautiful woman with windswept hair as yellow as the sun stood on the beach, smiling at the camera. She held the hand of a little blond boy in swim trunks, and he also smiled at the camera.

The woman was beautiful in that special way that old-fashioned movie stars were, and I wondered if I was looking at a picture of Mr. Clementine's wife Clytie and their son Brian.

It occurred to me then that it was a little odd that there were no other photos in the room, and I took a quick look around again.

But there was nothing—no other photos of family or friends, no photos of business associates—no photos, even, of Mr. Clementine shaking hands with the dignitaries he must have met.

It seemed to me that that was odd for a businessman of Mr. Clementine's stature.

I was just turning back to the photograph of the woman and the boy to see if there was an inscription on the back when I heard a sound on the stairs below.

Before I could move, there was a quick step outside, and the door suddenly flew open.

And standing in the doorway before me was Daphne Minton.

"Just what do you think you're doing?" she demanded.

Daphne had her hands on her hips, and her neat dark hair was as sleek and unruffled as it usually was.

But her slightly ambiguous, friendly but off-putting demeanor was gone.

There was nothing ambiguous about Daphne's mood now.

She was clearly angry.

"I—um," I said. "That is, I—"

"Yes? I can't wait to hear your explanation."

I stared down at the photo in my hands and tried to come up with a plausible reason for my being in Mr. Clementine's office, going through his things.

Nothing was coming to me.

Daphne stepped into the room.

I cast about for something to say, and my eyes landed on Mr. Clementine's bookshelves.

"I came to get our library books," I blurted out, as Daphne advanced toward me.

She stopped, startled.

"What?"

"The library books," I said, "that Mr. Clementine borrowed earlier in the week—I came over to get them."

Daphne stared at me.

"Are you serious?"

"Yes—we don't want to give him any fines," I finished somewhat lamely.

"I assume you waive those for parties who are deceased. It's very hard for the dearly departed to return books in a timely fashion."

Daphne's sarcasm wasn't lost on me.

"Yes ... I—um—" I actually didn't know what our policy was—it hadn't come up since I'd been at the library—and I had to assume that Daphne was right.

For her part, Daphne's hands were back on her hips.

"I suppose that little hussy Marianne let you in?"

It was my turn to be startled.

"Did you actually just call her a 'hussy'?" I asked.

Daphne had the good grace to blush.

"I didn't really mean—" she began.

Then she glanced down and saw what I had in my hands.

"What's this?" she demanded, and she snatched the framed picture out of my hands.

As she stared down at the photograph, her face grew even redder.

"What do you think you're doing with this? This was Mr. Clementine's private property."

I was in danger of losing control of the situation and getting thrown out, and I hadn't found out very much so far. Maybe I could keep Daphne talking and possibly learn something useful—something I might not find out otherwise.

Angry people sometimes said more than was wise.

"It's the only one," I said quickly.

Daphne looked up at me sharply. "What?"

"It's the only family photo in the entire office."

Daphne's expression softened just a bit, and she looked down at the picture again.

"Yes—they meant a lot to him. He sometimes told me they were his real family."

It seemed as if I'd struck just the right note.

"She's beautiful," I said. "Who is she?" I added—although I already had an idea who she was.

"That's Clytie Clementine—and Brian—her son."

Daphne's expression softened further still.

"This is a big house for just two people," I said softly, echoing my previous words to Marianne. "Just you and Mr. Clementine."

I hoped she wouldn't notice that I knew about the household already.

"Yes—yes, it is," Daphne replied. "He never meant to go into real estate, too, you know."

"No?"

"No. In the beginning there was just the one house—this one. He built it just for her. It was to be their castle on the hill, and they were going to raise their family here."

"What happened?" I asked, careful to keep my voice soothing.

"He wanted a big family—wanted to build a kingdom just for them—a dynasty. They could have been happy here if she hadn't been so stubborn."

I waited, and Daphne went on of her own accord.

"But she was younger than he was—had dreams of being an actress. She took off with their infant son—ran off to Italy. He—Mr. Clementine—never saw them again. Eventually, she sent back this photo. It was all he had of them."

"Didn't Mr. Clementine go after them?"

"He did—he told me so. He hired the best detectives and found them very quickly. But there was nothing he could do. She filed for divorce before she left, and once she was overseas, she refused to see him. Clytie was eventually granted sole custody of their son."

Daphne's mouth twisted with bitterness. "She told all kinds of scurrilous tales—through her lawyers, of course—of affairs that Mr. Clementine had had. After that, he had no chance of even visitation rights. He lost his wife and his son."

Considering what I knew of Mr. Clementine—even from my short acquaintance—I could well believe that the "tales" were true.

"So why did she go to Italy?" I said. "Is that where she was from?"

Daphne sniffed. "No, though I dare say she would have loved for people to believe that. Mr. Clementine actually met her in New York—she'd been working there, getting small parts in plays and appearing in a few TV commercials."

"Then why did she go so far?"

"Mr. Clementine always believed that she wanted the sunshine. There's not much sunshine in New York with all those big buildings."

"She could have gone to California if she'd wanted sunshine and an acting career."

Daphne simply shrugged. "Perhaps Clytie figured she needed to go abroad if she truly wanted freedom from Mr. Clementine. Here in the United States his power and reach was too great. But in Italy, she proved to be harder to get to. By all accounts, she was a smart woman. Maybe she researched it and knew that Italian law would protect her. Then again, maybe she had no plan at all—she was known to just follow whims. Clytie, apparently, could be flighty."

Daphne giggled, and there was a note of hysteria in the sound.

"Did you know her?" I asked.

Daphne paused. "I met her once."

She giggled again.

"She lived out there, she died out there. No one ever saw her again."

"And what happened to Brian?" I asked.

"No one knows."

"Did he—" I began. "Did he die, too?"

Daphne shrugged again. "Mr. Clementine looked for him for years after he received word of Clytie's death. He never found him."

I glanced down at the photo in her hands.

"He was very blond once," I said. "Sometimes children who are blond grow up to be a little darker. Do you know if he stayed that way?"

"I have no idea. Clytie never sent any other pictures. As I said, I don't know if he's alive or dead."

"What about Clytie?" I said.

"What about her?"

"I suppose there's no doubt that she's deceased?"

Daphne drew herself up stiffly. "Clytie had a congenital heart condition that was exacerbated by the trouble she had with *him*."

She spat the last word out.

"And that's how she died?" I asked. "Heart failure?"

"Yes."

Daphne's face had gone very red again.

"Forgive me," I said. "But I can't tell whose side you were on. Were you on Clytie's side or Mr. Clementine's?"

"Side?" Daphne said. "Side? In life there are no sides."

I could tell I was losing her, and I hurried on quickly.

"What's with all the King Arthur stuff?" I asked.

Daphne looked startled. "Excuse me?"

"What's with all the books?"

Daphne shrugged. "He thought he was a knight or a king or something. I told you he thought he was building a kingdom."

"And why is this street Arthur King's Court?" I asked. "Why not King Arthur's Court? Why the inversion?"

" 'Arthur' was Mr. Clementine's middle name—he was Otis Arthur Clementine. He sometimes referred to himself as Arthur the king. I suppose he thought it had a nice ring to it."

"It sounded poetic?"

"Yes, if you like."

"And what about the cameras?" I asked.

"What about them?" Daphne said.

"I know there's one out front, but are there others? Some at the back of the house, perhaps?"

Daphne bristled. "Are you with the police?"

"No," I said.

"Then that's none of your business."

I could tell that Daphne was rapidly losing patience, and I was very close to being thrown out now, and so I threw out one last question.

"What's the telescope for?" I said.

Daphne blinked. "What?"

I pointed to the metal cylinder that nestled near the window.

"Did Mr. Clementine like to look at the stars, or—"

"Or?"

"It's just that I noticed that you can see other houses in the neighborhood from here. Maybe he could even see right into their windows."

Two bright red spots burned high on Daphne's cheeks as she stared at me.

"Are you asking me if Mr. Clementine spied on people while they undressed? Or while they did—other things?"

"Uh—yes?" I said. I hadn't been thinking of anything in particular, but if Daphne knew something, then I needed to know it, too.

Daphne drew herself up severely. "I'm sure I don't know a thing about that. But what would I know? I'm just a good Midwestern girl."

Something about the way she said that drew my attention. It was almost as if someone else had said that to her once.

"Daphne, were you—were you in love with your boss?"

She gave me a long stare, and her voice when she spoke was level but dangerous.

"You need to get out *now*. If you don't, I will call the police."

I turned and left the room.

Chapter Twelve

As I drove home, I got a call from Mike.

I was too worked up to drive and talk—even hands free—so I pulled over and parked the car.

Then I picked up the phone.

"Hey, Mike."

"Hey." He sounded happy like he always did when he talked to me on the phone. "Do you have a minute?"

I glanced around at the quiet road I was currently stopped on.

It was still early on a Saturday morning, so I wasn't likely to be bothered much by traffic.

"Yes, sure," I said. "I can talk now."

"Good," he replied. "I wasn't sure if you'd be up yet."

Then he paused.

"Are you okay?"

I'd tried to keep the weariness out of my voice—my run-in with Daphne and even my interaction with Marianne had taken a toll on me.

I felt like I'd learned a lot of valuable information.

But I didn't know what yet.

"I'm fine," I said, trying to put a smile in my voice. "It's just been a busy morning."

"Well, if you'd rather—"

"No," I said quickly. "I'd rather talk to you."

Mike chuckled, and I could picture him smiling.

It made me feel warm inside.

"Oh, well, in that case," he said, "I found out some information about your mysterious witch—if you'd be interested."

"If I'd be interested?" It was a good thing I *wasn't* driving—if I had been, I would have slammed on the brakes just then. "I am definitely interested."

"Wonderful!" Mike said. And in that one word I could tell how pleased he was—he sounded like an excited little kid. "I can't wait to tell you all about it."

"Then don't wait—tell me right now."

Mike paused. "Well, now, as to that—"

He suddenly sounded nervous.

"I—uh—I would like—"

"Mike, what is it?"

He cleared his throat.

"I rather hoped—that is, I was wondering—could we meet in person?"

"You want to meet up so you can tell me what you've learned?"

"Uh, yes," Mike said. "Maybe over lunch? Then we'd be free to discuss my findings at our leisure."

"Over lunch?" I said. "Like a date?"

"No!" Mike said quickly, then recovered himself. "I mean, yes. I mean—it would be like an intellectual date. A meeting of the minds to share information."

"Sounds very romantic," I said. "And I would love to."

"You would?" Mike sounded deeply relieved and happy. "Oh, Chloe, I—"

He didn't seem to know how to end the sentence.

I came to his rescue.

"Where would you like to meet for lunch?"

"Well, I—"

Mike seemed to be struggling again.

"Would you like to go back to Salty Sweet?" I asked. "That was sort of our first intellectual date."

Salty Sweet was an ice cream parlor in the next town over, and Mike and I had gone there after I'd gone to confront him about some information that I'd discovered. Somehow we'd ended up walking over there to get some ice cream, and even though we'd run into my ex-boyfriend—who'd caused a scene—I still had good memories of that day.

"Uh, maybe not Salty Sweet," Mike said. "That's really more of an ice cream place—though they have sandwiches there, too. I actually had some other place in mind."

He paused again.

"So—where would you like to go?" I said.

"I'd like to make it a surprise. Do you mind?"

"No, I don't mind. Where do you want to meet up?"

Mike chuckled again, and I realized that I liked the sound.

"If I told you that, it would spoil the surprise."

"You don't have to tell me the exact location," I said. "We could meet somewhere neutral."

"How about this—how about I pick you up at your house? Or rather, your sister's house."

I felt oddly pleased that he remembered that I didn't have a place of my own yet.

"Sure," I said. "Do you need the address?"

"Yes—thanks. I'm not that much of a stalker. At least not yet."

I gave him the address, and Mike gave me a time.

"So you're going to pick me up," I said. "Just like on a real date."

"I thought we'd established that this was more of an informational thing."

"We did. I just like teasing you."

Mike sighed, but he didn't sound displeased.

"Goodbye, Chloe. I'll see you soon."

We both hung up, and then I started the car and headed for home.

When I walked into the house, I could immediately sense it was empty—Alberta must have left while I was out.

I was glad that she likely wouldn't be around when Mike arrived—I could already hear her "gentleman caller" jabs in my head.

But I did wonder where she had gone.

She hadn't mentioned anything about going out in the morning.

I sat down on the couch then and got out my phone. I knew that Alberta had claimed not to have a Facebook page—but I also knew that she'd said she'd been on it herself, just looking around.

I figured I would double-check.

I searched for Alberta on Facebook, and sure enough, she still didn't have a page.

Since I was already looking around, I decided to go to Rafaela's page—after all, that was what had drawn Alberta to Facebook in the first place.

So I scrolled through her feed looking for something suspicious.

But Rafaela just seemed like a normal, happy twenty-five-year-old with a very busy life.

I smiled to see how many smiley-face emojis she had on her posts.

In fact, she had a smiley face on all of her posts.

As I continued to scroll down, I saw that someone named B. P. Gotschall had left a smiley-face emoji on all of Rafaela's posts for several weeks. Sometimes the smiley face was accompanied by flowers, sometimes by rainbows or stars or moons.

But there was always a smiley face.

And on a post that Rafaela had made this morning, there was yet another smiley face from B. P. Gotschall and a comment: "See you soon, babe."

I stared at the comment for a long moment.

Maybe Alberta was right—maybe Rafaela was seeing someone.

At the same time, that didn't mean anything was wrong.

I clicked on "B. P. Gotschall," but the profile had been set to private, and no picture showed in the little box. That didn't necessarily mean anything—lots of people liked to keep their online profiles private and just for their family and friends.

But if Rafaela *was* seeing someone, it was a little strange that she hadn't told us.

I began to scroll down through the posts again to see if I'd missed anything when there was a crash from the kitchen, and Sibyl came running out in a streak of black and yellow.

She ran past me and zoomed up the stairs.

I jumped up from the couch and ran after her.

"Sibyl?"

I paused at the foot of the stairs and stared up at her.

Sibyl was standing at the top and staring down at me. Her face was ringed by a thick, yellow-brown paste, and her pink tongue flicked out to lap her nose as she regarded me.

"Sibyl, are you all right?" I said.

For her part, the cat simply sat down where she was and began to wash her face with one black paw.

I stared at her for a moment, and then figuring that she was okay, I went to the kitchen to see what damage had been done.

As I walked in, I could see that there was a nearly full jar of mustard lying on the floor on its side, its golden-brown contents spilling out in a round puddle with a splatter pattern all around it. A tall, plastic trash can was also lying on its side, its lid still mercifully intact. On the counter not far away was the lid to the mustard jar and a white china plate with a golden-brown tinged knife lying across it.

There was also one golden-brown paw print between the overturned mustard and the overturned trash can.

It seemed to me that I could piece together what had happened.

Alberta had made herself a sandwich, or something savory, and had left the mustard out. Then after Alberta had left, Sibyl had climbed up on the counter to lap at the mustard. She'd managed to knock it over, and then when the crash startled her, she'd jumped down and bumped into the trash can on her way out, knocking it over, too.

Why Alberta had left her things out, which wasn't like her, was a bit of a mystery—as was why Sibyl had been interested in the mustard in the first place. As far as I knew, cats didn't like that stuff.

And how she'd gotten it all over her face was also a mystery—unless she'd stuck her face into the jar.

I wouldn't have thought she would have done that—but then again, I wouldn't have thought she'd do that with tomato sauce, either.

I cleaned up the kitchen, and when I walked into the living room to see if there was any mustard residue out there, I found Sibyl on the couch fast asleep, her face clean.

"Crazy cat," I muttered to myself.

Then I went upstairs to get ready for my lunch with Mike.

Time seemed to fly by, and before I knew it, there was a knock on the front door.

I hurried down the stairs, keeping a wary eye out for Sibyl and any new mischief she might have gotten into, but luckily, she was nowhere to be seen.

I opened the door and found Mike standing just a bit awkwardly on my doorstep.

He seemed to be uncertain what to do with his hands, and for just a moment, I thought he was going to offer me a handshake.

"I knew I should have brought flowers," he muttered.

"What was that?" I said.

"Nothing," Mike replied. He swept out his hand in a grand gesture—as if he'd had a sudden inspiration. "Your chariot awaits, my lady."

I giggled and stepped outside.

Then Mike and I walked to his car.

Soon we settled in and drove off.

"So where are we going?" I asked.

Mike glanced over at me. "I told you—it's a surprise."

"And what about this information you have to tell me?"

"That can wait, too. Let's have lunch first."

I glanced over at Mike—it seemed to me that he was gripping the steering wheel just a little too tightly, and his face as he stared out at the road was just a little bit tense.

It seemed to me that Mike was nervous.

We drove on in silence, and I kept an eye out for possible restaurants.

But we drove past all the usual places, and soon, a wide, grassy expanse came into view.

It was the same spot where the Fourth of July fireworks were usually held—it was the square right by the old historic state house.

I looked at Mike questioningly.

"This is it," he said.

We both got out of the car, and he walked around to the trunk.

"I don't understand," I said. "There's no restaurant here."

"No—no, there isn't," Mike replied.

Then I saw what he was getting out of the trunk.

It was a picnic basket.

Mike smiled sheepishly at me.

"I thought we might try again."

I looked around at the bright, sunny day, and then I looked back at Mike.

He was staring at me, clearly concerned about what my reaction would be.

I understood now why he'd been nervous.

I had to smile.

"I love it, Mike. This is really thoughtful of you."

Mike's face lit up, and I could see the tension leaving him.

"You really like it?"

"I really do. I'm glad we finally get to do this."

Mike reached out a hand to me, and I took it, marveling at the little tingle that ran through me when his skin touched mine.

His touch had a magic all its own.

We walked across the wide green expanse of the square, and Mike wisely steered us toward a shady spot.

The day was beautiful—with not a cloud in the sky—but it was also hot and very humid.

We wouldn't last long out in the sun—or at least I wouldn't.

Under two broad, leafy trees, Mike unrolled a blanket he had brought with him, and we both sat down on the slightly bumpy ground.

Then Mike began to unpack the picnic basket.

He'd brought cheese, grapes, crusty bread, chocolate-covered strawberries, and a pitcher of cool, clinking lemonade.

I glanced at the chocolate-covered strawberries.

"Not a date, you said?"

Mike's sheepish look was back.

"I wanted it to be a complete surprise—I didn't want you to have any idea what I was up to. So I had to keep my whole approach low-key."

"Well, mission accomplished," I said. "You got your do-over."

Mike had brought two kinds of cheese, and they both paired well with the bread, which was crusty on the outside and soft on the inside and thoroughly delicious—Alberta would have approved.

The lemonade really helped take the edge off the heat, as did the grapes, which burst with tartness, and Mike had even brought tiny little smoked salmon sandwiches with the crusts cut off.

By the time we made it to the chocolate-covered strawberries, I was feeling serene and at peace with the world.

"I don't know how this compares to the picnic you packed," Mike said, wiping chocolate off his fingers, "but I think I did okay."

"You did a great job," I said. "You're a natural. I'd go on a picnic with you any day."

Mike looked inordinately pleased at this simple statement and stared at me for a long moment.

"Chloe—"

"So what information did you have for me?"

I hadn't meant to interrupt him, but somehow the words just tumbled out.

Mike blinked. "Information?"

"About the witch in the woods? That is why we're here, isn't it?"

"Yes—yes, it is," Mike said. "Though somehow that wasn't quite the reaction I was expecting at this point."

"What do you mean?" I asked.

"Well, isn't this a date?"

"Yes," I said. "But you said yourself it was an informational one. I believe you called it a meeting of the minds?"

Mike was rueful. "I did say that, didn't I?" He sighed. "So—the witch in the woods."

"The witch in the woods," I repeated.

"The funny thing is," Mike said musingly, "that this story was even harder to get a hold of than your family's story was."

I glanced at him sharply. "Yes—how did you get a hold of our story? I always wondered how you found out so much about us."

Mike shifted a little. "I told you I received those emails that were signed 'Charles Tyndall.' "

"I know—but you also said you found corroboration for everything that was in those emails. How did you do that?"

"I suppose I may as well give you the bad news," Mike replied. "Your family's history isn't as secret as you think—not even with your fancy symbol protecting everything.

"As I said last night, Henrietta College has a wonderful collection of local folklore—and an equally wonderful collection on local history and life. They've got letters and diaries and lots of firsthand accounts. There's even a rather marvelous book called *Magick in Our Dayes.*"

Mike paused to spell out the old-fashioned title for me.

Then he went on.

"It's all there. Your ancestor Mary helped a lot of people. And they were grateful, and they told other people. They wrote it down in those letters and diaries—and in that wonderful book. And Mary's descendants continued to help people. It's all there for anyone who cares to look—even your symbol is mentioned."

Mike smirked. "Magic is no match for the written word."

I continued to stare at him.

"Of course, not many people *do* bother to look. Until recently, the information was only available in dusty books. Now that it's been digitized, not many have access like I do."

Mike drew himself up with pride.

I sighed. I wondered if this magic thing was always going to be a sticking point between us.

Mike didn't really believe—and though he could discuss things in an academic way—he didn't really understand their importance.

But still, he was trying to help.

"So you have all these wonderful sources," I said. "And what did they tell you about the witch in the woods?"

"Nothing."

"Nothing?" I said, startled.

"There wasn't anything in them—I know them all nearly by heart. But I searched through them anyway. And I found nothing except for one phrase—'there will always be a witch in the woods.' "

Mike paused. "That was in *Magick in Our Dayes*, and it's not very helpful."

"No, it's not," I said. "So then you didn't—"

Mike held up a hand. "I didn't say I didn't find anything. I did find something in a place I didn't expect—kids' stories."

"Kids' stories," I murmured. "Detective Mia said something about that, too."

Mike nodded. "I conducted a series of interviews, and I came up with a remarkably similar group of stories."

"Wait," I said. "You conducted a series of interviews—and you did this last night? And you were interviewing kids?"

Mike colored. "No. It's nothing like that—I'm not a weirdo. I conducted a series of interviews when I first got here, and I only interviewed adults. I also sent out surveys. I asked people to tell me about local legends. And I asked them, if they had kids, to ask *them* what stories they'd heard, too."

"And the kids had heard about the witch?"

"Yes—well, at least I assume it's the same one the detective mentioned to you. None of the stories mentioned you or your sisters. But there were quite a few about a witch who lived in the woods."

"So what did they tell you? What witch? What woods?"

Mike frowned. "No one knew the name of the witch. But they all said she lived in the Old Forest. I tried to look that up at the time, but none of the maps showed a place with that name."

"That's because that's not the real name," I said. "At least not anymore."

"Are you saying you know where that is?"

"Yes," I replied a little abstractedly—the Old Forest was near the abandoned stone house where I had seen the pink dove.

I felt a sharp tug on my mind.

"So how do you find the witch once you reach the Old Forest?" I asked. "Or actually, Petit Mill Forest as it's known now."

"Well, that's just the thing," Mike replied. "It's a bit difficult. You have to follow a trail of breadcrumbs to the witch's house. And for the most part, only children can find them—though there were one or two exceptions. The stories call it the Hansel and Gretel house for those two reasons—the breadcrumbs and the kids. They say the witch is trying to lure children to her house with nefarious intent."

I shivered. "And then what happens? Once she lures them there?"

Mike chuckled. "Nothing. The stories aren't real. There's no witch in a gingerbread house trying to eat children."

I persisted. "But what do the stories say happens?"

Mike shrugged. "The stories say the witch has evil spells—some of them for sale. She tries to get the children to partake, and they run off."

"Partake? Partake in what?"

"The spells? A ritual? I don't know. The stories are all rather vague. The witch tries to get them to do something bad, and then they get scared and leave."

"Do you think—"

I hesitated.

"What?" Mike said.

"Do you think the witch in the woods could be part of the Crabtree Coven?"

Mike sighed. "So you still believe in that, do you? Well, you'll be relieved to know that my research never turned up any link between the witch in the woods and the coven."

I should have been relieved, but I wasn't.

I stood up. The tugging on my mind was growing stronger.

Mike looked up at me. "What's wrong?"

"I—I have to go," I said.

Mike stood up. "Then I'll go with you."

"No," I said. "I think I should go alone."

"Where are you going?"

"To the Old Forest."

Mike smiled. "Chloe, I *have* to go with you."

"Why?" I said.

"Because otherwise you'll never get there. I drove you here, remember?"

Chapter Thirteen

Mike and I did indeed drive out to the Old Forest.

And Mike had parked the car, and the two of us had tramped through the trees and the underbrush looking for a trail of breadcrumbs.

We didn't find one.

We also didn't find a house—with or without a witch.

The afternoon was very hot, however, and despite the cover of the canopy above, we were soon hot and sweaty.

Eventually, we were forced to give up.

As we walked back toward the car, Mike kept glancing over at me with a smug, I-told-you-so look.

But to his credit, he said nothing at all as we got back in the car, and he turned on the ignition.

Mercifully, the air-conditioning kicked in almost immediately, and I closed my eyes and listened to the very welcome *whoosh!* of cold air as it flooded in from the vents.

On the way back to my house, Mike tried to make conversation, but I was having trouble concentrating on his words.

Although we hadn't found the witch's house in the forest, I had felt *something* as I'd walked through those trees—I just didn't know what.

The image that had begun to grow in my mind a few days ago was suddenly growing again—becoming bigger, clearer.

It was changing.

"Uh, Chloe?" Mike said.

I looked around. "Yes?"

"We're here."

I glanced out the window.

We were indeed parked in front of my sister's house.

I hadn't even realized we'd stopped until that moment.

"Oh," I said. "Oh!"

"Chloe, are you all right?"

"Yes—I'm fine. I'm just a little distracted."

"I'll say," Mike muttered.

"Thanks, Mike," I said. "For everything. Thank you for the lovely picnic, and thank you for taking me out to the forest to look around."

"Any time," he replied. "Chloe—"

"Yes?"

"You've been really different since we came back from the forest. Are you sure everything's okay?"

"Yes," I said. "I just need to think."

Mike gave me a long look. "All right. Just take care of yourself. And if you want to go tramping around any more forests, please give me a call, okay?"

I smiled. "Okay."

I very nearly leaned over and kissed Mike right then.

But something held me back.

"Thanks again, Mike," I said.

Then I got out of the car, and with one last wave, he drove off.

As I went inside, I could hear someone rattling around in the kitchen.

"Alberta?" I said.

She poked her head out. "I'm in here."

I could smell something delicious wafting on the air.

But I ignored it.

"Alberta, you need to do some scrying right away."

She had disappeared into the kitchen again, and her voice floated out to me.

"Why?"

I set my purse down and walked into the kitchen.

"Because I've got a funny feeling," I said.

Alberta was fussing with something that sat on the stove, and she quickly whirled around and blocked it from my view.

She held out a little golden bite.

"Let's see if you like this as much as last time."

"What is it?" I asked.

"Just try it."

She sounded exasperated.

Since I was trying to stay on her good side at this particular moment, I accepted the proffered bite.

It was sweet, like a muffin, and then something deliciously tart burst in my mouth.

"That's wonderful," I said. "What is it?"

"Cherry muffin."

I made a face. "I don't like cherries."

"That's what you said last month when I had you try it. But you do like this?"

"Yes—I love it. That muffin's delicious."

Alberta smiled in satisfaction. "Good. Excellent. Just what I was hoping to hear."

Since she seemed to be in a good mood at the moment, I hurried on.

"You have to do some scrying, Alberta—and also I think you may be right about Rafaela."

She blinked.

"What?"

I'd thrown in the part about Rafaela to see if I could prolong Alberta's good mood.

Being told she was right often had that effect.

I decided to lead with that.

"Someone's been leaving smiley faces on Rafaela's Facebook page. And that same person called her 'babe' and seemed to be referring to a meeting."

I had Alberta's attention now.

"What? Show me."

"I'll show you right after you do some scrying."

Alberta shook her head and waved at her muffins.

"Can't. I'm busy right now."

"This is *important*, Alberta. This can't wait."

"What's so important about it?"

I told her quickly about the information Mike had given me—and about our walk through the woods.

And then I tried to tease out the idea that was in the back of my mind.

"I think … there may be a magical element to Mr. Clementine's death."

"Mr. Clementine was strangled," Alberta said firmly. "And the autopsy is available to the public. You can look that over if you want."

"Yes—but the autopsy isn't the end of the story, is it?" I said.

Alberta grumbled under her breath.

I could tell she'd been hoping I didn't know that.

"I've read through the autopsy report," I said. "Last night. And it doesn't say a lot that wasn't in the media reports. But there's a coroner's report, too, isn't there? One that takes longer and goes more in depth. That one's probably still in progress."

Alberta sighed. "Yes—that's likely true. So I suppose you want me to take a look at the coroner's report?"

"Yes. And we also need to find out about this mysterious witch in the woods."

"I don't know. To do scrying, it's really best if I focus on a specific person—their feelings and impressions."

"But you can do places, too, can't you?" I said. "Focus on the feelings and impressions that have occurred in a specific place?"

"Yes—but that's not so easy. And scrying isn't easy to begin with."

I hurried on. "Then that's perfect. I know the name of the local coroner—and I even found a picture of him online. Then after him, we can focus on the Old Forest."

Alberta stared at me. "Did you even hear what I said?"

"Yes, I heard you. But this is important."

"The coroner's report may not be complete, you know."

"I know."

"And it's much better if I do scrying on someone I've met and talked to—or even someone close to that person. Focusing on a stranger I've only seen in a picture is much harder."

"I know that, too."

Alberta sighed again—a big, dramatic sound.

"You're not going to let this go, are you?"

"No," I said. "No, I'm not."

"Fine." Alberta glanced longingly at her muffin pan. "I guess I'm done here for the moment anyway. But we'd better make this quick."

"Quick is good," I said. "I can do quick." I paused. "Can I sit with you?"

"Of course. I'm only doing this because of you."

"Should I get some tea, or—"

Alberta waved a hand. "I don't need anything. Let's just get this done."

I sighed to myself—I'd clearly put her in a bad mood.

But at least we were finally going to do some scrying.

As we walked up the stairs, Alberta grumbled about this being an invasion of privacy, but in my mind it wasn't really.

The coroner's report wasn't necessarily going to become a public document, but it wasn't really a private one, either. It was just a sensitive document that the authorities didn't want to get out because they didn't want the leaked information to interfere with their investigation.

But I wasn't interfering—I was helping.

And I certainly wasn't going to make anything public.

And as far as woodlands went, they didn't really have any privacy. If the Old Forest had a secret, it was fair game.

Alberta went into her bedroom where she always kept her scrying mirror, and I hurried to get the information I had printed out about the coroner.

I gave it to her, and she read it over carefully.

Then she got out a single tapering candle and moved to pull down the shades.

Scrying was fire magic, and it required darkness in order for her to focus on the flame properly. It was a form of divination, and it allowed Alberta to see what was hidden or unknown. And she performed it through the use of a candle and a special black mirror.

"Are you sure you don't want any tea?" I asked a little anxiously.

Alberta often drank tea—usually mugwort—before she did any scrying. The herb helped to promote clarity and the power of insight.

"No, no tea," she said shortly.

"But—"

"Do you want me to do this or not?"

I almost said "yes, ma'am," but I settled for a simple "yes."

"Close the door," Alberta said.

I hurried to do that, and she pulled two chairs up to her dresser where her scrying mirror sat.

Then she draped a cloth over the regular mirror that hung over her dresser, and unveiled the scrying mirror.

The mirror itself was smooth and black, and it rested on a rosewood stand. Alberta lit the candle in front of it, and then went to turn out the lights.

After that we both sat down—I sat at a little distance from Alberta so I wouldn't distract her, and she angled her chair so that she wouldn't see her own face in the mirror.

"This doesn't always work," she muttered, as she angled her chair a little more.

"I know," I said.

"And you're not a cop."

"I know that, too."

Alberta finally settled herself, and then the scrying session began in earnest.

She stared into the mirror, watching the reflected flame, and as I watched my sister, her expression grew distant and peaceful.

She looked as if she were looking through the mirror into a place beyond, and I knew that she was fully into the divination now.

She hadn't told me what questions she was going to focus on, but I supposed it didn't matter—as long as Alberta was clear about what she wanted to find, she'd find it. And I'd already told her that I believed there was a magical element to Mr. Clementine's death.

Despite her protestations, she really was very good at scrying.

Alberta frowned a little, and I quickly glanced at her. She tilted her head to one side and squinted her eyes as if she were trying to see something she couldn't quite make out.

Eventually, her face relaxed.

Her expression remained calm and peaceful, and after a little while, my attention began to wander.

I was just thinking about Mike and our car ride home after the forest when Alberta made a tiny noise, and my eyes snapped back to her face.

Her eyebrows were raised, and she blinked in surprise. She leaned forward, peering into the mirror.

I quickly looked at the mirror, too—but its smooth, dark surface was blank to me, and I saw nothing in it except the little arrow of yellow flame that rose from the candle.

After a moment, she blinked again and sat back.

She'd clearly come out of her trance.

I was bursting with questions, but I didn't want to jump on Alberta right away—I knew that scrying took a lot of mental and physical effort.

But Alberta continued to remain silent, and when she put the cover back on the mirror and rose from her chair, I couldn't contain myself any longer.

"So what did you see?"

Alberta didn't reply to me—instead she grumbled to herself as she flicked on the lights and blew out the candle.

"Does that mean I was right about something?" I asked.

Alberta grumbled a little more, and then she threw me a dark look.

"There was nothing in the Old Forest. No presence at all."

"Oh, okay," I replied.

Alberta continued grudgingly. "But that in itself is strange."

She paused, and I could see two emotions at war on her face—she didn't want to admit that I was onto something, but she also liked to tell the truth and disliked hiding anything.

Being truthful quickly won out.

"I should have been able to sense *something*," she said. "Some past events, some emotions—at the very least I should have had some impressions of animals. But there's nothing there at all. It's almost as if—"

I waited.

"It's almost as if someone's blocking me," she finished.

"So does that mean—"

"It doesn't mean there's a witch," Alberta said quickly. "But it does mean something's there that we need to investigate."

I smiled—not so much in triumph, but in relief.

"Then I'm not crazy."

"I wouldn't go that far. But at least it's not your imagination."

"And what about the coroner's report?"

Alberta's face darkened for just a moment, and I had to assume that that meant I was right again.

But her face quickly cleared, and she went on.

"It's not completed yet, but from what I can tell there are abnormalities."

"Like what?"

"Like—there's no bruising on the body. Mr. Clementine never fell down the stairs. He was strangled either in place, or he was strangled up in his office and then carried down."

"But we already knew he was strangled," I said. "We knew it wasn't an accident."

"But someone wanted it to look like an accident. They probably didn't know that the coroner could tell the difference."

"That's probably true," I said—but that certainly wasn't enough to have caused Alberta's bad mood. "And that's a good point. But that's not all, right? Surely there's something else?"

Alberta sighed and then spoke in a tone that implied that the words were being pulled out of her.

But all the same she spoke.

"Yes—there's a blue line—a stain, really—around the body's neck—"

"And?"

"And it glows in the dark. But under normal light, it doesn't glow at all."

"It glows in the dark?" I said.

"Yes."

"That—doesn't sound normal," I said.

"It isn't. And the coroner said as much. He's never seen anything like it."

"So, a glowing blue line," I said. "Could be magical in origin."

Alberta scowled. "Yes—it could be."

She sounded like she was being strangled herself.

But I wasn't interested in being proved right for the sake of being proved right—I just wanted to help Mr. Clementine.

And I now had proof that I was on the right track.

"Thank you, Alberta," I said.

She grumbled something that sounded a little bit like "you're welcome."

"No, I really mean it," I said. "I wouldn't have this information without you."

She grumbled a little more, but she seemed mollified.

"So I suppose I should call Mom about this," I said. "Unless you know something about spells that can strangle people?"

"No—I don't know anything about that—none of us do. You'd better call Mom."

I stared at her for a moment in surprise.

"Wait—you're not going to rush in ahead of me? You're not going to tell me *not* to call Mom so that you can secretly do it yourself?"

She did that sometimes—not to be dishonest, but because she was going into protective mode. As a big sister, she felt that scary things had to be kept from her littlest sister.

Alberta drew herself up with dignity. "Of course not. When have I ever done that?"

"You do it all the time," I protested.

"I certainly do not. Besides, I already know what she's going to say—she's going to tell you to stay out of it and let the police do their job."

"So it's all right for you to help the police," I said, rehashing one of my recent arguments. "But when it's me, I have to stay out of it?"

"I was helping to find missing people," Alberta replied. "This is a murder case. It's not the same thing at all."

"I'm still helping someone," I said stubbornly. "Even if that person is deceased."

"Fine. Whatever. Mom will agree with me—you'll see. Now if you'll excuse me, I need to get back to my baking."

"More baking?"

"Yes."

"Fine," I said.

Then I stood and turned to go.

"Oh!" I said suddenly, turning back. "I promised to show you Rafaela's Facebook page—"

Alberta waved a dismissive hand. "I'm sure I'll figure it out. I don't need you to show me."

"Fine," I said again, and left the room.

Alberta actually followed me as I walked down the hall, and when I reached my room, I very nearly slammed the door behind me.

But I realized that would be childish, and instead I closed the door quietly.

I heard Alberta continue down the stairs to the kitchen.

For my part, I stood by the door, still a little bit stunned.

It wasn't like Alberta not to try to take charge—and as I heard her rattling around downstairs, it seemed to me, once again, like she was doing an awful lot of baking, even by her standards.

And that was something she often did when she was stressed out.

I remembered once more that Rafaela had said she was worried about her.

And Alberta hadn't mentioned Peter in ages.

I sat down on my bed and wondered about her.

Chapter Fourteen

I'd meant to call Mom right away, but somehow I didn't.

Instead, I sat down on my bed and thought for a while.

Alberta's insistence that our mother would tell me to stay out of things was still ringing in my ears, but that wasn't really the reason I didn't call.

What really stopped me was the feeling that I would be calling too soon—I had to put things in order, and I couldn't do that properly with new information—at least not yet.

So I sat on my bed and let the facts I already had settle into place.

Mr. Clementine had been strangled, and whatever method had been used had left a glowing mark on him.

That was definitely magic, and I now knew that I was on the lookout for a magical killer.

I could feel the image in my mind growing, shifting—changing. Little bits of it were starting to come into focus, but the vast majority of it was still shrouded in shadow.

I sighed a little and got up to look at my flowerpots.

My family of flowers was still looking perfectly healthy, so whatever Alberta and Rafaela were both up to, it couldn't be *that* bad.

Unless, of course, the worst is yet to come, said a small voice in my head.

And it was true.

The connective magic of my plants only tracked the current physical state of the originals they were bound to.

If there was trouble up ahead, the plants would have no way of knowing that.

I shrugged the thought off and went back to concentrating on the image in my mind.

But as I meditated, eventually, my mind turned to more mundane things like cleaning and laundry, and I decided to tackle the dust bunnies under my bed.

After turns with both a long-handled duster and the vacuum, I was confident that Sibyl would no longer be able to pick up a wispy white beard from my room.

And then I went down to do my laundry, and I tried to tell Alberta about the incident with Sibyl and the mustard jar, but she didn't seem interested. Instead, she was busy whipping up something in a mixing bowl.

I offered to cook dinner that night, but Alberta nixed that idea, too, and shooed me out of the kitchen.

As I continued my cleaning frenzy, it occurred to me that if Alberta was using magic to keep the house clean that that probably wasn't a bad way to go.

Just when I thought I'd done all I could do for the day, I caught the scent of something delicious wafting out of the kitchen.

I hurried downstairs.

"Mmm … what's that?" I said.

"Open-faced turkey sandwiches," Alberta replied. "Hot ones with gravy. I thought I'd do something simple."

Soon I had set the kitchen table and poured out iced tea, and we sat down to eat the hot roast turkey sandwiches and some broccoli soup that Alberta had made.

I wasn't usually a big fan of broccoli, but Alberta's soup was good—I knew it had only three ingredients, broccoli, sea salt, and broth—and even the open-faced sandwiches were good. I suspected that the thinly sliced turkey was actually from the deli, and I'd seen a store-bought gravy packet poking out of the trash can, but the bread was Alberta's own, and even the prepackaged stuff was good.

It was all as delicious as the scent had promised, and I told Alberta so.

In response, a malicious twinkle lit up her eye.

"What did Mom say?"

"I haven't spoken to her yet," I admitted.

Alberta smiled smugly in response.

Then she glanced at the dining room table.

"I invited Rafaela over again tonight, but she turned me down."

I glanced over at the dining room table also—I knew what Alberta was thinking.

Just last month, the three of us had sat at that table many times, sharing many meals.

Now we barely seemed to see our sister.

The mood suddenly seemed somber, and Alberta stood up.

"I have something that will cheer us up."

She produced a blueberry cheesecake from the refrigerator, and soon both of us had a slice.

I still thought Alberta had been a little overzealous with the baking lately, but I had to admit that it definitely had its perks.

After dinner, I went upstairs to finally call Mom.

But as I put my hand on the phone, it suddenly lit up, and I turned it over.

She was calling me.

"Hello?" I said.

"Hi, honey." Maura's voice was warm, but there was an edge of emotion in it.

She sounded worried.

"Hiya, Chloe." My dad's voice rang out in the background.

He sounded worried, too.

I could picture the two of them—Maura blond and soulful with big eyes so full of feeling just like Rafaela's—and beside her, Richard with his black hair peppered with silver, and his black-rimmed glasses resting on his nose.

And both of them, concerned about me and focused on the phone that probably sat on the table in front of them in their Florida home.

"How are you doing, Dad?" I said.

"I'm fine. How are *you*?"

"I'm great," I said. "But you just had a doctor's appointment."

"It was nothing—just routine. But your mother here is worried about you. And when she's worried, so am I."

"Chloe, honey, I have the most terrible feeling—" Maura began.

"Also your sister called," Richard said, interrupting. "She told us the whole story."

"Richard, you know I am very sensitive. I could sense my daughter's emotional state—I could tell she was in trouble."

"Yes, you're sensitive—that's true—but that phone call didn't hurt. That's all I'm saying."

"Wait," I interjected. "Are you saying that Alberta called you about me?"

"Yes," Maura said.

"Then she's a lot sneakier than I realized," I replied. "What did she say?"

"She told us about the coroner's report," Maura said. "And about the glowing blue line. She also said she thinks you feel like you have an obligation to solve this murder."

"And she also told us to tell you to stay out of it," Richard chimed in.

"What?" I said.

"Honey, she may be right," Maura said.

"I don't believe this," I fumed. "Alberta made me believe that she wasn't going to get involved in this, and then she goes and calls you behind my back. I don't understand how she can be so straightforward and so sneaky at the same time."

"She's just worried about you," Maura replied. "And she's very protective of you. She feels like it's her job as your big sister to look out for you."

"But—"

"She doesn't mean to be sneaky," Maura added. "She just shuts down emotionally when she goes into protective mode. She wants to wrap both you and Rafaela in armor at times and shield you from everything. That's why she doesn't tell you these things straight out— she can't. To tell you would be to let you in on the danger. She has to shield you without ever letting you know that anything was wrong."

I had had similar thoughts, but I was still irritated.

"So she called you to do the shutting down." I couldn't help doing a little Alberta-style grumbling myself.

"I can tell that you're unhappy, Chloe, but it's not as bad as all that. Alberta wants to help you. *We* want to help you."

"Well, at the very least, can you tell me what you know?" I asked. "What does that glowing-in-the-dark blue line mean?"

There was a long pause, and I could picture my parents exchanging an uncomfortable glance.

"So I take it that means you do know something?"

"It's a strangulation spell," Maura said at last. "It requires an incantation and a powder mixed with several very rare herbs, and it always leaves that telltale blue mark. It's not at all an easy spell to cast."

"Then that's good, isn't it?" I said. "That will narrow down the number of people who could have cast it."

Maura sighed. "That's just it—I don't know anyone who could have cast it. And this really is a matter for the police. Please, Chloe, just let them handle it."

"But we know things they don't," I protested. "They don't know magic is involved—and that means they're missing a vital clue."

"And they won't be able to understand that," Maura replied. "You'll never be able to convince them. And they can still solve it without that. They're experts on murder—and we're not."

"But—"

"Chloe," Richard said. "Listen to your mother."

"Okay, fine," I said. "But what about the Old Forest? I assume Alberta mentioned that, too?"

There was another pause.

"It *is* strange," Maura admitted after a moment. "But you went out there yourself, and you didn't find anything, right? Maybe it's just a natural phenomenon causing this."

"A natural phenomenon?" I said. "The local kids tell stories about that place. They must have noticed something."

"The kids used to tell stories about Charles Tyndall, too," Maura said. "Before he died, they were all saying he was a member of the Crabtree Coven, and those stories were all false. The poor man had no knowledge of magic whatsoever."

"But what if this is the Crabtree Coven? What if they're blocking the forest? What if they're blocking our rune stones?"

Maura's voice was quiet. "I'm sorry I asked you to check on the rune stones. I'll look into that myself—later. Right now, we should let the police get on with their investigation—without our help. I fear that anything we do could actually get in the way."

"You mean anything *I* do," I said.

"Oh, honey, don't take it that way. We'll get this all cleared up— after the police investigation is over. Let's let all the hustle and bustle die down. We'll get to work once things are quieter."

"But aren't we supposed to help people?" I said. "Isn't that the reason the rune stones were set up in the first place? We did that so we could protect this town."

"I know—but murder is something else—it's beyond the range of healing and helping."

"But aren't we supposed to keep out bad magic? And this is definitely bad magic. Besides, I had an idea growing in my mind about this. And you told me once to hang on to that."

"Yes, I did—and that's important. But in this case—"

Maura broke off.

"Oh, honey, I don't want to say this, but someone has used magic to kill already. And I don't want you to get hurt."

"Last time—"

"Last time you were saving your sister. This time we need to keep you safe."

I fell silent. I could tell that her mind was made up.

"Now you're upset," Maura said gently. "But you can understand why we'd like you to stay out of this, can't you?"

"Yes, I can," I said, heaving a huge sigh.

"Is there anything else you want to tell me?"

"No," I said.

"Don't sound so sad, honey," Maura said. "It's really better this way. And I'll call you again soon."

"Take care of yourself, little witch," Richard said. "And stay out of trouble."

With that they were gone.

I sat for a few moments, stewing.

I could see why they wanted me to stay out of things.

But I also knew why I couldn't do that.

Detective Mia had asked me if there were magical means to do away with someone, but I knew that she didn't genuinely believe and that she wouldn't be able to investigate the magic angle with any degree of sincerity.

I knew things no one else knew, and I had to help.

I *would* help.

And an idea was coming to me as to how.

I couldn't put my plan into action right away, so I sat up in my room and stewed some more.

I usually went down for a snack in the evening, but I didn't want to see Alberta—I had a feeling she would be insufferable.

So I stayed where I was and thought and looked on my phone for anything I could find about the Otis Clementine case.

Nothing really jumped out at me, so I broke into the stash of granola bars that I always kept in my purse and drank a bottle of water.

I went to bed in a very bad mood.

In the morning, Alberta was already gone when I made my way downstairs—even though it was Sunday—and I was grateful to be able to drink my coffee in peace.

Then I went out into the hot, humid morning to work my usual Sunday shift at the library.

I'd have access to better research resources there than I had on my phone, so I was looking forward to doing a little investigation when things got quiet.

Stu was in as usual, and after a little flurry when we opened, things began to settle down.

I was just turning to my computer when the front door opened, and my sister Rafaela walked in.

She was smiling broadly, and her golden-brown hair was pulled back into a French braid—a style I had never seen her wear before.

Her face was turned, and she was looking back at a man who was following her in.

He was tallish, with chin-length blond hair, and he was grinning back at her.

The way they were talking, they seemed like they knew each other, and I couldn't help but wonder if this was the mysterious B. P. Gotschall.

Rafaela walked up to me, beaming, and the man followed close behind.

"Hi, Chloe," Rafaela said, and she giggled.

I stared at her in mild surprise.

I'd never seen Rafaela this giddy.

"Hi," I said.

Rafaela reached back to take the arm of the blond man, and he stepped up beside her.

"I wanted you to be the first to meet Bodhi," she said.

"I'm Bodhi P. Gotschall," he said. "The 'P' is for peace."

He extended a hand.

I stared at him in surprise.

So he was indeed the person who'd been leaving smiley faces on my sister's posts.

But somehow he wasn't at all what I'd expected.

He was deeply tanned, and he had a strong, square jaw with a cleft in the chin. He was wearing a light, collarless tunic in a pale shade of lavender and loose-fitting white pants that looked a little like pajama bottoms. His blond hair was slicked back from his forehead, and it curled below his ears and along his neck, accentuating the firm line of his jaw. He wore silver cuffs on both ears and silver rings on both of his thumbs. He also wore a medallion with an amethyst-colored stone in a chain around his neck. He looked to be about Rafaela's age, but when he smiled, the crinkles around his eyes made him look just a bit older.

In any large city, there would have been hundreds of Bodhis walking around—but here in our little town he would really stand out. And he wasn't Rafaela's usual type—she tended to go more for the rugged, outdoorsy kind of guy.

Eventually I found my voice.

"Bodhi?" I said. "Like the tree under which the Buddha found enlightenment?"

He smiled. "Exactly."

He was still holding out his hand, and I finally took it.

"Sorry," I said. "I didn't mean to leave you hanging."

But his handshake was warm and a little sweaty, and I recoiled just a bit.

Bodhi must have noticed my face.

"I just came from hot yoga," he said apologetically.

"Bodhi is a yoga instructor," Rafaela said, looking up at him.

He smiled at her and then produced a business card, which he handed to me.

It simply said "BPG" and had a lotus on it embossed in pink and gold. And below that was an address, a phone number, and an email address.

"Very nice," I said.

Rafaela looked up at him again, and he smiled and nodded.

Then he walked off toward the books.

I got the feeling it was a prearranged signal between the two of them.

Rafaela turned toward me.

"So what do you think?"

"About?"

"Him?" Rafaela nodded her head.

I turned to see the lithe figure of her male companion disappearing behind a bookcase.

"Very nice," I said—I couldn't think of anything else to say.

"And?"

I turned back to Rafaela. "The yoga seems to be working for him?"

She giggled loudly, and a number of patrons from nearby tables looked up and glared at us.

"Oh, right, library," Rafaela said, lowering her voice. "Sorry about that."

"That's okay," I said, glancing up. "I like your hair."

Rafaela patted the golden-brown braids. "Do you? Bodhi did it."

"Wow," I said. "A man of many talents."

I paused. "So what brings you guys here?"

"I told you—I wanted you to meet."

"Then Bodhi is your boy—"

Rafaela giggled again and slapped my arm.

"Don't say it. He's not my boyfriend. He's just a very good friend that I like spending time with."

"Whom you wanted me to meet," I said.

"Yes," Rafaela replied dreamily.

"So I assume this means we'll all be hanging out together?"

"Yes—I'd like you guys to get to know him."

She glanced at me furtively.

"And I'd like you to help me."

"Me?" I said. "How?"

"You know how Alberta gets. Can you help me smooth things over with her?"

"Wait—I don't understand."

"Alberta gets all mother hen-y about people we're dating."

I glanced back at the books that were now hiding Bodhi.

"What's wrong with him?"

Rafaela blinked. "What?"

"Alberta doesn't automatically object to any guy we go out with. She only objects when she thinks something's wrong. So what's wrong with him?"

Rafaela gave me an astonished look. "There's nothing wrong with him. Why would you say that?"

"I just think that you're being weird. Why would you think that Alberta would object?"

"It's just that I know how she can get," Rafaela said again. "And you do, too. And I'd appreciate your support."

"Okay," I said. "What do you want me to do exactly?"

"Just put in a good word for me—for us. Sort of pave the way to let her know that I'll be introducing her to someone."

"I think she already knows," I said dryly.

Rafaela was startled. "What? How could she know?"

I didn't want to tell her about my sleuthing on Facebook.

"Alberta just kind of suspected. She told me she thought you might be turning her down for dinner because you were seeing someone."

And that was true—she had suspected it first. I only went looking because Alberta had planted the idea in my mind.

Rafaela sighed. "Leave it to her to be sensitive at exactly the wrong moment."

"Alberta isn't insensitive," I said. "She's always there for us when we need her."

"I know—it's just that when you finally locate someone you really click with—someone who's special to you—you want everything to go smoothly with your family."

"You really think that?" I asked. "You think this is something special?"

Rafaela smiled fondly over at the spot where I assumed Bodhi was still hiding.

"I really do."

I frowned. "Why did you say it like that?"

"Like what?"

"You said when you 'locate' someone. You didn't say 'find.'"

Rafaela looked at me, perplexed. "I don't know why I phrased it that way. Are you sure that's what I said?"

"Yes."

"Maybe it's just because I met him online. 'Finding' sounds more like meeting someone in person."

She shot me a glance. "Is something wrong with that?"

"No," I said. "Not at all. It's just—that word makes me think of something."

"What?"

"I'm not entirely sure."

Chapter Fifteen

Monday morning found me waking up way earlier than I usually did.

Lee had scheduled the reading of the will for eight o'clock in the morning, and I wanted to get there early.

I didn't want to miss a single minute.

At the same time, an idea was gnawing at the back of my mind, trying to find its way into the light.

It had something to do with what Rafaela had said and something do with what my mother had said yesterday.

But I wasn't sure what.

So I hurried to get ready, and I wondered what I should wear to a will-reading.

I settled on a plain black dress that I could wear to work later.

Then I hurried downstairs and began to brew some coffee.

Alberta was already gone.

And that was really fine with me.

I hadn't told her about Rafaela's sort-of boyfriend—mostly because all she wanted to hear about was my conversation with our mom.

She only wanted to hear that both our parents didn't want me to investigate Mr. Clementine's murder.

But there was no way I could turn back from that.

So at the moment, that meant that we didn't have a lot to say to each other.

I ate my breakfast—just cereal and milk this time—and then I was out the door.

I stumbled just a little over the latest edition of *The Morning Cider*, which was sitting on the doorstep, and I picked it up and glanced at it.

Apparently, yet another jewelry store had been broken into.

I dropped the paper back inside the house and went down to my car.

I'd expected Lee to hold the reading of the will at his office, but he'd actually booked a room at one of the boutique hotels downtown.

Luckily, the hotel had a small parking lot, and I was able to slot into one of the spaces allotted for visitors.

The meeting was being held in a room with the rather elaborate name of the Crystal Palace Drawing Room, and as I arrived, a young woman in a dark-navy suit asked for my ID.

Once she'd matched the image on my driver's license with my face, she allowed me to enter.

The room was small but ornate, with crystal chandeliers, parquet floors, and lavish flower arrangements on little tables all along the walls—and there was even a crystal decanter with a row of crystal glasses nestled on one table, as if this were a real drawing room in which to receive guests.

There were also ten chairs with red-velvet cushions lined up in a row, and they all sat facing a table that presided at the front of the room.

Behind the table sat Lee Hurtzel.

I was a little perturbed at the seating arrangements—I'd hoped that we'd be in a much larger room and that I'd be able to hide out in the back without anyone really noticing me.

But this way I'd be front and center along with everybody else, and I wouldn't be able to observe without being seen myself.

I wondered if the room had been set up this way for that very reason.

I was the first to arrive, and Lee looked up from a set of papers he was perusing and smiled at me as I sat at one end of the row of chairs.

Very soon other people began to arrive—and two men who somehow gave off the impression that they worked with their hands came in and sat all the way at the other end of the row of chairs—as far away from me as possible.

After them came Daphne Minton and Marianne Mozer. Marianne smiled and waved and sat down next to me. Daphne didn't seem too pleased to see me, but she gave me a polite nod and sat down on the other side of Marianne.

Then the rest came in rapid succession—a tall, stunning, short-haired blonde whom I recognized as Mr. Clementine's girlfriend, Heather, another man who somehow seemed to belong with the first two who had arrived, and then two other men who clearly did not. They were both tall, blond, and bore a strong resemblance to the portrait of Mr. Clementine that hung in his front hall.

I figured they were likely his sons, Christopher and Bobby.

Once they were seated, there was still one empty chair.

Lee looked over the row and cleared his throat.

"Since we're all here, let's begin—"

Heather interrupted, her voice high and shrill. "We're *not* all here. *Someone* is missing."

Lee glanced at the empty chair. "I've received an email from Ms. Jackie O'Shea. She won't be attending today."

One of the blond men looked over at Heather.

"Our mom's in Bali. She couldn't make it back in time."

"Bali?" Heather sniffed. "Must be nice."

The other blond man looked over at Heather.

"Dad's done pretty well by you. I don't see that you have anything to complain about."

Heather sniffed again but didn't say anything further.

Lee looked over the row of chairs again, and when silence reigned, he started once more.

"Since we're all here, please allow me to say thank you for coming. My name is Lee Hurtzel, and I was the personal attorney to Mr. Clementine for many years. I know some of you, and others I have only corresponded with over the phone and through email. But all of you are here for the same reason: Mr. Clementine wanted you to be present at the reading of his will."

A rustle ran through those seated on the chairs, and I wondered why—surely they must all have known that that was the purpose of the meeting. But perhaps they hadn't known that others would be present, or perhaps they were all shifting in their chairs in anticipation.

After all, a great deal of money was at stake.

Lee continued. "I should caution you, however, that it will take a year or more for Mr. Clementine's estate to be settled. So if you hear that you have inherited something under Mr. Clementine's will, you won't receive it right away—and there is even a possibility that what is recorded here could change. The probate process allows challenges to the will. So I am making you aware now that neither I nor anyone else is currently authorized to award money or property. This is a simple reading of Mr. Clementine's most recent will. It will be a very long time before anything mentioned here is disbursed."

Another rustle went through those seated in the row of chairs, and I'd noticed that Daphne had looked up at the words "most recent."

Lee looked over the assembled group one last time, and when no one protested, he cleared his throat and began to read the will.

Mr. Clementine listed his full name—Otis Arthur Clementine—and then declared himself of sound mind and body.

Then there was a long list of bequests to various charities and local institutions—and the Crabtree Bay Public Library was one of these. I was mentioned as a representative of the library who would be present, and all eyes in the row of chairs swiveled to me as Lee read out a large sum of money that would be placed in a trust for the use of the library.

It was quite a large sum of money, and as everyone continued to stare at me, I felt myself shifting uncomfortably.

"At least we'll be able to buy some new furniture," I said.

Lee looked up at the interruption with the air of a disapproving teacher.

All eyes snapped back to him.

He continued the reading, and eventually, he came around to the bequests to individuals.

He listed several people I didn't know, and they were given bequests of prize possessions—a set of rare books, a statue, a painting.

Then Lee mentioned a name, and one of the three men sitting at the other end of the row stirred.

He sat forward as Lee read out a large sum of money and a collection of antique swords.

The man smiled, and the two men sitting near him seemed to be congratulating him.

Those other two men each looked expectant in turn as their names were called, and they were both bequeathed two equally large sums of money and an expensive wristwatch and a case of rare scotch respectively. All three of the men were thanked for working for Mr. Clementine for many years.

Then Daphne and Marianne were mentioned.

Both were gifted substantial amounts of money and presents of jewelry—Daphne was to receive an antique cameo that had belonged to Mr. Clementine's mother, and Marianne was to receive a gold heart-shaped locket.

They were also thanked for their service.

Lee then turned to the family, and people began to shift in their seats.

The room was noticeably tenser.

Heather, whose last name turned out to be Pim, was bequeathed a condo and a very substantial sum of money—more than four times what any of Mr. Clementine's former employees received. Managed right, it was certainly enough for Heather to live on for the rest of her life—but she scowled openly.

The sum was only a tiny fraction of what Mr. Clementine had been worth, and it was clear that she'd expected more.

Jackie O'Shea was gifted a house and the same amount of money that Heather had received.

There was no reaction from the two blond men who I assumed were her sons.

And then Lee announced that there would be a sale—Brian's Baskets, its subsidiaries, and all Mr. Clementine's real estate holdings, not including Heather's condo and Jackie's house—but including his own home—would be sold, and the proceeds would be divided equally amongst his four sons—Brian, Christopher, Robert, and Jaden. Also, all stocks and other investments Mr. Clementine had in other companies would be assessed and then divided equally amongst the four. The same was true of all cash and cash equivalents not disposed of elsewhere.

Jaden's portion of the estate was to be placed into a trust for him, and Lee Hurtzel was named as the executor of the trust.

And Brian's receipt of his portion of the estate was contingent on his being found. If he couldn't be located within one year, then his portion would be forfeit, and his share would be divided evenly amongst his three half brothers.

The effect of this pronouncement was electric.

Heather whooped and jumped out of her seat, throwing her arms up in the air.

Daphne also jumped out of her seat—but she was clearly less than pleased.

One of the blond men shouted, "All right!" and tried to high-five his brother, but his brother simply looked disapproving.

"This is outrageous!" Daphne sputtered. "Just outrageous!"

Lee looked at her in mild surprise.

"What is, Ms. Minton?"

"That is *not* Mr. Clementine's will. *I* witnessed his will, and I saw what was in it. He made provisions for his other sons—saw that they were well cared for—but he left the bulk of his estate—and Brian's Baskets—to Brian. He built that company for his eldest son, and he intended it to go to him. Where's *that* will? That's the one you should be reading."

"Shut up, Minton," Heather snapped. "Lee's a lawyer. Don't you think he knows what a proper will looks like? If he says that's the one, then that's the one."

Daphne turned a malicious face on Heather. "Don't think you'll get your hands on your son's money, my girl. That money's going into a trust, and it's going to be properly managed. You're not going to spend all of his fortune on frippery for yourself."

Heather looked startled, and she turned an accusing face on Lee as if he'd tricked her.

"Is this true?"

Lee held out a pacifying hand. "Now, now, everyone just settle down. As I said, it will be a long time before anyone receives any money or property of any kind. And Ms. Minton, to your earlier point, this is indeed the correct will. You witnessed one several years ago, but since then Mr. Clementine made a new will."

"When?" Daphne demanded.

Lee glanced at the document in his hand. "This one was signed and witnessed two months ago."

"Witnessed?" Daphne said sharply. "Witnessed by whom?"

"See for yourself." Lee stood up and held out the will.

Daphne walked over to the table and snatched it out of his hands. She perused it for a moment and then glared balefully at Marianne. "Marianne," she said acidly. "I might have known."

Then she turned her attention to one of the non-blond men. "And Ralph. I suppose you two were only too happy to get your hands on this money."

Daphne then waved the document in the air and swung around to one of Mr. Clementine's blond sons.

"And what do you have to say to this, Christopher? You heard what your father always said about Brian. What do you think about this—this travesty?"

At first glance, the two brothers looked very much alike, but now I could start to see some differences. The one addressed as Christopher was dressed in a plain white Oxford shirt and khakis, while the other—who I assumed was Bobby—was dressed in a well-tailored black suit that was clearly very expensive. Christopher sat stiffly in his chair, while Bobby lounged indolently in his.

Christopher regarded Daphne coldly.

"I think that everyone here has shown a deplorable lack of decorum. My father has *died*, and we should all show some respect."

Bobby chuckled—a nasty sound. "Yeah, Minton. Did you really think Christopher would object? He heard what Dad said about Brian—and so did I. Did you honestly believe that either one of us would mind getting a slice of the pie when we'd heard all our lives that everything was going to Brian? Even Christopher couldn't object to that."

Christopher turned a mortified face on his brother.

"That wasn't what I meant at all."

Bobby smiled and winked at him. "Sure it wasn't."

Daphne stared at Bobby, and two spots of color appeared high on her cheeks.

"I've got a good mind to tear up this will right now."

Bobby laughed. "Just be grateful you got something out of this, too, Minton."

She pressed her lips into a thin line, and she looked ready to make good on her threat.

"You may tear up the will if you wish," Lee interjected gently, "but I can assure you that will have no effect. This document is only a copy. And I have other copies—as well as the original—back at my office."

Daphne stared at Lee, and the spots of color remained on her face. But she handed the will back to him and returned to her seat.

Lee read out the last few sentences—mostly concerning the date of signing and the witnesses—and then he set the document down and glanced at his watch.

"Now I'm sure you all have questions—and I'll be happy to answer them for you. But the reading of the will has concluded now, and I need to get back to my office. Miss Mitchell, my assistant, will be happy to give you all the details you need to get in touch with me."

Lee held out a hand, and we all turned to look.

The young woman in the navy suit who had checked our IDs was standing at the back of the room, and she gave us all a polite, professional smile.

"Thank you all for coming today," Lee said, and he got out his briefcase and began to put his things into it.

It was clearly a dismissal.

Everyone in the row of chairs took the hint and began to gather up their own things—except for Daphne, who stood with her hands on her hips, watching Lee.

But after a moment, she turned to go, too.

I was one of the last to leave, and as I stepped out into the parking lot, I felt a tap on my shoulder.

I turned to find myself facing Heather Pim.

She was even more beautiful up close, and she had flawless, dewy skin and clear blue eyes. She wore eye-catching earrings with huge, clear stones that I assumed were real diamonds and an even larger diamond on a slender gold chain around her neck.

Her jewelry and her bright blond hair caught the morning light, and she seemed to be enveloped by sparkles.

What wasn't sparkling, however, was her expression.

Heather was scowling at me.

"Just what do you think you're doing?" she demanded.

I looked at her, confused. "I was just going to my car."

"Funny. You're funny, you know that? I know what you did, and I just want you to know that you're not going to get away with it."

"Get away with what? I don't know what you're talking about. So you'll have to enlighten me."

Heather stepped closer—and she was already pretty close.

Soon she was towering over me, and I noticed that even though she was thin, she was well-muscled. Sinewy cords and veins stood out on her bare, tan arms.

"You stole the ring," Heather hissed. "The big white-and-yellow diamond ring that Otis had from his first wife. He was going to give it to *me* when he proposed."

I nearly retorted that Mr. Clementine had told me he never intended to marry her—but I stopped myself just in time.

It was really better for me to stay out of this argument, and I'd promised Lee that I wouldn't say anything about the ring. Of course, I'd already told Alberta about it—but she was my sister, and Lee had said it might be wise to tell a family member—so I felt like that didn't count.

"I haven't stolen anything," I said.

"Yes, you did," Heather said, and she was so close that I could smell the mint on her breath. "You went into Otis's office, and you were snooping around, looking for something. Minton told me she caught you. She also told me that she didn't see you take anything out, but I *know* that that ring was in there—I saw Otis looking at it more than once. And how hard is it to hide a ring? You could have slipped it in your pocket and waltzed out with it without Minton being any the wiser."

"I didn't take anything out of Mr. Clementine's office," I said firmly.

Heather's eyes narrowed. "So you admit that you were there? What did you do with the ring? Do you have it now?"

She looked me over, and I thought that she was going to try to search me.

I took a step back.

Heather moved as if she were going to follow me, but then she seemed to think better of it.

"I'll get that ring," she hissed at me.

Then she turned on her heel and walked away.

Chapter Sixteen

Feeling just a bit rattled, I got into my car and drove to work.

Rita knew that I had the reading to attend, and she'd told me not to worry if I ended up being a little bit late.

As it worked out, however, I was only a little bit after my usual time, which was nine o'clock, and the library hadn't opened yet.

I walked in to find that Rita had already brought in the books from the book drop.

I was about to thank her when I saw that she was on the library phone.

And she was frowning.

I could hear a recorded voice buzzing in the silence of the empty library, and once it subsided, Rita hung up and looked at me.

She didn't look happy.

"There was a message in our voicemail—" she began.

"Sorry about that," I said quickly. "Sometimes I forget to check."

"It was from several days ago—"

"Yes," I said. "I figured that. It's just that there's no light or anything that goes on to let you know that you have a message. And sometimes it's so busy in here that I just don't think to do it—"

Rita shook her head. "It's not that. It's who the message is from."

"What do you mean?"

"It's from Mr. Clementine."

169

"What?" I said, startled.

"Maybe you'd better listen to it."

Rita handed me the phone and stepped aside.

I started the message up again.

"Hello, Chloe?" I heard Mr. Clementine say in his querulous tone. "Is that you, girl? No? Well, this is Otis Clementine, and I'm leaving a message for Chloe Bartlett. I imagine you're already on your way over here with that new book. I just want you to know that I appreciate what you're doing right now. I really do. And I really do need that book. I'm not just being difficult. All right, then. See you soon."

There was a click as Mr. Clementine hung up, and then a time stamp—Wednesday at eleven forty-five a.m.

I frowned as I hung up.

"But that doesn't make any sense," I said. "I was already back at the house by eleven forty-five. And the time stamp on Detective Ortiz's message was eleven thirty-five—that's when Mr. Clementine called him in distress."

Rita nodded. "I thought you had said something like that."

Her face was grim, and I could well imagine that mine was, too.

"Maybe the time stamp is wrong," I said slowly. "After all, our phone system's pretty old and unreliable."

"That's true," Rita replied.

"But all the same, I think I should share this with the police."

"I think you should, too."

I picked up the phone again, but I hesitated.

"What if they want me to go down to the station right away?"

Rita gave me a reassuring smile. "You can take time off if you need to. I can manage here."

I completed my phone call to the police station and asked for Detective Mia Coleman.

I knew that the Clementine case technically belonged to Detective Ortiz, but I also knew that he might still have the flu.

And I knew that I didn't want to talk to him.

After a few moments I was connected with Detective Mia, and I told her about the voicemail and the time stamp.

She seemed interested, but she also didn't seem to think the matter was urgent—she said it would be fine if I stopped by the police station after I got off work for the evening.

I was a little disappointed that she didn't want to see me right away, but after I hung up, I dutifully wrote out a transcript of the message as she had asked me to do, and then I made sure to save the message.

Then I went back to my usual work.

The day seemed to stretch on forever—but eventually five thirty rolled around, and I hurried out of the library and jumped in my car.

Then I drove down to the police station.

I waited for a little bit in the lobby with the bulletproof glass, and while I waited, I looked at a glass display case that held shelves full of trophies, awards, and pictures. I spotted the picture Detective Mia had mentioned of the teenage Detective Ortiz in the Police Athletic League. He was smiling and clean-shaven—naturally, as he seemed to be only about fifteen—and I only recognized him because of the caption below the picture.

I was squinting at the other names to see if there was anyone else I recognized when Detective Mia came out and ushered me through the metal door into the busy room beyond.

When we reached her desk, I was relieved to see that Detective Ortiz wasn't at the adjoining desk that I now knew was his.

Mia held out a hand to indicate that I should have a seat, and I began to feel slightly foolish.

I was busy worrying about running into Detective Ortiz, but he was probably still out sick. And actually, if he'd been coming down with the flu the day I met him, that could probably account for his surly behavior.

Mia seemed to think very highly of him—and the image of the smiling boy I'd just seen made me feel as if I'd been overreacting.

I'd likely just encountered him when he wasn't feeling his best.

I started to feel contrite, and I glanced over at his desk again.

I thought I should make up for my judgmental thoughts by at least asking about him.

"How is Detective Ortiz?"

Mia shot a rueful glance at his desk, too.

"He's pretty low at the moment. His wife says he sleeps most of the day right now. It'll be a little while before he's ready to come back to work. I try to keep him apprised of any developments, though."

"I'm sorry to hear he's still so sick," I said—and I meant it. "I hope he's feeling better soon."

Mia smiled at me. "Thank you. It's kind of you to be concerned."

"So have there been any? Developments, I mean."

Mia smiled again, but this time it was her polite, professional smile—an expression I knew well.

"Now, Ms. Bartlett, you know I can't answer that."

I did know—but I thought it was at least worth a try.

"So tell me about this voicemail message," Mia said.

I told her briefly about the message again, and then I handed over the transcript I had written out.

Mia perused it with a frown.

"And you say you just found this message today?"

"Yes—sometimes I forget to check the library's voicemail. My boss is actually the one who brought it to my attention. But the message is actually from Wednesday at eleven forty-five."

"Yes, I saw where you noted that," Mia murmured. She sighed. "On the face of it, it does appear to conflict with the message that Detective Ortiz received. Of course, we'll have to talk to your IT department and see if they can give us a copy of the message and authenticate the time and date."

"Our library is run by the county," I said. "I can give you the address and phone number of our administrative offices."

"Please do. That would be very helpful."

"Can I ask a question?" I said.

"Of course."

"Why did Mr. Clementine call Detective Ortiz when he was in trouble? Why not just call the main line? Or even 9-1-1?"

I expected Mia to brush off the question like she'd brushed off my earlier one, but instead she smiled.

"Mr. Clementine had a special relationship with Detective Ortiz—sort of like he did with you."

I blinked. "What special relationship? I barely knew Mr. Clementine, and he spent most of his time shouting at me."

"I understand that you used to bring Mr. Clementine library books."

"Yes."

"Well, Dave—Detective Ortiz—used to do something similar—help him out. And he put up with a lot of bad temper, too. Mr. Clementine had a knack for finding warm, caring people to help him out."

"Help him out how?"

Mia sighed. "Mr. Clementine was always a little paranoid. Every time he heard a bump in the night or some other funny sound, he would call Dave up and demand that he come over to check it out. He was always convinced it was some burglar trying to rob him, and Dave put up with it for years."

Mia frowned. "Lately though, it had been getting worse. Mr. Clementine seemed to be genuinely afraid of someone—he said someone was watching his house. In fact, he asked Dave to hurry to his home just a few days before he was killed. He was convinced he'd seen an intruder—he said someone was trying to kill him."

Mia stopped suddenly and drew herself up as if she'd said too much.

"Who?" I said. "Who did he think was trying to kill him?"

But Mia didn't answer me. Instead she just gave me a quelling look—I got the impression she felt like I'd tricked her into giving something away.

"Thank you, Ms. Bartlett, for coming down here to share this information with me. I'll make sure that it gets all the attention it deserves."

It was clearly a dismissal—but I wasn't done yet.

"What about the person I saw?" I said.

Mia blinked. "I'm sorry?"

"When we found Mr. Clementine, I saw someone running away from the house. Do you have any idea who that was yet?"

Mia gave me her polite, professional smile, but I thought I could sense some frustration in it—and not frustration that was directed at me.

"I'm not aware of anyone who fled the scene. However, we are pursuing all avenues."

"But I told you about that."

"I know." Mia's smile never wavered, but it seemed to me that it grew a little stiffer.

"So then you haven't found any corroborating evidence? No footprints? What about the cameras?"

"I'm not aware of any cameras."

"But there's one outside the front door," I protested. "I saw it myself. I would imagine there are others at the house, too, if Mr. Clementine was as paranoid as you say. What does the footage show?"

Mia's polite smile was starting to look pained.

"I'm not aware of any cameras, Ms. Bartlett."

"So does that mean there's something wrong with the cameras? Is the footage damaged? Did someone steal it before you got to it?"

"Ms. Bartlett!" Mia said sharply. Then she quickly lowered her voice. "You'll have to pardon me. I'm very busy, and I need to get back to work. If you have any further questions, I'm sure our clerk at the front desk would be happy to help you."

It was clearly another dismissal, and this time I took the hint.

"Thank you, Detective Coleman," I said, standing. "I appreciate your taking the time to see me today."

In response, she gave me a smile that told me how happy she was that I was leaving.

As I drove home, I could feel the image in my mind shifting and changing yet again. I hadn't tried yet to find the mysterious person whom I'd seen running away across the lawn on Wednesday, and it seemed to me that it was high time I did that.

So as I drove home, I made a brief mental checklist of everything I had to do. I had to start interviewing people to find out where they were Wednesday morning, I had to find the source of the murderous spell that had been cast—and that included investigating a possible link to the witch in the woods, and then I had to get a look at the footage from the cameras at Mr. Clementine's house—that is, if the footage was still available.

And I already had an idea how I was going to do that last thing.

But it might take some doing.

I reached the house, and I went inside.

As soon as I stepped in, I was struck by the most delicious, spicy scent.

I closed the door and stood for just a moment, inhaling the heavenly aroma, and then I set my things down and went into the kitchen.

Alberta was standing by the counter, presiding over a row of takeout boxes.

She turned as I walked in.

"Smells wonderful," I said. "Is that cumin and turmeric?"

"Yes. I hope you don't mind Indian takeaway. I'm just too tired to cook tonight."

Ordinarily, I would have kidded her about that, but she really did look tired.

"Is it from Palace of India?" I said instead.

"Yes."

"Then I don't mind at all. Their food's amazing."

"I got you some vindaloo," Alberta said.

"I love vindaloo."

Alberta smiled at me wearily. "I know."

We soon had plates of piping hot Indian food, and we sat down at the kitchen table to eat.

I started on my vindaloo, and Alberta had a chicken curry.

The two of us were silent for a few moments, and then I glanced over at Alberta as we enjoyed our food.

She had dark circles under her eyes, and I was surprised by just how weary she looked. Usually Alberta could stay up all night and then get up before dawn and be as fresh and energetic as if she'd had a good night's sleep.

She very seldom looked tired, no matter how hard she worked.

"Is everything okay?" I asked.

"What do you mean?" Alberta glanced up at me.

"It's just you look a little—"

"I'm fine," Alberta said hastily. "How was the reading of the will?"

"It gave me a lot to think about," I said.

I quickly told her about everything that had happened at the reading—all the bequests and arguments—and about Heather Pim confronting me in the parking lot about the ring.

"Considering her earrings and necklace," I said in conclusion, "you would think that she already had enough jewelry."

"Well, you *do* have the ring," Alberta said.

"Yes, but I didn't steal it. Lee Hurtzel entrusted it to me to dispose of properly. You know that."

"I do know that. But I imagine it wouldn't make any difference to Heather if she knew—she would still think the ring doesn't belong in your possession."

"Well, at any rate, at least I found several people who could have been the person I saw leaving the scene of Mr. Clementine's murder."

"No, you did not," Alberta said in a suppressing tone.

"You weren't there," I said. "You don't know what I saw."

"I know Mom told you to stay out of it."

"Well, as it turns out, I can't. I have knowledge the police don't. They don't know how to catch a magical killer."

Alberta sighed. "Did it ever occur to you that this is dangerous? If there's a person out there who used a lethal spell to kill someone, what's to stop that person from using one on you? They could, you know, and they just might if you interfere."

That had been mentioned to me—several times, in fact—and even though I should have been used to the idea by now, I still felt a chill run through me. But I was resolute.

"You're just trying to scare me."

"You should be scared. This is a matter for the authorities—not for you."

"But it *is* a matter for me," I said. "And I was hoping you would help me with something."

"I don't see why I should."

"It's important, Alberta," I said. "*Please*. Just hear me out."

"It's not more scrying, is it?"

"No."

Alberta looked very stubborn for several moments, but she continued to stare at me, and after a moment, she relented.

"Oh, all right. I suppose I can at least listen. What is it?"

"You have a lot of friends, right?" I said.

Alberta seemed startled but pleased. "Yes. I suppose I do."

"So I was hoping you could work with your network to see if you could get someone's phone number for me."

"Whose phone number?" Alberta said cautiously.

"Marianne Mozer's. She was one of the people who was at the reading of the will."

"Oh. I suppose you want to grill her?"

"No—it's nothing like that," I said. "I actually spoke to her once before—over at Mr. Clementine's house. We seem to be on pretty friendly terms, and I was hoping she'd help me with something. I just don't happen to have her phone number."

"What do you want her help with?"

I took a deep breath. I knew Alberta wasn't going to like this.

"I'd like her to get me into Mr. Clementine's house so I can view the footage from his surveillance cameras."

"What?" Alberta said. She was so startled she nearly squeaked. "I can't believe you."

"Why?" I said. "What's wrong?"

"This is way out of line."

"Why?"

"You're trespassing for one thing."

"No, I'm not," I said. "That's why I want to get a hold of Marianne. She'll let me in."

"It's not her house."

"She doesn't own the house—that's true. But no one does. It's going to be sold—I told you that."

"Hmmm." Alberta pressed her lips together. "I feel like that's sort of a gray area."

"Whatever it is, I'm going to try it."

"You'll be interfering with police work."

"No, I won't," I said. "I'm sure the police have already seen it. I'm just going over to view evidence they've already looked at."

"And what if it's no longer there?" Alberta said, and her voice was just a little smug. "That's common practice, you know, for them to take evidence away with them."

"I—" I stopped.

I hadn't thought of that.

Alberta was watching me triumphantly.

"I—I'll go anyway," I said. "I have to try."

"I can't talk you out of this?"

"No," I said firmly.

"So what will you do if I don't help you find this Marianne person?"

"Then I'll have to just drive up to Mr. Clementine's house and hope that I can run into Marianne over there. It worked for me once before."

"You're really that determined?"

"Yes."

"Okay—fine," Alberta said, making a big show of sighing.

"You'll help me?"

"Yes—I'll help you find this Marianne. It shouldn't be too hard—this is a small town, after all."

"And you do know everybody," I said.

Alberta smiled a little at the flattery, but she shook her head. "You're crazy, you know that? But at least this way you'll be going in in a semi-legal way. And please try not to get yourself in trouble. Mom will never forgive me if you do."

"Thank you, Alberta," I said.

And I jumped up and hugged her.

"You won't find anything," she prophesied darkly. "I already told you that."

"And I already told you," I said. "I still have to try."

Chapter Seventeen

That night I sat up in my room staring at the sunflower box Mr. Clementine had given me.

I had no doubt that Alberta would be able to track down Marianne's information—I had friends, too, of course, but my social circle was nowhere near as large as hers. Even though she didn't use social media, she seemed to know someone in every neighborhood and in every profession in town. My friends were mostly from the old days when I was younger—or they were up in New York.

I hadn't made many new friends since I'd been back.

But in my defense, I *had* been busy. First, there had been the move itself, and then I'd been settling into my new job.

And then mysterious problems began popping up that I needed to solve.

And I was in the middle of another one right now.

I opened the sunflower box and took out the ring.

It really was beautiful with its large, glittering white diamond and the two yellow stones on either side that sparkled like sunshine.

I supposed that the yellow stones were diamonds also, though I couldn't remember if anyone had said what they were or not. But even if they were only pretty pebbles, the white diamond alone would make the ring worth a king's ransom.

I looked inside the band and saw the initials "CC" and the motto, *For one who truly loves.*

Mr. Clementine had asked me to give the ring to someone who deserved it.

From the looks of his family so far, no one did.

I sighed to myself and turned to the other contents of the box— the glove and key.

The glove still bore its fake jewels proudly and the initials "GG" still winked at me in gold thread from the wrist. The key also still had its intricate scrollwork on the handle, but was otherwise inscrutable.

They were both pretty pieces of bric-a-brac—but neither one of them was giving up their secrets.

I puzzled for a moment over the initials "CC" and "GG."

"CC" was clearly "Clytie Clementine," but I didn't know who "GG" could be.

Perhaps it was just a mistake—perhaps it should have been "CC."

I wished I knew why Mr. Clementine thought the glove and the key were important, but since the objects themselves couldn't tell me, I eventually had to pack them up and put them away.

Then I went to bed.

Since I worked the later shift on Tuesday, I allowed myself to sleep in a little, and when I went downstairs, Alberta was long gone.

But there was a little sticky note on the refrigerator with Marianne's name and phone number on it.

I smiled as I took the note off.

Alberta hadn't disappointed.

After I drank a cup of coffee, I glanced at the clock.

I thought it probably wasn't too early to text, but I figured I would give it a few more minutes.

I had a light breakfast of yogurt, granola, and a banana, and then after I put my dishes in the dishwasher, I sat down to text Marianne.

My tone was a little apologetic—after all, she hadn't actually given me her number. But she replied readily enough, and she seemed happy to hear from me.

When I asked if she would do me a favor—and when she found out further that the favor was my sneaking in to watch Mr. Clementine's surveillance tapes—she readily agreed.

She seemed to relish it as a bit of mischief.

Of course, that wasn't why I was doing it, but if that appealed to her, then I wouldn't argue with it.

I gathered up my things and ran out of the house, tripping over the newspaper that was sitting on the step.

I left it where it was and hurried over to Mr. Clementine's house.

As I drove up the hill, I was disturbed to see that the vaguely question-mark-shaped pink cloud still hung in the sky over Mr. Clementine's house.

The first two days, it *might* have been a coincidence.

But this time I knew it meant something was wrong—something magical.

The problem was I didn't have any idea what.

Once I was about halfway up the hill, I turned onto a little side path that Marianne had told me about.

It led to a small, covered driveway where regular workers and service people who came to the house could park their cars.

Both Marianne and I thought it would be better if I parked out of sight and came in the back way.

There were a few cars in the driveway already, and I parked on the other side, giving them plenty of room.

As I got out of the car, my phone rang, and I saw with a pleasant tingle of anticipation that it was Mike.

I answered quickly. "Hey, Mike."

"Hey," he said. "How are you?"

"Good. What's up?"

Mike paused. "I know today is your 'later' day, right? You have some time off in the morning?"

"Yes," I said.

"Well, I was just wondering what you were up to right now."

"I'm—investigating."

Mike sighed. "I was afraid you'd say that."

I got the distinct impression he was hoping I'd say something else. Before I could ask what, he went on.

"So what are you doing exactly?"

I told him quickly about how I was hoping to get a look at the camera footage, and he sighed again and said all the things Alberta had said.

"I know," I replied when he had finished. "It might not work, and it might look weird to the police. But I'm doing it anyway."

Mike gave yet another sigh. "And then what will you do once you're done with the camera stuff?"

"I'll—" I thought for a moment—I had my next moves in mind, but I hadn't planned out their order yet. "I'll interview all my suspects, and then I'll go find the witch in the woods. I feel like she's important."

"So, interfering with a police investigation and witch-hunting." Mike's tone was light and joking, but I could tell he was disturbed.

But then I was disturbed, too.

"Witch-hunting?" I said. "Why would you call it that?"

"I'm sorry," Mike said quickly. "Poor choice of words. I just meant—"

He stopped.

"I know I've said this before," he said after a moment, "but if you need anything, please, please, give me a call—even if you just want to go tramping around in the woods again. It doesn't have to be something dangerous—it can be something mundane."

I smiled in spite of myself. "All right. I'll call you if something mundane comes up."

Mike chuckled a little. "Okay, then, I'll leave you to your sleuthing. Just remember, there's no rush. You don't have to hurry up and do everything right away."

"Why did you say that?" I asked sharply.

I found myself glancing involuntarily up at the pink cloud. I'd gotten out of the car and left the covered drive, and from my current vantage point, the cloud really did appear to be directly over the house.

Mike seemed flustered. "I didn't mean anything in particular. I was really just thinking that if you go slower, maybe the police will solve this before you get yourself into trouble."

I couldn't reply—I suddenly felt chilled.

"Chloe?" Mike said. "Chloe, are you okay?"

"Yes—I'm just glad that you reminded me of the urgency of the situation."

"That was actually the opposite of what I meant to do."

"Well, I appreciate it all the same," I said. "Thanks, Mike. I've got to go."

He sounded a little forlorn as he said goodbye, and I felt bad about the way the conversation had ended—I hadn't meant to sound so abrupt.

But I was worried as I glanced up at that pink cloud one last time and then headed toward the house.

That cloud just wasn't normal.

Marianne must have been watching for me, for she met me at the back door and ushered me inside quickly.

"Hurry," she whispered, her eyes sparkling. "Before Old Minton sees you."

I was a little irritated by Marianne's attitude—I wasn't there to play a prank—but I was lucky she was helping me at all, so I decided to quash my annoyance.

Instead, I simply followed her into a small room full of boxes and gardening equipment. There was a desk, a few chairs, and a laptop, but I didn't see any TV monitors or other electronic equipment that I assumed you would need if you were going to view surveillance camera footage.

I began to feel a sinking sensation—Alberta had been right.

There was nothing here.

But Marianne didn't seem fazed—instead she made a big show of looking both ways down the hallway, and then she shut the door.

She looked gleeful as she bounced over to the desk.

"So, Marianne," I said. "I don't see any screens in here or anything—"

"I know," she replied. "The cops took everything away."

"Oh." I felt disappointment settling on me heavily. "Then—"

Marianne's eyes danced with mischief. "That is, the cops took away everything they knew about. But all of Mr. Clementine's video files were backed up on his own server. And I happen to have—access—to it. That's a word Mr. Clementine taught me."

"Wait, what?" I said.

Marianne smiled in satisfaction. "Mr. Clementine explained the whole thing to me once—and I remembered his words nearly exactly—he complimented me on that. He said his cameras would record onto hard copy tapes that could be stored. They kept hundreds and hundreds of them on shelves in a big room. But those video files were also automatically backed up and stored as digital files on Mr. Clementine's own private server. He could watch them any time he wanted to. Here—I'll show you."

She opened the laptop and logged on.

"Pull up a chair," she said, reaching for one herself.

As she did so, I thought about the telescope I'd seen in Mr. Clementine's room.

I wondered if this was the same kind of thing.

After a moment, Marianne brought up a folder full of files with dates on them.

"What would you like to see?" she asked, her eyes bright and full of excitement.

"What are we looking at here?" I said.

"This is from the camera right over the front door."

"Can we go back to the day Mr. Clementine died?" I asked.

In answer, Marianne clicked on the file with that date, and a video began playing.

It showed Mr. Clementine's front door. No one was around, and the light was dim—it was clearly night.

"Let me rewind that to the beginning," Marianne murmured. She brought the video back to the beginning, and it was equally dark—but this time that was because it was early morning rather than late at night.

"Where do you want to start on this day?" Marianne asked.

"Can we go to when I arrived?"

"Which time?"

"What do you mean?" I said.

"I had it in my mind—you were here twice and the policeman was here twice."

"I was here twice," I replied, "but on two separate days. I was here on Tuesday first, and then I was here on Wednesday. Detective Ortiz probably was here twice on Wednesday—in fact, maybe more than twice."

Marianne frowned. "I guess you're right. I guess I got a bit muddled. So do you remember when you arrived? This video has a time stamp."

"Yes," I said, "it was—"

Then I suddenly thought of something—the message Mr. Clementine had left me at eleven forty-five.

"Let's go back a little before I arrived," I said. "Let's try eleven forty."

I figured Marianne didn't need to know about the voicemail—it wouldn't help the police if I began telling other people about evidence.

But Marianne didn't seem to find the request strange, and she dutifully moved the video forward.

As she reached the eleven forty mark, however, the video changed from images to static.

She pressed "play" and the static continued. At eleven forty, there were no images—only fuzz and distortion.

Marianne frowned. "Well, that's strange."

She rewound a bit, and the distortion remained. Then she began fast-forwarding, and the same thing was true—there were no images at all until eleven forty-three, and then shortly after that, I came into view.

I watched myself going into the house.

"Can we go back again?"

Marianne obliged, but no matter how many times we went over the footage between eleven thirty and eleven forty-three, we couldn't get any video to come into focus.

Those minutes were lost.

"What do you want to do?" Marianne asked.

"Let's just watch what we have," I said.

So we watched my arrival, and then Detective Ortiz's panicked arrival several minutes later, and then about ten minutes after that, we saw the ambulance and the paramedics arrive.

Eventually, we saw the paramedics come out that same door with a stretcher.

"I think that's good," I said.

Marianne stopped the video. "Did you find what you were looking for?"

"No, not really. But then again, I wasn't necessarily hoping for anything from this particular angle. You did say there were other cameras, right?"

"Yes—there are cameras covering the whole outside of the house."

"Is there a camera at the back? One that covers the back lawn?"

"Yes."

"Can I see that one?" I asked eagerly.

Marianne gave me a shamefaced smile. "No."

"No?" I said. "Why not?"

"Because I don't know where the files for that one are," she replied.

I glanced at the computer screen. "But—"

"I do have access to Mr. Clementine's server. But he only showed me how to get to that one camera. I don't know where the others are."

"Do you mind if I have a look?" I asked.

"No—go ahead."

Marianne slid the laptop closer to me.

I poked around a little, and I could soon see why Marianne could only see footage from one camera—she had only been granted permission to view one folder. All the others said "access denied" when I clicked on them.

"Mr. Clementine only asked me to keep an eye on this one," she said apologetically.

"Why did he do that?" I asked.

"I don't know. He just said to watch the video of the front door every day and tell him if I saw anything funny."

"Funny how?"

Marianne shook her head. "I don't know that, either."

"So what about the tapes from the other cameras?" I said. "I assume the police took those, too?"

"Nope." The impish glint returned to Marianne's eyes. "They couldn't find those. They took hundreds of tapes with them, but those were all from the front-door camera. Everyone can see the cameras, of course—they aren't hard to spot. But no one can find the tapes. Not even Old Minton knows where they are."

Marianne smiled maliciously. "I seen them questioning her. They really grilled her—but she didn't know anything."

"What about Mr. Clementine's server?" I asked. "Did they find that?"

Marianne frowned. "I don't know. I don't really know what a server is."

"It's basically just a computer," I said. "And other computers connect to it to access stored files and other data. It's a computer that's hosting those digital files you have."

Marianne brightened up. "Oh—it's a computer? Yeah—I overhead the police talking about that, too. They were looking for one—a special one. But Old Minton didn't know where that was, either."

She thought for a moment, and then she glanced at me furtively.

"I thought it was cool at first—that I didn't tell the police about my computer. But should I have told them about it? Can they use my computer to find that other one?"

"No," I said. "I think you're okay. You can't use one computer to track another. Mr. Clementine must have hidden it somewhere."

I glanced at her. "I don't suppose you have any idea where it might be?"

Marianne shrugged.

"No—I didn't even know what a server was."

I looked around in disappointment—I had hit a dead end, although it wasn't quite the one I had expected.

Instead of the police confiscating what I needed, what I needed was actually missing.

I now had yet another thing I had to find.

Marianne eyed me uncertainly. "What will you do next?"

"I'll have to look for either the tapes or the server."

Marianne's eyes suddenly lit up.

"Would you like some help?"

"What do you mean?"

"Well, you can't exactly wander around the house here without someone noticing—I can be your excuse for coming to the house. And I can even do some looking on my own."

She grinned—I could tell the idea really appealed to her.

"Thanks," I said. "That would be great."

"And Old Minton would really hate it."

That seemed to be the best part of all for her.

She looked over at her laptop.

"So are we done for right now?"

"Yes—I think so." I glanced at the clock on my phone. "And I have to get to work anyway." I stood up. "Can I just go out the way I came in?"

"Sure. I'll come with you. With any luck we won't run into Old Minton on the way out."

But as we reached the door, it suddenly flew open, and Daphne herself appeared in the doorway.

She stared at the two of us, and then put her hands on her hips.

"Just what is going on here?"

Marianne hurried to grab her laptop, and she hugged it to her chest.

"It's none of your business," she said fiercely.

"None of my business!" Daphne sputtered. "I'll have you know I'm in charge around here—"

"No, you're not," Marianne snapped. "This house doesn't belong to you. It doesn't belong to anyone anymore. I heard them say so."

Daphne started to say something, then stopped. She went on with an effort at composure.

"Well, anyway, it's supposed to be business as usual. We're supposed to continue our work just like we always did. And that means no—lollygagging."

Marianne giggled at the word, and Daphne's face went red.

"I wasn't lollygagging," Marianne said. "I don't even know what that means. Besides, I'm allowed to have a friend stop by. Mr. Clementine always said it was allowed."

"It's okay," I said hastily. "I was just leaving."

Daphne glared at me. "See that you do."

I hurried on to the open door, and as I walked out into the hallway, I glanced back.

Daphne was staring at me with ill-concealed dislike.

Chapter Eighteen

I left Mr. Clementine's house and drove down the hill, with the strange pink cloud still hanging high overhead.

I suddenly felt the need for more coffee, and I still had a little time before I had to be at work. So I stopped at Kyle's Teapot, a little tea shop nearby that was run by a friend of Rafaela's—I'd been meaning to go there for some time anyway. The focus of the china-filled shop was tea, of course, but they did have coffee, and the proprietor, a huge, well-muscled man with a bald head who looked out of place in the delicate surroundings, took my order himself, and he soon brought me a cup of coffee and a cheese danish.

He paused to extol the virtues of the local bakery that provided their baked goods, and then left me so he could see to the next customer.

As I bit into the danish, I could tell that it was fresh—the cheese was both tangy and sweet, and the pastry was light and flaky.

His confidence was well placed.

And the coffee was just what I needed—it was dark and smooth and somehow both soothing and stimulating.

I definitely felt like my mind needed a bit of a jolt.

As I sipped at the lovely, dark brew, it suddenly occurred to me that I still hadn't told Alberta about Rafaela's sort-of boyfriend Bodhi.

As I was staring at my phone, wondering if it would be weird to text her about it, a text suddenly came in from Rafaela.

Have you told her yet?

The text wasn't very specific, but it didn't have to be—I would have known what it meant even if I hadn't already been thinking about that exact topic.

Funny you should ask that, I texted back. *It was just on my mind. And no I haven't told her.*

There's no rush, Rafaela replied. *Bodhi was just wondering if he could take us all out to Peter's Table tonight. It's right down the street from his yoga studio, and he loves it. I know you guys love it, too. A late dinner, of course. I know it's your later shift.*

I frowned a bit—I wasn't sure how Alberta would feel about going to that particular restaurant and possibly running into Peter himself. But I thought I could at least try.

I'll see if I can get with her this afternoon, I said.

It's really no rush, Rafaela replied. *We don't have to do dinner at all if you don't think Alberta's ready for it.*

I'll let you know soon, I said. *I won't leave you guys hanging.*

I waited a moment to see if she would reply, and when nothing new popped up on the screen, I decided to text Alberta.

As Rafaela had said, the dinner wasn't urgent—but I figured I should get things started before the situation grew awkward.

The text I sent her was brief:

Can I stop by your office this afternoon?

Alberta immediately called me.

"No!" she said when I answered the phone. "Do *not* come to my office."

"What?" I said. "Why?"

"I won't be there. I have an appointment."

"An appointment? Like a doctor's appointment? You didn't mention anything about that last night."

Alberta didn't reply, and I sighed.

"Fine. You don't have to tell me if you don't want to."

"What's so important anyway?" Alberta said. "Why do you need to see me this afternoon? You know you'll see me when you come home tonight."

I felt irritation rising in me. "It's not super important. I just— forgot to tell you something."

"What?"

I thought for a moment and then decided just to plunge ahead. "I met Rafaela's new boyfriend two days ago, and they want to know if we want to have dinner with them tonight."

"You *met* Rafaela's new boyfriend?"

"Yes."

"And you didn't tell me?" Alberta sounded outraged.

"I forgot."

"You forgot."

"Yes."

"How could you forget something so important? I *told* you something was going on. Now you can see that I was right."

Alberta's tone still rankled, but she had noticed before I did that Rafaela had been acting a little different lately. A little voice in the back of my head reminded me that Rafaela had said the same thing about Alberta.

But I pushed that thought aside to focus on the issue at hand.

"What's that?" Alberta said. "You've been silent for a while now."

"I was just thinking," I replied.

"Thinking about how I was right?"

I let this go by, too—I still had an invitation to deliver.

"So Rafaela's new boyfriend is not exactly her boyfriend yet," I said. "She said they haven't quite reached that stage officially. His name is Bodhi, and he has a yoga studio."

I took a deep breath. "He wants to take us all to Peter's Table tonight."

"What?" Alberta screeched.

She was so loud that I had to move the phone away from my ear for a moment.

"I thought you wouldn't like that," I said.

"What? Why wouldn't I like that?" Alberta said.

"Because you seem to have a problem with Peter lately."

"I do *not* have a problem with Peter," Alberta replied with dignity.

"Oh, no? Then what's with all the screeching?"

This time, Alberta was silent.

"At any rate," I said, "I take it you vote no on Peter's Table?"

"It would be much better to make this more low-key," Alberta said. "Especially since tonight is your late shift."

"I don't mind going out afterward."

"Besides, he's not really her boyfriend yet," Alberta said as if I hadn't said anything. "So we don't really want to make a big fuss. We don't want to put any pressure on them."

She paused. "I really think it would be much better if everyone came over to my house for dinner tonight."

"And this has nothing to do with avoiding Peter?" I asked.

"Nothing at all. I just think everyone would be more comfortable that way."

"What are you going to cook?"

"Lamb chops," Alberta said promptly. "And baked potatoes. And then probably a second vegetable—maybe green beans."

"I don't know—" I said.

"I know how to microwave a baked potato, Chloe."

"I know. It's just that lamb requires a little extra attention—"

"I know how to cook a small cut of meat," Alberta said firmly. "You turn on the heat and then throw it in the pan. It's as simple as that."

"It's not really that easy," I said. "There's more to it—"

"Yes, it is that easy. And then I'll make something equally easy for dessert—an apple crumble. It'll all be nice and homey. What's-his-name is going to love it."

"Bodhi," I said. "And he and Rafaela haven't agreed to this yet."

"They will. I'll see you all around eight fifteen tonight."

There was a clattering sound in the background, and Alberta swore under her breath.

"What was that?" I said.

"Nothing," she replied. "I've really got to go now. Eight fifteen—don't forget."

In those few words, she managed to make it sound as if the entire thing had been her idea, and I felt a fresh wave of irritation as she hung up.

But at least she was agreeing to meet Bodhi, which was what Rafaela wanted.

I quickly texted her the news.

Dinner at her place? Rafaela texted back.

Yes.

So she's still avoiding Peter?

Yes.

I told you she's acting weird, Rafaela replied. *If she wants to break up with him, she should do it properly—not just disappear on him.*

You can tell her that tonight at dinner, I replied. *I'm sure that will go over well.*

Ha-ha.

So do you think Bodhi will want to come tonight?

I'm sure he will. He's very easygoing. He's pretty much perfect.

Even though it was a text, I could practically hear Rafaela sighing dreamily.

He was handsome, I texted back. *I'll give you that.*

Chloe! That's not all this relationship is about. I'm shocked at you.

Whatever you say, I replied.

Did she say what time? Rafaela asked.

Eight fifteen.

We'll see you then.

And with that she was gone.

I glanced at the time—I needed to get going, too.

Suddenly, I was in danger of being late.

I drank up the rest of my coffee, and then I hurried to the library.

As I drove, I had the weirdest feeling that I should call my mother. But I had no idea why.

I shrugged the feeling off and drove a little faster.

I reached the library just in time, and as I went to take over the circulation desk from Rita, she gave my shoulder a little squeeze in passing.

I think she could tell that I'd only just made it.

The day seemed to progress as usual—and except for an argument between two patrons over who should get to sit in a particular favorite chair—there was little excitement.

But even though the library was quiet, my mind certainly wasn't, and I could feel ideas churning, and images shifting and changing shape.

I had a feeling I needed to ask Rita a question.

But once again, I wasn't sure what it was.

As the afternoon changed to evening, and Stu's arrival time approached, I suddenly realized what I needed to know.

Rita had brought her things up to the front desk in anticipation of her changeover with Stu, and I turned to her.

"Did we ever get those books back from Mr. Clementine's house?"

Rita stared at me for a moment, puzzled, then she smiled.

"Those books you took over as part of your last special delivery? Yes—yes, we did."

"Who brought them?"

Rita frowned in thought. "It was someone who worked for Mr. Clementine. I think it was Denise? No—Daphne. She brought them back the day after he died. I thought was very generous of her, considering how upset she must have been."

I, on the other hand, found myself wincing.

Daphne would have known, then, that the library already had the books when she'd caught me searching Mr. Clementine's office, and she also would have known that my excuse was flimsy.

I was lucky she hadn't called the police on me.

"Are you all right?" Rita asked.

"Yes," I said quickly. "So we got all three back? I usually took over two, but this time I took over three."

Rita moved to the computer that we reserved for reference questions and brought up the catalog.

She scanned it quickly.

"Yes—*Volumes One, Two*, and *Three* of *Robertson's History of Rome*. They're all here."

As I looked over her shoulder, I nearly smacked myself in the forehead.

I hadn't really needed to ask Rita anything at all—I could have just looked the books up in the catalog myself to see if they were back in inventory.

Rita gave me another quizzical look. "Are you sure you're all right?"

"Yes," I said. "It's just that my brain seems to be overloaded with ideas at the moment—and I seem to be missing things I should see."

Rita smiled at me. "That's what makes you so much fun to work with—you're always full of good ideas."

"Oh, my, yes," said a new voice. Stu, the night librarian, had quietly appeared and come up to stand beside us. He was smiling at me in his vague, pleasant way. "Our Chloe always does have good ideas—some truly crackerjack ones. I keep telling you you'll make a fine librarian someday."

I smiled my thanks as Stu took over the circulation desk and Rita left for the day. Then I moved off to start shelving books—our page, Emily, wasn't coming in today—and I was very happy to be freed from the desk.

I needed to take a look at Mr. Clementine's books.

I took my cart with me, and I went straight to the history section—*Robertson's History of Rome, Volumes One, Two,* and *Three* sat quietly on the third shelf from the bottom, bound in faux red leather with gilt trim.

I picked up *Volume One*—a very hefty tome—and saw that its subtitle was *Politics and Warfare*. I flipped through its pages briefly before setting it down again and picking up *Volume Two—Art and Culture*.

I flipped through this one, too—not really sure what I was looking for—and then I turned with a frown to *Volume Three*.

The message Mr. Clementine had left me at eleven forty-five on Wednesday came floating back to me.

Mr. Clementine had rejected the first two volumes I'd brought and had demanded the third. I'd thought at the time that he was being difficult—according to his usual habit. But what if he'd actually wanted this third volume for real and not as a game? What if he hadn't been being difficult for once?

As I thought back to his message, it seemed to me that he'd genuinely wanted it—he'd said he needed it. And in hindsight, I realized that I'd believed him when he'd said that.

So what had he wanted it for?

I picked up *Volume Three*—this one was *Religion and Mysticism*. I flipped through its pages—not really knowing what I was looking for this time, either—and I noticed that one of the pages had been folded over in the top righthand corner—it had been dog-eared.

The dog-eared page was the first page of a chapter titled "Divination." I read through the chapter, and then I sat down on a nearby step stool to think.

The chapter dealt with divination and augury—ways to uncover events or knowledge that were hidden or in the future. Though the techniques were largely unfamiliar to me, the concept was very similar to what Alberta did when she scried for me—or when she'd helped the police find missing persons.

Mr. Clementine had said he was looking for his son Brian.

And he'd also mentioned following a trail of breadcrumbs.

Had he sought out the witch in the woods to help him find his son? Had he found her? And being found, had she been unsuccessful?

But Daphne had said Mr. Clementine's will had originally been almost entirely in Brian's favor.

And then recently the will had been changed so that all four of the children were to inherit equal shares—if Brian could be found.

Did that mean Mr. Clementine had given up on finding his son?

Or did it mean that something else had happened—something that caused him to continually look over his shoulder?

But all of that was just speculation.

I read through the chapter on divination one more time, but despite the section's subject, I was unable to uncover any secrets.

Chapter Nineteen

Eventually, the bright summer sunshine gave way to evening, and before I knew it, it was time to gently shoo the last few stragglers from the library and lock up for the night.

The evening had really flown by for me—shelving books always made the time pass, but adding in my ruminations on Mr. Clementine's interest in divination had made everything speed by in a blur.

I couldn't have told anyone anything about the books I'd shelved, or even what I'd had for an evening snack.

And to top it all off, my hours of cogitating hadn't given me any answers.

I still didn't know what Mr. Clementine had wanted with that book.

And the feeling that I needed to call my mother had returned.

I was glad to be leaving the library for the night—maybe I could get some more investigating done.

And then I remembered—Rafaela and Bodhi were coming over for dinner.

And I felt a brief flash of irritation.

It wasn't that I didn't want to see them—but I hadn't gotten much of anything from the camera footage at Mr. Clementine's house, and that meant that I would definitely have to interview all the possible suspects who could have been the tall blond person I saw running away from the house.

And there were at least three of them.

And I wasn't sure how to find any of them.

At the very least, however, Bodhi and Rafaela's presence would likely be enough to distract Alberta and keep her from asking me about the camera footage—and I wouldn't have to admit that I hadn't found anything.

Besides, if I was being realistic, I would have to admit that I probably couldn't do much investigating tonight anyway.

And Rafaela had every right to go on with her life as usual.

It wasn't her fault I had to solve a murder.

So once I'd talked myself into a good mood, I got in my car and drove home.

As I reached the house, it looked as though Bodhi and Rafaela hadn't arrived yet—there were no cars I didn't recognize parked on the street, and Alberta herself always parked in the garage.

I parked in my usual spot and went inside.

I was greeted immediately by the aroma of baked potatoes and sizzling lamb. It wasn't at all an unpleasant scent, and I felt a little spark of hope that dinner would actually be good. There was also the lighter, sweeter scent of baking apples, and I felt my mouth watering at the thought of dessert.

Alberta's voice floated out of the kitchen. "Which one of you is it?"

"It's Chloe!" I said. It was true that Rafaela had a key, but she seldom used it, preferring instead to knock.

"Oh, good!" Alberta called back over the sound of the sizzling. "That means we still have a little more time. Do you want to come back here and set the table for me?"

"Sure!" I walked back into the kitchen and found Alberta at work at the stove with an iron skillet.

Sibyl sat just behind her on the floor, her sleek, black body poised in readiness, her amber eyes turned upward, and her mouth opening in a silent meow to reveal a pink tongue.

She was clearly hoping for a tidbit of the lamb.

Alberta glanced back at her.

"Not just yet, baby. Wait till later tonight."

"So we're going to be in the dining room, right?" I said.

"Of course," Alberta said in irritation. "This is a special occasion. I doubt Rafaela would appreciate it if I tried to squish the four of us and a full dinner around the kitchen table."

Ordinarily, I would have been annoyed by Alberta's short-tempered answer to a simple question, but as I glanced at her intent face, I could tell that my adventure with the cameras today was unlikely to be on her mind.

She was obviously focused only on the dinner.

I was just glad I was going to get through the evening in peace.

Rafaela, on the other hand, was probably in for a grilling.

As I moved to the cabinet to get the dishes, I happened to spy something bright green and gelatinous in a bowl.

I stopped to sniff it. "What's this?"

"It's mint jelly," Alberta replied. "And I'll thank you to get your nose out of it."

"Mint jelly?" I said.

"Yes—it's traditional to serve mint jelly with lamb. Or didn't you know that?"

"I knew that," I said. "It's just that this doesn't actually smell like mint." I then glanced over at Alberta's skillet, where the sizzling was continuing. "And I think you might want to take the lamb off the heat now."

"I know what I'm doing," Alberta replied with dignity.

"Did you use Mom's recipe for mint jelly?" I asked.

"No—I used one I made up myself."

"Because Mom's mint jelly always smelled like actual mint—"

"I know what I'm doing," Alberta replied. "Leave the cooking to me—I believe *your* assignment was setting the table."

I cast one more worried glance at the lamb but said nothing further.

Instead, I got out the dishes, glasses, and silverware and set the table.

At eight fifteen, Rafaela and Bodhi still hadn't arrived, so Alberta took the chance that she had enough time to run upstairs and change, and I stayed downstairs in case they arrived while she was occupied.

I figured that the clothes I had worn to work were probably dressy enough.

Sooner than I would have thought possible, Alberta had changed into a little black dress, switched her casual flats for black pumps, and applied some smoky eyeshadow. Her red hair had been swept back into a chic updo, and all of that, coupled with the emerald earrings she usually wore, gave her an incredibly glamorous look.

I began to regret my decision to remain as I was.

Moments later, there was a knock at the door, and both Alberta and I hurried to answer it.

The door opened to reveal Rafaela in a simple dark-blue dress that somehow brought out both the blue in her eyes and the gold in her golden-brown hair. She looked positively radiant, and I was definitely regretting my decision not to change into something more elegant.

She seemed to float as she stepped into the house, and Bodhi stepped in just behind her. He was still just as handsome and athletic-looking as he had been when I'd first met him, but his overall look was now much more buttoned-down.

Gone were the silver rings and the other adornments, and he was dressed in a plain white shirt and black trousers.

He looked very solid and respectable, and for just a moment, I thought he looked familiar—like someone else I knew.

But the moment passed as quickly as it had come, and I was left to marvel at just how different he looked. He seemed much more like a lawyer or an accountant than a yoga teacher, and the only thing that potentially gave away his occupation was the man bun that nestled at the top of his head.

I glanced at Alberta to see how she would take that, but she didn't seem to notice it.

Instead, she was staring at his face, enraptured.

And Bodhi was staring back at her, equally entranced.

I glanced at Rafaela to see what she thought of this, but she, too, was staring at Bodhi.

"So, um, welcome," I said.

All the staring suddenly broke off, and Rafaela gave Bodhi's arm an affectionate squeeze.

"Where are my manners?" She giggled. "Chloe, you know Bodhi already, of course. But Alberta, I'd like you to meet Bodhi P. Gotschall."

Bodhi took Alberta's hand. "The 'P' stands for 'Peace.' And I must declare myself enchanted. Delighted to meet you, Alberta."

Alberta giggled, too. "Likewise."

Rafaela continued. "Bodhi is a good friend of mine."

Bodhi, who had been staring at Alberta again, suddenly turned to look at Rafaela.

"I hope we're a bit more than friends."

Rafaela giggled once more.

"Well, as Chloe said, welcome," Alberta said. "Rafaela, please show our guest into the dining room."

Rafaela and Bodhi went on ahead of us, and Alberta lingered and leaned toward me.

"So handsome," she murmured. "Just like a movie star."

The four of us were soon seated at the dining room table, and we passed the dishes around family style.

The microwaved green beans and baked potatoes were actually pretty good, and the Irish butter and chives for the potatoes really brought them up to the next level.

I couldn't have said the same thing for the lamb chops, however.

They were definitely overcooked, dry on the inside, and a little hard to chew.

I glanced over at Rafaela, and she glanced back at me.

Her eyes were watering from a bite of the lamb she'd just had that had been accompanied by a little smear of the mint jelly.

She began to cough, and she picked up her water glass and began to drink, apparently in hopes of quelling the coughing.

I eyed the dollop of mint jelly on my plate dubiously—I'd taken a little bit simply to be polite.

I looked up to see Alberta watching me, and I dutifully put a little smudge of the jelly on a dry piece of lamb and conveyed the morsel to my mouth.

I immediately wished I hadn't.

There was a little hint of mint, and then something pungent and spicy and strong rolled through.

It tasted like horseradish—but not in a good way.

I found myself coughing and reaching for my water glass, too.

I looked up, my eyes watering, to see Alberta beaming at me.

"So how do you like the mint jelly?" she asked. "It's good, isn't it?"

"It's—spicy," I said, struggling a bit to speak. "And exotic."

Alberta seemed to take that as a compliment.

"A little goes a long way," Rafaela added, her eyes still tearing.

Alberta's eyes darted to her suspiciously. "What does that mean?"

"Is it a new recipe?" Rafaela asked, getting up and walking into the kitchen.

"Yes, it's a new recipe," Alberta said, turning in her chair. "What of it?"

"Nothing," Rafaela said, returning a moment later with a bottle of Worcestershire sauce.

She set it on the table and returned to her seat.

"It's great that you're trying new recipes," she added kindly.

Alberta watched with eyes narrowed as both Rafaela and I poured the bottled sauce on our lamb chops.

"I've just never been a fan of mint jelly," Rafaela said hastily. "It's not you at all."

"I've never been one, either," I said. And it was true—I usually passed on mint sauce when it was served with lamb. I also usually passed on Worcestershire sauce, too, but this time the lamb really needed something to make it palatable.

Alberta transferred her suspicious gaze to Bodhi, but he seemed perfectly content with his lamb chop, and even added more mint sauce to it.

"Tastes like wasabi." He flashed her a grin. "I love wasabi."

Alberta seemed mollified—which made her next question even more astonishing.

"So Bodhi, how do you make money?"

"Alberta!" Rafaela looked mortified.

Alberta turned an innocent face on her. "What?"

"I'm sure Chloe already told you," Rafaela said as quietly as she could. "Besides, you can't just ask people questions like that."

"Why not? If I already know and you already know and he already knows, why can't we talk about it?"

"Alberta," Rafaela said in exasperation, "it's just not—"

"It's quite all right," Bodhi said smoothly. "I don't mind."

He turned to Alberta.

"I own a yoga studio here in town."

"And is there much of a future in a yoga studio?" Alberta asked.

"Alberta, please!" Rafaela said.

Bodhi smiled. "I don't mind at all. Sisters have to look out for one another, after all. Actually, I have been quite successful with my studios—I move from town to town opening them, getting them off the ground, and then selling them. And then of course, I have my workshops and my online presence. And this particular studio is doing very well—I've been able to attract some local celebrities."

"Local celebrities?" Alberta said. "Like who?"

"Well, Heather Pim for starters."

Bodhi seemed to puff up a little as he said the words.

"Heather Pim?" Alberta's forehead wrinkled in thought. "Why does that name sound familiar?"

I looked up, interested. I knew Alberta had heard about Heather from me—though she didn't seem to remember that—and I was curious to hear what Bodhi had to say.

Maybe I could find out a way to get to question her.

"Heather is quite a successful sports model," Bodhi said with a touch of pride. "She's even done some high-fashion work and been featured in some of the top magazines. And of course, lately she's been making a name for herself as a rock climber. She's been writing about how she scaled El Capitan in Yosemite on her blog."

"Oh!" Alberta said. "And she was also the girlfriend of—"

I could see comprehension dawning on her face as she glanced at me.

She stopped.

"Yes," Bodhi said. "It was a terrible tragedy. Heather has been really broken up by it. But she has to stay strong for their young son."

Alberta snorted. "That's not what I heard."

She shot another glance at me, and I tried to tell her with my eyes not to say anything further.

"Wait," Rafaela said, frowning. "How does everyone know about this Heather Pim except for me?"

"I don't know," Alberta replied. "I've never seen her myself, but I understand she's quite a beautiful blonde. Isn't that right, Chloe?"

I stared at Alberta. I couldn't tell if she was causing trouble on purpose, or if it was just her usual forthrightness popping up at the worst possible time.

And then I glanced down at my plate. I could see the dark Worcestershire sauce sitting in a brown puddle around the dry lamb, and I suddenly saw what was going on.

Alberta was getting back at Rafaela and me for rejecting her mint jelly.

And she was doing it in front of Bodhi.

"A beautiful blonde?" Rafaela was saying. "And she comes to your yoga studio?"

"She takes a few classes," Bodhi said soothingly. "Besides, I have a lot of beautiful students. She's hardly the only one."

"You do?" Rafaela said. She looked panicked—as if the thought had never occurred to her before.

Alberta looked on smugly, and I could tell she was hoping an argument would break out.

I stared at her hard, trying to will her not to stir up any more trouble. I hoped maybe she'd see my face and take the hint.

At that moment, Sibyl walked into the dining room and let out a plaintive meow.

We all turned to look at her.

Her face was coated in green goo, and a gelatinous green beard dripped from her tiny chin.

She had stuck her face into Alberta's mint jelly.

The four of us stared at her, and then we all began to laugh—Bodhi included.

Alberta got up to clean up her cat, and when she returned, she apologized to everyone for her irritability.

Dinner was more amicable after that, and by the time we made it to the apple crumble—which was delicious—it was easy to see that the meal with Bodhi had been a success.

Sibyl had saved the day.

As Alberta and I walked to the door with Rafaela and Bodhi at the end of the night, Rafaela drew me aside.

"Thank you for making this happen," she whispered, giving me a hug. "It's so important when you find the right person to make sure your family gets to know him, too. This meant a lot to me."

"When you find the right person—" I murmured.

"What's that?" Rafaela said.

"You said when you find the right person. You said something like that before—only you used a different word."

"And what does that mean?"

Something fell into place.

"It means I know what I need to do next."

Chapter Twenty

I helped Alberta clean up in the kitchen, and then I went up to my room.

It was getting late—but I knew my mom would answer when I called.

Find the right person, Rafaela had said.

Locate the right person, she had said earlier.

Something was in my mind, trying to work its way forward.

And I had to ask my mother a question.

I knew it would make a few things clearer.

I dialed, and Mom answered after just a few rings.

"Hi, honey," Maura said. "Is everything okay?"

"Everything's fine," I replied. "I just want to ask you a question."

"Wait a moment. Let me see if your father ... oh, no, never mind. He's fast asleep in his easy chair with his glasses sliding down his nose. You should see him—he looks so cute."

"That's okay, Mom," I said. "This question is really just for you."

"You're sure nothing's wrong? You are staying out of trouble, aren't you?"

"Yes, Mom, I'm staying out of trouble. I just need to know one thing. Why didn't you want us to use magic for housecleaning?"

"I'm sorry?" she said. She sounded surprised.

"Remember how you didn't want us to use magic to clean the house?"

"Yes."

"Well, why didn't you want that?"

"I—" Maura paused for a moment. "I guess there were two reasons, really. First of all, you'll forget who you are if you don't do mundane tasks. You'll start to think everything can be fixed with a spell—when in reality, everything takes hard work, including magic."

"And the second reason?" I prompted.

"The second reason was just as practical. Let's say you're using a broom—levitating it so it'll sweep the floor for you. That kind of magic is just too showy—it's more likely you'll get caught using it. It's much better to use magic to heal and to help. That's quiet magic, and it's easier to hide."

"That's what she's doing," I murmured to myself. "That's exactly what she's doing."

"What was that?" Maura said.

"Oh, nothing," I replied. "I needed to figure something out, and I knew you could help me to do it."

"Hmmm." My mother didn't sound happy. "Chloe, what are you up to?"

"Nothing—really."

"You've got an idea in your head, don't you? Something's growing there, isn't it? Like you told me before."

I couldn't deny that that was true, but I didn't want my mom trying to stop me.

"Nothing's fully formed," I said. "There's still no action I can take."

"Hmmm," Maura said again.

"Well, thanks, Mom. This really helped." I yawned theatrically. "Oh—look at the time. I'd really better get going—I've got work in the morning, you know."

"I do know. And you called me, remember?"

"Yes—sorry to call so late."

"Well, have a good night, honey. And just be careful. I think you can do a lot more than you know—and that can get you into trouble. Don't go leaping into anything. And please, please, please, leave the investigating to the police."

I made a few noncommittal noises, and then a little while after that, we both hung up.

I could feel my mind churning, and all the pieces of this particular part of the puzzle fell into place.

We all knew that we had to hide what we could do—anyone who could do magic knew that.

And the witch in the woods was no different.

Just as we couldn't enchant a broom because it might attract attention, so the witch in the woods had to hide herself and what she could do.

No one had been blocking Alberta when she'd magically searched the Old Forest.

The witch in the woods was actually hiding with a spell, and it would take another spell to break through it.

"Find" the right person, "locate" the right person.

That was exactly what I was going to do.

Truth to tell, spellcasting wasn't really my strongest area—at least not when it came to traditional spellcasting. I was always better when I was growing something—that was why the connective magic on my family of plants was so strong.

But I could do regular spellcasting in a pinch, and I tiptoed downstairs to get some matches.

I was going to cast a locate spell.

And that kind of spell drew on the element of fire.

I was glad to see that Alberta wasn't around as I slipped into the kitchen—I didn't want her to ask me what I was doing.

She wouldn't approve of my looking for the witch in the woods, and she would also give me a lecture about my use of fire magic.

It wasn't that she disapproved of my use of fire magic—she used it herself. But she didn't like the fact that I would draw on all four elements—earth, air, fire, and water for my magic.

She said I should just pick one and stick to it.

But I wasn't about to do that.

I liked drawing on all four elements, and besides, I needed all four to make things grow.

I found the matches and then gathered up a few more items I would need.

I then turned to go back to my room but soon thought better of it—the spell I needed to cast required smoke, and I didn't want to set off the smoke detector.

So I went out the back door instead.

The night was mercifully cool, and I paused for a moment to listen to the crickets singing and to gaze up at the bright stars above.

Somehow it seemed like a perfect night to cast a spell.

I left Alberta's patio and walked through the cool grass to her little stone birdbath. She'd purchased it recently, and so far, she hadn't actually put any water in it.

So it sat, clean and empty, the ideal spot for me to work my magic.

The locate spell was simple really—I had to create white and black smoke, speak the incantation over the two plumes of it, and then mix them together and peer into the center.

Then I would see the person I was searching for.

A little doubt tugged at the back of my mind—it seemed to me that I was forgetting something.

But I shrugged it off and got to work.

To create white smoke, I simply needed to burn a few sheets of paper, and I lit a match and watched them ignite. I dropped the sheets onto the gray stone of the birdbath, and as little tongues of orange flame lapped at them, white smoke rose up. Then I took a few rubber bands and set them on fire, dropping them quickly into the birdbath. Centuries ago, anyone who cast this spell would have used wood dipped in pitch. But since pitch was hard to come by nowadays, the rubber bands made a good substitute—they smelled terrible when they burned, but they did produce a lovely, thick black smoke. Once I had the two plumes of smoke going—one white, one black—I quickly spoke the incantation. Then I focused my mind on the Old Forest, and I swirled the two plumes together with my hand. I kept swirling and swirling, until I'd created a circle in the air with the smoke. Soon the smoke began to clear in the center, forming something like a window. And I looked through the window and saw the Old Forest.

And in the Old Forest I saw … no one.

I kept swirling, trying to make the image clearer, but it remained resolutely blank of any people.

I quickly put out both of the little fires and started once again.

I'd brought extra materials just in case.

I did the entire spell over again and came up with the same result: no person in my smoke-ringed image.

I had failed to find the hidden witch.

I was tired of breathing in smoke, so I put out my little fires and then got out the garden hose to wash the ashes out of the birdbath.

Then I went back inside.

The little nagging voice at the back of my mind had been right—there *was* something I'd been forgetting.

I might have gotten the incantation wrong—or I might have forgotten another ingredient that was supposed to go into the smoke.

The little voice piped up again to tell me that neither of those things was it.

But whatever the trouble was, I couldn't solve it tonight.

I resolved to go to my parents' house first thing in the morning and grab a few of my mom's old books.

I was sure to be able to find the right spell in one of them.

I went up to my room and fell asleep almost immediately—it had been a long day.

My alarm went off very early the next morning, and I hurried to get ready.

Then I went downstairs.

Alberta was startled to see me, and it was probably only the fifth or sixth time since I'd been staying there that I'd actually seen her at breakfast on a weekday—though the frequency had gone up a little lately.

"Fancy seeing you here," Alberta said.

"I've got something to do before work," I replied. "I needed to get an early start."

Alberta stood and finished the last of a glass of orange juice. "Well, I've got to do something before work, too. It's great to see you, but I've got to get going."

"That's okay," I said. "I'm really no good at conversation until I've had my coffee anyway."

She put her dishes in the dishwasher and then gave me a pat on the shoulder as she passed.

Then she was gone.

I sat down with my coffee, and it occurred to me that it was very strange for Alberta not to grill me about what I was up to—as she had said, it was unusual for me to be up this early.

And then I realized that if she'd asked me what I was up to, that would also open up the opportunity for me to ask her what she was up to.

Of course, it wasn't strange at all for Alberta to be up this early.

But she *had* said she had something to do.

And now I wondered what it was.

But I didn't have time to linger and ponder—instead, I quickly ate a bowl of cereal and had a second cup of coffee, and then I was on my way, too.

My parents' house was about fifteen minutes away, and as I drove, the quiet suburbs that Alberta lived in gave way to rural lanes and wide swaths of green fields.

Though the house wasn't that far away, it was definitely out in the country.

I reached the house and pulled into the driveway, my tires crunching on the gravel.

As I got out of the car, I paused for a moment to take in the view—there was a farm across the street, and a little gray pony and a long-legged brown horse always seemed to be standing out in a wide stretch of pasture. Today was no exception, and I watched the two of them switching their tails gently as they cropped the dewy grass.

I turned back to my parents' house and marveled as I always did at how cozy the house seemed. Though my mom and dad had been in Florida for several months now, the house didn't feel empty or abandoned. Instead, it seemed as if they had just stepped out and would be back at any moment. I knew that a neighbor looked in on the house every few days, and Alberta, Rafaela, and I stopped in from time to time to do a little dusting and other maintenance, but it seemed to me that something else might have been creating that comfortable, lived-in atmosphere.

I wondered if my mother had cast a spell on the house to make it seem that way—perhaps it was a precaution to deter would-be burglars.

Whatever the reason, the house did seem occupied and well-cared for, and I got out my key and went inside.

The last time I had been here looking for books, it had taken me quite a while. This time, however, I was just looking for basic spellbooks, and I knew that what I needed wouldn't be hard to find.

I went into the little room that Mom called her library, and I found a few books almost immediately—the books really were basic, and after decades of spellcasting, my mother would hardly have needed to take them with her.

She'd learned their contents by heart long ago.

I, on the other hand, was more than a little rusty—and Alberta always claimed that I wasn't as strong in the fundamentals as I needed to be.

And she was probably right—I hadn't had that locate spell on tap last night when I'd needed it.

I took two more books off the shelves, and then I remembered that my mother had all the books in the *Great Grimoire* collection somewhere in the house—those were the basic texts that witches used when they were first starting out, and they were very popular for schoolchildren—they were the texts of choice for the few witch schools that existed.

I finally found them on one of the bottom shelves, and they were just a little dusty. I selected one titled the *Great Grimoire's Book of Practical Spells*, and then I piled all six books I'd chosen on a table. I thought for just a moment of sitting down in one of Mom's comfy chairs and starting to read—after all, I still had plenty of time before I had to be at work.

But knowing me, I'd start reading and then wouldn't look up until several hours had gone by. I didn't want to risk being late, so I carted my armful of books out to my car and drove to work—even though it was still early. I would do my reading there.

Once I reached the library, I was surprised to see Rita and Barry, our handyman, already there.

It had rained during the night, and the ceiling in our old library had leaked in several places, and there were puddles and piles of plaster everywhere.

I quickly stowed my books in a closet and then hurried to help Rita and Barry clean up.

By the time we got everything back to normal—and Rita had put in a request to our head office for repairs—I had just enough time to get all my morning chores done before the library opened for the day.

My reading would have to wait till later.

Once our usual morning rush had died down, I found myself really longing to look at those books—but even in a library, reading while at work wasn't a good idea. I suddenly realized that there was something else I *could* do. Bodhi had mentioned that Heather Pim had a website—and that she had established a name for herself as a model and an athlete.

Maybe she also had a list of appearances or a schedule of events she was attending.

Perhaps I could pop up somewhere she was going to be and try to question her.

A brief search turned up her website easily enough, and I was delighted to see an "Events" section listed at the top.

I was even more delighted when I saw that Heather was putting in an appearance at a local country club tonight.

I was just wondering how I might be able to crash the event when I heard a creak, and the front door opened.

Mike walked in, and I felt my heart give a little flutter.

Sometimes I was surprised by just how handsome he was.

He looked around, and when his eyes landed on me, he broke into a grin.

He walked up to me at the circulation desk, and I felt my heart do another little flip.

He'd clearly come to see me—or at least I hoped he had.

Otherwise, I was smiling like a crazy person for no reason.

"Hi, Chloe," Mike said, and he lowered his voice so that it sounded just a little bit husky.

"Hey," I said.

"Chloe, I've missed—"

Mike stopped abruptly.

He cleared his throat and then went on.

"I've missed hearing about what you've been up to lately."

It seemed to me that Mike had been about to say something else.

And I wanted very much to know what that was.

I realized then that he was staring at me expectantly.

Apparently, he'd meant it when he'd said he wanted to know what I'd been up to.

"I've been busy," I said.

It was all I could come up with at the moment—I was pretty sure everything I'd been doing was stuff Mike wouldn't approve of.

"Doing what?" Mike sounded genuinely interested.

"Investigating." I tried to make my tone sound light.

Mike was rueful. "Investigating. I should have known."

He took a deep breath. "So is there any chance you might like to have dinner with me tonight? That is, if there's room in your sleuthing schedule?"

I felt my heart give yet another happy flutter, and then I glanced down at Heather's website, which still sat open on my computer.

"I would love to," I said. "I really, really would. But it's just that— I have to interview someone tonight. Otherwise, I would be happy to."

Mike's face fell. "You've got to investigate tonight, too?"

"I'm afraid so."

"Is there any chance I could go with you?" Mike sounded hopeful.

"I wish you could—"

I sighed—it would be hard enough for me to sneak into the country club myself. I didn't see how I could sneak him in, too.

"But you have to do this alone," Mike concluded.

"It's really just this one time," I said quickly. "This night is going to be tricky."

"Well, take care of yourself," Mike said. "And try to be careful."

With that, he was gone.

I felt a pang in my heart as the door closed behind him.

Chapter Twenty-One

I couldn't help being in a bad mood for the rest of the morning.

I cheered up a little when one of our regulars, Mrs. Chilcott, told me how much she liked a book I'd recommended to her.

Then I fell back into my gloomy thoughts, and I resigned myself to the fact that I'd disappointed Mike.

I'd have to see if I could patch things up with him later.

But right now I had some spellbooks to read through, and when my lunch hour arrived, I lugged my books downstairs to the break room and began to pore over them.

A Cauldron Full of Spells began with a dire warning against using curses for harm—it said using dark magic could cause the spell to rebound on the user, forcing the unlucky spellcaster to suffer the consequences he or she intended to inflict.

It further went on to say that curses should only be used in a defensive capacity, and it defined dark magic as any magic that was developed by using harm or that intended harm as an outcome.

It then went on with a list of ingredients that good witches were forbidden to use, and I flipped past several more pages of warnings of what *not* to do to see if there were indeed any actual spells, and I found that there were.

The spells, however, didn't appear in any particular order and appeared to have been placed randomly in the book. There was no table of contents or index, but there was a note at the end of the book that stated that any witch who was reading it should be able to use a spell to find anything he or she wanted—therefore no index was necessary.

I closed the book and moved on to the next one.

The *Big Book of Spells* was indeed a very big book, and it had a lock on it that I couldn't open. I tried a rudimentary unlock spell on it, but the spell didn't work—either I'd forgotten how to work the spell properly, or the lock required something more powerful.

The Only Spellbook You'll Ever Need was heavy on advice and empowerment slogans but light on actual spells, so I turned with a sinking feeling to the *Great Grimoire's Book of Practical Spells*.

So far I hadn't chosen my books very well.

To my relief, I discovered that the *Great Grimoire* spellbook was indeed full of spells, and they were arranged in alphabetical order with an index at the back.

As I flipped through, looking for a locate spell, another spell caught my eye.

It was a glamour.

A glamour was a spell to alter your appearance.

I suddenly had an idea.

But it would have to wait for a moment.

I continued flipping until I reached the locate spell, and I read through it eagerly.

It turned out I had actually done two things incorrectly with the spell I had tried to cast last night.

First of all, I had gotten the incantation wrong—I'd forgotten several crucial words.

And second, a locate spell wasn't meant to be used the way I had been trying to use it. A locate spell was supposed to be used to find someone you already knew—you had to have a very clear picture in your mind when you cast it.

And as I read through the description, I realized that was why Alberta hadn't used a locate spell when she'd worked on those missing person cases.

She could get a picture of the missing person, but she didn't actually know them, so the spell wouldn't work. She'd had to use divination to find someone who was unknown.

So now that I knew that a locate spell wouldn't work, there was no point in my using it.

But I memorized it anyway.

I then flipped back to the glamour spell and read through it.

It was exactly what I needed.

I could either use a glamour to look like someone else—that is, transform myself so that I had another person's appearance, or I could simply alter my appearance so that I didn't look like myself—I could look like someone I just made up.

I would never get into the event at the country club as myself—Heather Pim had already made it plain how she felt about me. But I could get in using a glamour.

I could transform myself so that I didn't look like me at all.

Satisfied that I had a solution to the Heather problem, I flipped through the book some more, hoping to find a way to uncover the witch in the woods.

While looking, I did find an unlock spell, and I tried it on the big, locked book of spells.

To my delight, I discovered that it worked—and I also discovered that, once again, I had gotten the incantation wrong when I'd tried it before.

I suddenly thought of the key up in my room at home—the one that rested inside a glove in Mr. Clementine's sunflower box.

I wished there was some kind of spell that could tell me what it was for.

I did find a reveal spell—but that was meant to be used to reveal magic.

And I didn't think there was anything magical about the key—it was just an ordinary object that happened to have a secret.

I set to work memorizing the glamour spell. I was taking the books home, of course, so I didn't need to memorize it—but I wanted to have it in my mind already when I tried to cast it after work.

I glanced at the clock on my phone—my lunch hour was almost up.

I quickly ate two granola bars and drank half a bottle of water.

Then I stashed my books on a nearby shelf and hurried upstairs. If Rita or anyone else found them, I knew they'd think they were fiction.

The day didn't go by as quickly as I would have liked, but eventually five thirty rolled around, and I went out to my car, lugging my spellbooks.

I probably could have taken just the one and left the others, but I felt like I should have them all with me—just in case.

As I settled the books on the seat next to me, my phone rang, and I was startled to see that it was Rafaela—she usually just texted me.

"Hello?" I said.

"Are you heading home now?" Rafaela sounded breathless.

"Yes," I said.

"I need you to do something for me tonight."

"I don't think I can—I'm kind of going to be busy."

"I don't need you to do anything exactly," Rafaela said. "It's more like I need you to find out something—from Alberta."

"From Alberta?"

"Yes—I saw her this morning."

"I saw her this morning, too," I said.

"But I saw her, and she didn't see me," Rafaela persisted.

"So? That happens sometimes. We do all live in the same town."

"She was meeting a man," Rafaela said with emphasis. "And he gave her a key."

"What? What does that mean?" I said.

"It means she met a man in the street, and he gave her a key."

"You already said that. So?"

"So she was happy about it," Rafaela replied. "*Really* happy."

"I still don't see what you're getting at."

Rafaela hesitated, as if she were reluctant to go on.

"Well, what do you think it means?" she said at last.

"Maybe it's something for work?" I hazarded.

"Maybe. Could you—could you find out from Alberta what was going on when you see her tonight?"

"Why didn't you just ask her yourself at the time?" I asked.

"It's just—I saw her, and she didn't see me—"

"And you didn't want her to know you were spying on her?" I couldn't help teasing her a little.

"I wasn't spying on her!" Rafaela sounded horrified. "I just happened to see her, and then she looked so furtive—"

"I thought you said she looked happy?"

"Yes, she did. But she looked furtive at the same time."

"So, she was happy," I said. "But she was trying to hide it?"

Rafaela sighed. "It sounds crazy when you put it like that. I'm just worried about her. Can you please find out what she was up to?"

I frowned. "You really are worried about her, aren't you? Just like you were before."

I paused. "What do you think she's up to?"

Rafaela hesitated again. "I'd rather not say."

"But there's something you suspect?"

"Oh, Chloe. Sometimes you seem so innocent."

"What's *that* supposed to mean?"

"It means you'll always be my little sister." I could hear a weary smile in Rafaela's voice. "So will you find out for me?"

"I'll do what I can," I replied. "But you do know as well as I do that if Alberta doesn't want to talk, she won't. And nothing will change her mind."

"I know. Just do your best. This is really important."

I promised I would try, and then Rafaela hung up.

I sat for a moment, trying to figure out what Rafaela could possibly think Alberta was up to, and vague suspicions of drug deals floated through my head.

That was, of course, completely ridiculous, and I quickly shrugged the idea off.

Whatever Alberta was up to—if anything—I was sure it probably wasn't that bad. But I had promised Rafaela, so I would see what I could find out.

I started the car and headed for home.

As I walked into the house, I could smell Chinese food, and sure enough, when I went into the kitchen, I found Alberta fussing with a bunch of white takeout boxes.

She glanced up as I came in. "Sorry to have takeout again so soon. I don't think I'll have time to cook tonight."

"That's okay," I said. "I have to go out tonight, so something quick is really perfect."

Sibyl meandered into the room and wound around my legs, and I was relieved to see that for once she didn't have any food on her face.

As I patted Sibyl, I waited for Alberta to start grilling me about where I was going.

But instead, she simply shrugged.

"That's good. I've got a lot to do tonight, and it'll be nice for me to have the house to myself."

Again, I got the feeling that Alberta was purposefully avoiding asking me what I was up to.

That way she wouldn't have to volunteer any of her plans.

I wanted to ask about what she was doing, but I already had Rafaela's question to ask.

And I didn't know how much I would be able to get out of her.

We dished out the Chinese food, and I was very happy to see that Alberta had ordered egg foo young and egg drop soup for me. She'd also ordered beef and peppers and wonton soup for herself.

There was also a little, sealed plastic bag with a handful of fortune cookies inside.

I eyed them nervously and decided not to take one.

It seemed to me that when you were a witch, innocent, mass-produced fortune-cookie fortunes could take on added dimension and power.

And even though the fortunes tended to be good, I didn't want anything written on that little slip of paper to interfere with my plans tonight—even "you will find true love" could prove catastrophic under the wrong circumstances.

And I noticed that Alberta didn't take one, either.

So while Sibyl ate her crunchies nearby, Alberta and I sat down at the kitchen table and began to eat our Chinese food.

I glanced at her a couple of times, trying to figure out how to bring up Rafaela's question, and just as I was about to speak, Alberta broke the silence herself.

"What do you think about pickle bread?" she said abruptly.

"Pickle bread?" I echoed.

"Yes—you know, bread with pickles in it?"

"What do you mean?" I said. "Like a whole pickle?"

"No," Alberta said, exasperated. "I don't mean a sandwich. I mean bread with little pieces of pickle in it—like zucchini bread."

I felt myself grimacing. "I don't know. I love zucchini bread—but somehow I can't see pickle bread being quite the same."

"It's just that I've been craving it lately." Alberta's voice had grown dreamy.

"But you hate pickles."

"I know. But I think they might be good in a bread. It's just funny—I've been having a lot of cravings lately."

"You know what else is funny?" I said. "Rafaela said she saw you this morning. She was wondering what you were up to."

I'd just thrown that in because I thought I'd found a good opening, and I wanted to get Rafaela's question out of the way. I assumed that Alberta would just shrug me off and not answer the question, but instead, the effect on her was electric.

Her eyes opened wide, and she froze.

Then all the color drained out of her face.

"Alberta?" I said. "Are you okay?"

But Alberta didn't say anything.

And she continued not to say anything for the rest of dinner, no matter how many times I asked her what was wrong.

So eventually, I gave up and went to my room—I had an event to get ready for.

And I was sure that Alberta was actually all right.

At least, I was pretty sure.

I got out the *Great Grimoire's Book of Practical Spells*, and even though I had the glamour spell memorized by now, I still kept the book open as I cast the enchantment.

I said the incantation and focused on how I wanted my features to change. I didn't want to look like anyone in particular—I just wanted to change myself so that I was unrecognizable to those who knew me.

So I focused on changing my dark hair to blond and my brown eyes to blue. Then I made the texture of my hair straight rather than curly, and I made my nose a little longer and my cheekbones a little more prominent.

Finally, I focused on making myself look taller and thinner—a little more like a high-fashion model.

And then I turned and looked in the mirror.

I was startled by what I saw.

Looking back at me was an unfamiliar face. My eyes were indeed blue, and my hair was actually blond and straight—just like I'd imagined. And in the simple skirt and blouse I'd worn to work, I looked tall and long-limbed—even a little gangly.

I wondered then if the glamour worked on clothes, and I said the incantation again while focusing on my work clothes. As I watched, my skirt and blouse transformed into a tight, fire-engine red minidress, and my sensible shoes became strappy, sky-high stilettos. Even my little gold earrings transformed into gaudy, eye-catching bangles.

I was just like Cinderella getting ready for the ball—only I was my own fairy godmother.

And Cinderella wouldn't have been allowed into the prince's palace dressed like this.

I went to get my purse then, and I realized that it wouldn't really match my outfit—and I didn't have one that would.

So as one final touch, I transformed my purse into a tiny little sparkly clutch.

The good thing was that even though the purse appeared to be smaller, it was actually the same size, so I could fit all my usual stuff in it.

I took one last look in the mirror, and satisfied with my handiwork, I tiptoed down the stairs—I didn't want Alberta to see me going out like this. In fact, I didn't want her to see me at all—she'd think I was a stranger until she heard my voice—and then I would have some explaining to do.

I peeked around the banister, and I could hear Alberta rustling around somewhere back by the pantry.

I realized the way was clear, so I slipped out of the house into the night to interrogate Heather Pim.

Chapter Twenty-Two

The drive over to the country club only took about twenty minutes, and along the way I passed Camelot, where Mr. Clementine's house rose on its hill above all.

It was only seven o'clock, and since it was summer, there was still plenty of light illuminating the evening.

I was disturbed to see that the question-mark-shaped pink cloud still hung over the house.

And I was no closer to figuring out what it was.

I continued on to the Belle Époque Country Club, and I was relieved to see that there was no gate or fence around it—I could drive right up through the circular driveway lined with twisting green topiary and wait in the line for valet parking.

As I waited, I suddenly felt a little stab of nerves—I'd never actually had a valet park my car before, and I was afraid I would do something that would mark me as a newbie—and I wanted very much to blend in.

And then I realized that I had cast a glamour on myself, but I had forgotten to cast one on my car—which was an unassuming and slightly beaten-up sedan. I could already see that my little car looked out of place in the long line of luxury automobiles, and it was too late for me to cast a spell now.

Nothing would attract more attention than my car suddenly transforming in front of everyone's eyes.

So I just had to hope I could brave it out and get through with my decidedly low-key car.

When it was my turn, I stepped out of the car and flashed the red-jacketed valet what I hoped was a dazzling smile. But the attendant barely glanced at me and simply took my keys without a word and gave me a ticket.

Then he got in my car and drove away.

I was left standing on a wide, stone terrace, and I watched people going up the steps into a big, white building that seemed to have a lot of French windows. The eventgoers were expensively but casually dressed, and I fit right in with my minidress and strappy heels.

I did notice one thing, however, that gave me pause. As the guests were going in, they all stopped by one of two white-jacketed attendants and handed over what looked to be an invitation.

I felt my heart sink.

I definitely didn't have an invitation.

I began to rummage in my purse to see if there was something in it that I could cast a glamour on. While I searched, I realized that I didn't know if a glamour would work the same on an object like a piece of paper as it did on my hair or my clothes. Could I make something like a receipt look larger just like I had made myself look taller? And what about the way it felt? If I made something like a matchbook look like one of the invitations, would the attendant be able to feel that it was the wrong size and shape when he handled it?

And then I realized that I had another problem.

I didn't know what the invitations actually said.

Even if all the other problems were ironed out, I didn't know what words to put on the card in order to make it look like a legitimate invitation.

I squinted up at the line ahead of me, trying to see if anyone had their invitations out in readiness.

As I did so, I happened to catch the eye of one of the door attendants—a dark-haired young man with a very deep tan. He smiled at me.

I quickly looked away.

The last thing I wanted to do was attract any attention.

Before I knew it, I had reached the head of the line.

I found myself standing in front of the dark-haired man who had smiled at me earlier. I was still searching in my bag as if I could find my nonexistent invitation, and so far I hadn't come up with a plan— I'd decided that casting another glamour was too risky.

The man smiled at me again.

"Mademoiselle finds herself in difficulties?"

I'd been trusting that I'd come up with a plan when I reached the door, but suddenly my mind went blank.

"Uh, yes," was all I could think of to say.

The man reached for a clipboard on a nearby table.

"It is no matter—don't think on it. Many of our guests find that they have forgotten their invitations. That is why we keep a list of our distinguished guests."

He winked at me.

I felt my heart sink again.

I knew my name wasn't going to be on that list.

The man ran his finger down the names.

"Ah, yes. I see Mademoiselle's name right here. But then we know you well at the Belle Époque."

I blinked. "You do?"

"Yes, of course. We remember all our loveliest guests. And the party would be much poorer without Mademoiselle."

The man held out his hand in a welcoming gesture.

"Entre, s'il vous plaît."

His accent was decidedly American, but the French words were still lovely.

"Thank you," I said, and I went inside.

I found myself in a long, cool hallway with lots of potted plants whose large green fronds reached up toward the high ceilings. There were ceiling fans that sent a slight breeze wafting through the entranceway, and a large sign sat on a stand surrounded by bright orange and red flowers.

The sign proclaimed an exhibit of pictures of Heather Pim, and I remembered that that was indeed the event that had been listed on her website.

According to the sign in front me, this was a special one-night stop before these same photos were shipped to a gallery in New York.

I heard an impatient rustle behind me, and I realized that I was impeding the flow of traffic.

I hurried to move toward the set of double doors that stood open in front of me.

As I approached them, however, a familiar blond figure came out.

It was Bodhi P. Gotschall, and he was talking in hushed tones on a cell phone.

Luckily, he hadn't seen me yet, and I ducked into another, smaller room that stood open nearby.

I watched as he went past me—he seemed to be going outside.

And then I remembered that I had glamoured myself, and he wouldn't have been able to recognize me anyway.

I happened to notice that there were several small, patterned mirrors hanging on the wall nearby, and I paused to check my reflection.

I was still blond and blue-eyed and unrecognizable.

But maybe it was best if I didn't talk to him anyway.

I felt a gentle tap on my shoulder, and I turned to see a slender, middle-aged woman with jet-black hair standing by my side.

She wore a little black dress with an unusual, geometric cut, and ochre-colored bangles clanked on her wrists. Something about her gave off a very artistic vibe, and she smiled at me with bright scarlet lips.

"Good evening, miss. Are you here for the silent auction?"

She had an accent I couldn't quite place—though I thought it might be Eastern European—and I blinked at her.

"Silent auction?"

"Yes. We are auctioning off a few select photos of our star tonight, Heather Pim. There are also some wonderful trips and a few other lovely prizes. But I would recommend the photos. Of course, I may be partial—I am, after all, the photographer."

She laughed loudly, startling me.

"Do not mind me," she said. "I am eccentric. But then again, I *am* Anna Anatole."

I hadn't heard of her before, but I took the hint and murmured a few impressed noises.

My first instinct was to excuse myself politely and move on, but then I remembered that I was supposed to be a guest, and I figured it might be better to play along.

And if she'd photographed Heather Pim, she might be able to "introduce" me to her.

"Yes, of course," I heard myself saying. "I'm definitely here for the silent auction."

"Wonderful!" Anna screeched, startling me again.

I guessed she wasn't into the silent part of the auction.

Anna linked her arm through mine and led me over to the auction, where other people were already browsing.

There was a row of tables, and each table had a glossy photo of Heather or a picture showing a prize propped up on a little wooden stand. On the table below each picture was a sheet of paper, and I could see that guests had already written down their names and how much they were bidding. Apparently, each new bid had to be larger than the last by fifty dollars.

"But look closer," Anna hissed in a husky whisper. "I'm in charge, and I've added a twist!"

On the sheet in front of me, up above all the listed names and bids, were two words:

HEAD

HEELS

"Head over heels?" I said.

Anna screeched with laughter. "Yes, my clever girl! How about this one?"

She dragged me over to the next table.

This time I saw:

F A R E D C E

I stared at the apparently scrambled letters for a moment.

Then it dawned on me.

"Red in the face!"

"Yes! You are a wonder! You are a jewel!" Anna cried. "How is it that we've never met before?"

I knew the answer to that, but I didn't think Anna would believe it, even if I were foolish enough to tell her.

But I was saved from having to answer by Anna herself, who dragged me over to yet another table.

"Now this one," she said.

I stared at the sheet of paper in front of me. It read:

WORL

"Worl?" I said. "I have no idea what that is."

"Come, my child, you must have figured out what these are by now."

"They're word puzzles."

"Ah, yes," Anna said with a glint in her dark eyes. "But what kind? They have a name, you know."

I frowned in thought. "These are—rebus puzzles."

"Yes!" Anna screeched, startling me for a third time, and a few people standing at the next table turned to stare at us.

Anna didn't notice them and instead poked me in the ribs.

As she did so, I felt a tug on my mind.

The rebus puzzles reminded me of something.

"Yes, my dear, that's exactly what they are," Anna said. "Do you know why they are here?"

"No."

"No, of course you don't! But I will tell you. It's a second chance at a prize. A person writes the answer to the rebus puzzle on a slip of paper along with their name. Then they put the slip in one of those boxes."

Anna pointed to a bright red cardboard box that sat on the table in front of us.

She continued. "After the main prizes are given out, we will do a drawing. Then if a guest's name is drawn, and they get the right answer, they will be eligible for a secondary prize related to the first one. So, if they bid on a picture of Heather, and their name is drawn, they get to have lunch with her and me. And all they have to pay is their original bid on the big prize. But they must have bid, of course, in order to be eligible."

"Ingenious," I said.

Anna laughed loudly. "Yes, I am. But, come now, you must know what this means."

She pointed to "WORL."

"It's 'world' with no 'd'?" I said.

"Yes—yes. And what does that say to you? What phrase is there like that?"

"Oh!" I said suddenly. "World without end."

"Yes!" Anna cried. "Yes! All the letters are important. You have it, clever girl!"

I felt the tug on my mind again—something about letters.

While I was thinking, Anna led me back to the first table.

"Now you are ready," she said. "You must bid on all the prizes and then answer all the rebus puzzles. I feel quite sure that you will win something. And you must stop by my studio. Someday I shall photograph you."

She turned swiftly.

"Darling!" she screeched suddenly, startling me yet again. "How good to see you!"

And she sailed off to greet a matron in a flowery caftan with a towering beehive hairdo.

I'd thought at first that Anna might prove hard to get rid of over the course of an evening, even if she could be helpful in getting me to Heather—but now I could see that she was really just a good saleswoman.

She hadn't actually been interested in me at all.

I pretended to scribble something on the first bid sheet, and then I drifted past the groups of people clustered around the other tables and headed toward the back of the room.

I could see another set of double doors opening onto a big room full of people.

I slipped into the room, and I realized that I'd finally reached the main event—the meet-and-greet with Heather Pim.

There was a jagged, towering ice sculpture in the center of the room, and three well-stocked bars were serving a long line of guests. The lights were low, there was a solid murmur of voices and laughter, and people stood in clusters, talking and gesturing.

I had expected to see Heather in a central area, perhaps with a sign, but I supposed an arrangement like that would be too inelegant for a place like the Belle Époque.

I made my way over to the ice sculpture and climbed up the few short steps that led up to it—first, so that I could get a better look at the room and possibly spot Heather, and second, so that I could get a better look at the sculpture itself.

I was having a hard time figuring out what it was.

Once I was up close, I could see that the craggy surface of the sculpture was meant to represent a mountain, and climbing up the rock wall was a tiny figure—presumably Heather herself. Cold was rolling off the massive sculpture in waves, and I shivered a little and stepped away from it.

I glanced around the room once more and finally spotted the original version.

Heather was standing in the midst of a group of people, in a short gold dress with a plunging neckline. Her short blond hair looked especially golden tonight, and in her gold platform heels, she towered over everyone in her little circle.

She was laughing—clearly enjoying being the center of attention—and I wondered how I could have missed her before.

I hurried over.

I barged right into the middle of the group, and when I found myself facing Heather, I suddenly realized that I didn't have a plan.

And I could hardly interrogate her in a room full of people.

"Hi," I blurted out.

Heather turned to look at me, and I was momentarily dazzled by the bright yellow jewels that hung in her ears. They were almost—but not quite—as bright as the yellow stones in Clytie Clementine's ring.

I wondered once again why she wanted that ring—she apparently had plenty of jewelry already.

Her eyes narrowed as she looked at me.

"You look really familiar," she said, swaying just a bit.

I felt a sudden flash of panic.

I wondered if the glamour had worn off—but Heather continued to look at me searchingly, so I figured it must be holding.

"What's your name?" she demanded.

I very nearly blurted out "Chloe," but I caught myself just in time.

I decided to trot out two of my other names.

"Anastasia Delaney," I said.

Heather stared at me for a long moment, then she nodded.

"I remember you. We both walked in the Gabrielle Janssen show at New York Fashion Week."

It wasn't so much a question as a statement, and I smiled noncommittally.

Heather's posture became less defensive and more relaxed, and when she relaxed, the people around us did, too.

I hadn't realized until that moment that everyone had been holding their breath.

"I didn't know you lived around here," Heather said to me.

"Well, I like to be mysterious," I said.

I didn't really know what I meant by that, but a ripple of admiration ran through our little group.

Apparently, I'd said the right thing.

"I—like your earrings," I said.

I winced on the inside—I'd followed up my unexpectedly successful comment with a decidedly uncool one.

But to my surprise, the little group around me murmured their assent, and one woman with spiky orange hair laughed.

"You're going to be able to buy a lot more like them when you get your money."

Everyone, Heather included, laughed in response.

"Don't you worry about that," Heather said. "I intend to get it. All of it."

Cheers from the group accompanied this pronouncement.

"So, Heather," I said. "Could I talk to you for a minute?"

I still didn't really have a plan, but I seemed to be getting along with the whole group, and I figured that now might be as good a time as any to try to get Heather by herself.

She eyed me a bit blearily for a moment.

"Sure," she said. "Let's go have a talk, model to model."

We walked off with Heather leading the way, and she guided us over to one of the bars.

There were several glasses of champagne lined up along one side for the guests to take as they chose, and Heather picked up two glasses and handed one to me.

Then she led me over to two large, overstuffed pink armchairs in a corner. She flopped into one, and I perched on the other.

We were partially hidden by two enormous potted plants, and I was grateful for the little bit of privacy.

She took a long drink from her champagne flute and then eyed me blearily once again.

She'd clearly had one flute too many already.

237

"So what do you want?" she asked.

"I just want to know how you are," I said. "It can't have been easy since your boyfriend died."

It felt strange using the word "boyfriend" to describe the elderly Mr. Clementine, but that was the right word to use.

Heather took another drink. "Oh, yes. I'm very broken up."

I felt weird pretending to console her when I was actually trying to get information out of her, but I had to do it.

I had to find out what she'd been doing the day Mr. Clementine died.

"The earrings," I said coaxingly. "Were they a gift from your boyfriend?"

Heather snorted. "These earrings? A gift from that old miser? Hardly. He barely gave me any jewelry at all. And that allowance he kept me on! It paid for the condo and for basic things, but if I wanted to spend—really spend—I had to make my own money. That's why I kept working. And then even after Jaden was born, he only gave me a few more thousand a month."

She took a swig from her champagne flute and drained the glass.

"But I'm going to get everything that's coming to me. And then I'll buy lots and lots of earrings like this—as many as I want."

"So you bought these earrings yourself?" I said.

Heather smiled smugly. "No. Let's just say I've got a friend. And I might have a new boyfriend before too long."

She set down her glass and looked at me, her eyes swimming.

"That's what I like about models. We look out for each other. I can't talk to anybody else like this—not really."

"Did you know about the will?" I asked. I figured she was drunk enough that it was safe for me to ask more pointed questions. "Did you know your boyfriend was going to split everything amongst his four boys?"

Heather's face suddenly darkened, and I saw a hint of the anger I had seen back at the parking lot two days ago.

All of the veins in her neck and arms seemed to pop out against her tanned skin.

"No," she spat. "He was supposed to marry *me*. He was supposed to give *me* that ring. And he was supposed to give everything to me and Jaden. *We're* his family now."

"Did he actually say that?" I asked gently.

Heather flung herself back against her chair. "Oh, that man. He never *really* said anything. But he implied things. He made me think—"

She broke off abruptly.

"Heather?" I said.

But she didn't seem to have heard me.

She was staring straight ahead, her chest heaving.

Her big, strong hands convulsed, and I noticed that there was a strange blue stain on one of them.

She looked ready to strangle someone right now.

"Heather?"

Her eyes swam in my direction.

"Heather," I said, "I have to ask you something."

"What?"

"I heard—that is, there's a rumor going around that on the day your boyfriend died, someone was seen running away from his house—someone tall and blond and athletic. Was that you?"

Heather stared at me, and her breathing grew even more labored.

I thought for a moment that she was going to lunge at me.

Instead, she stood up and grabbed my hand.

"Come on. Let's dance."

Music had started up somewhere nearby while we'd been talking, and Heather pulled me into a room with no overhead lights but a floor that was lit from below. We danced to loud techno music, and afterward, Heather kept me by her side the rest of the night, whether she was talking to friends and admirers or getting yet another drink from the bar.

Every time I tried to sneak away, she'd grab my hand in her big, strong one, and I found myself unable to get away.

Eventually, she collapsed into a chair and seemed to fall asleep.

A small group crowded around her and woke her up.

I could hear people offering to take care of her and take her home as I slipped away.

Once outside, I breathed in the cool, clean air gratefully.

Then I hurried down to the driveway. I'd only had a few sips of champagne and that had been hours ago, so I was perfectly clearheaded to drive—I was just a little tired.

As I looked around for the valet, I heard the clink of metal on metal, and I saw a man silhouetted against the moon, working under the hood of a sleek white car parked right out front.

He was swearing loudly, and I hurried past him.

I found the valet parking in an underground lot and turned in my ticket.

Then I jumped into my car gratefully when it was returned to me.

As I drove out, I had to pass by the man who was tinkering with the car again.

My headlights illuminated him, and he swung around to look at me.

It was Bodhi.

Chapter Twenty-Three

Of course, there was nothing wrong with Bodhi taking a look at his car if it wasn't working properly.

But somehow he'd seemed so sinister that it had given me pause.

I'd really had to wonder what he'd been up to, but it always led me back to the same question.

What could possibly be wrong with a man working on his own car?

As I drove home that night, I undid the glamour, and I decided to put the question out of my mind.

I had plenty to think over without that.

After I reached home, I found myself on my phone, doing as much research as I could.

Alberta had a laptop that would have been much better to use for that purpose, but I could tell she'd retired for the night, and I didn't want to disturb her. So, on my phone's little screen, I swiped through website after website, reading more about Heather, and about her deceased rival, Clytie Clementine. I found archived photos of Clytie's ring, and I read about her childhood in Ohio—her parents had divorced when she was young, and her mother had remarried. The new marriage produced a half brother and sister, and when Clytie was still a young teen, she left for New York City and never looked back. Clytie's marriage was chronicled quite a bit in the press as Otis

Clementine was extremely wealthy even back then, and her flight to Italy with their infant son, Brian, had made for some splashy headlines.

Brian himself, however, wasn't very much in evidence. There were a few rumors that he had married and divorced a makeup artist in Italy, but there were no pictures of him, and he seemed to have lived quietly, avoiding appearances in both gossip magazines and scandal sheets.

By contrast, Otis's later romances and the activities and antics of his sons Bobby and Christopher had attracted quite a bit of media attention. Both of his younger adult sons owned businesses right here in Crabtree Bay—and conventional wisdom held that they remained in town because their father wished it rather than because they'd chosen to do so—Bobby in particular was known to be something of a jetsetter.

Both sons had quarreled with their father over money, and Christopher had actually been completely cut off. Bobby had still been in his father's good graces at the time of his death, but there were rumors that he was in financial difficulties, too.

After Heather's strange behavior at the country club, I was mostly convinced that she had been the blond intruder at the Clementine house.

But now it was pretty obvious that Christopher and Bobby had strong motives, too.

I would have to talk to them both—just to be sure.

I shut off my phone and closed my eyes, but my head kept spinning with ideas.

Somewhere in the middle of all the furious thinking, I fell asleep.

I awoke in the morning to find sunlight on my face, and the first thing I thought of was the rebus puzzles from last night.

I suddenly knew what they reminded me of.

I scrambled to find my phone, and I called Mike.

I felt bad about brushing him off yesterday, but I genuinely hadn't been able to take him with me.

But maybe he could go along with me this morning—if he was free.

Mike answered on the first ring like he always did, and I wondered briefly if he kept the phone nearby just in case I would call.

But just as quickly I realized that that was a ridiculous idea—he probably just kept his phone handy in case his students needed him.

"Hey, Chloe."

"Hey," I said. "So I'm sorry about yesterday—"

"That's quite all right," he said quickly. "I shouldn't have asked you at the last minute like that."

"No, that was fine," I said. "I just wish I could have gone, and since we're on the topic of last-minute invitations—"

"Yes?"

"I was wondering if you might be free to do something with me this morning." I glanced at the clock—it was nearly ten a.m. "That is, if you're not busy already. I know you still have classes and office hours in the summer."

"I could take some time out this morning," Mike replied. "What were you thinking of?"

"How would you like to take a little drive?"

"Where?"

"Up to Mr. Clementine's neighborhood. I think I've figured something out."

"Ah—so you're letting me go along on your sleuthing?" Mike's tone was teasing.

"I suppose you could put it that way."

Mike sighed dramatically, but I could tell he was kidding.

"Why is it that you never want to go to dinner and a movie like a normal girl?"

"It's too early in the day for either of those things," I said. "Does that mean you want to go along?"

"Sure, I'll go along. Somebody's got to keep you out of trouble. When do you want to meet?"

I glanced at the clock again. "How about eleven?"

"Sounds good—I can do that. Where do you want to meet?"

"Are you at school?" I asked.

"Yes, I'm in my office."

"Okay, then. I'll come by and pick you up."

"I think that's supposed to be my line," Mike said dryly.

I ignored that, and we both said our goodbyes.

Then I hurried to get ready and went downstairs to get some coffee.

Alberta was long gone, of course, but she'd left a note on the coffeemaker that directed me to a plastic container sitting on the kitchen table.

After I'd had my first cup of coffee, I opened the container and found a dozen doughnuts lying inside—glazed, powdered, and chocolate.

It was a delightful surprise.

I ate a glazed doughnut and then half of a powdered one—my eyes turned out to be bigger than my stomach—and I wrapped the second half up for later.

And later, I would also try one of the chocolate ones.

Then I picked up Mr. Clementine's sunflower box, which I had brought down with me, and then I was out the door.

The morning was hot yet again, and I was grateful that my air-conditioning kicked in quickly as I drove over to Henrietta College.

When I reached Mike's building, I found that he was already waiting outside, and as I drew to a stop, he opened the passenger's side door and got in.

"I was going to get out and open the door for you," I said.

Mike just threw me a look, and I drove off.

"So you said we're headed to Mr. Clementine's neighborhood?" he said.

"Yes," I said. "We're headed over to Camelot."

"And what's there?"

"Honestly, I don't know yet," I said. "But I have a hunch."

"Then this will be a voyage of discovery?"

"Something like that. But I really hope we find what I think we'll find."

"And what's that?"

I shook my head. "I'll tell you if I'm right."

"So I take it your investigating went well last night?"

I paused. "I talked to Heather Pim."

"And how did it go?"

"Let's just put it this way—she didn't come across as innocent. In fact, I kind of thought she was going to kill *me* there for a moment."

Mike sighed. "This is what I'm talking about, Chloe—or at least what I'm always *trying* to talk about. This stuff is dangerous. Someone has been killed, and someone else surely wants their identity to remain a secret. And then you go poking around, stirring everything up. It's a miracle you *haven't* been killed."

I felt myself growing stubborn. "I have to do this."

"I know," Mike said wearily. "That's why I want to come along— why I always want to come along. Like I said, someone has to keep you out of trouble."

I felt like I should have been irritated, but instead I found myself giggling.

"You're kind of like my bodyguard."

Mike looked over at me. "Your bodyguard or your dad—I'm not sure which."

"You're only four years older than I am," I said.

"Really? It feels like a lot more than that."

I glanced at Mike and saw that he had a smug, superior look on his face.

Again, I felt like I should have been irritated, but instead I just found it endearing.

Mike really was sincere about wanting to look out for me.

I smiled at him, and he looked back at me, puzzled, as I continued to drive.

We soon reached Camelot, and I was disturbed to see that same pink cloud still hanging over Mr. Clementine's house up in the distance.

But his house wasn't where we were headed.

I slowed the car.

"There are a lot of interesting street names in here," Mike remarked. "Roundtable Terrace, Lancelot's Love Lane. Nice houses, too. I've never been in here before."

He looked over at me. "So when are you going to tell me what we're up to?"

"Very soon," I said. "Would you mind opening the glove compartment and getting something out for me?"

"Sure." Mike leaned forward and obliged. "Will you tell me what I'm looking for in here? Or do I have to guess that, too?"

I did have to smile at that—there was a lot of stuff in the glove compartment.

"There's a box in there with sunflowers all over it," I said. "Could you take that out for me, please?"

"Okay. I've got it."

The box sat in his lap.

"Now open it," I said.

He opened it to reveal Clytie Clementine's diamond ring and the fake-bejeweled glove.

Mike whistled. "That's quite a sparkler."

He picked up the ring. Then he made a strangled sound.

"First, you pick me up, then you offer to open the door for me. Chloe, are you going to propose?"

I stared at him—I couldn't tell if he was kidding or not.

"What? No. I just forgot I'd left that in there. I meant to take it out before I left."

Mike chuckled. "I know—I figured it was something like that. But you do have to admit that it would have made a pretty good proposal. I would have been completely surprised."

I snorted.

"At any rate," Mike said, "would you like to tell me what I'm looking at? If it's not the ring, then what is it? Could you clear up that little mystery for me?"

"The glove," I said.

"The glove?" Mike picked it up, and the key with the ornate handle fell out of it.

He then picked up the key. "Am I supposed to know what this means?"

"That's what I said when I first saw it," I said. "And then last night, I went to a party for Heather Pim, and I happened to see some rebus puzzles. And then it hit me."

"What?"

"Look at the glove," I said. "What do you see?"

Mike turned it over. "A lot of fake jewels."

"And?"

"Two letters—it looks like 'GG' "

"Exactly," I said. "Now look up at the street sign next to us."

I had slowed the car to a stop, and we were idling with the brake on.

Mike looked at the sign and then looked at me blankly.

"I don't get it. But then again, word puzzles aren't exactly my thing."

"It's not really a word puzzle," I replied. "It's just that the puzzles reminded me of this. The glove says 'GG,' and this street is Guinevere's Gauntlet. And that's a glove."

Mike looked down at the glove. "Oh." Then he looked up at the street sign. "Oh!"

"And there was a key inside the glove," I said.

Mike nodded. "I get it now. So you think that key unlocks something on this street."

"Yes."

"Do you know what it is?"

"I think it's one of these houses," I said. "But I don't know which one. But once we find the right one, I'm pretty sure I know what will be inside it."

"And what's that?"

I smiled. "Like I said, I'll tell you if I'm right."

I pulled the car over to the curb and then parked it.

"So why exactly did you bring me along?" Mike asked. "Did you want me to help you locate the right house?"

"No," I said. "I'll do that. I just wanted you along for the company."

After Mike stashed the box with the ring back in the glove compartment, we both got out of the car, and Mike handed me the key.

I glanced back at the car—I was a little nervous about leaving the ring in there—but I figured it was safer in there than it would be if I carried it around.

Then I glanced down at the key—as before, I admired the intricate scrollwork on the handle, but there were no markings of any kind to indicate what house or building it might belong to.

I looked at the grand houses that lined either side of the street known as Guinevere's Gauntlet.

I could hardly go from door to door, trying each lock to see if it fit.

That was probably a great way to get arrested.

Mike and I were standing at the corner of the street, and I glanced over at the street that came just before it.

"You know," I said to Mike, "the street right next to this one is Lancelot's Love Lane. I don't think that's a coincidence."

"Don't look at me," Mike said. "I'm just here to look pretty."

"That's not quite what I said."

"Well, I'll fill in for the eye-candy role anyway. And to show you I'm not just a pretty face, I'll ask a question—what does it mean if those two streets are near each other?"

"It means I may have an idea about which building this key goes to," I said.

"But you're not going to tell me which one, are you?"

"Let's just say, I saw it through Mr. Clementine's eyes."

I started down the street and walked past stately home after stately home with Mike in tow.

And then I saw the little cottage that I had glimpsed once through the small telescope in Mr. Clementine's office.

I now had a pretty good idea of what it was for.

I walked a little faster.

We soon drew in sight of the little cottage, and it was a pretty place.

It was dwarfed by its much bigger and grander neighbors, but it had a charm and an individuality that the cookie-cutter mansions that surrounded it lacked.

The cottage was made of white brick, and climbing roses in shades of light pink wound their way up trellises on either side of the bright yellow door, and a riot of sunflowers with yellow petals and brown faces populated the front lawn. A trail of flat, oval stones led up to the little house, and a sign by the front step read, "Model Home."

I turned up the stone path and hurried up to the door.

"Are you sure you want to go in here?" Mike said, coming up behind me. "These places are never very interesting."

"This one is different," I said.

"Oh?"

"Just look around you. Notice anything?"

Mike gave a deeply exasperated sigh. "Well, obviously this house is much smaller than the others, but—"

"But what?" I fitted the ornate key into the lock, and to my delight, it turned.

"Well, surely the model home has to be smaller than the others? If you built one the normal size, you'd be wasting a lot of space and real estate. The model is just here to give buyers a taste of what's possible."

"I'm sure that could be true," I replied. "And it makes a lot of sense. But I am equally sure of one other thing—this is *not* a model home."

I opened the door and went inside.

"Oh, no?" Mike said.

And I really couldn't blame him.

We were standing in a cheerful, sunny living room. There were chairs and sofas in shades of pale cream, and three seashells sat in a row on a pale wood coffee table.

The little living room looked in on a bright, cheery kitchen done in shades of yellow.

"But this has to be the place," I said. "There are sunflowers outside."

"And what does that mean?" Mike asked.

"He—Mr. Clementine—associated them with his late wife, Clytie. It's from the legend about Clytie and Apollo."

"Oh, I see," Mike said—and this time I could tell he really did. He was a professor of folklore after all. "But the idea of her turning into a sunflower didn't come about until later. In the earliest stories she became a—"

"Heliotrope. Yes, I told Mr. Clementine that once."

Mike smiled at me like I was a student who had pleased him.

"Yes—heliotrope. Very good."

I ignored the condescending look on his face—I knew he meant well.

Instead I simply continued.

"So this is his house for her—he was guarding it, protecting it. There's something here."

I continued on through the rest of the house—though there wasn't much of it. There was one small bathroom and two tiny bedrooms.

There appeared to be no more to the house.

"This can't be right," I said to Mike as we returned to the living room. "Does this look like a model home for a luxury development to you?"

"To be fair, it does not," he replied. "I would have expected more chandeliers and grand staircases. This looks more like a beach house."

"Yes, it does," I murmured. Then I spotted some photos on the wall.

I hurried over to them.

There were four of them—all of Clytie Clementine, looking movie-star beautiful as she frolicked on the beach with the sun behind her.

I glanced around. There were several more photos on the accent tables scattered around the room.

They were all of Clytie.

"No, I wasn't wrong," I breathed. "This was his house for her. Like I said, there was a reason the Lancelot and Guinevere streets were near each other. Clytie was Mr. Clementine's Guinevere—but she didn't leave him for Lancelot—she left him for the sun."

"Technically, Guinevere didn't leave Arthur," Mike interjected. "She just cheated on him—she still lived at the castle, though."

"It's close enough," I said. "Perhaps I should say she betrayed him for the sun. So he brought both of them back here."

"So—"

"So that means it *is* here—I just have to find it."

I looked down at the key in my hand.

Maybe it opened more than one door.

I began to go over every door in the house.

Mike followed me.

"I'd ask you what you were doing, but I know it wouldn't do any good."

I barely heard him as I continued to look—and then I found it.

It was a door in the living room that I'd overlooked—it had a hook on the back with a jacket and a net bag full of seashells hanging from it.

It looked like a closet—it was probably meant to.

I tried the door, but it was locked.

Then I fitted my key in the lock and it turned.

I opened the door and found a dark staircase leading down.

Mike peered over my shoulder. "Intriguing. Is this what you expected?"

"Not exactly," I said. "But I realize now that it makes more sense than having it on the main floor where anyone could see it from the window."

I flipped on the light and hurried downstairs.

Mike trundled down after me.

We found ourselves standing in a room full of screens. Images from all over the neighborhood flickered on rows and rows of monitors that sat above a long table that wrapped around most of the room. A single chair sat by one cluster of monitors.

Mike looked around.

"This is quite the surveillance setup."

He looked at me.

"You knew all this would be here?"

"It took me a little while to figure it out," I said. "But I remembered that Mr. Clementine had a small telescope in his office, and it seemed to be trained on this cottage. And then neither the police nor anyone who frequented his house knew where he kept all the footage that came from his many cameras. And then he'd left the glove and the key with his lawyer to give to me. He didn't leave any explanation, but maybe he thought it was obvious."

"So all of this was set up by Mr. Clementine?"

"Well, I imagine he had help, but for all intents and purposes, the answer to your question is yes. And it appears that he was the only one who came into this place."

I pointed to the single chair.

"So what did he use all this for?" Mike asked. "Was he spying on people?"

"I think he was trying to keep himself safe—though I did wonder about that myself when I first saw the telescope. But then I heard that he was afraid someone was after him—and it looks as if he was right."

"So why did you want to find this place?"

"I needed to get a look at that video footage."

I suited my words to my actions, and I pulled out the lone chair and seated myself in front of the banks of monitors.

"Wait," Mike said. "Aren't you going to call the police?"

"Oh." I was startled. "I hadn't thought of that." And it was true— I really hadn't. "I guess I'll call them later."

"Later?" Mike was stunned. "Chloe—"

"I'll call them, I promise. But I need to get a look at this first."

"Chloe, this is tampering with evidence."

"How is it tampering? I'm going to put everything back the way I found it. And I'm not going to erase anything. It's going to be fine."

"You're getting fingerprints all over everything for a start."

I paused and looked down at my hands. I was in the process of opening up a laptop I'd found, and my fingers had indeed been all over it.

"Can't be helped now," I said. "I've already done it."

"You could stop."

"No, I can't," I said stubbornly.

Mike sighed. "What are you looking for anyway?"

"I'm looking for the camera at the back of Mr. Clementine's house. And I'm looking for the day he died. I want to see if I can find footage of the person I saw running away from the house after we found the body."

I glanced up at the monitors. They were all labeled, and I had located the one at the back of Mr. Clementine's house. But that camera was currently showing what was happening at the house at this moment, and I didn't know how to rewind it—there was a panel in front of me with a dizzying array of controls and switches, and I was afraid to try anything.

Which was why I had turned to the laptop when I'd spotted it. It looked a lot like the one Marianne had showed me, and I could see a black box sitting nearby that I assumed was the missing server.

I wouldn't be able to figure out the video equipment any time soon, but I had a feeling that I could get the digital copies to work.

I powered on the laptop, and I was relieved to discover that there was no password on it—Mr. Clementine likely had never thought that anyone would use it but him.

And I had a feeling that even if the laptop had been password protected that I would have been able to figure it out.

I had a feeling that Mr. Clementine's obsession with his ex-wife, Clytie, extended to his taste in passwords.

"Well, that's really not a bad idea," Mike was saying. "If that person you spotted can be found on tape, that would be very valuable for the police. But I really think you should let them do that."

But I was already looking through the folders, and I was pleased to find that everything looked just like it had on Marianne's laptop—only this time I had access to everything.

I quickly clicked through to the camera at the back of Mr. Clementine's house.

Then I found the day he died.

I clicked on the video in that folder, and it began to play.

The footage began at midnight, however, so I fast-forwarded to later in the morning.

I kept going, in fact, until I saw a gray-clad figure running away from the camera. I quickly hit pause.

Then I caught my breath and clutched Mike's arm.

"That's it! That's the person I saw!"

I expected Mike to grumble a bit more about the police, but instead he leaned forward.

"There really is someone there," he murmured. "You really did see someone."

I glanced at him. Had he not believed me? But I didn't think that was it—instead he seemed to be simply astonished to see actual evidence in a murder case.

I rewound until we couldn't see the figure anymore, and then I kept rewinding.

I was looking to see when the figure had arrived.

Oddly enough, that proved hard to do, so I just rewound a full twenty minutes.

And then I watched.

I could soon see why I hadn't been able to see the figure's approach in rewind.

When I finally spotted the gray figure coming toward the house, it was at the far end of the camera's range of vision.

The figure had its head down, it was wearing a baseball cap and sunglasses—and it was wearing a surgical mask over its mouth.

Whoever it was, he or she didn't want to be seen.

The figure moved swiftly to the wall and then scaled it, moving out of the camera's range quickly.

About fifteen minutes later, the figure came back into the camera's view, moving down the side of the building swiftly and then running away across the back lawn.

The figure was clearly in a hurry to get away.

I leaned forward and squinted, but it was impossible to tell much of anything about the figure. It was someone tall with short blond hair—or possibly longer blond hair pinned up—wearing extremely baggy gray sweats and a baseball cap. I couldn't even tell if it was a man or a woman.

I sat back in my chair.

It was impossible to tell who it was.

Chapter Twenty-Four

Mike had to leave to get back to school—and he called a local ridesharing service since I'd driven—but before he left, he made me promise that I would call the police and let them know what I'd found.

He also pointed out that the police would probably have technology that would enable them to enhance the video—maybe they would be able to see something we couldn't.

But even though I agreed with Mike wholeheartedly, I felt like I needed to wait just a little bit.

I was sure I would be able to see something the police couldn't.

So I watched the video footage a few more times. According to the time stamp in the corner, the gray figure in the ball cap first appeared on the screen at eleven thirty-three and soon reached the wall and began to climb it. Then the figure reappeared at eleven forty-eight and began to run away.

That was plenty of time for someone to have cast that strangle spell and then left.

As the footage continued, I was pretty sure I was watching the killer run away.

But no matter how many times I watched the video, I couldn't figure out who it was.

This really was a matter for the police.

But I *still* had a feeling that I needed to wait just a little bit.

I shut down the laptop and put it away, and then I got out my phone.

I was going to dial Detective Mia.

But somehow I just couldn't.

I left the little cottage, and I locked it up again.

I would call the police—and soon.

But first I needed to talk to my other two tall, blond suspects—Mr. Clementine's sons, Christopher and Bobby.

And thanks to my internet searches, I knew just where to find them.

I got into my car and drove into town.

Christopher Clementine's office sat just down the street from Peter's Table—the restaurant owned by Alberta's possibly estranged boyfriend—and the restauranteur himself happened to be standing outside as I parked the car nearby.

As I got out of the car, I saw him throw something small and white onto the sidewalk.

Then he walked over to me.

Peter Gambelli was a tall, handsome man with thick black hair and an olive complexion, and a slight tendency to plumpness around the middle.

He turned large, sorrowful eyes on me.

"Good afternoon, Miss Chloe."

"Hi, Peter," I replied.

"It's been quite some time since you and your oh-so-charming sisters have patronized my establishment."

His tone was mournful, and I felt sorry for him. I missed seeing him—and I also missed his restaurant.

"So how have you—"

"It's your sister, isn't it?" Peter said suddenly. "The fiery and beautiful Alberta. She doesn't love me anymore, does she?"

"Oh, Peter," I said. "I really don't know—"

I stopped and looked over at the little white object he'd thrown to the side.

"Was that a cigarette?"

Peter looked shamefaced. "Yes."

"I didn't know you smoked. Isn't that bad for a chef? Doesn't it interfere with your palate?"

I stopped abruptly, realizing that it was actually none of my business.

But Peter didn't seem offended. Instead, his shoulders slumped, and he hung his head.

"You're right. I shouldn't be smoking. I gave it up years ago. But now that my heart hurts—now that I have lost the one I love, I find myself taking solace in it. I am ashamed."

"Peter, what happened between the two of you? Alberta won't tell me anything."

He shook his head and looked at me with eyes full of anguish.

"That's just it—I don't know. I have gone over that day many times in my head, trying to figure out what I did wrong, but I just cannot fathom it."

"What day?" I said.

"That fateful, rueful day—the last time my Alberta ever spoke to me."

"So what happened?"

Peter shook his head again. "I don't know—everything seemed to be going so well that night. She was happy, she was smiling—I always like to see her smiling. And then I said something about one of my competitors, I think. And then her face seemed to fall. She didn't look really unhappy—just a little disappointed. And then she never spoke to me again."

"That's it?" I said. "There was no big argument?"

"No."

"What did you say about your competitor?"

A look of shame crossed his face again. "I believe I said something disparaging."

"Do you know what?" I asked.

"I said I couldn't believe that they had the gall to try to compete with me. They had added something new to their menu—it was something that was a specialty of mine."

"Well, that doesn't seem like enough to—"

"That's it, though! It must be!" Peter suddenly cried. "I can think of nothing else. My poor, sweet Alberta, angel that she is, couldn't bear to hear me speak ill of another. I should have kept my opinions to myself. Then she would still be with me."

"You think Alberta's been avoiding you because you bad-mouthed a competitor?" I said doubtfully.

"Yes—Alberta is too high-minded and good to be able to tolerate such things."

I could think of more than a few times when Alberta had said some less-than-generous things about her colleagues and competitors.

But I decided to keep those examples to myself.

"And that's really all you can think of?" I said.

"Yes—I have racked my brains. I have been over everything."

Peter stepped toward me suddenly and took my hand. Along with him came the smell of cigarette smoke.

"Will you help me, dear Chloe? Will you help me win my Alberta back?"

"I will do what I can," I said, coughing a little. "I'll talk to her. But you have to promise me one thing."

"Anything. Name it."

"You have to give up smoking."

"I will do it!" Peter declared. "I will stop smoking. Soon my breath will be as pure as my heart. And my heart *is* pure because it belongs to the dearest, sweetest soul that has ever walked this earth."

I had my doubts about Alberta being quite that good, but I would certainly do my best to help Peter out—at the very least, I could try to find out what had really happened with Alberta.

Although it was entirely possible that nothing *had* happened.

Perhaps she had simply realized that she wasn't in love with him after all.

But that wasn't a possibility that I wanted to voice to Peter.

Fortunately, I was saved from further comment by a black-clad server who came out of the restaurant and beckoned to the owner.

Peter turned to me. "I must go, dear Chloe. But I feel a little lighter knowing that you will now advocate for me. You have given me a tiny ray of hope on an otherwise dark day."

He gave me a sad smile and turned to go into his restaurant.

I continued down the street past a yoga studio named Bodhi Yoga, and sure enough, I saw Bodhi himself through the large windows, leading a class.

He was dressed all in black with his blond hair in a man bun again, and I paused to watch as he set his hands on the floor and then placed his knees on his elbows.

His class, with varying levels of success, attempted to mimic his pose.

One of the people in the class, a woman dressed all in purple Lycra, glanced up at me.

I hurried along.

I soon reached Christopher Clementine's office, and the sign outside declared him to be an accountant, a fact I already knew from my internet research.

The building was small and unassuming, but this was a fashionable street, so I knew that Christopher had to be doing pretty well with his business.

Of course, "pretty well" was a far cry from the massive fortune that his father had had.

And if the stories were right, Christopher had been cut off from all of it.

Until now.

I stepped into the office and found myself in a small room with an empty desk.

A sign propped up on the edge of the desk read, "Out to Lunch— Be Back Soon," and an answering grumble in my stomach told me that it was indeed lunchtime.

I stood staring in disappointment at the sign for a moment, and then was just turning to go when I heard a rustle from the next room, and a man stepped out.

He was tallish and blond with bright blue eyes and a striking resemblance to the late Otis Clementine—right down to the cleft in his chin.

I'd noticed that he and his brother Bobby looked a lot like their father at the reading of the will, but I suddenly felt for just a second like I was looking at their father—I got a strong impression of a willful, powerful personality that wouldn't be denied. And as the man popped the last bit of a sandwich into his mouth, the impish smile on his face was uncannily like the one his father had worn whenever he'd been giving me a hard time about a library book.

The man wiped his hands on a napkin and then held one of them out to me.

I noticed that it had a strange blue stain on it.

I hesitated, and he pulled it back.

"Sorry," he said with that same impish grin, "I'm just finishing up lunch and my secretary's still out at the moment. I'm Christopher Clementine—how can I help you?"

I realized that once again, I hadn't really thought out my approach, and I found myself fumbling for words.

But before I could get out a full sentence, Christopher gave me a keen look that would have suited his father well.

"You're that librarian—the one who was at the reading of the will."

I didn't think it was worth explaining that I was actually a library assistant rather than a librarian, so I just plunged ahead and took the opening he gave me.

"Yes," I said. "Could I talk to you for a minute?"

A faintly puzzled look came into his eyes, but he nodded.

"Sure. We can talk in my office."

He led me into another small room with a desk and a lot of filing cabinets.

He waved me toward one of three guest chairs that looked as if they had seen better days and then sat down behind the desk himself.

I took a quick look around. There were quite a few pictures on the wall by the desk, and several of them showed two young blond boys—clearly Christopher and Bobby—with a middle-aged Otis Clementine and a blond woman who I assumed was the boys' mother.

There was also a large portrait which appeared to be a copy of the one that hung in the foyer at Mr. Clementine's palatial house—it showed the elder Mr. Clementine in all his youthful, leonine glory. And there were several photos of a raven-haired beauty, including one that sat in a prominent place on Christopher's desk.

The young woman had perfect hair and perfect makeup, and the sparklers in her ears would have made Heather Pim envious.

She looked like someone who might have very expensive tastes.

"She's beautiful," I said.

Christopher smiled. "Yes—that's Reina. We hope to be married someday, but right now we don't have enough, well, resources."

"And I recognize your dad, of course."

Christopher turned to look at the big painting on the wall, and then his attention seemed to fall on one of the family portraits with four people in it.

He stared at it for a long time, and a strange look came into his eyes.

I had a fancy that I recognized that look.

But somehow, I couldn't place it.

Christopher seemed to snap out of his daze, and he turned back to me.

"So how can I help you, Miss—"

"I'm Chloe—Chloe Bartlett."

"How can I help you, Chloe?"

Once again, I decided just to plunge ahead.

"I've heard you're in some financial trouble."

Christopher went very still.

"I beg your pardon?"

"I heard you argued with your father, and he disowned you."

Christopher's face flushed.

"That's not exactly what happened."

"So what did happen?"

Christopher shifted in his chair, and though he went on in a polite, professional tone, it was clear he was angry.

"Look—who are you? Are you a cop?"

"No, I—"

He interrupted. "No—of course you aren't. You were at the reading of the will as a representative of the library. Are you a librarian?"

"Well, no—"

"Then what are you doing here? What right do you have to ask me these questions?"

He stared at me, and I figured it was best to come clean—even if he didn't believe me.

I took a deep breath. "You see, your father—he sort of spoke to me—"

Christopher laughed suddenly, a short, sharp sound.

"I don't believe it—you're a PI."

"A what?"

"A private investigator. I should have known—I see enough of them here."

"I'm not," I said. "Like I was saying, your father came to me—"

Christopher chuckled—a real laugh this time.

"It's all right. I'm sure my father made you sign some kind of nondisclosure agreement. I suppose you're reporting to Lee Hurtzel?"

"I have spoken to him, yes, but I'm not—"

Christopher cut off my protestations.

"It's funny—you don't look like a private eye—or act like one."

I was startled. "What do you mean?"

Christopher smiled. "Your approach was decidedly amateurish."

I was a little irritated by this, but then I figured I might as well just go with it—I seemed to have stumbled on a way in.

"So you say I've got a hold of the wrong version of this story," I said. "In that case, why don't you tell me what really happened between you and your dad? It *is* true that you don't currently receive any of his fortune, isn't it?"

Christopher stared at me, and an angry, stubborn look came into his eyes. Then he seemed to grow resigned, and he sighed.

"I suppose you have to go into all of this," he said ruefully. "My dad suspected something before he died, didn't he?"

"Apparently he was in regular contact with the police," I said carefully.

"Well, to be honest, I don't have anything particularly spectacular to tell you. But I can tell you this—the press has got it wrong."

I waited patiently, and after a moment, he went on.

"We did argue—that is true. But not the way you think. And I did stop receiving money from him. Again, not for the reason you think."

"And what do I think?"

Christopher's rueful look was back. "You think we argued about money. You think I wanted more—and he said no. But that's not the way it was at all."

"So what *did* happen?" I said.

Christopher suddenly drew himself upright in his chair, and he looked very staid and proper.

He looked every inch the accountant.

"*I* told my father that I wanted to be independent. I told him that I didn't want his money anymore and that I wanted to make my own way in this world. I further told him that I didn't like the way he treated me—he acted like I was a pet he could just keep on a leash."

His chin trembled just a tiny bit.

"And then I told him that I didn't like the way he treated our mother. I told him that he should have married her. I believe in marriage, you see, and then—"

Though his chin trembled again, he somehow drew himself up even straighter.

"I was angry at that point—really angry—and I told him that his money was filthy and he was, too. And I wanted no part of either of them."

"I bet that went over well," I said dryly.

"That's just the thing," Christopher replied, sounding aggrieved. "He wasn't upset at all. He just kept laughing at me. He said a moralizing puritan like me would never be able to succeed in this world. He said I'd be back begging him for money in a week."

"And were you?"

"No, I was not. That was over a year ago. I'm proud to say that my business is doing quite well."

"Have you talked with your father since then?" I asked.

Christopher hesitated. "Not much."

"What did you say to each other when you did talk?"

"My father disparaged my business. He said I made peanuts. I suppose it is peanuts compared to what he made, but it's enough for me."

He glanced involuntarily at the picture of Reina on his desk.

"But I had no reason to kill him, if that's what you're asking. I'm quite happy the way I am."

"Then that wasn't you?" I said nonchalantly.

"What wasn't me?"

"The blond man who was seen leaving your father's house right around the time he was killed."

Christopher went very still.

"What do you mean?"

"A blond man about your height and weight was seen leaving your late father's house on the day he was killed—right around the time of the murder, as I said. Apparently, he entered and exited through a window."

I paused.

"We have the whole thing on tape."

The color drained from Christopher's face, and he pressed his lips together until they turned white.

After a moment, he looked up at me.

"You're bluffing."

"No, I'm not. I've seen the tape."

Christopher froze once again.

Then he swallowed.

"It's not what you think," he said.

"And what do I think?"

"I was there," Christopher said in a rush. "I saw my father—we argued again. But when I left, he was fine. I did sneak in there—but I didn't kill him."

"Why did you go there?" I asked.

"Just to talk."

"You couldn't talk on the phone? Or use the front door like a normal person?"

Christopher went white again. "I—I—"

He stopped and licked his lips—apparently his throat was dry.

"I did go to my father's office," he said at last. "But I didn't think he'd be in there. I went in there looking for something, and my father surprised me."

"What were you looking for?" I asked.

"A—a ring," Christopher said with a sideways glance at his girlfriend's picture. "My dad had a beautiful ring with two yellow diamonds and one big white one. It belonged to his first wife. I was going to find it and give it to Reina. I was going to use it to propose."

"You were going to steal it, you mean."

Christopher winced. "No—yes. I suppose so. I didn't really think of it that way at the time."

"So you sneaked into your dad's office looking for the ring, and when he found you, you quarreled and then you killed him."

"No!" Christopher cried. "No—that's not what happened. He found me, and we argued—he was ashamed of me—for—for stealing. Then I left. I ran—I wanted to get out of there as fast as possible. But he was still alive when I left."

Christopher stared hard at me, and there were tears brimming in his eyes.

"You have to believe me—he was fine. I swear to you when I left, he was still alive."

Chapter Twenty-Five

When I left Christopher Clementine's office, my head was spinning.

After the party with Heather, I'd been pretty sure she was the person who I'd seen running away across Mr. Clementine's back lawn.

But now I wasn't so sure.

After all, Christopher had just confessed—a turn of events which had really startled me.

I'd said I'd seen a "man" when I was questioning him rather than a person because I thought there was an outside chance he might have known about Heather's visit and the use of the word might startle him into a reaction. Then, too, I'd also thought there was an outside chance that the figure in gray had been Christopher himself, and my use of that specific term might shake him up.

And did it ever.

I stood for a moment on the sidewalk as the image in my mind began to change and shift—and grow.

But it was still hazy, and I still had another person to grill.

So far two suspects had had strong reactions to the mention of the fleeing figure in gray.

I wondered if Bobby Clementine would make that a third.

I started toward my car, and I passed Bodhi's studio once again.

This time Bodhi was standing in the tiny parking lot that nestled against his studio, and once again, he was tinkering with that same white car and swearing.

I paused for a moment to watch him, and then a glint of light overhead caught my eye, and I looked up.

The amethyst medallion Bodhi had been wearing when I'd first met him was hanging in a window above the studio, catching the sun's rays.

I wondered if he lived above the studio, and I wondered why he had hung the medallion in the window.

Something about it struck me as malevolent.

Bodhi swore again, and I hurried to my car.

As I drove off, I told myself that I was being silly—there was no reason for me to be worried about Bodhi, and in fact, I didn't even know what I was worrying about. It wasn't a crime to be upset with a malfunctioning car—that was actually perfectly normal. And anyway, I knew my sister wouldn't be dating him if he were a bad person.

But somehow those rationalizations didn't satisfy me, and I began to feel goosebumps rising on my arms as I drove along.

I told myself that was just the air-conditioning.

I soon reached my destination—it was a sports bar owned by Bobby Clementine, which was called, appropriately enough, The Sports Bar.

I couldn't help thinking that the name showed a certain lack of imagination.

But according to my research online, Bobby spent quite a bit of time there. I'd also learned that even though he was the owner, he didn't have much to do with the day-to-day running of the place—that was done by a manager, who, by all reports, did an excellent job. Bobby mostly drank and socialized all day—and all night.

The Sports Bar was located in a neighborhood that was verging on the old section of downtown, which was very exclusive.

So Bobby, like his brother, was doing pretty well for himself.

But Bobby hadn't given up his father's money.

There were vague rumors, though, that the bar wasn't doing as well as it appeared to be—that it was actually losing money and was being propped up by funds provided by Bobby's father.

There were further rumors that someone—possibly the manager, but more likely Bobby himself—was skimming money off the top, and that was the real reason for the bar's money troubles.

Bobby, though he had just turned thirty, was very dependent on his father for money.

He was, as his brother had said, like a pet on a leash.

Luckily, since the bar was adjacent to the old section, but not actually in it, there was still a decent-sized parking lot, and I was able to find a spot.

The building itself was white stucco with a green-shingled roof, and I could see TV screens tuned to various sports channels.

I went inside.

It was the tail end of the lunch hour, but there was still a pretty good-sized crowd inside The Sports Bar.

There were people with beers at the bar staring up at the TV screens—most had sports news shows on, but one was broadcasting a baseball game that appeared to be live.

There were also booths and tables where people sat having lunch—The Sports Bar was really more of a bar and grill than just a bar.

I could smell french fries, and my stomach grumbled just a bit.

In all my investigating zeal, I had forgotten to eat lunch.

I glanced around the room, and I soon spotted Bobby Clementine at the corner of the bar with what looked like a martini.

He was staring up at the TVs, and even though I was suddenly acutely aware of him, he seemed to have no idea that he was being watched.

He took a casual sip of his martini, and I paused before I approached him.

This time I was going to have a plan before I started questioning him.

Surprise had worked for me before, so I was going to try it again.

I walked over to the bar, and I sat down in the empty spot next to him.

"Hi, Bobby," I said. "Do you remember me?"

He turned in his chair and threw a lazy look my way.

"No, I don't. Should I?"

Bobby, like his brother, looked a lot like a blond version of his father. He had the same strong chin with a cleft in it, and he gave off an aura of strength and power. But also like his brother, that strength of personality didn't seem to have been channeled in the same direction as his father's. While Otis Clementine had used his energy to build an empire, Bobby Clementine seemed to have channeled his into having fun.

He was every inch the hedonist from the toes of his expensive loafers to the top of his well-coifed head.

"Think back," I said. "You might remember me after all—I was at the reading of your father's will."

Bobby lounged back against the bar and looked me over.

He was wearing a plain white shirt and khakis, but something about them screamed expense, as did the large gold watch that glinted on his wrist.

He gave me an insolent smile.

"No, sorry. I don't remember you at all. I suppose because my father threw you a few dollars, you think that gives you an in?"

Bobby's superior tone stung, and I frowned.

So far this wasn't going the way I'd hoped at all.

Bobby turned back around on his stool and resumed watching TV.

"This isn't what you think," I said. "Your father didn't give me any money. Actually, he gave the money to the library I work for."

Bobby turned on his stool and stared at me in shock.

"You're a librarian? You've got to be kidding me."

"Well, no," I said. "I'm not a librarian exactly, but I do—"

"Honey," Bobby said. "You are *not* my type."

He jabbed a finger at the nearest TV screen where a beautiful model was cavorting on a beach in a beer commercial.

"*That* is my type. Glamorous is my type. I would never—and I do mean *never*—date a librarian."

I felt my temper flare. "I'm not interested in dating you. And just so you know, you're not my type, either. I'm not interested in narcissistic, empty-headed pretty boys with inflated egos."

Bobby turned back to me and smiled—a real smile this time.

"Maybe you might be worth talking to after all. You're cute enough in a buttoned-up kind of way, and it's still several hours till happy hour. I've got some time to kill."

I felt my temper still simmering, but I'd finally gotten through to Bobby, and I figured this was about as polite as he was likely to get.

"So," I said, trying for the element of surprise again, "I'm here to ask you about your father's murder."

Bobby's eyebrows rose. "A librarian detective? I have to say, I've never heard of one of those."

"No, I'm not—"

"You know what you should have done, though? You should have come in here wearing glasses with your hair in a bun. Then you could take off the glasses and shake out your hair and look all sultry. You should also have worn a trench coat—"

"Bobby!" I said sharply. "This is serious. Your father's been murdered, and you're a suspect."

He glanced around uneasily and gave me another appraising look. His eyes grew wary.

"So is this what the police call a friendly chat?"

"You could say that."

"Well, I've had enough of those lately. But I'll play along. What do you want to know?"

"Where were you last Wednesday afternoon between eleven thirty and eleven forty-five a.m.?"

Bobby grinned wryly.

"You get right to it, don't you?"

I waited, and after a moment, he went on.

"As it so happens, I was right here in my own establishment. Ask anyone—they'll tell you."

"I'll bet they would." It was my turn to smile wryly. "As you said, this is your place. And what employee would deny their boss an alibi?"

Bobby shot me a glance. "Just what are you implying?"

It might have been my imagination, but I thought I detected a note of unease in his voice.

"A tall, blond man was seen scaling the wall of your father's house. Shortly thereafter, he was seen climbing down that same wall and running away across the lawn. And it just so happens that this was right around the time your father was murdered."

I paused.

"And we have the whole thing on tape."

Bobby stared at me.

All the color had drained out of his face.

He sat very still for a long time.

"Bobby?" I said.

After a moment, he stirred—it was as if he had come out of a trance.

"Should you be telling people these things?" he said lightly.

But even though his tone was light, there was an edge of censure and disapproval in it, and I winced on the inside.

He was right, of course, I shouldn't have been giving away information to a suspect—but I'd been hoping for a reaction, and I'd gotten one.

But it was a bit hard to decipher under all the arrogance.

One thing was certain, however.

Bobby could have given even Mike lessons in the superiority department.

He was staring at me now, his eyes half closed.

"I think I do remember you—you were sitting down at the other end. What's your name, by the way?"

"It's Chloe Bartlett." I didn't really want to tell him, but I supposed I owed him that.

"Yes, Chloe," he said. "It was just a little hard to notice things over the sound of my stepmother screeching for joy."

He gave me a grin. "Oh—sorry. She's not my stepmother—she's just my father's much younger girlfriend who had his baby, who is now my half sibling, nearly thirty years my junior."

He grinned again.

If he was trying to make me uncomfortable, it wasn't going to work.

"Would it interest you to know that your brother confessed?" I said.

The smile froze on Bobby's face.

"What?"

"Your brother—your full brother, that is—confessed to being the individual who climbed up into your father's office."

Bobby stared at me, stunned.

"You mean Christopher?"

"Of course I mean Christopher."

Bobby shook his head.

"That's not possible."

"But it *is* possible," I said. "I heard him say so myself."

Bobby stared at me again.

Then he made a tiny movement—so tiny as to be almost imperceptible.

Then he smiled and leaned back, his eyes hooded once again.

"If I were you, I wouldn't put too much stock in what my brother said."

"Why not?"

"My brother's what you might call chivalrous."

"And what does that mean?" I said.

Bobby leaned forward. "Did it ever occur to you that the blond figure you saw *wasn't* a man?"

It had, of course, but I wanted to see where Bobby would go with this.

"What do you mean?" I said again.

"You didn't see a face, right? Otherwise, you wouldn't be here questioning me. And you wouldn't have needed my brother to confess."

"That's very logical of you," I said. "So what are you proposing?"

"It was my stepmother," Bobby said firmly. "That is, my wannabe stepmother. My father's girlfriend."

"Heather Pim?"

"Yes—she's the one. That rock-climbing rhinoceros. I'm sure she scaled that wall like it was nothing."

"Rhinoceros?" I said. "Rhinos can't climb—"

"Have you seen her hands? She's a beast, I tell you, an absolute beast."

I noticed that Bobby had his father's way with an insult, but I pushed that thought aside.

"So what does that have to do with Christopher?"

Bobby leaned even closer, and this time he tapped me on the knee.

"Don't you see? Christopher is covering for Heather. He told you he did it, but it was really her."

"And why would he do that?" I asked.

"He's trying to protect her. He's taking the blame for her. He's chivalrous, like I said. He has all these high-minded, moral ideas."

"But why—"

Bobby interrupted. "Because he's a good guy. That's why."

"How did he know?" I said.

Bobby looked at me, startled. "What?"

"How did he know it was Heather?"

Bobby continued to stare at me, and he looked stricken.

He couldn't seem to think of anything to say.

I waited.

"He must have figured it out," he said at last. "Christopher's good like that—he's smart."

"So let me see if I understand what you're saying," I said. "You think Christopher is protecting Heather Pim—but she's actually the one who climbed up to your father's office?"

"Yes."

"And then she killed him?"

Bobby blanched. "What? No—I never said that."

"But surely she must have," I said. "That's why I'm looking for this mysterious wall-climber. He—or she—is a suspect in the murder. So you're automatically implicating her."

"No—"

"Then what do you think happened?"

Bobby didn't reply right away.

"I think," he said slowly, "that maybe she went up there to talk to him. Maybe he just wouldn't listen any other way. So she had to sneak into the house. And then when she got there—they argued. When she saw she wasn't getting anywhere, she left."

I watched his face as he spoke.

"That's basically what Christopher said—with one minor addition. He said the argument was over a ring."

Bobby seemed relieved. "See? I told you Christopher was smart. He figured this all out, and he did it to protect her."

"There's no chance it was you?"

"No. Absolutely not. Scout's honor."

"You were a Boy Scout?"

"Once, a long time ago."

"So, if it wasn't Heather who killed him," I said, "or whoever the mysterious blond visitor was, then who was it?"

Bobby shrugged, completely at ease once again. "I don't know. You tell me."

But I was suddenly out of ideas—and I had a feeling that Bobby had told me everything he was going to tell me.

And then he suddenly leaned forward.

"But I do remember one thing Dad said. He said he was going to a place called the Midnight Market."

"The what?" I said.

"The Midnight Market. It's some kind of meeting of black-market dealers. I imagine he met some really shady characters if he went."

"Why would he go there?"

Bobby's lips twisted into a bitter smile.

"He was looking for Brian, his lost golden boy. Apparently, Christopher and I weren't good enough for him."

I frowned. "How would going to this market help him? Hasn't he been looking for Brian for years?"

"Yes—but this place was supposed to be special."

"How?"

Bobby lowered his voice.

"It was supposed to be magical. He was looking for a spell."

"A spell?" I said. A thrill of shock ran through me.

"I know—it sounds incredible. But it's true. He was looking for a spell that could help him find Brian. But you know what I think?"

"What?"

"I think he found a lot more than he bargained for."

Chapter Twenty-Six

Not long after that, I left The Sports Bar, and I left Bobby Clementine to his martini.

I began to walk toward my car and then stopped where I was on the sidewalk out front.

Ideas were churning in my head, like shoots from a seed pushing their way through the soil.

I hadn't told Bobby that his father had been killed by magical means, and yet he had volunteered that as a possibility—even though he himself seemed to think the idea was on the wild and fantastical side.

Bobby seemed to genuinely believe in the Midnight Market and to believe that spells could actually be purchased there, although there was a distinct possibility that Bobby knew this because he himself had purchased a spell from it and used it to finish off his father.

But it was also possible that he hadn't, and he still believed in the market anyway.

However, Bobby had had no idea where it was located—or if it even had a fixed abode—and no amount of questioning on my part could elicit a different answer.

He stuck very firmly to his claim that he was entirely ignorant of where it might be found.

He also said that his father had spoken about visiting it right before he died.

I knew it was theoretically possible to mix up a magical "packet" that a nonmagical person could use—sort of like a spell in a box.

But I'd never heard of anyone doing that, and I couldn't imagine an entire market made up of spells for the nonmagical.

And if such a thing did exist, how was it possible that my family didn't know about it?

A voice broke into my reverie.

"You've got to be kidding me."

I looked up to see a familiar figure.

It was Detective Ortiz.

He stared at me through red-rimmed eyes, and his nose was equally red.

As he continued to stare, he brought out a tissue and dabbed at his sore appendage gingerly.

He clearly wasn't over the flu yet.

And he clearly hadn't gotten over his anger with me yet.

His eyes flashed, and his lips were pressed into a thin line—even his beard seemed angry.

"Detective Ortiz," I said, a little startled. "I'm surprised to see you. Shouldn't you be at home resting?"

"And I'm surprised to see you," he replied. "Though I suppose I really shouldn't be. I can't believe you're—"

His face had gone very red—but he suddenly stopped himself and took several deep breaths.

His color slowly went down, and after a moment, he actually smiled at me.

"I'm sorry, Miss Bartlett. I must apologize to you. I've been pretty horrible to you since I met you, haven't I?"

The word "yes" was hovering on my lips, but I didn't want to be rude—and besides, it seemed as if the detective was trying to be nice.

"That's quite all right," I said. "You were just doing your job."

Detective Ortiz glanced over at The Sports Bar.

"Speaking of doing my job, I'm here to talk to Bobby Clementine. Is there any chance that's what you were here doing?"

I felt myself coloring.

"Uh, yes," I said slowly.

Anger flashed in Detective Ortiz's eyes again.

Then as quickly as it had come, it was gone.

"Miss Bartlett," he said with an obvious attempt at composure, "this is exactly what I'm talking about."

"And what were you talking about? I don't think you said."

"I'm talking about your visiting Marianne Mozer," Detective Ortiz said with an air of forced patience. "And Daphne Minton. And asking a lot of questions about the murder of Otis Clementine. And now you're here."

"Oh," I said, coloring again. I'd had a feeling that's where he was headed. "So you know about that?"

"Yes. And do you know what's wrong with all your visiting?"

"You ... think I'm interfering?" I said.

Detective Ortiz smiled, but the smile didn't reach his eyes.

"Exactly, Miss Bartlett. I think you're interfering. In fact, I know you're interfering. And I'm going to have to ask you to stop. Please, please, leave the investigating to the professionals."

He gave me a stern look—which I supposed was meant to impress on me the importance of his request—but I just made a few noncommittal sounds in response.

"I'm sorry," he said. "What was that?"

"I said, I'll do my best to stay out of your way."

Detective Ortiz gave me another long stare.

"That's not good enough. This needs to stop. *Today.*"

He wagged a finger at me and then walked off as if he'd won an argument.

I watched his retreating back, and I resisted the urge to stick my tongue out at him.

He was, after all, a duly sworn officer of the law.

And it was just as well that I decided against it because Detective Ortiz abruptly swung back.

"Oh, and Miss Bartlett?"

"Yes?"

"I've already been to visit Christopher Clementine this morning. But I'll be extremely disappointed later on if I hear that you've gone to visit him, too. So do us both a favor and stay away from him. Understand?"

He turned again and walked off with the air of someone who'd just won a great victory, and I permitted myself a secret smile.

His parting shot was just a little too late.

I hurried to my car and headed for home.

The afternoon was wearing away, and I figured I'd done enough investigating for one day.

Now I needed to digest what I'd learned.

And speaking of digestion, I hadn't eaten lunch, so when I arrived home, I made myself an extra cheesy grilled cheese sandwich and a bowl of tomato soup.

As I ate, the patterns and shapes in my mind kept shifting and changing.

An image was definitely emerging, but it was still hazy, and pieces of it were missing.

I just had to keep looking until I found all the pieces.

After lunch, I thought about calling Mike, just to see what he was up to.

But then I decided that talking to him might be too much of a distraction—and I needed to let the picture in my mind grow undisturbed.

So I reluctantly put my phone away, and I went upstairs to look at the spellbooks I'd brought home from my parents' house.

I was wondering if there was a spell that might help clarify my thoughts.

But I supposed that was what divination was for, and unlike Alberta, I didn't know how to do that.

So I opened the *Great Grimoire* book again, and when a second perusal didn't turn up anything I could use, I looked up the unlock spell from that same book to use on the old-fashioned hinge lock that bound the *Big Book of Spells*.

I'd unlocked it once before, but it had locked itself up again.

I cast the spell, and to my delight, the lock sprang open once more, and I could leaf through the pages freely.

This book began with a warning, just as *A Cauldron Full of Spells* had done—it cautioned the reader to be very wary of casting hexes or curses.

It warned that such a spell—powered by dark magic—could potentially rebound on the user—especially when being cast by a new magic user or fledgling witch.

Not having much experience with curses myself, I wondered if that was true, or if it was simply meant to deter young witches from casting curses on each other when they were just learning.

I could easily imagine two little witches getting mad at each other and casting curses when they really didn't mean any harm—so a warning was probably in order.

I could also understand why a book containing such things would need a lock.

And the *Big Book of Spells* did indeed have a long list of curses and hexes.

I flipped past those quickly.

I was looking at a reveal spell, which I thought might be useful, when I heard my phone buzzing.

I fished it out of my purse and found a text from Alberta.

She said she wasn't going to be home for dinner, and she probably wouldn't be home until after I had gone to bed.

I felt a twinge of disappointment.

I'd been looking forward to some company—and I'd even been hoping to bounce a few ideas off her, despite the fact that I knew she wouldn't approve and would protest the whole time.

I turned back to my book, and I realized that the reveal spell I was looking at wouldn't help me with clarifying the images in my mind—it was actually a reveal magic spell, and it could be used to reveal magic that was hiding. It was, in fact, nearly identical to the reveal spell that I'd already seen in the *Great Grimoire* book—it was just that the summary above the spell had somehow led me to expect something different.

I decided to give up on my research for the moment and get to work on dinner instead.

I'd always wondered what chicken cacciatore was, and I decided to look up a recipe on my phone.

It seemed like we had all the ingredients on hand, so while Sibyl feasted on crunchies in the kitchen, I got out peppers, onions, and cooking wine, and then dredged some chicken breast that Alberta had just purchased in flour and got cooking.

I figured Alberta wouldn't mind too much.

And besides, whatever she had planned to do with it, it probably wouldn't have been pretty.

I ate dinner at the kitchen table with Sibyl sitting near my feet, purring contentedly.

After dinner, I gave her a little piece of unbreaded chicken breast that I had saved for her, and she purred even louder.

Then I packed up the rest of the chicken cacciatore and put it in the refrigerator, and I left Alberta a note to let her know it was in there.

Then I went up to my room.

I had just settled on my bed with the big spellbook again when my mother called.

I picked up my phone.

"Hey, Mom."

"Chloe?" Maura said. She sounded rushed and worried.

"I'm here. What's wrong?"

"Someone cast a glamour, Chloe. Is everything all right?"

"Yes," I said. "Everything is fine. I cast that glamour myself. Don't worry—nothing really happened." I paused. "How did you know it was me, by the way?"

"I don't think it was you," Maura said.

"Sure it was. I cast it last night."

"See—that's exactly what I mean. This glamour wasn't cast last night. It was cast last week—I only just found out about it. I'm still using my jerry-rigged reporting system, and it can take days to get proper results."

I shifted uneasily. "So why are you calling me? I assume you called me first and not Alberta or Rafaela."

"Well, honey, it seemed more likely that you would be mixed up in something, shall we say—unusual—than your sisters would be. Especially since you seem to be determined to involve yourself in the search for Mr. Clementine's murderer—even though both Alberta and I advised you to stay out of it."

"Mom—"

"Now, Chloe, it's no use your protesting. You would be better off staying out of everything and letting the police get on with the investigation. But that is neither here nor there at the moment. What I'm most interested in is this glamour. Are you really all right? Did anything strange happen that you need to tell me about?"

I thought back. "Nothing comes to mind."

"Nothing strange?"

"Not really—at least, nothing's been any stranger than usual."

"Think carefully," Maura said. "I should tell you that this wasn't a normal glamour."

"What do you mean?"

"This glamour was much fainter—and rarer. It didn't show up as strongly as it should have. That tells me one thing—this wasn't a visual glamour."

I was puzzled. "What other kind is there?"

Maura sighed—not so much in exasperation, but as if she were puzzled herself.

"As you know," she said, "you can use a glamour to look like someone else, right?"

"Right."

"And you can also use a glamour to make one object look like another—for example, you could make a chair look like a table or vice versa."

"That is also true," I said.

"So a glamour typically affects your vision—your sight. And it does just a little with your sense of touch, too, depending on the skill of the spellcaster. You can create an illusion of 'feel,' too, to go with your new appearance. If you're someone who's very slender, and you're impersonating someone bigger and more robust, you can create a field around you that makes you feel to the touch as if you've got a bigger body. And the same is true in reverse."

"So what are you saying?" I asked. "Did someone cast a glamour that only affects touch and not sight?"

"Not quite," Maura said. "But you're on the right track. What I'm saying is that a glamour can be cast that affects any or all of the five senses. You can create a visual glamour or a touch glamour. But you can also create a glamour that affects hearing, taste, or smell."

I wrinkled my nose. "Who would want to create a smell glamour?"

"Someone who wants to brew a powerful potion and wants to keep the scent hidden. Or someone who's selling a so-so love potion—an infatuation potion, really—and wants to have a more enticing aroma for it in order to attract buyers. Maybe even someone who wants their cooking to smell more delicious than it is."

I very nearly made a quip about Alberta, but I quelled it just in time.

"So you think one of these other glamours has been cast?"

"Yes."

"Which one?"

Maura paused. "I don't know. I'm getting some indications that the spell was cast clumsily—so that might leave some kind of mark on the surrounding area. I really need to be there—in fact, there's a book in our house called the *Big Book of Spells*—"

"I've got it right here," I said, interrupting.

"You do?" Maura sounded surprised.

"Yes—I stopped by the house and picked it up—along with a few other books."

Maura chuckled. "Thought you'd do a little light reading?"

"Something like that," I said.

"Well, whatever you're up to, the answer to this glamour is likely in there. Read through the section on glamours, and if you see anything that looks familiar—maybe something you've seen around town—give me a call and we'll go over it together."

Maura stopped, and she seemed to be thinking something over.

"Now, honey, I don't want you to get frustrated, but there is a lock on that book, and it can only be opened with an unlock spell. I know you aren't always good with basic spells—"

"Mom," I said, "it's okay. I've opened the lock already—I found the unlock spell in one of your *Great Grimoire* books."

"Oh, Chloe!" Maura exclaimed. "That's wonderful! Good for you! I always said you had a lot of talent and you just needed to harness it— to believe in yourself—"

She stopped abruptly.

"Of course, in this particular case, you really should be letting the police get on with their work, but I don't think there's any harm in your looking into this glamour."

"Why not?" I said. "Don't you think it's related to the murder?"

"Oh!" Maura sounded surprised, and I could picture her blue eyes opening wide. "I hadn't really thought about that. I was mostly worried about its possible effect on *you*." She paused. "I take it you *do* think they're related?"

"When was the glamour cast?" I asked.

"Give me a minute. Let me just look over everything." Maura was silent for a moment. "Near as I can tell, it was cast last Wednesday."

"That was the day of the murder," I said. "In that case, I do think they're related."

"Of course, I could be off by a day one way or the other."

"I have a terrible feeling you aren't."

Maura sighed. "I have a terrible feeling you're right. Oh, honey, just read up on the glamours, and then give me a call. We'll figure out what it was together. And try not to do anything rash in the meantime."

"I'll do my best," I said.

But my mind was already spinning.

My mother had given me another clue, and I couldn't wait to follow it up.

"Well, don't stay up too late, Chloe," Maura said. "You have work in the morning, after all."

I had to smile. "How is it that you remember my work schedule? My hours are a bit irregular."

"I'm your mother, dear—it's a very old habit. Now don't worry—all will be revealed. We just have to put our heads together. And don't forget to call me."

"I won't."

"And if you need to call again tonight, you can."

"Thanks, Mom."

"Good night, honey."

"Good night."

After we both hung up, I lugged the *Big Book of Spells* onto my lap again and began to read.

The section on glamours was fairly lengthy, but the gist of it was this: glamours, just like other spells, derived from one—or sometimes two or more—of the four elements. The most common type, the visual glamour with elements of a touch glamour, came from earth. An auditory—or hearing—glamour derived from water and air. A full-blown touch glamour—one that really made one person feel like another—derived from earth and fire. A taste glamour derived from earth and water, and a smell glamour derived from air.

And a glamour that wasn't cast properly could cause a disturbance in any of the elements related to it.

So that was what I had to look for—a localized disturbance in any of the four elements could point to the type of glamour that had been cast.

After all, my mom had said that she thought the spell had been clumsily done.

As I looked over the list of glamours again, I could see why the visual one was cast most often—first, it was the most useful. And second, aside from the smell glamour, the visual was the only one that derived from one element alone and didn't require two.

Most witches stuck pretty firmly to their strongest element and didn't really work on developing the others.

As I continued reading, and my eye landed on the word "air," an image of the vaguely question-mark-shaped pink cloud that hung over Mr. Clementine's house popped into my head.

The cloud was definitely a disturbance in the air, as it actually hung in the atmosphere.

But somehow I couldn't see a smell glamour being useful to the person who had killed Mr. Clementine.

However, a cloud wasn't just made up of air—it was also composed of water droplets.

So a strange cloud in the sky—that wouldn't go away—was water and air.

It was a hearing glamour.

I was puzzled for a moment, and then it hit me.

There could have been a struggle when Mr. Clementine was killed with the strangle spell.

And a hearing glamour could have been used to cover up the sounds.

As I thought about the spell hiding the struggle, I felt a tug on my mind, and a few words floated through my head—words spoken by my mother and Rafaela recently.

Reveal … find … locate.

It suddenly occurred to me that I might be able to use the reveal spell I'd found to locate the witch in the woods.

I could use the spell to peel back her magic and find just where in the Old Forest she was hiding.

And maybe she could lead me to the Midnight Market.

Maybe she was even part of it.

Suddenly, there was a bounce on my bed, and I looked up, startled.

Sibyl had jumped up beside me, and she now had a thick, little white beard extending from her furry black chin, and two little white tufts like eyebrows over her amber eyes.

She looked even more like a little Santa Claus than she had when she'd gotten some dust bunny wisps on her face.

I peered closer.

This time her beard and eyebrows appeared to be made out of a thick paste—it looked like frosting.

"Sibyl," I said, "what have you got on your face?"

As if in answer, she turned and ran from the room.

I pushed the heavy spellbook to the side and went after her.

She ran nimbly down the stairs and then sped off to the kitchen.

I hurried after her and was just in time to see her disappear through the door of the pantry, which was standing open.

"Sibyl, stop!" I said, though I knew it was pointless. The pantry was full of shelves with heavy cans and jars—not to mention enormous sacks of flour. There were lots of things that could get knocked over and hurt Sibyl, and it was also the place where Alberta kept her latest baking experiments—things that she wasn't quite ready to have anyone taste yet.

There were a lot of ways a cat could get into mischief in the pantry—as evinced by her current frosting beard—and we usually kept the door firmly closed.

And as a result, Sibyl was often desperate to get inside it.

"Sibyl!" I said as I hurried into the pantry after her.

But as soon as I stepped in, I stopped in shock.

The pantry was completely full of cupcakes.

There were chocolate cupcakes with white frosting as far as the eye could see—there were easily two hundred of them, if not more. As I walked past the rows of cupcakes, I found dozens of cakes beyond them—all decorated in frosting of varying colors—white, pink, yellow—even red. And at the end of the cakes were dozens of loaves of bread—all of them with little bits of green in them.

I lifted the plastic cling film off one of the loaves of bread, and I caught the unmistakable aroma of pickles.

Alberta *had* said she'd been craving pickle bread lately.

Sibyl gave a tiny mew, and I looked down at her.

"That must have been some craving she had."

Chapter Twenty-Seven

I did indeed call my mom that night as she had asked, and she agreed with me that the strangely shaped pink cloud was likely the sign of a clumsily cast hearing-based glamour.

She also agreed that it was theoretically possible for a spell to be "boxed up" and given to a nonmagical person to use—and that would certainly explain the clumsiness.

She hadn't, however, heard of the Midnight Market, and I could tell that she doubted its existence.

My mother believed that the market—like the witch in the woods—couldn't exist in our town without her knowledge.

I wasn't so sure.

Of course, it was entirely possible that some unknown magic worker was actually responsible for Mr. Clementine's death.

But my three main suspects—Heather, Christopher, and Bobby—didn't appear to have any magical abilities.

And while it was possible for them to be cleverly hiding it, somehow I really doubted that.

If any of them were to cast a spell, they'd certainly need a lot of help.

And I really did believe any of the three could have done it. Heather was certainly strong enough to have climbed up to Mr. Clementine's window, and Christopher had actually confessed to it—

the climbing, at least, though not to the murder. And Bobby hadn't confessed to anything, but he appeared sporty and athletic and seemed to be capable of doing the climbing himself.

And while it was possible that Christopher was covering for Heather as Bobby had claimed, it was also possible that Christopher was actually covering for Bobby.

All three were capable, and all three had a motive.

And it seemed to me that the fastest way to find out which one it was, was to find out if a hearing glamour or a strangle spell had been sold at the Midnight Market.

And the only lead I had on *that* was the witch in the woods.

I had to find her.

Naturally, I hadn't told my mother about that, but I had a feeling she suspected I might be up to something like that—especially since she told me several times not to do anything rash.

She also told me that now that we had identified the glamour and the accompanying disturbance, that I should just keep an eye on it—from a distance, of course.

It wasn't an immediate threat to me or my sisters.

My mom had great faith in the police, and I did, too.

I just knew that this time, I had knowledge that they lacked.

After I finished talking with my mother, I sat up and waited for Alberta—I really needed to ask her what she planned to do with all those baked goods in the pantry downstairs.

But time passed, and Alberta didn't show up.

And before I knew it, I fell asleep.

I awoke in the early morning to hear someone clattering around downstairs.

I hurried to get downstairs myself, and I made it down just in time to see the front door closing.

I wasn't quite dressed yet, so I scrambled for a jacket, and by the time I made it outside, Alberta was already taking off down the road.

I had just missed her.

I turned back to the house, and as I did so, I tripped over the copy of *The Morning Cider* that was sitting on the step.

I nudged it to the side and went inside, grumbling to myself.

There were still a few doughnuts left from the other day, so I had a chocolate doughnut and a glass of milk for breakfast, and then I rounded it off with an orange.

Alberta always thought it was weird when I had milk with an orange, but I didn't have a problem with the difference in tastes, and the lingering chocolate from the doughnut gave it a nice chocolate-and-orange flavor.

Sibyl sat beside me in the kitchen, washing her face with her paw, all traces of the frosting from last night long gone.

I glanced toward the pantry.

Part of me wanted to check to see if all of the cupcakes, cakes, and loaves of bread were still there, but the other part was more worried that it would all be gone.

It was far too much for Alberta to have taken into the office—she only worked with about twelve people—and it was also far too much even if she were participating in a bake sale.

If I went in and found it gone, I was more than a little afraid that that would mean she'd eaten it all.

I put my dishes in the dishwasher and then gave Sibyl an affectionate pat on the head.

Then I hurried to finish getting ready.

I was up way earlier than usual, and I still had several hours before I had to be at work.

I would go out to the Old Forest and see if I could finally find the witch in the woods.

This time I was determined—and I wouldn't leave until I found her.

Even if that meant that I had to skip work to do it.

As I stepped outside, I tripped over the paper again, and this time I picked it up in irritation and prepared to toss it into the house.

But a headline on the front page made me pause in shock.

Heather Pim had been in a car accident.

And the police were investigating it as attempted murder.

Apparently, her brakes had been tampered with.

I quickly read on, and I found out that Heather and her young son, Jaden—who had been in the car—were miraculously unharmed.

Heather, however, was afraid for herself and her son.

She believed someone was after their new-found fortune.

I read on, and *The Morning Cider*—never one to ignore a juicy, "big-city" story—had gone into great detail.

The article spilled over to the next page, and it had even bumped the story about the latest jewelry theft to page three.

Apparently, Heather had been leaving her afternoon Mommy and Me yoga class yesterday when the accident occurred. The article detailed what Heather and Jaden had been wearing, which hospital they had been discharged from this morning, and it even went into detail about what had been done to the brakes to cause them to malfunction—apparently the brake line had been punctured, introducing a slow leak. And it further disclosed that the lug nuts on her tires had been loosened—something else that could also potentially cause an accident if one of them were to come off entirely.

The author of the article even speculated that it wouldn't take any great expertise to damage the brakes that way or to loosen the lug nuts, and that the information was readily available on the internet.

The rest of the article was further reactions from Heather, and also reactions from her friends.

I read through the whole thing, and then I got in my car.

I sat for a moment to think.

I didn't know how the author of the article knew all of that information, but if it was true, it meant that there was a serious leak in the police department.

I couldn't imagine that they would want the public to know that they were treating the accident like attempted murder. And I would think that they were even less happy that the details of the brake-tampering had been leaked—especially if they had a suspect in mind.

I had to wonder, too, about Heather's assessment of the situation—that someone was trying to kill her and her son. And I had to conclude that she was right—especially if the information about the brakes was correct.

So did that let her out as a suspect? It seemed so at first glance.

And did that mean that Christopher or Bobby was trying to get Heather—and especially Jaden—out of the way so that their share of the inheritance would come to one of them?

That was a distinct possibility.

Then a little voice at the back of my mind whispered, *there could be someone else.*

I started up the car.

As I drove to the Old Forest, my mind became entangled again in speculation.

I'd thought about calling Mike to see if he'd like to come along, but I discarded the idea quickly—it was far too early in the morning.

Then, too, I might not find anything, and we might end up tramping around in the woods again with nothing to show for it.

I told myself not to think that way.

I *would* find the witch.

But it might be better if I looked for her by myself—just in case anything went wrong.

My thoughts then turned to Mr. Clementine and the remark he'd made about breadcrumbs. The fact that he'd known the term the town children used made it sound as if he'd found the witch himself. But then Bobby had said that his father had also planned to visit the Midnight Market—and Mr. Clementine had been very insistent about receiving that book that I now knew was about Roman mysticism.

Did that mean, as I'd once thought, that he'd sought the witch's help, and she'd been unable to assist him, so he had to look elsewhere?

Or was the witch just a front of some sort, and she and the market were one and the same?

Whatever the answer was, I told myself I'd find out soon.

After a few more minutes, I saw the Old Forest stretching up ahead of me, and I pulled over onto the narrow shoulder.

Then I got out of the car.

Alberta had left the house just before five thirty, and it was about an hour later now. Dawn was peeking over the horizon, but the vast bulk of the forest largely obscured it, and the trees loomed ahead of me, dark and forbidding.

I stepped into the woods, and there was a rustle in the trees nearby.

I turned quickly, but I couldn't see what had made the sound.

I waited a moment to let my fluttering heart calm itself, and then I reached into my purse and pulled out a piece of paper.

I'd copied down the reveal spell, and I unfolded it now and read it over.

I had the contents largely memorized, but I wanted to make sure that I didn't leave anything out.

The notes on the spell really recommended using a wand, but I had never used one, and now didn't seem like the ideal time to start.

I glanced back toward the car and the road, and then I glanced beyond it to the trees on the other side. The forest stretched on either side of the road, and I had no idea if I'd even picked the right side.

I had to hope that if I found the breadcrumbs, that they would lead me in the right direction.

I realized then that I was stalling.

I put the piece of paper away, and then I closed my eyes and recited the spell.

As I finished it, the rustling sound came again, and my eyes snapped open.

I was just in time to see a pale pink dove burst out of the foliage nearby and streak off into the distance.

I wondered if it had been watching me.

As the bird disappeared into the trees, I saw a light appear in front of me on the ground. It was bright and golden and tiny—no bigger than a crumb. But it shown out clearly through the leaves and other debris on the forest floor.

I walked toward it, and as I did so, another one lit up just a few feet away.

I walked toward that one also.

Soon a line of tiny, glowing lights stretched ahead of me, trailing deeper into the forest.

I followed the trail through the still-dark woods, and where each light sprang up, it created a tiny gray halo that looked a little like fog.

I glanced behind me and saw that the tiny lights disappeared after I passed them.

A trail of breadcrumbs indeed.

Eventually, I came in sight of a little square structure.

It appeared to be part house, part tent. From where I was standing, I could see that the back, sides, and roof were made of wood. But where there would have been a front and a door, there were actually two large canvas flaps, like tent flaps—and they were a deep, gingerbread brown.

The front flaps were tied together with a little white canvas bow that somehow looked like icing.

As I approached, the bow untied itself, and the canvas flaps hung open a little.

"Come in!" called a voice.

I glanced behind me.

The trail of lights had disappeared.

"Now, now, don't be shy," called the voice, which was light and female. "Come on in!"

I hesitated for just a moment, and then I plunged through the canvas flaps.

Inside, it seemed to be just a bit bigger than it had appeared from the outside—but that could have been my imagination.

It was light and airy, and a soft breeze seemed to blow through from somewhere. There were standing shelves filled with all kinds of strange, metal objects—all comprised of hoops and bent wires—and several globes hung in the air without apparent support and filled the room with a soft, golden glow.

And in the center of the room, behind a table covered with books and what looked like a red-and-blue quilt, was a woman.

The woman had faded hair of a beige hue, and she was clad in beige overalls with a loose-fitting white shirt. I would have guessed her age to be about sixty, and she had pale skin with a network of fine lines around the eyes and mouth. Beside her on a perch sat the pale pink dove I had glimpsed earlier, and the woman's head was bent as she looked down at something below the table.

A *clack, clack, clack* sound filled the air.

The woman was apparently working on something with her hands.

"I was wondering when you'd finally get here," she said.

She didn't look up.

"You were wondering when I'd get here?" I said.

"Yes."

"Who are you?"

The woman looked up. Her eyes were a faded blue.

"I thought you knew, dear. I'm the witch in the woods."

"Yes, but—"

"I know what you meant," the woman said, twinkling a little. "It's just that I don't get many visitors, and I have to use my impressive opening lines when I can. You can call me Mistress Mabel. Most people do."

"I'm—"

"Chloe Bartlett," Mistress Mabel said. "Yes, I know."

As she spoke, her hands continued to work, and the clacking sound continued.

"You look puzzled, Chloe. Why is that?"

"It's just that—you're not quite what I expected."

Mistress Mabel smiled. "You thought I'd have a green face, and I'd be cackling over a bubbling cauldron? You of all people should know better."

"I—"

I stopped. I actually *had* been picturing someone kind of sinister.

Mistress Mabel smiled again. "So what can I do for you, Chloe?"

I was startled. "You don't know?"

"No, of course not. How could I?"

"But you said you were expecting me."

"Yes, but I'm not clairvoyant, my dear. Let's just say that a little bird told me."

She glanced fondly at the pale pink dove that sat on the perch next to her.

I felt a little spark of temper.

"I've seen that bird a lot lately. Did you send it to spy on me?"

" 'That bird' has a name," Mistress Mabel replied with a trace of asperity. "It's Elise. And I can't help what she tells me. She likes to keep an eye on the town, and whenever something interesting happens, she comes back and tells me all about it. She's such a little gossip."

"Are you serious?" I said.

"Certainly I am."

"You think that bird—Elise—talks to you?" I said.

But even as I said the words, I felt a little funny.

After all, I was there in the first place because I thought a deceased man had been communicating with me.

Mistress Mabel was silent for a moment, but she didn't seem to be offended.

Instead, she seemed to be thinking the question over.

The strange clacking continued in the silence.

"You know," she said, "Elise definitely doesn't talk to me—at least not in the usual way. But I do get thoughts, feelings, impressions. I do know that there's communication going on—I can understand her and she can understand me."

Mistress Mabel paused and looked up at me.

"What of it?"

"Nothing," I said. "I just didn't know anyone had the ability to do something like that."

Mistress Mabel tilted her head to the side, and I got the impression that she was pleased by my reply.

"But that still doesn't explain how you know my name," I said. "Elise didn't tell you that, did she?"

"No, of course not, my dear. You're a Bartlett, of the famous and powerful Bartlett family. All the magic workers around these parts know you and your sisters and your lovely mother."

"Famous and powerful?" I said.

"Yes," Mistress Mabel replied. "Your ancestor Mary was a very powerful and very good witch. And your family has watched over this region for centuries. Everyone knows about you—and recognizes you."

"You said other magic workers," I said slowly. "Are there others around here?"

"Yes, of course."

I froze. "Are you part of the Crabtree Coven?"

"Oh, my, no. But they're around."

I was startled. "They are? What I heard last month was really true?"

"Yes, my dear," Mistress Mabel replied. "But then, you already know that. This can't have been news to you."

And she was right—it wasn't. The evidence I'd found of their magic was far too obvious to ignore.

It was just that hearing someone else confirm their existence so casually came as a shock to my system.

Mistress Mabel continued. "But their power is greatly diminished, and they aren't really what they once were. They're largely playacting really."

She took a deep breath. "Now, my dear, won't you tell me why you're here? And please do have a seat. Your standing there like that does make me nervous."

I looked down and happened to see a chair on the side of the table that was closest to me.

I couldn't remember having seen it before.

But Mistress Mabel nodded at it encouragingly, and I sat down.

"How about some light refreshments?" she said. "It's quite early, and I imagine you haven't eaten anything yet."

I glanced down.

In front of me was a cup of tea and a plate of gingerbread men that I was positive hadn't been there a moment ago.

"Gingerbread?" I said. "Really? Isn't that a little Hansel and Gretel?"

Mistress Mabel smiled. "I couldn't resist. You did follow a trail of breadcrumbs to find me."

"What about the children?" I said suddenly. "Do they really come to see you out here?"

"Sometimes."

"How do they find you?"

"They follow the breadcrumbs just as you did."

"And then what happens to them?" I said.

Mistress Mabel's pale blue eyes opened wide. "Why, my dear, nothing at all!"

"The stories say that you try to make them take evil spells with them."

"Nonsense. I do nothing of the sort. In fact, most of them run off as soon as they see my house appear."

"And what happens to the ones who don't run?" I said.

Mistress Mabel tilted her head and clicked her tongue, a sound that was nearly drowned out by the steady clacking noise that still continued to fill the room.

"Such suspicion," she said. "Most of the children who come here are lost—I sometimes try to use a little magic to help them find their way home again. And children can be very melodramatic when they tell their stories later on."

"How do they find their way to you in the first place?" I asked. "I had to use a spell to make your breadcrumbs appear."

Mistress Mabel smiled. "All children have a little magic in them. It's a shame that it often disappears as they grow older."

She nudged the plate toward me a little. "Now why don't you have something to eat and tell me why you're here."

I glanced down at it.

"No thanks."

"Suit yourself," Mistress Mabel said. She reached out and took one of the gingerbread men and bit into it.

The clacking sound abruptly stopped.

"You know," I said, "my mother wouldn't approve of the way you just conjure things."

"I imagine she wouldn't. But there's no one else here but you, and you'll hardly be shocked by it. Now are you going to quit stalling and tell me what you want?"

There was no asperity in her tone, but her point was well made.

I was stalling.

And I wasn't sure why. Perhaps I feared she wouldn't tell me anything.

Or perhaps I feared that she would.

So I pushed myself to talk.

"Did Otis Clementine come to see you?" I blurted out.

"So that's it," Mistress Mabel said with a glance at Elise. She offered the bird a tiny crumb of gingerbread, and she took it. "I've heard you've been hanging around his house. I'm glad someone is looking into it. What happened to him wasn't natural."

"What do you mean looking into it?" I asked.

"Why, his murder, of course."

"Who said I was looking into his murder?"

"Well, aren't you?"

"Yes," I said. "But I don't know how you knew."

Mistress Mabel gave me a level look.

"Chloe, dear, it's really the only logical explanation for your presence here. So please stop acting so jumpy, and stop acting like you've never seen magic before. Just get on with your questions."

"I *did* ask you a question just now," I pointed out a little peevishly. "And you didn't answer it. You're the one who got us into this little side exchange in the first place."

"Why, so I did." Mistress Mabel finished her gingerbread, and the clacking sound started again. "Please proceed, and don't mind me. This helps me to relax."

"So, did Otis Clementine come to see you?" I asked.

"Yes."

I felt a little thrill of excitement—my guess had been right.

"And what did he come to see you about?"

Mistress Mabel smiled. "Do you really need to ask? Don't you know already?"

"Please just answer the question," I said. "I can't just go off my assumptions. I have to have confirmation."

"Yes, I suppose you do. In that case, Otis Clementine came here to see if I could help him find his son Brian."

Mistress Mabel shot me a sharp glance.

"And I can see that you already knew that."

"I guessed something like it," I replied. "And were you able to help him?"

"No."

"Did you try?" I asked.

"Yes."

"What went wrong?"

Mistress Mabel sighed.

"The boy—well, I shouldn't really say boy, should I? He's a grown man. The son, Brian, that is, couldn't be found."

"Why not?" I said.

"Well, first of all, as you well know, a locate spell is out. You use that to locate a person *you* know. Not a person someone else knows."

I did indeed know that—my memory on this topic had been refreshed very recently. And I knew that that was why Alberta had to use divination rather than a locate spell when she had worked on her missing person cases. A locate spell was far more exact, but you couldn't do it for someone else—it was very specific to the spellcaster.

Mistress Mabel continued. "So I had to turn to divination. But what I found was a great dark cloud."

I frowned. "What does that mean?"

"All I could feel was anger and resentment when I looked. The boy—Brian—has set his face against his father. He doesn't want to be found."

"Brian can really block you?" I said. "How did he even know you were looking for him?"

"I don't think he did," Mistress Mabel replied. "I don't think he had any idea. But when emotion is that strong—that powerful—it can create a barrier like a shield. The son's negative emotions toward his father will block anything that is done on his father's behalf."

She paused. "In fact, 'negative emotion' is probably the wrong term. I'd venture that 'hatred' is actually a better word."

"Hatred?" I said. "But Mr. Clementine told me he'd had no contact with his son since he was a baby. How could Brian possibly hate his father?"

Mistress Mabel shrugged. "Who knows? But it was there. And emotion has a profound effect on magic. Love is strong enough to change it. And so is hate."

"So then you really couldn't help Mr. Clementine at all?"

"No."

"Then he had to go somewhere else," I murmured.

"What was that?" Mistress Mabel said—it was possible she couldn't hear me over the sound of the clacking.

"So he left here after that?" I said a little more loudly.

"Yes."

"How did he seem?"

Mistress Mabel paused to think.

"He was distraught—yes, definitely distraught. He insisted that I could do something if I really wanted to—but ultimately, I couldn't."

She paused again.

"I think the idea that his son didn't want to see him upset him greatly. Especially since he's spent so many years searching for him. It probably made him realize exactly why all his conventional attempts at contact had failed."

"So when he left," I said, "did he give you any indication of what he might do next? Where he might go, perhaps?"

"No. I'm sorry—he didn't."

"I know this calls for speculation on your part," I said slowly. "But if you had to guess, where would you think he might go?"

Mistress Mabel shook her head. "I really couldn't say."

"What about the Midnight Market?" I asked. "Is it possible he could have gone there?"

Mistress Mabel's eyes twinkled.

"So you've finally found out about that, have you?"

"Yes," I said. "So what do you think? Could he have found what he was looking for there?"

"Well—I couldn't really say if he went there or not. I'd really have no knowledge of something like that. But it's possible he found his way there—though it's not easy to get to. And if he did—he wouldn't have found any help there, either. No spell he bought there would be able to find his son for him—the animosity the son is harboring would stop anything in its tracks."

I was startled. "So nonmagical people can really buy spells there?"

"Yes."

"And do they work?"

"Sometimes. Some of the stuff there is just gaudy junk designed to fool the unwary. But some of it will work even if you don't have a drop of magic in you."

I found myself frowning. "I've heard of things like that. How do they work—when they actually do work?"

"Well, now, let me see," Mistress Mabel said, blinking. "It's not really my area of expertise—but I have heard of one thing. They call it 'fairy dust,' and it's actually some form of distilled and powdered magic. I don't know how it's created, but I have some very unpleasant theories that I'd rather not discuss at the moment. And despite the fanciful name, fairy dust apparently isn't very pretty stuff. I've heard it described as gray grit."

I shuddered just a little.

I had no idea how magic could be powdered myself, but somehow I didn't like the concept.

"So what kind of place is the Midnight Market?" I asked. "Is it all dark magic?"

"Oh, no!" Mistress Mabel said, her eyes opening wide. "I didn't mean to give you that impression at all. It's really just a market—it's a market for magic workers, of course—but aside from the unusual wares, it really isn't much different than the farmers' market they have here in Crabtree Bay on the weekends. The iffy stuff—like the premade spells—is a tiny part of it. And you have to know the right people—that is, the right shady people. And as I said, a lot of it is actually junk."

"So how can I get there?" I asked.

Mistress Mabel smiled—but it was unlike any of her other smiles. This one was condescending.

"You won't be able to find it—at least, not this time."

"What do you mean?" I asked.

Mistress Mabel gave me that condescending smile again.

"Look how hard it was for you to find me—and you knew I was here. Both Elise and I saw you that day when you and that handsome young man were stomping around looking for us. If you couldn't find me then, you won't be able to find the market now. The time has not yet come."

"But—"

"My dear, it doesn't matter if Otis Clementine went to the Midnight Market or not, and it doesn't matter if anyone saw him there or not. He wouldn't have been able to find any means to find his son there. The only way Brian Clementine would have been found is if he wanted to be found—that is, if he went looking for his father himself."

"And how would he do that?" I said.

Mistress Mabel gave me a level look.

"Chloe, my dear, Otis Clementine was one of the richest men in the country, and he lived in a castle that he built for himself. It wouldn't have been hard for Brian to find him at all. Like I said, he didn't want to be found by his father."

"I suppose that's true," I said.

"Oh, Chloe," Mistress Mabel said, "don't look so defeated. I'm not ordering you not to go to the Midnight Market—you can do anything at all that you wish. I'm just saying I doubt you'll find out how to get there any time soon, and you'll just be wasting your time. What really matters is that someone killed poor Mr. Clementine through magical means, and you—and you alone—can figure this out."

"How did you know he was killed by magical means?" I asked, suddenly suspicious.

"Your presence here, first of all. You're doing work the police can't—you're in a unique position to be able to work in both the magical and nonmagical worlds. You've been called to do this—no one else can do what you do. And like I said, I could tell that Otis Clementine's death wasn't natural—I just had a feeling. That and the fact that some very unusual details—including a strange glowing blue stain—have been revealed in that local paper of ours—someone on the staff seems to have a *very* good connection on the police force."

Mistress Mabel's eyes twinkled as she said this, and I rose to go.

I had a feeling that there was nothing more I could learn from her.

"Goodbye, my dear," she said. "And take heart. You really can do this. And you don't need me or the Midnight Market to show you how."

I mumbled a reluctant thanks, and then I turned toward the tent flap doors with that strange rhythmic clacking still echoing in my ears.

I turned back.

"Can I ask you one last question?"

"Of course, my dear."

"What *is* that sound?"

"Oh!" Mistress Mabel said. "I had no idea you didn't know."

The clacking sound abruptly stopped, and she held up a tiny blue sweater and two silver knitting needles.

"I was just knitting this for my godson."

Chapter Twenty-Eight

Whether or not I could find my way to the Midnight Market was an academic point at the moment.

First, I had to find my way back to my car.

Then I had to go to work.

Luckily, finding my way back wasn't so hard. I had a good sense of direction, and even though I wasn't really an outdoorsy person, I could see signs of my passage through the woods.

Somehow I even found a button that I'd dropped on the forest floor.

I examined my lightweight cardigan, and sure enough, one of the decorative buttons from one of the sleeves was missing.

Before long, I found my car again, and I began the drive back to town.

I felt frustrated—apparently I had hit another dead end.

But somehow it didn't feel like it.

The image in my head kept growing—it was changing, getting clearer.

But there was still a piece missing.

I had to agree with Mistress Mabel—Mr. Clementine probably hadn't found Brian—even if he had found the Midnight Market.

I only knew of divination through Alberta, but I did know it was very tricky and even a slight miscalculation could make it go wrong—

so I had no trouble believing that a son with negative feelings toward his father could be hidden from any divination done on that father's behalf. I also didn't have any trouble believing that any other spells performed to find Brian would also misfire—especially if they were "out of the box" spells.

So the Midnight Market probably wouldn't have helped Mr. Clementine out.

But it might have helped someone else.

Now that I knew that the Midnight Market indeed existed, it seemed like the kind of place where someone so inclined might be able to pick up a fatal spell.

Despite Mistress Mabel's insistence that I wouldn't be able to find the Midnight Market, I had a feeling that I could find it anyway.

However, as she'd said, it might not actually do me any good—and not just because Mr. Clementine probably hadn't met with any success there.

Whoever it was who was selling lethal spells was unlikely to come right out and admit that they were doing so—admitting to assisting murder wasn't a good idea for anybody, even if I'd have a very hard time making the charge stick.

And ferreting out who was doing it was likely to take some time—and I wasn't sure how much time I had.

That car accident involving Heather and her son had me worried.

I had a feeling that she was right that someone wanted them both out of the way.

And I wasn't sure that they'd be so lucky next time.

I was feeling decidedly gloomy as I arrived at work.

The morning started normally enough, but I felt my spirits plunge still further when both doors to the library swung open and Daphne Minton walked in.

Her lips were pressed into a thin line, and her eyes oriented on me angrily.

As I'd thought once before, there was nothing ambiguous about her now.

I didn't know what she wanted, but I knew it couldn't be good.

She walked right up to me where I stood at the circulation desk, and she was so angry that her sleek, dark bob actually trembled.

She placed her hands on her hips.

"Just what do you think you're doing?"

Her voice was loud, and it carried all over the library.

Everyone stopped what they were doing and looked up.

"I'm sorry?" I said.

"Just *what* do you think you're doing?" Daphne's voice was even louder.

"Daphne," I said in a firm, calm voice, "I'm happy to talk about anything you'd like to discuss, but this is a library, and I'm going to have to ask you to keep your voice down."

"No," she said.

"Daphne, please. I'm going to need you to be quiet."

I glanced around. Rita wasn't here this morning, and Stu and Emily wouldn't be in for hours.

I would have to defuse this on my own.

"No, I will not be quiet," Daphne said, her voice rising louder still.

"How about we step outside—"

"I will *not* step outside."

"All right," I said. "Why don't you just tell me what's wrong?"

Maybe a little venting would help her to calm down and be reasonable.

"What's wrong is *you*," Daphne spat. "I've just heard that you've been to see both Christopher and Bobby."

"Yes—" I said.

"And you've been asking them questions about their father—as if they're guilty of something—"

"I'm just—"

"You're just what?" Daphne demanded. "Doing your job? Last time I looked you were a librarian."

"You don't understand—"

"You've got no right to go snooping around, sticking your nose where it doesn't belong. And all this comes after you were over at *my* house, poking around, trying to dig up nonexistent dirt."

"I wasn't trying to dig up anything," I said firmly. "And that house isn't yours."

Daphne stared at me, and her mouth opened and closed several times.

Then she pressed her lips into a thin line again.

"You're impertinent," she hissed. "You're not part of the family, and this is none of your business. Stay away from Christopher and Bobby. Stay away from Mr. Clementine's house, and stop slinking around peeking into other people's windows."

Her voice had risen again as she said this last part, but she stopped abruptly and stared at me.

"Why are you looking at me like that?"

"It's just that you said 'windows.' "

Daphne drew herself up. "Yes, I certainly did. And I meant what I said."

"Okay, then," I said abstractedly—my mind was suddenly somewhere else.

"Okay?" Daphne looked both outraged and confused.

"Yes—okay."

She stared at me a moment longer—but she seemed to have run out of things to say.

"Just remember what I said," she hissed.

Then she turned and walked out of the library.

I looked up to see Mrs. Ludlow staring at me.

I could feel her anger radiating across the desk toward me, but I was too distracted at the moment to be fazed by it.

"I'm sorry, Mrs. Ludlow," I murmured.

"No, you're not," she replied.

I blinked and came out of my reverie. "I beg your pardon?"

"No, you're not," Mrs. Ludlow said again. "If you were sorry, you'd stop."

"Stop what?"

"You'd stop bringing those hooligan friends of yours in here—always shouting and waving their arms."

She then turned with a great deal of dignity back to the book she'd been reading and ignored me completely.

After that, the library soon settled into silence again, and I was free to let my thoughts flow.

Though Daphne had meant it as an insult, I *had* been peering into a window recently.

And I had a strong feeling that it was important.

But I just couldn't remember what I had seen.

So I let the idea take root and then grow.

I let it grow in any direction it wanted to.

Suddenly I saw a window—but I wasn't so much peering into it as looking up at it.

I was standing on a sidewalk looking up at a window, and something in that window had caught my attention.

I knew now that I had to get inside that building and see what was in that room.

I glanced at the big, round clock that sat over the front doors.

As I'd noted before, I had several more hours before Stu and Emily came in—and besides, *he* was likely to be there.

In fact, he was likely to be there all day.

A woman walked up to the desk to check out a book, and I felt a flash of impatience—but I quickly squashed it and smiled instead.

As much as I wanted to go rushing out of the library, my doing so would do no good.

He was likely to be at his place of business all day, and there was no way I'd get past him and his clients without being seen.

So I would have to wait.

As the woman left with her book—and mercifully didn't complain about the recent scene with Daphne—I felt a sinking sensation. My quarry was likely to have evening hours, too, so I would have to wait until very late in order to be able to sneak in.

And then I felt a further sinking sensation—it was possible that the room I was interested in—the room above—was actually his apartment. So if I waited until late at night to sneak in, he was likely to be there himself, trying to sleep.

I realized gloomily that no time was a good time to sneak in.

And then it occurred to me that he would have to eat dinner at some point, and as I recalled, he liked one of the restaurants on that same street.

Maybe, with any luck, he would head over there tonight, and if my luck held further still, maybe I would be able to spot him going over there.

That was a lot of luck, however, and I realized it was entirely possible that he would simply go up to his apartment and have dinner there.

But I had to try, and I glanced at the big clock overhead again.

I still had several hours to go, and it seemed to me as if the hands on the clock had barely moved at all.

I waited in an agony, and I worried that he would leave for a meal or some other kind of break before I had a chance to go over there.

But eventually Stu and Emily arrived, and I went tearing out of the library.

They probably thought I was crazy.

But I didn't have a second to lose.

I jumped in my car and drove as fast as I could downtown.

My heart sank when I saw that the lights were on, but no one was in the front room where all the classes seemed to take place.

I was staring at Bodhi's yoga studio.

But no one was there.

I was afraid that I had missed my chance.

And then it occurred to me that this *was* my chance.

I parked the car at a distance that I judged to be discreet, and then I got out and sauntered as nonchalantly as I could over toward the studio.

I had to make this look as natural as possible—I had to look as if I had every right to go into the studio.

But just as I reached the door, Bodhi himself came out, his hair tucked up under a baseball cap.

I swerved quickly to the side, and then turned and walked right back to my car.

I listened for sounds of pursuit, but I didn't hear anyone's footsteps following mine.

Once I reached the safety of my car, I ducked down behind it and peered out.

Bodhi had continued down the sidewalk and apparently hadn't noticed me.

As I watched, he turned toward Peter's Table and went inside.

As he'd told Rafaela, he did like the place.

I waited a few moments to make sure he wasn't coming out again, and then I hurried back over to the yoga studio.

The front door was naturally locked, and there was a sign in the window that declared that Bodhi would, "Be back soon."

I glanced quickly overhead to see that Bodhi's violet-colored medallion was still hanging in the window just like it was the last time I had seen it.

Then I searched in my purse like I was looking for my keys, and as I did so, I recited the incantation for the unlock spell.

After a moment, there was a click, and the door to the studio opened at a touch.

I quickly went inside and locked the door behind me.

There was no one around, but the walls at the front of the studio were all glass, so I knew that anyone who looked inside would see me.

I hurried toward a door at the back of the room.

This door opened easily, and beyond it stretched a short hall.

I peeked into the rooms on either side, but I only saw another, smaller yoga room and the restrooms.

Then I spotted a staircase at the end of the hall.

I hurried up the stairs, and each step creaked loudly as I trod on it.

I winced and looked over my shoulder, but as far as I could tell, I was still alone.

If Bodhi was ordering dinner at Peter's Table, then I probably had at least an hour before he came back.

However, if he was just picking up a carryout order, I might only have a few minutes.

I hurried up the last few protesting stairs and encountered another locked door, which I took to be a good sign.

This was very likely his apartment, then.

I recited my incantation, and the door sprang open.

I stepped inside cautiously, but the room seemed to be empty.

I walked further in and glanced around.

I appeared to be in Bodhi's living room.

The entire room was done up in soft shades of lavender and white, sort of like a high-end spa, and I crossed quickly to the far side where the amethyst medallion was hanging in the window.

I took it down and examined it.

The tiny silver frame that held the amethyst stone had one word etched into it: protego—latin for "protect." Now I knew what the medallion was for—there was something in here he wanted to shield. Or to be more accurate, there was something in here that he wanted to hide.

A quick sweep of the living room turned up nothing extraordinary apart from the medallion itself, and my search of the expensively appointed kitchen next to it showed only that he had a refrigerator full of energy drinks and excellent taste in utensils and cooking implements.

I moved on to the next room.

Bodhi's bathroom, like his living room, was done in shades of white and lavender, and there was a stunning array of personal-care products lining his sink and shelves. There were moisturizers and lotions and face creams, and I glanced at a bottle with a label that said, "Bright Lights." Apparently, it was spray-in color to keep blond highlights looking their blondest.

It appeared that Bodhi's golden tresses owed a little something to artifice.

But other than that, the bathroom concealed no secrets, and the only room left was Bodhi's bedroom.

As I walked toward it, I felt the image in my mind changing and shifting.

I had a feeling I knew what I might find.

The problem would be proving it.

Heavy shades were down in the bedroom, and it was dark as I entered it, so I flipped a switch and turned on the overhead light.

The room was strangely utilitarian after the simple, spa-like luxury of the rest of the apartment, and I looked over the bed, two dressers, and a few assorted storage boxes without finding anything.

Then I turned to the closet, which turned out to be a walk-in, and I found nothing in that but two long rows of neatly pressed clothes and several racks of expensive leather shoes and sneakers.

I searched through the closet, puzzled, but no matter how many times I looked, I couldn't find what I'd expected to find.

And then I spotted it—there was a little distortion in the back wall of the closet. The bottom corner didn't quite fit, and I could feel a little draft of air coming through it.

It was a false wall.

There was actually a door here.

I recited the unlock spell for a third time, and as before, the door sprang open.

But this time there was no need for me to search.

What I was looking for was right in front of me.

And it was not at all what I'd expected.

Chapter Twenty-Nine

I ran out of Bodhi's apartment, and I didn't stop running until I'd reached the safety of my car.

Then I quickly peeled out and began to drive home.

It was there now—all the pieces were there.

It was the last clue I needed.

The image in my mind shifted and changed and came into focus.

There were a few things I wanted to check—a few things I wanted to make sure that I'd seen correctly.

But if everything held up, then I finally had the right picture.

And it wasn't at all what I had anticipated.

I reached home in record time, and then I shut and locked the door behind me.

I was pretty sure Bodhi hadn't seen me leaving his apartment, but it didn't hurt to be sure.

And just for good measure, I peered out the front window.

There was no one on our street.

Sibyl came out to greet me, but Alberta, it seemed, wasn't home yet. And that was just fine with me.

I needed some time alone to think.

I fed Sibyl, and while she settled down with her bowl of crunchies, I ran upstairs to use Alberta's computer.

I waited impatiently for the laptop to boot up, and then I was on the internet.

The facts were all there—just as I remembered them. And I knew from my own work that a lot of newspapers—even small ones—had digital archives now. So I did some further digging, and I found exactly what I'd hoped to find.

The wife, the half siblings, the pink cloud—I understood how they all fit together now.

I also looked up a few other things—mostly on YouTube. And I was satisfied with what I found.

After that, I shut the computer off, and then I sent Marianne Mozer a text.

I waited impatiently, knowing it could be a while before she answered—or she might not answer at all. But after a few minutes, I heard a very welcome buzz, and I read her response.

I'd been right.

I thanked her, and then I called Mike.

I was going to need his help.

"Hey, Chloe."

He answered right away.

"Hey, Mike. Sorry to call you out of the blue like this—"

"No—it's quite all right."

"But I need your help with something."

"What is it?" he said quickly. "What's wrong?"

"Nothing's wrong exactly. I was just hoping you'd deliver a message for me. On paper if possible."

I could picture Mike frowning. "What are you up to, Chloe? Is it something dangerous?"

"No—it's not dangerous. It's just—unusual. I was hoping you'd deliver a message to someone because I don't think this person will come if I deliver the message myself. You have a lot more prestige. You should definitely introduce yourself as a professor of folklore."

"I don't quite understand," Mike said. "Where do you want this person to go?"

"To a little gathering I'm having," I replied. "You're invited, too."

Mike's tone grew even more disapproving.

"Somehow I don't think this is a party you're having."

"No—it definitely isn't."

Mike sighed. "What's the message?"

I dictated it for him.

Mike made a scoffing sound when I was done.

"And what's that supposed to mean?"

"The person the message is intended for will know."

"Fine," Mike said. "And whom am I giving it to?"

I told him.

"I don't know who that is," Mike said.

"I'll give you the address," I replied. "And when you deliver the message, be *sure* to introduce yourself as a professor of folklore."

"All right. I'll do it. But I have no idea where you're going with this."

"Don't worry," I said. "It will all be clear soon."

"So what are you going to do while I'm inviting your friend to this little gathering?"

"I'll be inviting everyone else," I said. "And this person is definitely *not* my friend."

"Chloe—" Mike said suddenly.

"Yes?"

"Did you call the police about the video footage like you said you were going to?"

I drew in my breath sharply.

"No, I didn't."

"You didn't?"

"No—I forgot."

"You forgot?" Mike was clearly exasperated.

"Yes—I just forgot. Things were so busy."

"Chloe—"

"But I'm going to call them right now."

"That's what you said last time."

"I really am," I said. "This time I need them."

Mike sighed yet again.

"I hope you mean that."

"I do—I really do," I said.

"All right, then," Mike said. "I'll deliver your note. I don't suppose you'd care to tell me what this little gathering is all about?"

"I can't just yet."

"I had a feeling you'd say something like that. Well, take care of yourself, Chloe. I imagine that whatever this is, it's more dangerous than you realize."

"Don't forget," I said. "You're invited, too."

"I wouldn't miss it. Believe me."

As soon as Mike hung up, I called Lee Hurtzel.

I *was* going to call the police, but first I needed a little help with my gathering.

Lee answered, and when I explained my proposal to him, he agreed.

Then I called someone who had a room, and texted Lee the results.

And then I called the police.

Everything was set now.

I just had to wait until tomorrow.

Saturday morning rolled around bright and clear, and I hurried out of the house while Alberta was still in the shower.

I didn't want her to ask me what I was up to.

I hurried out to the venue I had chosen—a private room in the quaint tea shop that I had visited earlier in the week—the one run by an unexpectedly big and burly proprietor. Since he was a good friend of Rafaela's, I thought there might be a chance that he'd agree—and he didn't balk at all, even when I told him what the room would be used for.

He was happy to let both me and Lee in early so we could set up.

And he even told me he'd be happy to back up the police in case there was any trouble.

There wasn't much to do, really, but Lee—who had arrived just after I did—and I busied ourselves rearranging chairs and tables.

And Kyle, the massive proprietor, very kindly brought us tea and scones on fragile china decorated with blue and red flowers.

"This is a little unorthodox," Lee said as we both sipped at the sweet tea—somehow he looked even more like a lawyer than usual.

"Do you disapprove?" I asked.

Lee reflected for a moment. "I suppose I should. But nothing about this entire business has been normal. I think, perhaps, this may be the only way."

"I'm just glad you don't think I'm crazy."

"I never said that."

I couldn't tell if he was kidding or not.

Before we knew it, we had company.

People were supposed to arrive at eleven, but they began arriving much earlier.

I imagined they were eager to hear what I had to say.

Daphne Minton arrived first, followed closely by Christopher Clementine and Bobby Clementine. Heather Pim came into the room next, looking no worse for wear after her ordeal, and behind her were Mike and Bodhi P. Gotschall. Detective Mia and Detective Ortiz arrived separately.

Detective Mia sat in the front, while Detective Ortiz sat in the back.

Everyone refused refreshments.

"Looks like your rogue's gallery has assembled," Lee said softly.

"Shall we begin?" I said.

Lee gave me a brief nod and moved to the back to close the door.

I stepped to the front of the room.

"I want to thank you all for coming—"

"Hold on just a minute," Daphne said, her voice tinged with outrage. "I thought Lee was in charge here."

"Lee has been instrumental in bringing you all here," I said. "But—"

Daphne turned in her chair.

"What's this all about, Lee?"

The lawyer walked past her and came to stand by my side.

"If you would all give Miss Bartlett a few minutes of your time, I would be most grateful."

Daphne pressed her lips together in disapproval, but she said nothing further.

I started again—this time I decided to dispense with the pleasantries.

"As you all know," I said, "Otis Clementine was murdered last Wednesday sometime between eleven thirty-five and eleven fifty a.m. His death was briefly considered to be a fall, but then it was determined that Mr. Clementine had been strangled. Someone very deliberately choked the life out of him."

It might have been my imagination, but it seemed to me that several people in the room shifted uneasily.

I continued. "We've all read, I'm sure, the accounts in the local papers and in the national press. The autopsy was pretty straightforward, but the coroner's report allegedly detailed some anomalies—and those details leaked to the media. You might have heard about a strange blue stain—a blue line around the dead man's neck that couldn't be identified, but seemed to have something to do with the manner in which he'd been killed."

I noticed then that Heather Pim looked down at her hands.

I went on.

"There was even some talk that the blue stain might have something to do with witchcraft or spells."

There was more rustling from those assembled in the room.

"But all that aside," I said, "a man was still strangled. It doesn't matter if the method used was magical or not. What matters is that someone stopped him from breathing."

This time the room was completely silent.

I turned to look at one person in particular.

"The first person I ever suspected of the murder was Daphne Minton."

"Now see here!" Daphne rose to her feet. "That's outrageous!"

She turned to Lee.

"Are you going to allow this?"

Lee was leaning against a table with his arms folded.

"Ms. Minton, please hear her out. All will be made clear in time."

Daphne sat down again.

"As I said," I continued, "Daphne was the first person I suspected. She was on the scene when it happened, and she objected to Detective Ortiz going up to investigate the call he received. On the days I came over to the house, I always had to come over twice. Mr. Clementine always said the first book I brought was the wrong one, and I'd have to come back the next day with the right one. And Daphne knew this. All she had to do was let me go up the first day and see Mr. Clementine alive. Then on the next day, she ran up to strangle him and then placed him at the bottom of the stairs like he'd fallen. Then I would return and find Mr. Clementine, who'd apparently died accidentally of a fall."

"Ridiculous," Daphne said. She didn't get up, but her face betrayed her disgust. "You told me yourself you saw someone running across the back lawn. You couldn't possibly have suspected me."

"Which brings me to the next person I suspected," I said. "Heather Pim."

Heather's face instantly went red, and I saw a vein standing out on her neck.

"You little—"

She stopped.

"Daphne is right," I said. "I did see someone running away from the house. Someone who had apparently just been in Mr. Clementine's office. Someone strong enough to climb up the side of the house. Someone like Heather Pim."

Heather gripped the arms of her chair and narrowed her eyes, but she said nothing.

I went on. "I saw someone tall with a baseball cap and what appeared to be short blond hair. And I couldn't tell from a distance if it was a man or a woman. This person had plenty of time to climb into Mr. Clementine's office, strangle him, and then climb down and run off."

"I'll strangle you," Heather said through gritted teeth. "Why would I kill my hus—"

"But that's just it," I said. "He wasn't your husband, was he? And he was never going to be. In fact, he was quite vocal about the fact that he would never marry again. And that meant that you would never get full access to his money—or that ring you want so badly."

"You have it, don't you?" Heather hissed. "I know you stole it from the house. That ring should be mine. I *deserve* it."

"You love jewelry," I said. "You love it with a ferocious intensity. But you couldn't quite afford to buy everything you wanted."

Heather reflexively clutched the large diamond necklace she wore.

"So you had to find another way to get it."

Heather froze.

"You decided it was easier to steal jewelry," I said. "And you had an accomplice—Bodhi Gotschall—hide the jewels in his apartment."

Heather jumped to her feet.

"I never stole anything! It's a lie! A filthy lie!"

Bodhi, for his part, had gone very pale.

"But stealing jewels is dangerous," I said. "And the police were closing in on you. Besides, you'd found someone new, someone younger—someone you could spend your life with. And that was Bodhi. And so Otis had to go. You knew there was a new will—one that mentioned you and Jaden and not just Brian. And you figured that you would get your money and your freedom all at the same time."

"You're insane!" Heather screeched. "Someone is trying to kill *me*. Or did you forget that?"

"Ah, yes," I said. "Your accident. Which you staged. Because the police were on your trail, and you thought they would back off if a young mother and her son appeared to be being stalked by a murderer.

You tampered with your own brakes and were very careful to crash at a low speed."

"I almost died!" Heather screamed.

She ran at me, and Lee stepped in between us.

Heather subsided, and Lee turned to me in disapproval.

"I hope you know what you're doing," he said.

"I didn't kill Otis," Heather sobbed as she sat back down.

"Then why is there a blue stain on your hand?" I said. "A stain just like the one on Mr. Clementine's body?"

Heather looked down at her right hand.

All the color drained from her face.

"I told you she did it," Bobby interjected into the silence that ensued.

Bobby Clementine was lazing back in his chair, with one arm extended over the seat next to him.

As I turned to look at him, he smiled and waved at me.

"Isn't that interesting?" I said. "Because the next person I suspected was you."

"Oh, did you now?" Bobby's good humor was undimmed.

"Your brother confessed," I said, "and you said he did it to protect Heather. But I actually think he did it to protect you."

Bobby shifted uneasily.

"You were the one who climbed up the wall," I said. "You slipped into your father's office, you strangled him, and then you fled. And you told your brother about it afterward."

Bobby sat forward then. He rested his elbows on his knees for a moment, and then he sat back and looked up at me as I went on.

"But you told your brother a different story, didn't you? You told him that you just went up to talk to him—you just needed a little money, and your father wouldn't return your phone calls. But when you found him in his office, you startled him. He was angry—you argued. Then you left, and he was very much alive. But it wasn't true, was it? Your father met his fate at your hands."

Bobby stared at me steadily, all amusement banished from his face.

Then his lips spread in a slow smile.

"You've forgotten one thing."

"Oh? What's that?"

He held up his hands.

"No blue stains. Only my wicked stepmother—sorry—the girlfriend—has that."

But even as he said the words, the smile faded from his face.

I could tell that he was trying very hard not to look at his brother.

"Which brings me to the next person I suspected," I said quietly. "After all, Christopher Clementine does have the blue stain on his hand."

"No!" Bobby said sharply. "It's not true!"

"I'm sorry, Bobby," I replied. "But Christopher confessed."

I glanced over at him. Christopher was staring steadily down at the floor.

"He didn't," Bobby said. "He may have confessed to going into Dad's office. But he never confessed to murder. I know he didn't."

I went on in the same quiet voice.

"Christopher, like Bobby, had heard all his life that he was largely cut out of his father's will—everything was going to Brian. But Christopher has a very expensive girlfriend, and he needed money desperately—he wanted to get married—to give his girlfriend the life he thought she deserved. And there was only one place he could get that kind of money from. But Christopher had quarreled with his father, and he knew he'd never get any money from him again—not while he was alive, at least. So Otis Clementine had to be disposed of."

"You're wrong," Bobby said, folding his arms across his chest. "You've already said that Christopher and I grew up hearing about Daddy's golden boy Brian and how he was going to get everything. So Christopher had no reason to believe Dad's death would benefit him. We didn't know he'd changed the will."

"No, *you* didn't know your father had changed the will. Christopher did."

Bobby couldn't help glancing over at his brother.

Christopher was still staring at the ground.

"Christopher put on a very convincing show," I said. "He confessed to part of it, but stopped short of admitting to the actual murder. And he did so in the most suspicious way possible, making it clear that he was trying to cover for someone else—and he was relying on his reputation for moral rectitude to bolster this. He confessed, knowing that I'd likely blame you, Bobby. And I'm sure he put on the same act for the police."

I looked over at Detective Ortiz.

"You did go to visit him this past Thursday, didn't you?"

The detective simply nodded his head.

"So once Christopher learned that his father had changed the will," I said. "He set about making plans to get his father out of the way. He even went so far as to go to a place known as the Midnight Market. It was a place where he heard that he could get items that would kill— spells even. And then he used the means he bought there to get rid of his father. And once that was done, he decided to get rid of the others in his way—to be the last man standing and get all his father's money. And the first person he turned on was Heather Pim."

Heather had been glaring at me steadily, and now she turned her baleful glance on Christopher.

"Christopher tampered with the car," I said, "hoping to get rid of her and her young son, Jaden. Jaden would only have his mother as next of kin, and since she would be gone, too, Jaden's inheritance would then go to his brothers."

"No!" Bobby shouted. "No! Christopher would never kill an innocent child! *Never.* If anyone tried to kill Heather, it was her thief of a boyfriend. He tried to kill her so he could keep all the loot."

"It's funny you should say that," I replied. "Because the next—and last—person I suspected was Bodhi P. Gotschall."

Everyone turned to look at Bodhi.

He was sitting very still.

"Bodhi is the right height and coloring," I said, "and he's certainly athletic. He would have had no trouble climbing the wall to get to Otis

Clementine's office. And he certainly knows how to get to the Midnight Market."

I looked over at Mike.

"Would you read out the note I asked you to write?"

Mike looked up at me, and I saw uncertainty flash in his eyes.

But he cleared his throat and read it aloud.

"The medallion you bought is a dangerous fake. Come to Kyle's Teapot on Saturday at eleven in the morning, or a terrible curse will descend upon you."

Bodhi had gone very pale.

"You went to the Midnight Market, didn't you?" I said.

Bodhi didn't reply.

"And you bought more than one spell there, am I right?"

Bodhi remained silent.

"You bought more than one spell, including a glamour. And for anyone who doesn't know, a glamour is a spell that creates a disguise. And you used that glamour to create a vocal disguise. It was that vocal glamour that created that pink cloud over Mr. Clementine's house."

Bodhi still didn't reply.

"And then you climbed up into Mr. Clementine's office and you strangled him. And after that, you used your vocal glamour—you called me at eleven forty-five pretending to be Mr. Clementine. And then you ran away. But what you didn't know was that Mr. Clementine had called Detective Ortiz at eleven thirty-five to tell him someone had attacked him."

Bodhi shook his head.

"No."

His voice was barely a whisper.

"And incidentally, Heather," I said, "I owe you an apology. You didn't steal any of those jewels—Bodhi did that on his own. But you may have to return the ones he gave you—I don't think you're allowed to keep stolen property."

Heather had risen to her feet again.

"You're crazy."

"I'm not—"

"You're insane," she said. "You think Bodhi killed Otis?"

"Yes."

"You think he tried to kill me?"

"Yes."

"Why?" Heather shouted. "Why would he do that? Give me one good reason."

"Because Bodhi is Brian," I said.

Heather looked startled. "What?"

"Bodhi is Brian Clementine."

Bodhi stood up.

"I've had enough," he said quietly. "I'm leaving."

"You are out of your mind!" Heather screeched. "Bodhi is Brian?"

"Yes," I said quietly.

"Prove it," Heather demanded. "Give us one real fact—one real piece of evidence. And I don't want any more of your deductions."

"All right," I said. "Bodhi's got coloring just like Mr. Clementine's other two sons—and despite how young he looks, he's just the right age to be Brian—he's easily thirty-six. He owes his youthful looks to his skincare regime."

"I see. Anything else?"

Heather's voice dripped sarcasm.

"He's got a cleft in his chin," I replied. "Just like Bobby and Christopher—and the late Mr. Clementine."

"Millions of people have a cleft in their chin. You'll have to do better than that."

"And he tampered with your car—I saw him."

Heather froze and then looked over at Bodhi.

He'd been moving toward the door, and now he stopped where he was.

"The first time I saw it was over at the country club the night of your photo party," I said. "I was outside, and I saw Bodhi tinkering with a car. I thought at the time it was his."

Heather was still staring at Bodhi.

329

"And then the second time was outside his studio. He was tinkering with the same car. I believe you, Heather, were inside taking a class from his assistant."

I paused.

"You did let him drive your car, didn't you? It's white and very sporty looking?"

Heather turned toward me slowly.

Then she turned to Bodhi, and her voice rang out in the room.

"You tried to kill me?"

"No, baby, no. You said you heard a funny noise—"

She screeched and rushed at him.

Bodhi turned and ran.

But Detective Ortiz stood and got in his way.

"Not so fast," he said. "I think you should come down to the police station with me for a little chat."

"I suppose that would be a great idea," I said, stepping forward. "If you were a real cop."

Chapter Thirty

"Excuse me?"

Detective Ortiz turned on me angrily.

"You aren't a real cop," I said.

The detective advanced on me.

"Are you trying to be funny?"

I turned to Detective Mia.

"Do you know this man?"

I pointed to Detective Ortiz.

"No," she said.

"Would it interest you to know that when I first met him—at Mr. Clementine's house—that he claimed to be Detective Dave Ortiz of the Crabtree Bay Police Department?"

"Yes, that would interest me quite a bit," Detective Mia said.

"And why is that?"

"Because I know Detective Dave Ortiz very well. And this man is a stranger."

"You don't know who he is?" I asked.

"No."

"Then I'll tell you. This man is Brian Clementine."

"You just said Bodhi was Brian Clementine," Heather interjected sardonically. "So which one is it? Or do you see Brian everywhere you go now?"

"When I said Bodhi was the last person I suspected," I replied. "I really did mean it. But I only suspected Bodhi because I thought he was Brian. Bodhi the yoga instructor would have no reason to kill Otis Clementine. But Bodhi, who was really Brian Clementine in disguise, would have plenty of reason to kill him. So I suspected Bodhi, but only because I thought he was Brian—Brian was the one I truly suspected."

"Thank you," Heather said sarcastically. "That really clears things up."

"But then I realized I was wrong," I said, ignoring Heather. "I was wrong about the jewels *and* the phone call. And don't get me wrong— Bodhi *is* guilty, but not of murder. I thought you, Heather, might be the jewel thief—but as I said, you had nothing to do with that. But once I saw all the jewels in Bodhi's closet and realized he was actually the thief, it made a lot more sense. I remember now how he had been staring at my sister Alberta—and I thought that was because she was beautiful. But he was really staring at her emerald earrings—they're a fine pair, and they would have made an excellent addition to the haul he's already made here."

I glanced over Bodhi. "I knew then that there was no way he was secretly Brian. In some ways the timing was right—he'd been here a few months and that would have given him some time to learn about Mr. Clementine and his household. But it was also the right time frame for him to be our jewel thief. And he was a thief on such a grand scale that I knew he couldn't have any time for Mr. Clementine—his mind was entirely focused on jewels. And then I saw something that made me realize who the real Brian Clementine was. Bodhi's blond hair owes something to art—he colors his hair."

I turned to Detective Ortiz.

"And so do you."

"This is ridiculous," he said. "*You're* ridiculous."

"I noticed the first time I met you that there was something dark under your fingernails—"

"A cop's hands get dirty," Detective Ortiz said. "It's a hard job— something you wouldn't understand."

"But we've already established that you're not Detective Ortiz," I replied. "Detective Mia doesn't know you—and she sits right next to the real Detective Ortiz."

Detective Ortiz fell silent.

"So as I said, there was something dark under your fingernails—and I realized it was hair dye. I don't know if your hair is blond like your brothers' or if it's auburn like your late father's. But you did dye it dark—less to disguise your hair color and more to make yourself look like Detective Ortiz. And I'm also guessing he has a beard, too, which you spent several months growing to complete your disguise. And it doesn't hurt that it disguises your chin, does it? I bet you have that same distinctive cleft your father had. And I saw a picture of the young, clean-shaven Dave Ortiz—his chin is smooth."

Detective Ortiz barked with laughter. "And why would I want to impersonate Detective Ortiz?"

"So you could get into the Clementine house," I said. "So you could get close to your father and kill him."

"Ridiculous."

"You've been watching the house for a few months. You knew that Detective Ortiz had a special relationship with your father, and that he was always being called to the house. You also knew that I made a visit to the house every month—and that I always came twice. So you figured that I would be the ideal witness—I could testify that I saw Otis Clementine on my first visit, and then I'd be back the next day when the 'accident' was discovered."

"You're dreaming," Detective Ortiz said.

"But you had to make sure that Detective Ortiz was there, too, because he was your way into the house—and you wanted to make sure that the police knew about it. So you're the one who lured him to the house—you're the one who used the vocal glamour. I'd originally thought that it was Bodhi impersonating Mr. Clementine on the second call—the one to me at eleven forty-five—but I was wrong. That call was real. The glamoured call—the fake one—was actually the first one. You impersonated Mr. Clementine and called the real

Detective Ortiz—and you got him to come running out here because he thought there was an emergency."

Detective Ortiz smirked. "A spell? Are you serious? Do you even hear yourself?"

"Yes—it was a spell," I replied. "And it wasn't the only one you used. You visited the Midnight Market, too, just like Bodhi did. Only the spells you bought there weren't fake. Not only did you buy the glamour, but you also bought a spell to make Detective Ortiz sick. You intercepted him as he came up to the house, and you gave him the flu—a very nasty case of it that knocked him out on the spot."

Detective Ortiz laughed. "I gave him the flu?"

"Yes—and I should really say it was a curse rather than a spell—and it rebounded on you, giving you the flu, too."

Detective Ortiz paused.

I could see that his eyes and nose were still red.

"So the real Detective Ortiz came up to the door, inquired after Mr. Clementine, and then was turned away. And either right before or right after you hit him with the curse. He likely didn't remember too much of what happened afterward. And then while he tried to make his way home, you waited nearby to make your appearance when I came back with my book that day."

"Nonsense."

"No, it isn't," I said. "And I can prove it."

"No—you can't."

I turned to Detective Mia.

"Detective Ortiz's cell phone went missing, didn't it?"

Detective Mia blinked. "Yes. And we haven't been able to track it."

"Well, you've found it now," I said. "This man right here has it—and I know because I called him on it. He took it off the real Detective Ortiz, and he used the message that was on it to push his way into Mr. Clementine's house. And he knew the message was there because he placed there himself."

"This is getting more fanciful by the minute," Detective Ortiz said. He chuckled, but his sardonic smile was starting to look strained. "How did I make the phone untraceable? Did I use magic on that, too?"

"No," I said. "You used YouTube. I found out how to disable GPS tracking with a very simple search. I imagine you could have done the same."

Detective Ortiz took a step back. He glanced over his shoulder toward the door.

I continued.

"Marianne—who works at Mr. Clementine's house—told me that 'the policeman' had been there twice that day. I assumed that meant that Detective Ortiz had been there first when we all found the body and then came back later to supervise things. But she actually meant that the detective had been there *before* the time that I saw him—I just confirmed that with her last night. He was there first when he was turned away some time around eleven forty. Then the *second* time he was there was the time with me. The first time 'the policeman' was the real Detective Ortiz. The second time it was the fake one. And Marianne told me she didn't know the detective very well. So she didn't recognize the substitution, and she wasn't the one who answered the door either time. And the really funny thing is right at that point on the video footage from the front-door camera—that is, right before eleven forty when the real Detective Ortiz would have come to the door—the footage disappears and there's only static. I suppose you cast some kind of spell at that point, too, to cause the interference."

Detective Ortiz's confident smile returned. "You know what I think is interesting? Everything you've come up with is pure conjecture. You don't have any proof—you say I was caught on camera, and then the footage magically disappears."

I answered with a smile of my own.

"At the risk of sounding juvenile, I'm going to have to say that's what you think. You think all the video footage was erased. But I'll bet you were only focusing on the one camera—however, there are cameras all over the grounds of Mr. Clementine's house. And up until now, no one knew where the footage was from those other cameras. But I've found it—and I'm sure it will be no problem to find unaltered footage of the real Detective Ortiz coming up to the door at that time."

The smile slipped from the detective's face.

"So I'll tell you what happened," I said. "After the real Detective Ortiz was gotten out of the way, you waited somewhere nearby. Then when I arrived on that second day, you waited for a few moments and then burst in and played the phony message from eleven thirty-five. Then you rushed past both Daphne and me and ran up the stairs. But Mr. Clementine was very much alive at that point and had not been attacked—unbeknownst to you, he left me a message at eleven forty-five. So you ran upstairs and strangled him with the choke spell that left that blue mark on his neck. You didn't have to touch him—you just had to cast it. Then you carried him down the stairs to make it look like he fell. Then Daphne and I came up just in time to see you supposedly finding the body."

"And why would I do that?" Detective Ortiz said. "Why would anybody do that? Why strangle someone and then try to make it look like a fall?"

"Because you thought the spell wouldn't leave a mark," I said. "You didn't quite understand how it would work. You thought you could just kill him without actually touching him, and then make it look like someone had pushed him. That's why your fake message mentioned being pushed."

"And why—"

"Because you were trying to take out your competitors," I said sharply. "You deliberately slurred your words so that anyone who heard the message wouldn't know if you said, 'he pushed me' or 'she pushed me.' You were hoping that Heather or one of your two half brothers would get the blame for the murder. Once convicted of a felony, they wouldn't be able to collect on the money—it would be divided amongst the next of kin—which in this case would be the other siblings, including you. When the strangulation was discovered by the coroner, things grew murkier, so you couldn't be sure any of the others would get the blame. So you had to take matters into your own hands. And you started with Heather. You're the one who punctured Heather's brake line in order to induce a slow leak—and disabled the brake light so it wouldn't alert her. And you hedged your bets, also loosening the lug nuts on her tires, hoping to induce an accident that way if the other way didn't work. When that didn't happen fast enough, you thought you'd make the leak in the brake line a little bigger—speed things up."

"I would never—"

"You were downtown the day of Heather's accident, not far away from the yoga studio where she was taking a class. I saw you. I ran into you, remember?"

Detective Ortiz chuckled, but he took a step back. "This is quite a little fantasy you've cooked up. But you still have no proof I'm this other man. And you say I've disguised myself when you don't even know me—"

"Your mother was an actress," I said. "You were around actors all your life, and your wife was a makeup artist. You learned more than enough to disguise yourself to someone who didn't know you. And most of the staff at the house, like Marianne, only saw the real Detective Ortiz from a distance and wouldn't have known—"

Christopher interrupted.

"Daphne would have known."

"What's that?" I said.

"Daphne would have known," he repeated. "She mentioned Detective Ortiz to me before. She would have known who he was— and if there was an imposter."

"Yes, she would have known," I replied. "And she did."

I turned to look at her.

"I remembered that Daphne looked angry when the detective burst in that day—and it occurred to me that she looked a little too angry. She wasn't a-cop-just-burst-into-my-house angry. It was something else—something deeper. And then I remembered that

337

she'd called herself a good Midwestern girl. And Clytie Clementine was originally from Ohio. And she had two younger half siblings—a brother and a sister. It didn't necessarily mean anything, but I thought it was worth looking into."

I glanced at Daphne again.

"Does any of this sound familiar?"

She was staring at me steadily.

"Nonsense," she said. "You said yourself you saw a blond intruder—"

"That was Bobby," I said. "The version of events he told his brother was true—he climbed up to his father's room, they argued, he ran off. And Christopher was trying to protect his brother, so he confessed to being the intruder. In fact, Bobby can now attest to the fact that his father was still alive at eleven thirty-five, the time of his supposedly panicked message—"

"I believe *that* is for the police to decide," Daphne said coldly. "The show you've put on here won't stop the authorities from doing their job."

"And your little show won't stop me, either," I said. "As I was about to say, I did a little digging. And there was plenty of information on Clytie—after all, she was famous. There was much less about her siblings, of course, but most sources noted that Clytie's parents divorced, and her mother remarried—and it was that union that produced Clytie's siblings. But there were no names, no pictures, nothing to identify them. And then last night, in a burst of inspiration, I did indeed find an engagement announcement in a small Ohio newspaper from several decades ago. It mentioned that Clytie's mother, whose maiden name was Sharp, was marrying a man with the last name 'Minton.' I can't prove it at the moment, but I have a hunch that they named their daughter Daphne."

I paused. "It's amazing what you can find online these days. Everyone's digitizing their archives."

Daphne was still staring at me.

This time, she said nothing.

"I wasn't sure what to make of the theory at first," I said. "I was pretty sure there was a good chance that Daphne was Clytie's half sister—and as I said, I had suspected her in the beginning before I even knew about that possibility—but I didn't see how she would benefit from her employer's death. She seemed to have a strong attachment to Mr. Clementine, and she was possibly even in love with him. So she might have killed him out of jealousy—he kept turning to other women and didn't seem to see her as a romantic possibility at all. But if that was the case, then casting a spell seemed unnecessarily showy and dangerous—especially since she could have quietly poisoned him any day of the week. Then I thought Brian could be in the picture somewhere—after all, he was her nephew—but I didn't see any sign of his presence. And then when I began to suspect Bodhi of being Brian, a possibility emerged—but he and Daphne didn't appear to have any connection."

I paused for breath.

"And *then*, when I realized that Detective Ortiz was Brian, it all made sense—even Daphne's anger. Daphne and Brian had planned all this together—only originally they had planned it just to look like an accident. And unfortunately, I was part of that plan, too. I was supposed to see Mr. Clementine alive and give him his book. Then I would come back the next day and give him the second book, and Daphne and I would discover him together—and he would apparently have died of a fall. Then Mr. Clementine would have died a seemingly normal death, and Brian would have emerged shortly afterward to claim his fortune and take over the business."

I looked at Daphne again.

"But Brian ruined all that, didn't he? He decided to show up at the door and proclaim the death a murder—and that's what made you so angry. He wasn't following the original plan, and he was making things much more complicated. Now you had to pretend that he was Detective Ortiz even when you knew he wasn't, and now you had to cooperate in a murder investigation. Everything was much harder than it would have been if it had all looked like an accident and if Brian had just waited in the shadows like he was supposed to—casting the spell quietly and just hiding in the house."

Daphne suddenly found her voice.

"Complete nonsense," she said sharply. "I worked for Mr. Clementine for years. Why would I suddenly plot against him now?"

"Because you met Brian," I replied. "I don't know if you found him, or if he found you, but I'm inclined to think he found you. And he hated his father, and I think he went to work on you, eventually convincing you to go along with his plan. You began to see that you could have it all—you could have the grand house and the vast fortune—you could be the one to travel the world and end up on a sunny beach in Italy."

"Nonsense, why would I—"

"Because you went to work for Mr. Clementine in the first place. You knew who he was—you knew he was your half sister's ex-husband—but he had no idea who you were. You were jealous of your sister who left the Midwest long ago for stardom. You wanted her lifestyle—you wanted it all. But the closest you could get to it was as an employee in the house that was meant for her. And you'd resigned yourself to that—until Brian came along. And then—"

"And then I killed him with a spell," Detective Ortiz said. "You've already said that. But that's not going to hold up in court."

"Maybe not," I said. "But it doesn't matter that no one will ever believe me about the spell. The fact remains that Mr. Clementine was strangled. And he has a blue stain on his neck. And you have a blue stain on *both* your hands."

Detective Ortiz glanced down at his palms. They were indeed tinged blue.

"You set me up!" he snarled.

"I did nothing of the kind. It was your own use of a lethal spell that set you up. You hated your father—but it was more than that. You hated everybody—that's why it was so easy for you to move from killing your father to trying to murder his girlfriend."

I looked at the fake detective and Daphne.

"And I'm sure we'll have no trouble IDing you. I'm sure your ex-wife can identify you, Brian. And I'm sure that your parents or your brother can ID you, Daphne."

Brian sprang for the door, but Kyle, the burly proprietor, who had quietly entered the room, moved swiftly to stand in his way.

Soon the two of them were grappling.

But Detective Mia was already on her phone and calling for backup.

Within minutes, uniformed police officers arrived.

"This is all your fault," Brian snarled at Daphne as handcuffs were placed on him.

"My fault? You should have stuck to the plan," she said.

The rest of us were ushered out after them, including Bodhi, who was also taken out in handcuffs.

As Mike and I stepped out of the tea shop, I was startled to see my sisters standing outside in the bright morning sunshine.

Rafaela and Alberta were both staring at me, panicked.

"What is going on here?" Alberta demanded.

"And why are they taking my boyfriend away in handcuffs?" Rafaela had transferred her attention to Bodhi.

"What am I doing here?" I said. "What are you guys doing here?"

"Mike texted us," Alberta said shortly. "He said he thought you might be getting into trouble. And from the looks of things, he was right."

I looked up at Mike.

"What?" he said. "You gave me their numbers once in case of emergency. And this certainly seemed to be an emergency to me."

I glanced over at Bobby and Christopher—they were getting into a car together.

"Wait right here!" I shouted to Mike and my sisters as I turned and ran. "I'll be right back."

I caught up with them, and after a few tense moments, Christopher agreed to what I asked.

Then I ran back to Mike and my worried siblings.

"All right, Chloe," Alberta said, her eyes flashing fire. "You're going to tell us everything. Now."

So I did. I told them all about Brian and Daphne—and Bodhi.

When I finished, both Alberta and Rafaela were staring at me in shock.

"I'm sorry," I said quietly to Rafaela. "I don't think you did find the right one—at least not this time."

"It's—going to take me a while to process this," she replied, equally quiet. "But I'll be all right. If I'm being honest with myself, I think I realized that something was off. I think I wanted it to be wonderful, and I saw what I wanted. You know how I can get—I was in love with being in love."

I gave Rafaela a hug.

Then I turned to Alberta.

"And while we're all being honest, I think it's time you were, too."

Alberta opened wide, innocent eyes.

"Me? Whatever do you mean?"

"You've been acting strange," Rafaela said. "Sneaking around. You're keeping odd hours—even for you."

"It's true, Alberta," I said. "I've noticed the signs, too."

"Signs?" Alberta put her hands on her hips. "And pray tell, what signs are those? Come on now—out with it. What are you accusing me of?"

I looked at Rafaela, and she looked at me.

"I know what it was for me," I said. "It was all the baking and the odd craving for pickle bread."

"For me," Rafaela said, "it was the fact that you've been avoiding Peter—and the fact that you got keys from another man."

Alberta's face was growing stormier by the minute.

"Don't keep me in suspense," she said. "Just what do you two think I've done?"

"You're pregnant," I blurted out.

"You're cheating on Peter," Rafaela said, rather louder than was necessary.

Alberta exploded.

"Pregnant? Cheating?"

"Yes," Rafaela and I both said quietly.

"Can't you two geniuses think of anything else?"

We both remained silent.

"Well, I'm neither one. I can't believe you two. Don't you know me better than that?"

"Then what—"

"I'm opening a bakery!" Alberta shouted, throwing her hands up in the air. "A bak-er-y. That's why I'm baking all the time and experimenting with new things," she said looking at me. "And the man with the keys was giving me the keys to my new *storefront*," she said, looking at Rafaela. "It was hardly for some clandestine tryst."

The two of us fell silent.

It suddenly all made sense.

"But what about—" Rafaela began.

She stopped suddenly.

I could tell by the look on her face that she thought her line of questioning wasn't wise.

"Yes?" Alberta said impatiently. "Go ahead. It can't be any more ridiculous than what you've said already."

"What about Peter? Why have you been avoiding him?"

Alberta's face fell and her shoulders drooped a little.

"Alberta," Rafaela said gently, "please tell us."

"It's just that—I overheard Peter telling someone how much he hated competition—specifically, someone who'd just introduced a new dessert menu. Peter said no one could compete with him on desserts. And I was afraid he'd see me that way, too. And I don't really want to compete with him—it's just that this bakery is important to me, and it's something I *have* to do. I didn't want him to leave me because of it."

"So you shut him out," I said. "Before he could shut you out."

"Oh, Alberta," Rafaela said. "You should give Peter a chance. Tell him the truth. Let him know what's bothering you."

"And if he doesn't like the idea of the bakery?" Alberta said.

"Then he doesn't deserve you," Rafaela replied.

"And we'll both be here for you," I said.

We wrapped her in a hug.

After a few minutes, my sisters turned for home, and I turned toward Mike.

His lips were twitching suspiciously.

"What?" I said. "What's so funny?"

He grinned.

"It's good to see that your wild guesses aren't right all the time," he said.

Then he put his arms around me, and he hugged me tight.

And I hugged him right back.

Chapter Thirty-One

"Thanks for coming with me," I said as Mike got in the car.

It was Monday evening, and the heat of the day had in no way, shape, or form dissipated.

"I wouldn't miss it for the world," he replied. "Though you still haven't told me where we're going yet. I do have to say, though, that the air-conditioning feels wonderful."

I'd picked him up at his office, and I glanced over at him questioningly.

"The air-conditioning's broken in my building," Mike explained. "I've been sweltering in there all day."

He shut the door, and I started to drive.

Mike glanced out the window.

"So am I just supposed to guess where we're going?"

"I'm tying up one last loose end from the Clementine case," I said.

"That much you told me already." Mike arched an eyebrow at me. "And it's a case now, is it?"

I sighed. "I don't really know what else to call it. And I feel a little funny about what I'm about to do. But I'm also sure that it's right— that I've come to the right decision."

Mike frowned. "You feel funny?"

"Yes."

"Funny how?"

"Like I'm about to do something momentous. That's why I wanted you to come along. And it probably doesn't hurt to have a witness."

"So far your explanations are making me feel worse rather than better," Mike said. "Why won't you just tell me what it is?"

"Like I said—it makes me feel funny. I don't want to talk about it—I just want to do it."

Mike shifted in his seat uneasily. "This isn't going to end with the cops showing up again, is it?"

"I—don't think so," I said. "But I have to admit it's a possibility— depending on how he takes it."

"That doesn't inspire confidence," Mike replied.

After a moment, he looked over at me.

"I have a few questions for you—not about our current excursion—but about what happened on Saturday. Or rather, what led up to it."

"Okay," I said. "Go ahead."

Mike took a deep breath. "I'm not saying I buy all this—the murder happened, obviously, and the guilty party was apprehended. But the magical parts are still difficult for me to comprehend."

"That's understandable," I replied. "For you anyway."

"But assuming I accept the magical elements for the moment, I still have a few things I'd like to know."

"Like?"

"Like—the glamour. You said Brian used that to disguise his voice."

"Yes, and that's what caused the funny question-mark-shaped cloud over Mr. Clementine's house." I glanced over at Mike. "It's dispersed now—almost as if it knew it was no longer needed. But you saw it yourself."

"Yes, I know I saw it. But I seem to recall that there was a hint somewhere that a glamour could actually be used to disguise an entire person—let that person take on a different physical appearance."

"Yes."

"Then why didn't Brian Clementine just use that glamour and make himself look like Detective Ortiz instead of using makeup?"

"I thought about that," I replied.

"And?"

"And, well, it wasn't necessary," I said. "A normal disguise was enough. The only person who would know the detective well was Daphne—and she certainly wasn't going to tell anyone. No one else at the house would be able to tell the difference from a casual sighting. And he wasn't planning on hanging around long. And then once his little performance was over, he didn't have to use the disguise again unless he wanted to. The real Detective Ortiz had gone to the Clementine house and then gone home and collapsed, and one of his colleagues took over. No one would have been any the wiser."

"If not for you," Mike said. "The brilliant amateur detective."

I shot him a look—I could tell he was teasing me.

"Besides," I said, "he might have feared casting a spell on himself to alter his appearance. Casting a spell on your vocal cords is one thing. But casting it on your whole body could have other consequences. And Brian *did* know spells could be lethal. After all, he'd purchased one specifically to kill his father."

"That's a good point," Mike conceded. "I'm not sure I'd cast a spell on my whole body, either—provided I believed in such things."

"And there's a third possibility," I said.

"Oh? What's that?"

"A full visual glamour might not have been available," I said. "He bought the spell at a black market—they wouldn't necessarily have a full complement of spells. They have what they have—it's not like they're getting shipments in from a warehouse. But I'm inclined to believe it was actually the first reason—Brian just didn't think it was necessary."

"And what about the blue hands?" Mike asked.

"Brian's hands had a blue stain on them from using the strangle spell. There was also a blue stain on Mr. Clementine's neck. That was caused by the spell—which was actually a curse. A lot of curses are tricky, and they'll do something that rebounds on you—kind of gets back at you. And I imagine they're especially tricky if you get them out of a box."

"Yes, I understand that," Mike said. "But Brian wasn't the only one with blue on his hands. How did the others get it?"

"From contact with Brian," I said. "Both Heather and Christopher had blue on their right hands. They got that when they shook hands with Brian. I saw him around town pretending to be Detective Ortiz, and he must have gone to interview the two of them—probably to scout out ways to get rid of them. But he was the only one with blue on *both* hands—and that was from contact with the curse."

"Ah, I see," Mike said. "It makes sense—assuming you accept the original premise."

"And there was blue at the scene of the crime, too," I said. "I saw it—along with gray grit. The blue was the curse—and the gray was the powdered magic used to activate it."

"Naturally," Mike said. His tone was a little arch, but his voice when he went on was normal enough. "So to ask you a more down-to-earth question—"

"Yes?"

"What about this will? I think you told me a few days ago that Daphne was surprised at the reading of the will—that she didn't know it had been changed to include all four sons."

"Yes," I said. "That's true."

"So then Brian didn't know it had been changed, either?"

"No, he didn't."

"Then he believed he would inherit everything?" Mike said.

"Yes—I believe he did."

"So why the elaborate ruse, then? Why impersonate a police officer and try to frame one of his siblings—or Heather—for murder? As far as he knew, they weren't going to get anything anyway. He didn't need to get them out of the way. Why not just go with the accident plan?"

I was silent for a moment.

"I wondered about that, too," I said at last. "And what I came up with wasn't good."

"What was it?"

"Brian hated his father," I said slowly. "And as far as I could tell, it was for no good reason. His dad wasn't around, but that wasn't his fault—it was Brian's mother who left and broke off all contact. Mr. Clementine didn't abandon him. And from all reports, Brian had a pretty privileged life—his mother was a movie star after all. So it's not like he grew up with privation."

I paused.

"And then Mistress Mabel—"

I glanced at Mike. "I found the witch in the woods, by the way."

Mike's eyebrows rose. "Indeed?"

"Yes—but I'll tell you later. Anyway, Mistress Mabel said that Brian hated his father and had turned his face against him—all without actually knowing him. And then it was so easy for him to turn on the others, even though—as far as he knew—he didn't need to to get all the money."

I paused again.

"I suppose it's possible he wanted to eliminate competition just in case—"

"But?"

"I think it's also possible that he was just a bad person—there was a strange quirk in him somewhere. There's a good chance he might have tried to kill them all no matter what."

I couldn't help an involuntary shudder.

"I think that's why Mr. Clementine was so desperate to contact me."

"After he died?" Mike said.

"Yes, after he died," I said, sighing—Mike sounded skeptical. "But I really do mean it. Mr. Clementine had spent his whole life ignoring his other children and mooning after Brian—the son of his true love. He'd built Brian up into something wonderful in his own mind, and I imagine he thought if he could only find his lost son that his life would be complete. And then the reality—when it happened—must have been a terrible shock."

"Do you think he recognized Brian?"

"I don't know," I said. "But I'm pretty sure Brian told him before he killed him—he wouldn't miss an opportunity like that. And then the fear—the terrible fear—Mr. Clementine must have felt for the rest of his family. I'm sure he could sense the great darkness in his son, and he reached out for someone—anyone—who could stop him from killing again."

"And he found you," Mike said softly.

"You don't believe me?"

Mike gave me a small smile. "As I said to you once before, I believe you believe."

He glanced over at me.

"So one last question—what was with all the surveillance cameras?"

"Well, I think that was really just practical," I said. "A man of Mr. Clementine's wealth and influence had to be careful."

"No, I mean, it sounded like Mr. Clementine thought someone was after him—hence having a police officer on call and always checking the front-door camera. Do you think he knew?"

"I can't really speak to whether or not Mr. Clementine had any clairvoyant abilities," I replied. "But Brian was lurking around here for months—and plotting with Daphne. I think he sensed *someone* was after him—having two people nearby who mean you serious harm has to give you some bad vibes, even if you aren't particularly sensitive. And he was right—what he feared marched right in through his front door."

Mike sighed. "It's sad that that's how it ended."

"Well," I said, "like I mentioned, it wasn't quite the end. The last thing Mr. Clementine did was reach out to help his family. I think his true final act was to realize how much he loved them."

I pulled the car into a parking space and stopped.

"And that's why we're here."

Mike glanced up.

"An accountant's office? Aren't we a little late to do our taxes? Or a little early, depending on your perspective?"

I smiled. "We're in the right place. Would you like to come in with me? I know you said you would do this, but you don't have to if you don't want to."

"I still don't know what 'this' is," Mike said dryly. "But of course I'll come in. I'm happy to help you if I can."

"Thanks," I said. "It's good to have the moral support, and like I said, I figure it couldn't hurt to have a witness."

Mike shot me an uncertain glance. "You were kidding before about the possibility of the police being called, right?"

"Sort of," I said. "And there's one other thing you should know that you probably would never have guessed at."

"Oh?"

"I think my sister's cat, Sibyl, may have given me a clue to solve all this."

Mike stared at me.

When he didn't say anything, I went on.

"She kept appearing with little beards made of dust bunnies or frosting. I think she was trying to tell me something."

"Tell you something?" Mike said in a strangled voice.

"Yes."

"Like what?"

"Like I should look for someone in disguise."

"You're right," Mike said. "I never would have guessed that." He sighed. "When we get in there, would you do me a favor?"

"Of course," I said.

"Whatever you do, don't mention the cat thing."

I got out of the car, and Mike followed me.

For the second time in the last seven days, I was going to have a talk with Christopher Clementine.

This time as I walked in, I could see that the receptionist was at her desk, even though it was after five thirty.

She asked Mike and me to have a seat, and then she called Christopher.

After a moment, she said we could go back to his office.

Christopher didn't come out to meet us.

Instead, we found him sitting behind his desk.

He looked at us warily.

"Won't you have a seat?" he said as we walked in.

The words were polite and professional, but he clearly wasn't pleased to see us.

"Hi, Christopher," I said as I sat down. "Thank you for seeing us. I hope you don't mind that I've brought along—a friend. This is Mike Fellowes. He—"

"I saw him on Saturday," Christopher said shortly. "He was at the event you staged."

"Yes," I said. "Mike's not in law enforcement or anything—"

"Why don't you just tell me why you're here?"

Christopher had a pencil in his hands, and he was gripping it tightly.

"The last time I was here," I said slowly, "I saw you looking at that picture of your father. And it seemed to me that I recognized that look in your eyes."

I glanced up at the portrait that hung on the wall.

"And then you looked at that picture of your girlfriend on your desk," I said. "And I thought I saw the same look in your eyes."

Christopher was staring at me steadily.

"And as I thought about it, I realized that I did indeed recognize that look—it was a look of love."

Christopher was still staring at me.

"I said some unpleasant things about you and your girlfriend, Reina," I said. "And I want to say I'm sorry."

Christopher looked startled. "You came here to apologize?"

"Yes," I said. "And to give you this."

I opened my purse and took out a little black-velvet bag.

I handed it to Christopher.

He looked at it, mystified. "What is it?"

"Open it," I said.

Christopher opened the drawstring neck and pulled out a ring—it had one large white diamond in the center and two sunshine-yellow diamonds on either side.

Even in the weak fluorescent light of Christopher's office, the stones glittered dazzlingly.

Mike gasped—I could tell he recognized the ring.

Christopher looked over at me, his eyes clouded with suspicion. "What's this all about?"

"Read the inscription inside the band."

He squinted at it.

"For one who truly loves," he said.

I took a deep breath.

"You were the only one," I said. "The only one who seemed to truly miss your father. And I know the two of you argued, but that's because you wanted freedom—you wanted to go your own way. And you *didn't* want his money—you just wanted him to be your dad."

I reached into my purse again.

"And then there was the way you tried to take the blame for your brother. He was the one who climbed into your father's office, and you pretended it was you—you were trying to protect him. You knew his history of lavish spending and asking for money would make him a prime suspect."

I looked up at him.

"Everything you've done, you've done for your family."

I handed him the original ring box, along with the letter I had received from Mr. Clementine—the one asking me to dispose of the ring. The original had been burned by Lee, but I had recreated it from memory and written it in my own handwriting.

Christopher read the letter over, and then he handed it back to me.

He still looked wary.

"Sometimes a young couple can't get married when they want to," I said, "because they can't afford the ring they would really like. Well,

I believe this ring will take away that problem. You can either give it to your future wife, or you can sell it, and then buy a ring you both would prefer—you should be able to get more than enough to buy any ring you wish."

Christopher grew wide-eyed.

"You're—"

"I'm giving you the ring," I said. "I think your father would want you to have it."

I paused.

"You are one who truly loves."

Christopher sat up in his seat.

"I don't know what to say. This ring must be worth a fortune."

"Just say you'll keep the ring. And that you'll do your best to be happy with Reina."

Christopher smiled. "I will."

"And for what it's worth, I think your father was actually really proud of you. He admired courage."

Christopher looked up at the portrait of his father.

"Thank you," he said softly. "That means a lot."

Soon after, Mike and I left the office, and Mike turned to me as we reached the car.

"I can't believe you did that."

I was feeling elated, and suddenly, I felt my spirits sinking.

"Why? You think I shouldn't have given the ring away?"

Mike grinned at me. "No—that's not what I meant at all. I was just thinking—Christopher's right. That ring's worth a fortune—and not a small one. There aren't many people who would have given it away—whether they liked jewelry or not. And you just did."

"And you think—"

"I think you're amazing," Mike said, laughing. "You're the most wonderful, strange, bewitching woman I've ever met. And I'm happy to be under your spell."

I could tell he was kidding with that last part, but I had to correct him anyway.

"I didn't cast a spell on you," I said. "Besides, love spells don't actually work."

"Then I cast one on myself," Mike replied. "And I'm glad I did."

He looked at me for a long moment.

"You remember that first kiss we had?"

"Yes," I said. "It was divine."

"Would you like to see if the next one will be just as enchanting?"

I laughed and threw my arms around him.

And then somehow—magically—it was.

Other Books by Catherine Mesick

Pure, Book 1 of the *Pure* series

Firebird, Book 2 of the *Pure* series

Dangerous Creatures, Book 3 of the *Pure* series

Ghost Girl, Book 4 of the *Pure* series

A Maryland Witch, Book 1 of the *Witches of Crabtree Bay* series

Coming soon!

Little Sun, Book 5 of the *Pure* series

A Maryland Witch Takes the Cake, Book 3 of the *Witches of Crabtree Bay* series

About the Author

Catherine Mesick is the author of *Pure, Firebird, Dangerous Creatures, Ghost Girl, A Maryland Witch*, and *A Maryland Witch in Arthur King's Court*. She is a graduate of Pace University and Susquehanna University. She lives in Maryland.

Visit the author's website at catherinemesick.com and her Facebook page at facebook.com/PureBookSeries. You can also connect with her on Twitter at twitter.com/CatherineMesick.

Sign up for Catherine's newsletter at http://eepurl.com/cXS5_z.